Dinosaur Lake VII:

~

By Kathryn Meyer Griffith

~

(The seventh Dinosaur Lake book... prequels Dinosaur Lake, Dinosaur Lake II: Dinosaurs Arising, Dinosaur Lake III: Infestation, Dinosaur Lake IV: Dinosaur Wars, Dinosaur Lake V: Survivors, Dinosaur Lake VI: The Alien Connection)

~

(Note: This book is not based on any scientific dinosaur data...it's a make believe story about make believe dinosaurs and more a thriller than science fiction.)

Dinosaur Lake VII:

The Aliens Return

By Kathryn Meyer Griffith

by Kathryn Meyer Griffith

Cover art by: Dawné Dominique

Note: This book is not based on scientific dinosaur data... it's a make believe story about make believe dinosaurs. More a thriller than science fiction

This book is for my beloved husband of forty-three years, Russell Griffith, who passed away on August 27, 2021 and took my heart with him. Rest in peace, sweetheart, I will love you forever and always. See you on the other side.

~

This book is also for my sweet brother Jim Meyer, who passed away on May 27, 2015. He was a great singer/musician/songwriter. If you'd like to listen to some of his songs, here they are: http://tinyurl.com/pytftzc

Chapter 1

Henry woke that morning with the first rays of dawn, got out of bed, stretched, and stumbled into the kitchen for coffee. His plan for the day was to nail up the squirrel house, he'd finished building the night before, hang in the backyard Oak tree. And paint it. He'd put it up high enough, partially hidden among the leaves and branches, so the squirrels would feel safe, yet low enough he could easily fill the container hanging beneath it with food without having to use a ladder. The spring had come late this year, and he was glad to see it. He'd had enough of snow and ice; enough of an Oregon winter. He liked hearing the birdsong; seeing the racoons and squirrels darting around the yard once more. He welcomed the baby critters and the new warmth of spring. He and Ann had always loved this time of year, only second to fall.

He'd been building a variety of comforts for the wildlife the last couple months since he'd left Area 52. It gave him something to do, and kept his mind and hands busy. He enjoyed creating things with his hands. It gave him a sense of accomplishment when he finished a wooden birdhouse or, in this case, a large squirrel family condo with many entrances. He not only built the structures himself, but enjoyed prettying them up with trim and painting them in bright colors. It tickled him to watch the antics of the flying creatures and the fluffy-tailed squirrels visiting, or living in their new houses. He'd sit on the rear porch for hours, with a cup of coffee, and observe the creatures scurrying or flying from tree to tree. Smile at the way the creatures would frantically chase each other around the yard like gleeful children. It soothed him. Ann would have loved it, as well. He wished she'd be there to see it with him. His sigh was so soft, it was almost soundless.

As the ex-chief park ranger waited for the java to brew, he looked out the window into the woods that ran along the edge of his property. There were a bunch of bushy tails playing tag along the topmost branches of the trees.; jumping from limb to limb, tree to tree. They were acrobats extraordinaire. There was–as clearly as he could make out from inside the house–what had to be a baby squirrel, it was so tiny, launching itself from branch to slender branch; practically sailing through the air precariously high above the ground from tree to tree. Its jumps fluctuated so wildly it was as if it were flying. Once or twice, Henry held his breath, fearing the little fella wouldn't complete the jump and would plummet to the ground, but it didn't. It flew through the air and its tiny claws caught the fragile limbs, clamping on, and swung its wee body into another branch each time. Astounding. He watched the miniature daredevil for a while until it vanished into the wall of green. The smile it brought was a good way to start his day.

On the perimeter of his property, there was also a deer, a small doe, standing perfectly still staring back at him, ears twitching. Then another one materialized behind her. A majestic male with the beginnings of a rack on its head. Standing up, Henry was about to go fetch his camera and try to get a picture of them, but he was already too late. An instant later both deer merged into the trees again. Henry loved that about his home. He was surrounded with nature, and he enjoyed watching the wildlife move through, and around, his yard. It made him think sometimes he was still in his beloved park in that cabin he and Ann had cherished so much. Ann at his side. A long time ago. Another life. At least now, he could look back and cherish the good memories.

He opened the window above the sink, and deeply inhaled the flower-scented air. Ahhh. So sweet. A warm breeze drifted in and lightly brushed his face. June. His eyes strayed to the cat calendar on the wall. The June page had a cute tuxedo cat, a lot like Sasha, on it playing in a garden. A frown touched his lips. Ann had been gone exactly a year and a half ago today. Eighteen months. Where had the time gone? He'd known the date was coming, but he'd tried to ignore it. Justin kept telling him to stop marking the dates. All it did was depress him. But Henry couldn't stop. Six months…twelve months…eighteen months. So much had happened since then. His life had gone on and, at times, a year and a half later, he was almost happy. Almost. He shook his head and looked away. Had it really been that long? It had gone by so quickly. Sometimes it seemed as if she'd been gone forever; sometimes, when the anguish of her loss still overwhelmed him, as if she'd just died. He missed her so much, but he tried to be as content day to day as he knew she would have wanted him to be. The way he would have wanted her to be if he'd been the one to die. He figured he'd appreciate and enjoy the life, the years, left to him; for someday he'd be with Ann again. In time. So, he tried to spend time with his friends, his family, kept up his photographic hobby Ann had always been so proud of him for, built squirrel and bird houses, enjoyed his home, was a faithful servant to his demanding cat Sasha. Remembered the days and years with his wife. It wasn't a lot, but it was enough. No use in complaining. He wasn't alone in his widowerhood. Millions of people lost their spouses every year. Now was just his time.

This being the day he'd dreaded Henry had arranged to spend it with Chief Ranger Collins up at Crater Lake. He'd been invited for lunch with Collins and Henry's old ranger friends. He'd be driving there as soon as he nailed up that squirrel condo, painted it, and stocked it with nuts and corn. That shouldn't take long.

He poured his coffee, carried it to the table, and drank it. The squirrel house was sitting in the middle of the table, and he drew it to him. The smell of fresh wood and paint–he'd given it a first base coat of white, to be able to see the squirrels better against it, bordered in red and blue stars–were strong. He rotated it in his hands, inspecting it; rubbing his fingers along its edges. One last check to be sure it would be rain proof. "Looks good," he muttered, taking another gulp of his coffee. He was forgoing breakfast because he was saving his appetite for lunch at the Crater Lake Lodge. He planned on having a huge meal. The Lodge served great food and he had missed it. He looked forward to eating there again.

His cat, Sasha, padded into the kitchen and jumped into his lap.

"I guess you want to be fed, huh, Puss-Cat?"

The feline meowed. *Yes, feed me. That's why I'm here in your lap being so affectionate.*

Henry got up, opened a can of one of Sasha's favorite wet foods, dished it out, and placed it on the floor. The cat wasted no time and woofed it down in minutes. Henry freshened the cat's liquid in her bowl. After Sasha lapped up some of the water, she waddled out of the cat door and into the backyard, and around the house. Henry knew the cat wouldn't stay outside long; and would keep close to the house, away from the woods at the end of the yard, and the dangers that lurked there. Part of the day she'd sleep beneath the porch, one of her favorite places. She always came inside once it was dark.

The feline being taken care of, Henry

collected the squirrel house, the wooden braces, nails and the hammer, can of paint and brush, and went out the rear door. Walking out to the end of the yard he spent the next fifteen minutes hanging up the squirrels' home. Gave it its second coat of paint. When he was satisfied it looked good enough and would support a multitude of critters he returned to the house. He wanted to get on his way to Crater Lake.

As Henry was getting ready to leave the house, a knock came at the door.

"Scott," Henry greeted the man with a friendly pat on the back, as he let him in. "What are you doing here so early in the morning? Anything wrong? Are Sherman and the kids, okay?"

Scott Patterson exhaled. "No, nothing is wrong. Everyone is fine. Sherman is spending the week at her mothers with the children. They'll be gone until next Monday. I could have gone with them, but I passed. I like my in-laws well enough, but I need some me time. I want to do something I want to do before I start my next job. So far, I've spent most of my vacation with the family; doing family things. They left this morning and I'm bored. So, I thought, with the whole week on my hands, I would join you for lunch today at the Lodge. If it's all right with you?"

"Of course, it is. How did you know I was going up there today?" Henry was surprised, yet pleased he'd have his friend along for company. He didn't see enough of Scott since the government had closed down Area 52.

"Actually, Chief Collins called and invited me. Said some of the old gang were getting together for lunch and wanted to know if I'd like to join all of you. I said positively yes. I haven't seen Collins or the other rangers for a while. It'd be nice to catch up with some of them."

"I didn't even know you were going to be home this week," Henry said. "I thought you were getting ready to fly off on some top-secret consulting job?"

As usual when talking about any of his jobs, Patterson's face went blank. He never divulged anything about his jobs, unless he received permission to. "The job has been delayed for another two weeks, maybe more. Paperwork snafu or something. I don't mind. Sherman's happy to have me home for as long as she can. As you know, once I take a job I can be gone for quite a while."

"Your wife is all right with having you

home longer, even after she's had you home for months? After the family went on that long fancy vacation? Where was that again anyway?"

"Disneyland, and after that we spent three weeks at a rented beach house on the ocean. Nice bungalow right on the water. It was great. You know Sherman. She'd love it if I'd just finally hang up my badge, consulting, too, and retire once and for all. But I want to make sure that the kids have money for college, and we're well set for retirement. I figure I need to work another decade at least. Families are expensive."

Since their stay at Area 52 had ended so abruptly, Henry had returned home and resumed his leisurely, boring, life while Patterson had taken time off to be with his family. To have a long rest, some fun, and to spend quality time with Sherman and the children. But the ex-FBI agent, he'd told Henry, as much as he loved his family, was more than ready to resume work.

Patterson ambled into the kitchen and made a beeline for the coffeepot. He was in his slumming clothes. A clean T-shirt and brand-new jeans. "Good, coffee is still warm." He grabbed a cup from the cabinet, filled it nearly to the top, went to the refrigerator and, taking the carton of milk out, poured a little into his cup. He didn't take sugar. "I needed some friend time, and when Chief Collins telephoned I was glad to accept the invite. Glad to see the old Lodge again, and be with the rangers."

"They'll be happy to see you, too. Why don't you pour your coffee into a go cup," Henry took one from the cabinet and handed it to him, "and let's go. I'm anxious to get out into the fresh air, the sunshine, of the park and the woods. I've been hanging around alone here in the house entirely too long. I'm growing roots to the floor. My brain is turning to mush."

Patterson gave him a thumbs up. "You got it, buddy, I'm right behind you." Patterson dumped his coffee into the go cup as Henry refilled Sasha's food bowl, and then trailed Henry outside to the porch.

"I'll drive." Henry locked the door behind them.

"I won't squawk about that. It means I can sit back and enjoy the scenery. Let you dodge all the wildlife that will scamper across the road." Patterson laughed. "At least these days you don't have to worry about rogue dinosaurs popping up everywhere; jumping on our vehicle, or lying in wait to attack from behind a boulder. They're all gone. Forever. Thank goodness."

"No, we don't have to worry anymore about dinosaurs." Henry felt a little uneasy keeping the truth of Oscar's existence from Patterson. From everyone really, except his son-in-law Justin, who he'd told months ago about seeing Oscar out in the deep woods of Crater Lake. That had been a mistake, too late now, but he trusted his son-in-law to keep his secret. Henry had thought it was best if he didn't reveal Oscar and his family's survival to anyone else. Bad enough Justin knew about it. Secrets had a way of getting out and he wanted the intelligent creatures left in peace to live their lives without being hunted, rounded up, captured, and experimented on. Better if no one else knew the creatures were in the deep woods of the park. Safer for them that way. He hadn't meant to tell Justin, but the secret had slipped out one night when the two of them were reminiscing about Oscar and his bravery; how the dinosaur had saved their lives many times, and Justin seemed so miserable that the courageous little beast was dead. Henry had to tell him that, no, Oscar wasn't dead. He was alive and well. He'd seen him. Justin had been overjoyed.

Thinking of Oscar, Henry wondered, as he had so often lately, if the small dinosaur was still living out in the far reaches of the park's woods; if he and his descendants were all right. Henry had searched for Oscar many times since that day Oscar and his progeny had surrounded him in the back forest, but hadn't run into Oscar again. It was possible that the dinosaur and his family had moved further up north into a wilder and more isolated territory to escape humans altogether. Maybe they'd moved up into Canada. He wouldn't blame them. If people knew Oscar and his family existed, the dinosaurs would be mercilessly hunted.

The men got into the truck and headed towards Henry's previous stomping grounds. As usual, he felt better, freer, when he knew he would soon be in his old park among the rangers, the landmarks he was familiar with, and the soul-healing nature of the park. Crater Lake had been home for so long, Henry, since Ann had passed away, often felt happiest there. When he was there, he could almost believe Ann was still alive somewhere else. Their cabin in the park. Her job at the newspaper, or out running down a story. Shopping in Klamath Falls, or visiting friends in town. And he was only out in the park working his job. It was a nice illusion, for a while anyway, until reality reared its ugly head, and he had to go home. Then he knew the truth.

It was also good, on a warm summer's day in the sunlight dappled by the tunnel of passing shade trees, to be driving through the entrance of Crater Lake National Park again. Just as he'd done so many times before over his park ranger career. His face was smiling. The drive revived so many happy memories. Before the dinosaur plague, of course.

The year before, in the depths of a snowy winter, months before he'd been rescued and had been saved by the timely miracle of going to Area 52, he'd grieved Ann's loss while he'd been in the park. Lost in a fevered delusion that she was still alive and with him. Those had been dark days. Strange, now, he could recall little of those first six months after her death. A lot of crying, anguish, and lost days and nights. He had to admit, he felt better now. Different. He missed Ann every second of every day, would never forget her, and would love her the rest of his life, however long that would be, but he had accepted he would be alone until he went to join her one day. He could wait. Eventually he and Ann would be together again. Forever and always. Until then he'd promised himself, and Ann, that he would live the best life he could; not let the sadness cripple him. He'd spend time with family and friends. Try to be happy. Him and Sasha.

"I guess," he snidely directed his query aside to his passenger as he guided the truck down the highway, "you can't talk about your new government project, right?"

"Nope. Classified. Top-top secret of the highest level. Unbelievably classified. Sorry. The government would put me behind bars me if I told anyone anything about it." But his friend's tone was tinged with a deeper disquiet that Henry, knowing Patterson as well as he did, could sense, perhaps, when most people wouldn't.

"That bad, huh?" Henry slowed the vehicle down to let a fox skitter across the road in front of them. Even foxes had the right to live. He avoided creating roadkill whenever he could. The creature halted on the other side, looking back at them, then ran off into the woods.

"You have no idea." The other man glanced away, pretending to care about the fox. Henry knew then something really scary was going on in the world. "I wish I could tell you, Henry. I really do. It would do me good to get it off my shoulders a bit."

"Is Russia about to start a nuclear war, World War Three, perhaps? Or possibly North Korea, or China, is preparing to launch their missiles at us? Wipe us out for good and for all? Take over the world order?"

Patterson purposely gazed out his window, head turned away, and muttered, "Henry, I can't talk about my new assignment. I'm so sorry. I wish I could, but *I can't*. Please stop pressuring me. We're friends, and, you know, it hurts me to keep things from you. I don't want to end up in jail, or see you locked up either, if I tell you something I'm not supposed to."

Henry couldn't stop himself. "Would you tell me if there was a real danger to those I love, humanity, the world, if that came to pass, so I could prepare?"

Patterson released a sigh, still studying the passing scenery. "No matter what the government said, Henry, I *would* tell you. They can shoot me afterwards, but I would warn you, and those I care about, if a great catastrophe was coming. *Government be damned*."

Henry's curiosity was a hungry beast, but he reined it in. Patterson's job, as an FBI agent and later as a consultant, had always been all about secrets, and Henry respected that. It was enough for him that Patterson would risk his job if he believed things were grave enough that he'd shatter his pledge to not divulge the secret and confess it to Henry. It was enough.

The park was as gorgeous and calming as always in June. The nights would be chilly, and the days a little cool, except warmer in the sunshine. Once they'd gone through the entrance, Henry rolled down the window and breathed in the fresh air filled with the scent of trees, grass, and everything that smelled like home to him. He was glad to be back in the park.

"I missed this place." Patterson's eyes were taking in their surroundings, a big smile on his face. "Even if, along with the good memories, it has a ton of harrowing ones."

"Like when we were running for our lives from Godzilla, or fleeing from those flying banshees? Shooting at One-Eye, or those little glowing red-eyed devils that infested the night woods?"

"Fun times indeed. I remember them all well." Patterson stretched his legs before him, raised his arms, and moved his neck back and forth. "I need to get out and move around. Been sitting too long, I'm stiff."

"That's what happens when you get old, buddy."

Patterson humphed. "You should talk. You're a heck of a lot older than me."

"And don't I know it."

When they arrived at ranger headquarters, and strolled in, Chief Collins met them outside his office. "You two made it here in record time. It's good to see both of you." The man thrust out a hand for them to shake, which they did.

"It's good to see you, too, Chief Ranger." Henry was gazing around at the station. There were no other rangers there. They were out patrolling the park, or leading groups of summer tourists on hiking tours; or already at the lodge waiting for the three of them. Late June was the beginning of the summer season. Most of the snow had melted, except in the far reaches of the park or up in its mountains. The visitors' numbers were larger. Though Henry did wonder why headquarters was completely empty. That was unusual.

"The rangers are out on tours spieling tales to the visitors, huh? Patrolling the park, or out checking the campgrounds?" Henry inquired of Chief Collins, as he peered into the other offices. They were empty, too.

"Some of them are. Truth is, we're down a couple rangers right now. One, the new guy Ranger Perkins, the one I hired right after you retired, already quit, and moved on to be a cop in Ashland, and another of my rangers, Thomason, is out on extended sick leave."

"What's wrong with Thomason?" Henry inquired.

"He broke his leg in two places while leading one of the trickier tours a week ago on Mount Scott. He slipped and fell. It happens, as well you know. All the extra rain we've had the last month had loosened the shale on the path. He took quite a tumble, but saved a visitor from falling instead of him. Good ranger. He'll be out a while."

"Ouch. Poor Ranger Thomason. I had a broken bone once. It was no fun." Henry made a sympathetic face. "Tell him I hope he heals quickly, and well."

"I'll do that, Henry. He'll like that you thought of him. After the dinosaur wars, you're his hero."

"No more a hero than any other dinosaur fighter, man, woman or child," Henry said, "who stepped forward and fought the prehistoric beasts. As far as I'm concerned, there were a lot of heroes during those years."

Chief Collins lifted an eyebrow at him, slightly amused. The man stood there, hand on his leather gun belt. "Not according to most of the rangers here. You were the hero."

Henry shrugged the compliment off. A lot had happened since his *hero days*. He preferred to live in the present. It wasn't as fulfilling, or even as exciting, but it was real.

His eyes roaming around, Henry thought the station looked about the same as when Henry had been Chief Ranger. Though it was the rebuilt, nicer headquarters, he'd worked from in the last years of his career before he'd retired. The dinosaurs had destroyed the original one. The newer station was larger; more fortified, surrounded in tall metal barricades, because it had been built towards the end of the dinosaur wars, and no one was sure the dinosaurs were completely gone. And, of course, they weren't. But the new headquarters, and its protections had never been tested. The dinosaurs had stayed away from it. Pure luck, Henry had always thought.

"Let's not dawdle." Collins closed the door to his office. "Some of the men are at the Lodge right now waiting for us. And I'm ready to eat." The man patted his ample stomach.

"I second that." Patterson was already on his way to the exit.

The three men left headquarters and, following each other in their vehicles, drove up to the rim and the Lodge.

As Henry got out of the truck his eyes scanned the familiar panorama around him. Memories flooded in. This park had been Ann's and his home for so long. How many times had they stood right on this spot, holding hands, or arms around each other, staring out over the beautiful lake, in all kinds of weather, sunshine, rain, snow, on their way to the Lodge? How many times had they had lunch or supper here? Too many to count. The food had at all times been excellent and it was their favorite place to dine in the park. The lake was below, the water shimmering, azure diamonds sparkling among the white tipped waves. He could almost feel Ann beside him as he and the other two men made their way into the Lodge. The building also, during the dinosaur years, had been partially rebuilt. Another victim of dinosaur destruction years ago. Yet the décor had been lovingly and faithfully restored. It was like going back in time when he walked into its lobby and into the main dining area. Oh, the memories.

Waiting for them at the large round table next to the wall of windows overlooking the lake were Rangers Finch, Cutters, and Samuel Cromwell. Ranger Cromwell had been hired after Ranger Perkins had quit. He was a short man with a radical crewcut, sharp brown eyes, milk chocolate skin, and a smile that never seemed to leave his face. Collins had told Henry on an earlier phone conversation that Ranger Cromwell was a dependable, competent, and very sociable ranger. The other rangers liked him. The visitors adored him. He was a good fit for the department.

Hellos, big smiles, handshakes all around, and catching up with what everyone had been up to, were made, and the men settled down to their meals, after ordering them, when the plates were brought out. Henry, as he always felt when with the rangers or in his park, was happy. He beamed, listening to the rangers' entertaining park stories of wild animal encounters or crazy visitors doing even crazier things. Most, if not all, experiences had happened to him once, if not more, over the years he'd been Chief Park Ranger there. Everyone contributed their own comical or poignant tales of the job, laughed and enjoyed the comradeship of the other rangers. Henry was at home. For a short while he wasn't a grief-stricken widower. He belonged. He was a ranger again in the park he loved.

Ann was probably smiling down at him from the great beyond. *Hi Ann. Here I am having fun back in the place where we were our happiest…and most terrified. I am trying to live the best life I can without you. But, don't ever forget, I will love you forever and always. I will never forget you, Sweetheart. I miss you.*

As Henry socialized with his old and new friends, his eyes kept revisiting the lake and the landscape around it. It was so beautiful with the sun shining down on the water. The rim of rock circling and containing it presented the water as if it were an exquisite sapphire jewel. The beauty of the lake and the land around it was breathtaking. Henry never got tired of gazing at it. He missed it. The lake, the park…the past. Yes, even the horrific dinosaur days, because Ann and Laura had been there with him.

"I heard that the California and Oregon wildfires are getting dangerously close to the park's perimeters?" Henry was in a conversation with Chief Ranger Collins as they were eating their desserts. Henry had chocolate cake and Collins was working his way through a bowl of ice cream.

"I'm afraid they are," Chief Collins admitted with a scowl. "We're watching their approach and making preparations for when and if they get into the park's land."

"You're not worried," Henry pressed, "that you'll have to shut the park?"

"Oh, I'm more than worried. The wildfire in the southern regions of Oregon looks to be as massive and destructive as the one we had here in twenty-fifteen. You remember that one? You were still chief then."

"I remember it." Henry's concern had ratcheted up at the mention of the twenty-fifteen fire. It had been horrible. One of the worst ones Crater Lake had ever had, other than the two thousand and six one. Both had closed the park for months, during the height of its summer season. "And throw in that we were in the middle of the dinosaur troubles, I can't easily forget it. You think what's coming will be as bad as twenty-fifteen?"

"It could be worse. The wildfire is moving incredibly fast and already nibbling on our outskirts." Chief Collin's face pivoted to the window as if he could see the smoke out there somewhere above the trees already advancing on them. "I'm praying the fire is stopped before it gets here. The fire in twenty-sixteen alone ate up over twenty thousand acres in the park. Doesn't look good so far, though the Oregon National Guard has been deployed to aid the firefighters and emergency operators. You know what that means, Henry."

"I do."

"They're throwing everything they have at it. But as you know, it's a last-ditch effort when they bring in the Guard."

Henry knew the truth of that. The wildfire talk had unsettled him. No matter how long he was retired he still cared about Crater Lake and the rangers. They were a part of him. "Let's hope they bring the fire under control then for all our sakes, and the park is spared…this year."

There was a murmur of agreement from the rangers at the table. By then the men were drinking their last cups of coffee, most having finished their desserts. Two of the rangers had to return to their shift and get back out in the park. Lunch was about over. For Henry, it had been a nice respite from his lonely life. He was more than grateful that the park, and his friends, were always here for him. He could come visit whenever he desired.

Then the conversation took a weird turn. One of the rangers, Ranger Finch, said in a hesitant voice to Collins, "I meant to ask about this when I came in later, Chief, but since you and some of us are here, I'll do it now. Has anyone," and here the ranger glanced around at everyone else at the table, "seen those strange lights that have been hovering and blinking over Lightning Springs and Dutton Creek areas the last few nights? Have any visitors mentioned seeing anything *unusual* in the skies at those locations, especially at night?"

"Strange lights? In the skies?" Chief Collins repeated, a confused expression on his face.

Ranger Finch exhaled, his face becoming a little red. Apparently, talking about what he was talking about was uncomfortable for him.

"Go on, Ranger," Chief Collins encouraged the man.

With furtive looks around him, Ranger

Finch did. "I was out driving along the trail out there the other night at the end of my shift, I like to take that route before I go home as it's so calming, usually anyway, and I saw these creepy multi-colored orbs playing around in the sky above me. They were spinning in lazy circles around each other. There had to be ten or twelve of them. Spheres of different colors. Quite pretty, in fact. Then after a couple minutes, they scattered and shot up into the sky. Gone. Just like that. In a flash, moving faster than anything I've ever seen." He snapped his fingers. "Never seen the like of it. And I've been a ranger here for, as you all know, a heck of a lot of years. To be truthful, they kind of spooked me. They moved so quickly and exited even quicker. I thought it was just my imagination. First time. It was late, I was tired. Then…two nights later I saw them again, or I thought I saw them again. Also, at the end of my shift.

"This time when I was driving past Dutton Creek right after sundown. This time there were more of them. I think, I'm not sure, but they seemed to be a different *shape*. Hard to tell because they were pretty far up." The Ranger pointed upwards at the rafters. "A little more triangular, I think. They made these weird noises as they chased each other. There was something about them that gave me the creeps. They made me feel…anxious. I drove away and, I swear, at a distance, they followed me for miles. Then, just as abruptly as they'd appeared, they were gone. Again."

Henry caught the sudden interest on Patterson's part. He was listening intently to what Ranger Finch was saying. Very intently.

"I haven't seen anything like that." Collins scratched the side of his neck, thinking. He turned to the other rangers. "Anyone else seen Finch's strange lights in the sky anywhere else in the park? Anyone seen anything unusual anywhere?"

"No. I haven't." Ranger Cutters had pushed his empty dessert plate aside, and moved his coffee cup into its place. He picked the cup up and drank.

Ranger Cromwell was shaking his head. "Me, neither. Haven't seen any spooky orbs dancing around in the skies anywhere in the park. Maybe you were seeing some campers' flashlights bouncing around through the trees? Their car headlights perhaps? Lights sometimes do peculiar things in the dark woods, especially in the fog. And it has been foggy out there in the hollows the last couple nights."

Ranger Finch appeared perplexed. "They weren't campers' flashlights or car headlights. I know what those look like. I was hoping someone else had seen them. So as to prove I wasn't crazy."

"I can check with the other rangers, Ranger Finch," Chief Collins offered, "and see if any of them have seen anything like that. But I imagine if they had they would have reported it. Don't you?"

"Not really," Finch murmured. "I almost didn't. I didn't want you and the other men to think I'd gone mad cow."

Seeing how upset Finch seemed to be over the sightings, no one laughed. Patterson's face had a pensive look on it.

The group finished their meal and began to break up. The rangers returned to their shifts and Chief Collins, the last one to leave, back to the station.

"Hey, we need to do this more often," Collins remarked affably as he trailed Patterson and Henry out the door and into the sunlight. "Patterson, you need to keep in touch more. You don't live that far away."

"I know. Been busy, though." Patterson shrugged. "Work, you know."

Chief Collins nodded. "I know, I know. Work you can't talk about."

"You got it. Government secrecy, you know."

"Yep. Don't we all know. You FBI, secret agent, types are all so enigmatic. I guess it's part of your charm, Patterson."

The Chief swung around to Henry. "It's always nice to catch up with you, Henry. Come on by for lunch anytime. Or supper. Or just when you want to chat. I'm usually here."

"I know," Henry replied. "And I'll be sure to do that. You're a good friend, Todd. Thanks for today."

Henry suspected it was Collin's attempt to get him more out into the world; see more people and not bury himself alone in his house all the time. But Henry wasn't alone. He had family and friends. Since Area 52 had been dismantled he had stayed in touch with Doctor Isabel. She often came to visit him. They had become fast friends. Sometimes, when he was visiting the grandkids in New York, he and Isabel did things together, like see a movie, go out to dinner, or just sit and talk for hours. Just friends, so far, but Henry grew fonder of her all the time. He wasn't ready to love anyone again yet. Ann was still, to him, his great love, and always would be. But it was nice to have a woman friend, though, to talk to, especially about things concerning his granddaughter. Phoebe. Phoebe was becoming a woman and sometimes Henry needed advice on dealing with the girl. The other scientists from the base he'd gladly let go. He'd never gotten really close to any of them.

Since Henry had left Area 52, though, he had accepted the truth that he needed to expand his friend circle. He needed more people in his life. He was working on that. These days he never missed a chance to make a new friend.

Justin, Delores, and the grandkids also visited him often, too. Then there was Patterson, Sherman, and their kids. He invited them over for get togethers all the time. Patterson and him had also gone camping once or twice since the weather had warmed up. Henry was trying.

And now June was winding down, Henry was thinking of planning a fourth of July barbeque, and inviting Isabel, Justin, and his family, Patterson and his, and musician Steven James, now a full-fledged nurse who worked alongside his doctor wife, Emily, in Nampa. Make it a weekend affair because Justin and

James lived too far away just for a one-day get-together. Henry had decided to make it a real big event. He was excited about it.

*****

Stuffed with fine food and good companionship, Henry and Patterson took their leave of Chief Collins and climbed into the truck.

Patterson glanced over at Henry. "How would you feel about taking a short camping trip with me down around Lightning Springs for a few days? Just us, our backpacks. Traveling light. Leave your Scamp home, and do it the old way? On foot. Look like you could use the exercise."

"Thanks." Henry wasn't surprised, he'd almost expected the invitation. He'd seen how attentive the ex-FBI agent had been during Ranger Finch's discussion of the strange orbs he'd glimpsed. Henry had seen the eager glint in his friend's eyes. Something was up all right.

Henry took a wild guess. "You want to check out those first sets of strange lights Ranger Finch saw there, huh? See if they do a repeat performance?"

"You know me too well, Henry. Sherman and the kids are gone for a whole week, the weather is supposed to be pleasant, so this would be the perfect time to go out camping with my best friend. After our stint at Area 52, I'm interested in all things unexplained and mysterious."

Patterson's declaration had touched Henry. "I'm your best friend? Really?"

"You are, with Justin a close second." The man gave Henry a sincere look, and then patted him on the back. "We've been through so much together, Henry. Going way back to when Dylan Greer and I first met you when you were Chief Park Ranger. When we were going after that first water dinosaur. Godzilla, as you called it, if I recall correctly. Then through the years after when there seemed to always be more dinosaurs to fight. And in my line of work, one doesn't get the opportunity to make and keep many friends over the years. They keep dying. So, yes, you're my best friend. Living anyway.

"And I've been wanting to take a camping trip anyhow. Get out in the wilderness, with nature, trees, and streams around me again. Breathe clean forest air. Sleep in a tent and sit out by a campfire under the stars. Just what I need before the next top-secret job claims me, and the working world closes in again. My soul cries out for a freeing wilderness excursion."

"When do you want to go on this little camping *excursion*?" Henry started the truck and pulled out of the Lodge's parking lot. The afternoon sun shone down on them. There were light shadows flickering through the trees around them. It was a lovely afternoon.

"How about first thing tomorrow morning? Why wait? The weather, they say, is going to remain nice for the next four, five days. I'm a bachelor for at least the next seven days. Perfect timing."

"Good weather, huh?" Henry thumped his fingers on the steering wheel in thought. "That means clear night skies, then. You're hoping you get a glimpse of Finch's eerie orbs, aren't you?" Henry maneuvered the truck down from the rim and onto the road that wove through the park. Maybe discover what they are?"

"Maybe."

"You going to tell me the real reason you're interested in these lights?" Henry probed.

Patterson didn't say anything at first, then, "I wish I could, but…"

"I know, I know," Henry muttered, "it's classified, top secret, right?"

"Maybe." Patterson was being evasive so Henry suspected the man knew more than he was saying, or was allowed to say. It was hard for Henry, after being privy to the secrets at Area 52, to now find himself on the outside again. He didn't like it. His curiosity was killing him. But he also respected Patterson's need to protect his occupational secrets. During the dinosaur wars, Henry himself had kept many a secret…to save people he loved from worry. Sometimes secrets were necessary to give people you love peace of mind.

On the other hand, Henry already had his suspicions to what the eerie illuminations in the night sky might be. After all he'd experienced and seen at Area 52, he couldn't help but wonder if those glowing spheres weren't extra-terrestrial in nature. The inhabitants of the orbs, if they were spaceships, could be even the ones who had stolen the two crafts from Area 52, or conceivably another species from a different planet? If there was one alien civilization roaming the cosmos out there, why not others? For years and years, humans had seen different shaped alien spacecraft flitting around in our skies…so there could be more than one variety. It was possible, wasn't it? More than possible. Of course, if true, that would create another problem altogether. Earth had become a target. Not all aliens, his invisible alien friends at Area 52 that night had warned him, were friendly. Henry felt a shiver creep through his body.

As the ex-chief park ranger drove through the park, he found himself with nagging thoughts. If the orbs were extra-terrestrial in origin, he didn't believe it was a good thing. After all, the ancient descendants of the Area 52 aliens, and every creature and bit of DNA evidence connected with them worldwide, except for Oscar and his clan, had been mysteriously swept from the planet. If his Area 52 aliens had returned, what did they want? And if it *wasn't* the invisible dinosaur aliens, it might just be another extraterrestrial variety that might actually present a real threat. The dinosaur aliens had told him there were many other aliens in the universe. Some not so friendly, either. It made sense therefore that another alien species might be clandestinely spying on the human race, for one purpose or another. Inwardly, he shuddered. The planet had just survived a war with viciously intelligent dinosaurs, a close encounter with dinosaur aliens, and he really didn't want to be faced with another possible world destroying menace. He'd gotten used to mundane normalcy again. He just wanted to live the remainder of his solitary life in tranquility and peace. Then die.

Henry was a patient man. So perhaps, if they spotted the lights and Henry was personally witness to them, Patterson might be convinced to reveal a part of the mystery he was hiding–*if* Patterson's secret had to do with aliens. Henry really had no idea.

For a short time, before they'd exited the park, Henry and Patterson talked about the lunch they'd had with their old friends, and how great it had been to catch up with everyone; to be in the park again at the Lodge, without ravenous dinosaurs chasing or trying to kill them. How delicious the food had been.

Once they were on the highway towards Klamath Falls and Henry's place, Patterson stopped talking. Henry had respected that, and the remnant of the journey was quiet. Henry didn't mind, because he was busy thinking about what he'd have to gather and pack for the morning's camping trip. How much food and water he'd have to leave for his cat. It kept his mind busy. It would be good to get out in the woods again with his friend. It had been a while.

*****

Once at Henry's, after agreeing what time they should leave in the morning, what they should bring, Patterson went home to also pack up his camping stuff.

"See you about eight a.m. tomorrow," Patterson spoke before he walked out the door, and drove away. "And bring your rifle and gun."

"I typically do when I'm camping in the wild. Bears and wolves, you know."

"Yeah, bears and wolves." Patterson had flashed Henry a sardonic grimace as he'd stepped off the porch; headed for his car. Over his shoulder, he sent a wave back at Henry.

In the kitchen, Sasha was sharking around Henry's feet begging for supper, and he gave the cat a large hunk of her favorite wet shrimp and tuna food. He'd have to leave a plentiful supply of dry, canned food, and water for the feline when he left the following morning. Patterson had estimated they might be gone for three or four days. Though Henry could easily leave Sasha alone for longer, if need be. She had a couple of automatic cat feeders and a ceramic cat fountain he'd bought. She had her cat doors to allow her to come and go. The cat was an independent little cuss, but she would miss her human if he was gone longer than that.

Henry was pleased to be preparing for a camping trip with his old friend, in the woods he loved so much. He was fairly sure that they were going so Patterson could search for those mysterious orbs. It didn't matter to Henry. They were going camping. He seized any chance he could to go into the wild with a friend. He was also curious about what Ranger Finch had reported. Hmm, maybe they'd see those strange lights for themselves. That would be interesting.

So he would be ready in the morning, and not have to rush his morning coffee and quality time with Sasha, Henry packed everything he'd need for the next three or four days camping and then headed to bed. Eight o'clock would come soon enough.

Chapter 2

Henry and Patterson leisurely traipsed through the forest's undergrowth in the vicinity of Lightning Springs, dodging the trees and rocks, and carefully trudging through the leaf covered dips in the earth. The fading sunlight filtering through the trees, though, was still warm. For a while yet anyway. When the night came it would cool down considerably, and it was getting late. June in the park was still not summer. There remained snow on the high ridges and upper elevations of the mountains. The nights could get down into the thirties. Both men had brought warm clothing and winter sleeping bags. They'd build a roaring fire once they set up camp.

It was invigorating to be hiking out in the woods again. He'd let weeks go by without going out; it had been too cold in the park until recently. Henry knew the exercise would do him good, but he'd most likely be sore as all get out tonight.

Henry halted, and peering behind him, met Patterson's eyes. "When do you want us to pitch camp for the night?"

Because where they'd been hiking was too dense for a vehicle to pass through, they'd left

Henry's truck, covered in a heavy dark green tarp, in an open spot they would remember, and would return to it on their way out of the woods. Opting for primitive camping, they carried single-man tents with them, and were traveling light. When Patterson hadn't wanted to bring the camper, Henry assumed it was because the ex-FBI agent desired to keep a low profile, because as Patterson put it, the camper would be too easy to see. Seen by whom, the ex-agent hadn't said. Yet Henry had a notion, so he went along with the game. Sooner or later, he'd learn what was going on.

"I guess this site is as good as any," Patterson declared as they came up to an open area surrounded by trees with a stream nearby. "With the creek down there, we'll have water. With the trees, we have tons of shade. It's the perfect camping spot. We'll roost here for the night, if it's all right with you?" Patterson struggled out of his too-heavy, and bulky, backpack, and dropped it to the ground with a groan of relief.

"Fine with me. It is a pleasant spot…and isn't this where Ranger Finch had one of his sightings?" Henry slid out of his backpack, laid it on the ground, then began to unpack it and set up camp. His tent came out first.

Bedroll, and cooking equipment he brought out last.

"You never miss a thing, do you, Henry?" Patterson chortled softly, pulling his tent out of his backpack.

"I try not to. Tell you the truth, I have a suspicion why we're out here in this exact area. You're hoping to get a glimpse of those strange lights yourself, aren't you?"

The other man flashed Henry a cynical look. "I won't lie to you, I am. I must admit, what Ranger Finch claimed he saw, intrigued me. As you know, I've been interested in UAPs way before they were called that, and way before Area 52." He shrugged, yanking his tent out of its cotton sleeve. A pan slid out of his backpack to the ground, and Patterson scooped it up.

I knew it, Henry thought.

"Greer got me hooked on all alien stuff when I partnered with him," Patterson continued. "Even back then, he believed the aliens were here on Earth, watching and abducting us, so he was always on the lookout for any signs of their presence, or their ships. He was absolutely paranoid about aliens. Do you remember when he told us that story about the whole town being abducted by aliens, and how the government covered it up?"

"How could I forget. It was quite an ominous tale. He maintained the government has been hiding the alien *visitations*, as he called them, for decades." Henry grinned, shading his eyes from the setting sun.

"That wasn't the creepiest of Greer's extraterrestrial stories, let me tell you." Patterson's eyes got an uneasy gleam in them. "Over the years he told me other wild stories about aliens, too. Lots of them. Scared me silly sometimes. Can you imagine what he would have thought of Area 52 and those two spaceships?"

"It would have freaked him out, I'm sure."

"Yep, Greer was a true believer. Now, especially since Area 52, I am, as well. He's the one who got me addicted to closely examining the skies."

Henry remembered Dylan Greer very well. "Good old Greer. Brave man. He was quite the character, with many sides to him. I miss him." And all the others that the dinosaurs had taken way too early. "So if you're searching for glowing spheres in the sky, I imagine after we leave here, we'll mosey on over for a night or two at Dutton Creek, correct?"

"You got it."

"Okay with me. I wouldn't mind getting a gander at those mysterious glowing orbs myself. See what they are. If we're lucky enough to see any, it'll be an extra bonus. For me, camping with a friend I haven't seen enough of lately is the main attraction."

Patterson didn't say anything to that, yet he sent a quick smile Henry's way, before he started to put his tent up. "Same here, Henry."

Henry wasn't sure that was as true for Patterson as for him. Patterson never did anything merely for the fun of it. He was always working, one way or another. Henry respected that work ethic, even though he wasn't part of that world any longer. He was just happy to be out in the woods with a friend, catching up.

The men had their simple camp complete, tents up, with a roaring campfire going, by the time full twilight arrived. After they made themselves supper and ate it, they lounged around the fire with cups of coffee, and talked.

"So, how's Sherman doing these days? I haven't seen her for a while" Henry had pulled a plastic bag of cookies from his backpack and was eating them with his coffee. He shared them with his friend.

"She's doing great. Been really busy with the children, they run her crazy sometimes, and that new government job of hers. She needed to visit her parents…when she's with them, they take over care of the kids and let her rest, get her hair done, or go shopping alone, have some time to herself. Since Ann died, there's no one to spell her watching the children, and it's nice for her to go have time with her mom and dad. They're good people."

"Sherman told me about her new part-time government job the last time I saw her. Doing paperwork, forms, documents and classified stuff, for the government, online, a couple days a week. It sounds like a convenient set-up for a stay-at-home ex-military mom."

"It is. It allows her to be with the kids while they're young. Though, when they both get into school, she plans on going back to work full-time somewhere."

"Doing what?" Henry took another cookie out of the bag that was between them on the ground. "Probably working at the military base she once served at. It's close. Office work, I think. She has the clearance for it."

"How are the children doing?"

Patterson smiled then in the firelight. "Dylan at almost six is already quite the little man. Very independent. Smart as his mom, and just as stubborn. Willow, barely two, seems to be the opposite. Sensitive, a mama's baby. She's a real good child. Hardly ever cries. Totally laidback. Smiles all the time. Pretty as a picture. I couldn't ask for two better kids."

"Cherish them, especially when they're young, and you and Sherman are their whole worlds, my friend. You're a lucky man."

"Don't I know it. I'm working as hard as I can because of them. I want them to have good lives. College or trade school someday, if that's what they want. Raising a family, if you do it right, takes a lot of money. But I wouldn't trade it for anything. My family is everything to me."

Henry bobbed his head. He understood that all too well. His thoughts touched on his late daughter, Laura, and his wife. He missed both of them so much. He'd been his happiest when they'd both been alive.

The evening morphing into the night was clear, and chilly, with a brisk breeze. The stars were shining like tiny fireflies high up in the heavens. They weren't moving, though. Not even a shooting star. Still no eerie lights yet. Ranger Finch had said he'd seen the lights early in the night.

"I miss Area 52," Henry confessed to his friend a while later as the night's shadows and the forest's animal symphonies closed in around them. The firelight flickered across his face, as he leaned into the warmth of the flames, and he rubbed his gloved hands together over them, careful not to get burned. The night, as he knew it would, was growing cold; he could see his breathe on the air, a wispy white cloud. The men were wearing their coats, gloves, and hats. The vegetation was a solid ebony around them. No moon, just stars. An excellent night to see dancing globes of light–if they showed up.

"I thought you would miss the base. You fit right in. It was quite the adventure, wasn't it, Henry? You and those aliens had a real connection. It spooked me out, I'll tell you. Almost feared I'd lost you there for a time, when that last spaceship vanished, and you along with it. I was so relieved when you showed up hours later. The military is still trying to figure out what happened. Where the spaceships, alien DNA samples, and everything went to in the blink of an eye. It's driving them bonkers." The man chuckled as he sipped the coffee from his metal cup. "I loved it." As he spoke, Patterson's eyes never seemed to leave the skies around them.

"I miss being included; being a part of something bigger than myself, and my own life. It felt really good," and Henry's voice lowered, "after Ann's death and all. Being there, I believe, saved my sanity. It just ended too soon. I was sort of enjoying myself."

"Chasing more voracious scheming dinosaurs that took over the base, and being haunted, and then contacted, by aliens?"

"At the time, I must admit, some of that was frightening…now in retrospect it was also exciting. I felt more alive in those months at the base than I had for a long time. Even now when I think about those two spaceships and what I experienced inside them…I still almost can't believe it. Being communicated with by aliens, how and what they told me, were some of the most astonishing things to ever happen to me. I can still hear their voices in my head. Sometimes. I miss the scientists that were there, too. I grew to like a couple of them. Not all, just some. And," here he paused, "I met Isabel. We've become really good friends. And since Ann passed, I need all the friends I can get. So, yes, I do miss Area 52."

"In some ways, I miss the place, too. It was

great having Dr. Maltin, you, and me together again. Short as it was."

"By the way," Henry threw more wood on the fire, stoked it with a stick, and the flames licked up, "did the military, and General Wallace, ever unravel the mystery of the missing alien spaceships–to their satisfaction? What, in their limited view of the world, happened to those ships?"

"Oh, General Wallace finally acknowledged, but in my opinion has not accepted it one hundred percent, that actual aliens returned to our planet and reclaimed their ancient ships. That the military didn't see it coming, and even if they had couldn't have stopped it. He still doesn't like to dwell on the fact that every piece of evidence of those ships' existence, the extra-terrestrial DNA samples, as well as every remaining trace of dinosaurs across the globe disappeared at the same time. You know the military. They only see black and white. General Wallace, if you don't know, was reassigned to a base out in the middle of nowhere. The higher ups don't look kindly on failure."

"I know that. Poor General Wallace. He did the best he could. I liked him. He was a pretty good Joe–for a military man."

Patterson, eyes continuing to inspect the night sky, changed the subject. "Speaking of Doctor Isabel, have you seen much of her lately? I know she lives and works in New York. A long distance away."

"On and off. When I visit Justin and the grandkids in New York, I often see Isabel, as well. As you know, she is a close friend with Delores and has been for years. Isabel has also become my friend. She's an amazing woman."

"Only a friend?" Patterson reached over to where the coffee pot was hanging above the fire and poured himself another cup.

"Right now, yes, simply a friend."

"Uh huh." Patterson tossed him a skeptical glance.

"A good friend, that's all. I still and will always only love Ann.

"By the way, Scott, I wanted to ask you something. I'm going to have a barbeque over the Fourth of July holiday. The usual crowd. You and your family are invited. I'll invite Isabel, as well. The more friends the better."

"That sounds like fun. Me and the family will definitely be there. You know how Sherman loves a party. And I'll still be here. I shouldn't be called to my new position until the week after."

They spoke of other things as the night went on. The past, some of their plans for the future. Friend stuff. They didn't hear or see anything odd out in the woods, or up in the sky. It was a normal camping night. No strange shimmering orbs, either. Henry could tell Patterson was a little disappointed.

Four hours before dawn, they retired to their sleeping bags. They'd sleep late and do some fishing until night arrived. Then do the same thing again. Sit in front of the fire and watch the skies. Waiting.

Two days later, having seen nothing, they packed up, retrieved the truck, and drove to a new camping spot near Dutton Creek. They spent two nights there, eyes glued to the night skies, staying up most of the night to do it, sleeping late, and hiking and fishing the rest of the time.

Henry didn't care that they'd spied no strange lights in the sky, he had a fine time hiking, fishing, and camping with his friend. He always enjoyed being out in the woods. It was his second home.

"I'm sorry, Scott," Henry said as they lounged around the dying campfire on their last night, "that we didn't see any of those strange lights you wanted to see."

"Yeah, me, too. I would have liked to see them. Curiosity, you know."

"So," Henry asked, "are you going to finally tell me what your passionate interest in these so-called lights are all about? Does it have something to do with your new assignment?"

Patterson was examining the darkness around them. "I can't say."

"Ah, top-secret, right?"

"Right. Sorry. I'd tell you if I could, but I signed a nondisclosure contract. You know about those."

"I do." At that, Henry let the matter drop. He was fairly sure he could guess what the whole thing was about anyway. Aliens. Again. And he was fairly sure that Patterson knew that he knew.

The following morning, they folded up camp, and trekked to where they'd left the vehicle. It was a farther distance, being in a denser area of the forest, than their last camp site was from where they'd parked, and abandoned the truck the first time. At least three hours.

The day had started out sunny, but thick gray clouds, and a wicked wind, had swiftly scudded in. The temperature had dropped considerably. That was weather in Crater Lake. Unpredictable. Henry found himself leaning into the suddenly cold wind, fighting it, as he and Patterson marched their way through the deep woods trying to get to their vehicle.

Now the clouds were lowering, dark and threatening. The wind whipping the limbs and trees around them. There was heaviness, a scent of fresh moisture, in the air. Henry smelled the rain before it came.

"I think we better slip on our rain ponchos. And we'd better hurry," Henry advised as he felt the first raindrop. "I think we're in for a heck of storm."

"I think you're right."

They dug their ponchos out of their packs and put them on.

"Follow me, Scott, I know a short cut. It's not used too often, because it's a difficult terrain, lots of creeks, and unlevel ground, so be careful, but it'll be faster."

"I'm game. I'll be careful. I'm right behind you!"

They picked up their speed, thrashing through the woods, trying to return to the truck, as the lightning flared around them, and the thunder boomed. The rain was now coming down in a solid sheet of icy water, more sleet than liquid. Hitting hard. Henry wouldn't have believed how quickly the storm had moved in on them, except he'd often seen and been caught in many just like it over his time in the park. In the heart of Crater Lake, sometimes severe storms could materialize and rise up in minutes.

Soon after that they ran into the man who lived in the shack, or he ran into them.

*****

Henry, with Patterson behind him somewhere, stumbled as the wind and rain pounded them. He saved himself from a tumble down a hill, by grabbing onto the trunk of a small tree. The ground had become slippery with the rain. The storm was now so loud, Henry couldn't hear anything but the falling water and the wind. So, he didn't know he'd lost his hiking companion until he glanced behind him, and didn't see Patterson, anywhere. He carefully retraced his steps, and found his friend on the water-soaked ground, moaning, holding his leg; obviously in pain.

"I must have stepped into a hole or something. I didn't see it," Patterson yelled over the storm's noise, as Henry stooped down to help him up.

The wind suddenly fell into a lull, so Henry was able to hear what else Patterson had to say.

"I can't believe it. I think I either sprained or broke my ankle; maybe pulled something higher up in my leg when I tripped. I'm not sure I can walk on my own," Patterson told Henry, leaning against him. Rain was pelting the man's pained face, cascading down his body.

With Patterson's injuries, Henry wasn't sure he could get him across the rough landscape by himself, through the storm, to the truck. The man was solid built, heavy. He couldn't walk.

Patterson moaned, after a few wobbly steps, and conceded what Henry had already figured out, "I'm not sure I can make it to the truck."

"Maybe we ought to find a spot for you to rest for a bit," Henry said, "out of the rain. Let me check that leg of yours."

"We need to get to the truck, Henry. I know this park almost as well as you. This storm is only going to get worse. We need to get out of here. Get to the truck. Get home."

The wind returned in force with a series of shrieks so loud Henry could barely hear himself think, much less talk above it. Patterson was right, the storm was getting worse. They needed to get moving.

Then, out of nowhere, a man in a hooded poncho, a sheathed rifle hanging from his shoulder, and a pistol at his waist, stepped out of the rain. He reached over and helped support Patterson on the opposite side of Henry. "I'll help you," he shouted over the storm.

The man in the poncho, close to Henry's ear, addressed Henry. "I have shelter–it's not much but it will get us out of the storm–not too far from here. Let's take your friend there, until the storm lessens a little. Until he can walk."

Henry didn't question the Good Samaritan; he nodded, and took the man's lead. It was easy to see that, at the moment, Patterson wasn't going to get far without help.

Minutes later they arrived at a shack, nearly hidden by the heavy rainfall, butted up against the base of a low cliff. The Good Samaritan had been correct. It was barely a hovel. A heavy tarp, nailed along the top, open at the bottom, functioned as a door.

The poncho man ushered them through its canvas-flap door, and they left the storm behind them. The shelter, more a primitive lean-to, was not very big. The three men barely fit together inside. But they were free of the freezing rain, and the wind. Outside thunder clapped and the world continued to be illuminated by lightning bolts.

The man, who'd rescued them, knelt down and switched on a lantern setting on the ground, and Henry could see what was around them. There was a tiny table, a sleeping bag on the floor, along with piles of what looked like clothes, and supplies, crammed against the walls in bags. Something in one corner that looked like a telescope.

The stranger said, "Put him on that sleeping bag there. Get him off that leg and foot." The stranger then switched on an electric lantern in the rear of the lean-to, and there was light.

Henry gently lowered Patterson to where he was directed. "How you feeling, Scott?" he asked.

"My ankle, my leg, hurts like all get out, but I'll live. It feels good to get off my leg, and out of the rain."

"It does."

Henry somberly regarded the stranger. "Thank you for helping us. You showed up at just the right moment. What I want to know is, how did you come across us in this rainstorm?"

The man, who once he'd flipped his hood off his head, and swung his face to Henry in the lantern's light, Henry could see was an older rugged appearing guy with long white hair and beard to match. Face crowded with wrinkles. A scar down the right side of his jaw. Eyes so pale a blue they almost glittered in the dimness. He had to be eighty if he was a day. But his eyes shone with craftiness, and humor. He was grinning at them as if he knew something real important they did not.

"Knuckleheads, I've been tracking you for a while, stealth like," he spoke in an old man's gruff voice. "I noticed you camping at Dutton Creek a few nights ago, and was ready to come introduce myself this very morning, but when I got there you had already picked up stakes and taken off. I was following, trying to catch up, so I could talk to you when the squall hit. I kept tracking you to make sure you both were okay. I saw your friend here, er, misstep, and go down hard. I could see he was truly hurt, so I reckoned I should help. Least I could do. You know the rest."

Knuckleheads? Henry snickered to

himself. What a crusty old bird. "And we thank you for the help. Thank you for offering this shelter. Who are you?"

"I could ask the same of you two. You seem to know your way around the woods all right. But first…let me introduce myself. My name's Nehemiah Hescott. Astrophysicist, Astronomer, multi-talented scientist–and college teacher. Partially retired, but not completely. I still sometimes teach a reduced schedule of classes at the local college up past Klamath Falls. I'm on summer break at the moment." He held out his hand, an amiable expression completely transforming his face to a friendlier one, and Henry shook it. Then the scientist shook Patterson's hand. He had a very firm grip for an old guy.

Afterwards, Henry introduced himself and Patterson. Briefly explained who they were and why they were out in the park.

"You both were just camping, you say? Ex-park ranger, huh, and a government agent? Explains your authoritarian attitude, stomping through the forest as if you own it. Cops are cops to me.

The old man was perusing Henry keenly and then, abruptly, his expression beamed. "Ah, but now I recognize the name! You're the ex-Crater Lake *Chief* Park Ranger. *That* Chief Park Ranger? Aren't you? The one who so bravely fought the dinosaurs during our darkest hours. Sorry I called you two knuckleheads."

"No problem. I guess we did look like knuckleheads stumbling around out in the storm." Henry shook some of the rain off of himself.

"I'm a huge fan, Chief Ranger," Professor Hescott proclaimed. "I think I read every newspaper story your wife, Ann I think her name was, wrote. I loved those dinosaur pictures she doodled on most of them. You are world famous."

With a humble smile, Henry confessed, "Yes, I can't deny it. I am *that* ex-Chief Park Ranger. I don't know about being famous, though. I only did my job like all the rangers in the park did to protect our visitors and ourselves." He didn't feel the need to tell the old man that Ann had died. What would it matter. The man was a stranger after all. "Patterson here, though, as well as a vast gang of scientists and courageous dinosaur-warriors, fought at my side through those times. I didn't defeat the dinosaurs on my own. Now…I'm also retired. Living the good life. You know how it is."

"Well, you're a hero to me, Henry Shore, as I know you are to the whole world, or anyone who's read those articles or that book of your wife's. After reading for years about your exploits against those monsters, the title fits. Same to you, Scott Patterson, if you fought by his side. I'm tickled pink to meet the both of you."

"So," Henry shrugged off the embarrassing flattery, and brought the discussion around again to the old man, "Mr. Hescott–"

"Doctor or Professor Hescott, if you please," the elderly man corrected Henry politely. "I have three masters degrees. But I prefer the title Professor. Teaching has been my life. And different lines of research and exploration to seek out universal truths, of course. I am a student of the human condition as it pertains to…the unsolved mysteries of our world or universe. And I'm an avid alien hunter."

Uh-huh. "Professor, it is." Henry's eyes scanned the man's shabby make-shift abode as he helped Patterson get his boot off, and bent over to examine the hurt ankle and leg. "As you thought, Scott, it's probably only a bad sprain. I don't believe it's broken, though.

There's swelling. A lot of redness. I don't see any skin breakage."

"That's good." A relieved sigh escaped Patterson's lips, as he pressed his fingers gingerly into the area around his ankle, and then further up on the calf of his leg, groaning a little.

"I don't know about the leg, though," Henry stated. "I don't see anything that could be wrong with it. You say it hurts?

"More a weakness in the leg, than anything else. When I try to stand on it, the muscles in the rear of the leg doesn't want to support me. Now the ankle, it hurts as all get out. Sharp bursts of pain. I don't believe I can hike on it right now. I don't think I can even make it to your truck. That is, on foot, anyway, another hour away. Possibly tomorrow. Bad timing all around. I hope this isn't a permanent injury. I need to be a hundred percent healthy for my next placement or they won't accept me."

"I think you will be fine, Scott. As far as I can tell, your ankle isn't broken. You might have just pulled a muscle in your leg. See a doctor when we get home to be sure, though, if it keeps hurting. Hopefully, both will heal quick enough. By what you said, you still have another week or more before you have to sign in."

Outside, the storm had hit a new peak, and was wailing like a banshee.

Professor Hescott, who'd been listening to their conversation, made Henry an offer. "I have a dandy full-size Gator UV out back that holds up to four people. I use it out here in the deep bush. It can get places a regular vehicle can't. It's how I got out here. Has great traction in the mud, too. When the storm passes, I can drive you both to your truck. It'd be no trouble at all."

Patterson looked up at the old man. "Thank you. We could use the lift, what with my leg and all."

"Now," Henry twisted around face their host, "*Professor* Hescott, what are *you* doing here in the park? Seems, with this little lean-to, your supplies, and all, you've been here a while."

A curious expression transformed the old man's countenance. "I guess I'm here for the same reason you two are. I've been searching for these strange glowing balls of light that have been riding the night skies around here lately. I've been chasing them all over the park."

Henry caught the startled glance Patterson

flashed Professor Hescott.

"What," Patterson demanded, "glowing balls of light?"

The old man chuckled. "Oh, you know. The alien lights that have been visiting us for, er, I would imagine…centuries, if not longer. Thousands of years. They've been I've been following the orbs now for weeks. Going from spot to spot here in the park on their trail."

Weeks?

"You have?" Patterson interjected. "Why?"

"Because those orbs are positively alien spaceships, that's why. Aliens have been an obsession with me since I was a young man. I have traveled all over the country, even all over the world, whenever there are alleged sightings of alien spaceships or strange orbs or lights. I know aliens exist and, doggone it, I want to prove it. Meet some of them. Take selfies with them, if they are friendly and they let me. I've never been so close as I have this time. I almost caught up to them a couple of nights ago. I got to the spot they'd just taken off from. They beamed up like Captain Kirk from those old Star Trek shows when he used the transporter. Poof!" he snapped his fingers in the air. "And the ship vanished into the stratosphere. I got *so close*. I was in such a hurry, so flustered, that I'd caught up to one of them, I didn't have time to get any photos." He shook his head. "Darn, maybe next time. They're still here somewhere in the park, I can feel it, and I'm not giving up, not leaving, until I catch one of them red-handed landing or leaving some place. And get pictures this time for proof."

Henry exchanged a secretive look with Paterson. *Wouldn't the Professor do a backflip if he knew about Area 52?*

Professor Hescott lowered himself, cross-legged, to the dirt floor very close beside the other men; grunting with the difficulty of it. "Old man, old bones." A sound a lot like a chortle escaped his lips.

Henry and Patterson were staring at the bearded elder. It was then that Henry realized who Hescott reminded him of. Zeke Johnson. The old curmudgeon who had originally owned the Klamath Falls Journal Newspaper, where Ann had first worked when they'd been living in Crater Lake Park where he had been a ranger, before she had inherited it. Zeke. The man who had loved squirrels and even had had a little pet one he'd called *little boy*. In the end, after years had passed and he had softened, Zeke had been a good friend to Ann and him.

A good man. Henry missed him. Gone now, as many of his old friends and acquaintances were. That was life. Sooner or later only one would remain, and that could be anyone. Could be him. Someday. He hoped it wouldn't be.

"If they are aliens, and I'm not saying the strange lights you've been witnessing in the skies are or are not," Henry countered, "what are they doing here in the park? What do they want?"

"Ah, ha." The professor winked at them. "I believe they are hunting for something, or someone. Here in Crater Lake. They've been all over the place. Searching. Or…the aliens are getting ready to invade us and their scout ships are searching for the perfect place to land the fleet. Could be either reason." Hescott chuckled.

God, I hope not, Henry brooded. The dinosaur invasion had been bad enough. He had no desire for an alien invasion. He merely wanted to live the rest of his life enjoying a peaceful retirement. No more wars. No more drama or tribulations. Of any kind.

Patterson remained silent, but Henry could tell his friend was weighing every word the professor had uttered.

The rain continued to pummel against the exterior of the shed, but the thunder and lightning had ceased. The storm had morphed the day dark, and it wasn't that late.

"Until the storm abates, you two are welcome to stay here for as long as you like." Professor Hescott was smiling at them now. "I know this shelter isn't much; I only threw it up for as long as I'm here. It provides better protection, though, than a tent. It won't blow away–or I hope it won't. I also have a small generator and a portable heater if you guys get cold tonight. I'm usually toasty in my insulated sleeping bag so I don't need the generator or the heater unless the temperature goes below twenty.

"Then, if you'd like, we could join forces, so to speak. I could use the company. I'm a sociable fellow. I enjoy convivial conversation and human companionship. Good discussions or healthy debates. I also imagine you two, after what you've gone through the last ten years, have some real interesting stories to tell. I'd like to hear some. And, let's face it, three sets of eyes on the skies hunting for these alien lights every night would be better than two sets."

"*If* we were looking for those lights."

Patterson had put his sock and boot back on. Henry wondered why he was denying what they'd been doing. But he had an idea why.

The old man laughed. "Fiddlesticks. *Of course*, you were. I've been spying on both of you. Your eyes were glued to the night skies each night you were in your camp. You're chasing the same spaceships I am. Don't even try to convince me you weren't. We alien hunters recognize our own kind." There was a soft snicker in his throat. "It's the madness in our eyes. Though I am surprised that two old dinosaur hunters would be so interested in extra-terrestrials."

The man had been spying on them? That was a bit creepy. How had he been doing that? Neither he nor Patterson had any idea they were being watched. Sneaky old man. For a moment, Henry did question if the old guy had all his marbles. Except aliens did exist. He and Patterson, of all people, knew that for a fact, since they had dealt with the whole alien and alien spaceship situation firsthand at Area 52. Henry had *spoken* with aliens. They still weren't allowed to talk about any of that, and he would have loved to with the professor. It would blow the old one's mind for sure. But, no.

"Aren't a lot of people interested in if there are aliens out there, are there?" Henry's eyes looked upwards, his hands spreading out.

"Yep, that is true. A lot of people believe there is life on other planets. I'm one of them. Yet many don't want to believe some of those aliens are here and have been for a very long time. They're abducting humans and torturing them with their tests. Ever see that nineteen-seventy-five movie, *Fire in the Sky*? Yikes! Those aliens were real sadists. First time I saw that movie, I was terrified of being taken. I kept a gun with me everywhere and by my bed at night for years…just in case they tried to take me. That sort of thing scares the bejesus out of most people." The professor shuddered visibly.

Henry knew there was no use in fibbing to the old guy about what they had really been doing the last couple nights, if the old guy had been spying on them. He nodded at Patterson and once more looked to the professor. "Yes, we were looking for the lights, as you are."

"Excellent." The old man slapped his leg excitedly. "Then let's join up. Combine and compare what we each know. I can help. I've been chasing these alien moonbeams for a very long time. I know their sneaky tricks.

You can stay here with me. Especially if it keeps storming. It'll be a tight fit, but we can make it work. Or you can use your own tents. Up to you." The old man seemed eager for them to stay.

Henry is the one who answered. "We'd be happy to combine forces, as you say, if we could. But we're supposed to be heading home now. Our camping trip is over. We'd be grateful to accept a ride–"

That's when Patterson interrupted. "Henry, I wouldn't mind staying another night or two. Sherman and the kids won't be home until Saturday. You could head home if you like."

"And leave you alone in the wilderness?" Henry huffed. "I don't think so. You're not leaving me behind. If those orbs are spaceships, I'd like to try to catch those shifty extra-terrestrials, too, you know. Possibly, if we're real lucky, get a glimpse of their ships or them. I can stay another night or two. There's no one waiting at home for me anymore. Except Sasha."

"Who is Sasha?" the professor wanted to know.

"My cat." Henry was sitting on the floor beside Patterson. "And I left her enough food and water to last her another week. As long as she's home, has her sustenance, her cat doors, and her yard, she's happy. She won't miss me. Too much. She's real independent, as long as she's home and has her normal surroundings. I'll make it up to her when I get back. Lots of treats."

"It's decided, then, we'll stay a few more nights here," Patterson announced. "We accept your hospitality, Professor."

"Good. Good.

"I imagine you two alien hunters are hungry, after slogging through the wet underbrush, mud, and fighting the storm and all?" Professor Hescott had gotten up from the dirt floor and, slightly crouching, because the shack wasn't tall enough for him to stand up straight, he moved over to one of the bags tucked up against the wall. "I have cheese and crackers. Wine. For now. I was going to cook some hot dogs over the campfire later tonight when the rain stops. Weather people say this little storm," he waved his gnarled hand at the outside world, "shouldn't last through the evening. It's supposed to clear up by nighttime. I have enough of the hot dogs to share."

"Sounds good to me." Henry gave the old man a smile. "We have leftover food we can share, as well. Canned beans, and canned fruit."

"That'll make us almost a proper supper." Hescott was digging in the bag and brought out a large box of crackers, cheese, and a bottle of wine. Paper plates, and plastic utensils. Styrofoam cups. The man sure was prepared.

The three men lounged around, eating cheese, crackers, drinking wine, and talking as the rain continued its onslaught. Henry was grateful to be out of the it and the chill. Grateful that they'd been saved by the professor. He accepted that he wouldn't have been able to get them to the truck otherwise. Also, the old man seemed to be an interesting fellow.

Henry inquired of Hescott, "You're a college professor, huh?"

"Yes, sir, I've been a teacher of astronomy now, oh, for over forty years." Prescott cut off another slice of cheese and sandwiched it in between two crackers. He stuck it in his mouth, smacking his lips. "When I'm not researching or chasing down UFO's–or what they want you to call them now, UAPs, Unexplained Aerial Phenomena."

"You enjoy teaching?"

"It's my calling, my career, but chasing UAPs is my passion. I wouldn't give up either of them."

But," Patterson echoed, "you only do it part-time now, right?"

"I do. Until the college makes me retire completely. They just can't get rid of me." He chortled. "I also give Astronomy lectures at other colleges. I travel. Makes it easy to side trip like this whenever I hear about…sightings."

"How long have you been here in the park?" Henry was listening for the rain. He couldn't hear anything. The rain had either stopped, or had slowed down to a drizzle.

"A week. In different sections of it, though. Following the trail. Looking for clues."

"Searching for the Unexplained Aerial Phenomena?"

"You got it." The professor bent over and did something to the lantern. The light glowed a little stronger into the gloomy corners of the shelter.

"How did you find out about them? The aliens? Their ships?"

"I'm part of an online UAF organization, *The Search for UAPs*," Hescott supplied, "that tracks any sightings of strange lights or UAPs from all over the world. I follow the leads. In America, at least. Once, though, I traveled to Mexico when there was a flurry of sightings. I saw plenty of weird lights, none landed. It's a private, closed group, though. Not just anyone can get access to it. You have to be invited. You have to be an astrophysicist, astronomist, or connected somehow to the science world."

"I have a son-in-law, Doctor Justin Maltin, who's a paleontologist. Lives in New York with his second wife, and my two grandchildren. Maybe he can help me get on that exclusive website."

"He might."

"You married, Professor?" Patterson asked.

"Used to be. Once," Hescott's voice took on a grave tone. "Her name was Geraldine. I called her Gerry. She died five years ago. Cancer. She was a good woman. The love of my life. We'd been married for over forty years. We didn't have any children."

Henry felt a stab at his heart. Ann. He suddenly felt a sad kinship with the other widower; looked at the old man differently.

"Sorry," Patterson said, "for your loss, Professor."

"It's all right. It has been five years. The wound isn't as painful as it once was. Yet, I'll always love and miss her. I'll see her again one day."

"You will." Henry put his empty wine cup in the bag that had held the snacks and wine. The cheese and crackers hadn't filled him up much. He was still hungry. He could have said something about losing his wife, his Ann, to the professor, but, for some reason, he didn't.

"Ex-Chief Park Ranger Henry Shore," Hescott said with a touch of admiration, "I know your story, or some of it. I read where you and a brave gang of ranger dinosaur hunters, barricaded in ranger headquarters, were besieged by and held off reoccurring attacks of rogue dinosaurs. You were one on the front lines during the dinosaur wars. What was that like? How long did you have to fend off the monsters?"

Henry answered the inquisitive man's questions patiently. The man obviously had a case of hero worship for him and Patterson. They talked about dinosaurs and what he and Patterson had gone through in the last decade. The old man sat, spellbound, as Henry spun his tales. Sometimes Patterson would tell his side of things. The old astrophysicist couldn't get enough of their stories. The day went by.

As night was falling, Hescott got up,

brushing cracker crumbs off his pants. "We can check, but I'm pretty sure the rain has passed us by. I can't hear it anymore. No wind, either. Why don't we go outside, build a fire, make us a real supper, and start gawking for those strange orbs? It's time."

Henry got up, too; bending at the waist because he was too tall, as well, to come to a full stand up in the shelter. He cast a glance at Patterson. "Yes, it's time. And I don't know about you two, but I could use a solid meal myself. Crackers and cheese are fine for a snack, but they can't take the place of real food."

The men left the shack and moved out into a beautiful twilight. The Professor and Henry, on either side of Patterson, helped him limp outside. The storm, the rain was gone.

*****

A short time later, as full night dropped its curtain, the three of them encircled the campfire, conversing among themselves about dinosaurs and aliens. Telling anecdotes of their lives. Professor Hescott had had a colorful life, too. He was not only a teacher, but he was a very respected scholar in his field, and had published a score of academic papers during his career. What would Hescott have thought if he would have known what he and Patterson had experienced at Area 52? What they had seen, the alien spaceships they'd been in? They probably wouldn't have been able to get rid of him. He'd most likely would have followed them home and wanted them to adopt him.

Because of Patterson's injuries, Henry put up both his and Patterson's tents. The Professor helped. They'd decided to sleep in their own tents, not wanting to intrude on the old man's privacy. That and the lean-to would have been really cramped if all three had tried to squeeze into it. The rain had stopped, so that would be no problem.

The three of them had made their supper over the campfire and had eaten. Made strong coffee and were drinking it. Henry felt much better with a full stomach. Almost human again.

"How's your ankle and leg doing?" Henry inquired of Patterson as the fire lapped at the night air.

"They feel somewhat better," Patterson replied, rubbing his leg. "I think you're right; I only sprained the ankle."

"That's good news, then," Henry remarked. "Right?"

"It is." Patterson bobbed his head. "In another week when I have to report to work, I should be fit enough."

Henry was glad to hear that.

The men hung around the fire most of the night observing the skies, when Henry and the professor, leaving Patterson to protect the camp site, weren't stumbling around in the nearby woods with flashlights, trying to get a different view of the skies, until near dawn. None of them spotted anything, not even a shooting star. They grabbed breakfast and naps as dawn crested over the trees of the woodland and filled the air with a tawny golden light. Henry loved meeting dawn in the woods when he was out camping. There was nothing else like it. It always made him feel so grateful for the gorgeous world they lived in.

The same thing, nothing, happened the next two nights. They eagerly inspected the skies, but saw nothing out of the ordinary. No strange dancing lights. No space ships. No aliens. Henry was beginning to believe the mysterious lights or orbs Ranger Finch and the Professor claimed to have seen, were just that. Blobs of bouncing lights that were unexplainable. Perhaps they had been a stray sliver **of a nearby aurora borealis, a case of** foxfire, or natural gas leaking out of the earth? There were always inexplicable phenomena occurring in the deep woods of Crater Lake. It was a mysterious place and always had been.

*****

Henry and Patterson took their leave of Professor Hescott, having bonded with the elderly scientist as a new friend. Henry had felt, at times, when the two were conversing, that he was speaking to old Zeke. It was uncanny how much the Professor reminded Henry of the late newspaper publisher. Once or twice, he'd almost called the man Zeke, and had to catch himself.

They would have liked to camp longer with Hescott, ogling the night skies for the lights and enjoying the friendly camaraderie, but Patterson's family was coming home in the morning.

"I'd promised Sherman I would be there waiting for them when they got home," Patterson said the last night they'd been camping. "I'll have hell to pay if I break that promise. With me leaving again next week, she doesn't want to lose any more of my off time. It was sweet enough of her not to make me go to her parent's house. I mean, I like both of them and all, they're sweet people, but they are so set in their old people routines, they bore me silly. They do the same things every day. Regardless of having company or not. Sherman and the kids have a lot more fun when they go without me."

"And I need to get home to my cat," Henry disclosed. "She's a selfish little mistress. She'll be mad enough at me for leaving her alone so long the way it is. She's probably rush out and bite me the minute I walk in the door. Her way of saying, *I'm mad at you. Where you been so long?* It's time I go home, as well."

"You two," Professor Hescott said, as Henry and Patterson were packing up to leave, putting their backpacks in the bed of the Gator UV, "even though we didn't see those orbs, have been very welcome companions. I've so enjoyed our camping experience. Best time I've had in a long while. I hope we can do it again someday."

"Same here, Professor." Henry climbed into the rear seat of the UV beside Patterson. "I had a good time, too, even if we didn't spy any mysterious lights, or meet an aliens."

"So did I. You were both real entertaining company." Hescott scooted behind the wheel, turned the key, and the machine roared to life.

Good thing, they had a ride, because, though Patterson's leg had ceased aching, his ankle was still sore, hurting, though not as bad as when he'd first injured it.

Unlike a few days before, with the rain and storms, the sun was shining. The temperature was temperate. The first hint of an Oregon spring. The air was sweet with the natural scents of grass and trees. The birds were jabbering up in the branches; coasting through the clear skies. All was well in the park.

The ride wasn't as smooth as Henry would have liked. The UV bumped forward with a lurch and tore through the forest. The old man drove like a maniac, and Henry and Patterson held on for dear life. Henry grimaced as the wind whipped across his face. *Maybe they should have walked back to the truck? He could have made Patterson a makeshift cane–or carried him on his back. Might have been safer.* Yet within a short time, not short enough for Henry, they arrived at the vehicle. Shaken, but still in one piece, or Henry hoped so.

"I think," Patterson informed the professor as he dropped them off by the truck, "we should stay in touch. In fact, if you want to give me your cell number, I'll give you mine.

That way if you ever do see or catch those mysterious lights of yours, you can let me know?"

"Sure," the old man replied with a grin, giving Patterson, and then Henry, his telephone number, and they gave him theirs. "I'll let you know if I see any more of them. I'm going to be here for some time. Got nowhere else to go, or anything else to do. I'm staying. Hoping to see those lights, mayhap, or, if I'm real lucky, an actual alien spaceship. Or–if either one of you are in the park camping again, and you happen to spot those crazy orbs, or anything else a little off, let *me know*. I'll be right there. But, no matter what, let's keep in touch anyway. Okay?"

Again, the elder reiterated, "I've had more fun these last couple days, enjoying your stories and your company, then I have had in a long time. I count you two as friends now. And I don't take friendship lightly, not at my age." There was a look of pleading in Hescott's gaze that wasn't lost on Henry. *The man must be lonely.* Henry knew about loneliness.

"I can do that." Henry shook the old man's hand. "We'll stay in touch."

Patterson nodded affirmatively. "Same

here, Professor. It was nice meeting and spending time with you."

As almost an afterthought, Henry wrote down his address and handed it to Hescott. "Or stop by and see me anytime, if you're in my neck of the woods. I'm retired. I'm home a lot. I like guests. I often invite them in for lunch or supper. I'm learning to like cooking for my friends."

The old scientist's face broke into an even bigger grin. "I just might do that, *Friend*." Then the professor drove off in a cloud of dust, bouncing up and down on the UV's seat as if he were on a bucking horse, waving at them until he was out of sight.

"What a character." Henry laughed.

"Yeah. What a character," Patterson echoed. "Some of the academic stories he regaled us with were hilarious. Who would have thought that university life was so competitive or cutthroat? Nice guy, though. Entertaining."

"He was that. Lonely, though, I think."

"I caught that, as well, Henry. Did you see the look on the old guy's face when you gave him your address and said he could stop by anytime? I thought he was going to hug you or something. But, *oh, great dinosaur hunter*, you're his hero. He couldn't get enough of your dinosaur fighting tales."

"Or yours," Henry reminded Patterson.

"True, but it was easy to see he worships you."

Henry shoulders rose slightly and lowered. "Just because I fought dinosaurs, like you and thousands of others during the wars, doesn't make me a hero. I only did what I had to do."

"That's what most heroes would say."

"Anyway, mysterious dancing orbs or no mysterious dancing orbs, it was an eventful camping trip. I enjoyed myself. Oh, except for you hurting yourself in the storm. How are you feeling now, Scott?"

"Not bad. My ankle is still a bit sore, but my leg is almost as good as new this morning."

"Great. Now you're ready to begin your new job."

"I guess I am."

Henry tugged the heavy olive-green tarp off the truck he'd left protecting it, and stuffed it in the back.

Once Henry and Patterson were sitting in the truck, Henry spoke aside to his friend. "Now that the old alien hunter is gone…are you finally going to tell me what connection those strange lights in the sky Ranger Finch and Professor Hescott have sworn they've seen have with your new assignment? *I know* there is one, or you wouldn't be so interested in these orbs. I mean, you were the one who announced we were staying days longer when we were already supposedly on our way home. Right?"

Patterson stared out the window, pretending he had heard Henry's questions.

"I *think* your new job has something to do with alien ships perhaps being sighted in the skies lately. Maybe you, or the powers that be, fear they are even here on Earth now. Up to no good. So, no sense in you trying to hide it. You can trust me to keep the secret to myself if you need me to. Remember, I talked to aliens at Area 52. Is the military in on this? Are they afraid we're about to be visited by a flock of aliens?"

Patterson expelled a tortured sigh. "Sorry, Henry. Though I'd like to, I really can't tell you anything. It's –"

"–I know, classified, *top secret*.

"*Some friend*," Henry mumbled under his breath, as the truck rumbled to life, and they headed home. But he understood. Patterson was merely doing his job, and secrecy was part of it. He couldn't hold it against him. This time Henry wasn't part of the secret team. He had no right to know the secrets. Darn.

Henry didn't really need an answer from Patterson. Something *big* was up. He felt it in his cop bones. It had to do with aliens, and the military, he was sure, was in on it. If it were big enough, one way or another, he'd end up hearing about it sooner or later. All he had to do was be patient and wait. That waiting was hard for him, ever since he'd been part of the team at Area 52. He hated being on the outside again.

When he got home, Henry would call his son-in-law, Justin, and see if he knew anything about what was going on. The scientist had been so deep in the mysteries of Area 52, and on top of it had a high military classification, Henry wouldn't be surprised if he wasn't part of this new development. Possibly he could get his answers from Justin. He couldn't wait to call and talk to him.

They drove into Henry's driveway late that night. Patterson took his leave.

Sasha was overjoyed to see him, didn't bite him once, and was soon purring in his lap–after he fed her and gave her her favorite treats. Cats!

Tired, Henry was glad to be home. It'd be an early night for him, for sure. He didn't even care that the house was empty. No Ann. Strange, he mused, how the longer she was gone, the more the house became a true sanctuary for him. It meant safety, comfort, and contentment now. He was so happy he had it.

CHAPTER 3

"So, son-in-law, you don't have even an inkling as to what Patterson is involved in right now, huh?" Henry was taking a break, from house cleaning, on the rear porch, drinking his third cup of coffee that morning, and watching a gentle rain fall across his back yard. In his other hand was his cell phone.

"Sorry, Henry, I sure don't. The last six months since Area 52 shut down, I've been at home base here in the New York lab, documenting what we went through there, and writing final reports for the government on our experiences. I've also been taking some time for myself and the family. I sort of neglected them the year and a half I was at the bunker."

Henry had no reason not to believe Justin. Whatever Patterson was part of now, Justin apparently wasn't. Darn.

Justin continued talking. "The family and I have been going on weekend trips around New York. Seeing the sights. We've been having a great time."

"How is Phoebe and Timothy doing?" Henry had his eyes on a couple of squirrels eating at the squirrel house, when they weren't chasing each other around the tree or knocking one another off the feeding tray. Squirrels didn't like to share.

"They're doing well. Phoebe is a normal teenager, and can't wait until she turns sixteen. By the way, she's got a new boyfriend."

"Alfonso is yesterday's news, huh? She has a new one?" Henry enjoyed hearing about his granddaughter. About both his grandchildren.

"She does. But she'd pretending she doesn't. She's so secretive when it comes to her private life. You know teenagers. Alfonso is still a friend, though. He's over a lot. They study together."

"Does she still want to be a scientist like you?" Henry stretched his legs out before him. The rain made the day soft, and tinted with a bluish gray color. Pretty. There was warm breeze that made him wish that Ann was there sitting beside him. She had loved rainy days. He hadn't seen her spirit for a while and he missed her; missed talking to her. Yet he knew, on some level, that it was better that he didn't see Ann. Afterall, she was dead.

"She does want to be a scientist, for her career, of some kind. She hasn't decided what field she wants to go into yet. She'll have her choice. She's in the honor society; is almost a prodigy in math," Justin's voice was full of pride.

"She's given up wanting to be an artist then, huh?"

"No. She draws and paints all the time. She's really good at it. She says she'll be an artist on the side, as well as a scientist. She says she can do both. Why not, I tell her. You can do, be whatever you want to be. She drew you something special she wants to give you next time she sees you."

"Of what?" Henry inquired, curious.

"That's a surprise. Phoebe made me promise not to tell you. You are going to have to come for a visit soon if you want it."

"A bribe, huh?" Henry laughed. "Talking about visiting. I was going to talk to you about that. Could you and the family get away next week for a Fourth of July weekend barbeque here? I'm inviting all the old gang and some new friends. Do you think you could make it? As you know, I have the extra rooms, and I'm inviting anyone who wants to stay here, to stay here."

"Sounds like an excellent idea. I'll pass it by Delores and the kids and get back to you. But I'm sure we can make it. We can fly over on Friday and fly back Monday morning."

"That'd be fantastic, Justin. I miss all you guys. I want to see my grandkids."

"And you will. Now enlighten me. What have *you* been up to Henry?"

"A mess of nothing, really. Doing odd upkeep jobs around the house. I built a squirrel home last week. It's already occupied by a bunch of the critters. They put on a good show, gives me something to watch while I'm on the porch.

"Oh, I also went camping with Patterson…searching for eerie glowing orbs in the night skies that some people have said they've spied in the park."

"Really?" Justin excitement was obvious in his voice. "Did you see any of them?"

"No, not a one. We had a good time anyway." Henry went on to tell Justin about Patterson spraining his ankle and hurting his leg in the storm and, then, running into Professor Hescott.

"Professor Hescott had this little shack, and luckily, he found us floundering around out in the rainstorm when Patterson could barely walk, and he helped me get Patterson to it. Gave us shelter during the worse of the weather. Turns out he was searching for the same bizarre lights in the skies Patterson was.

The Professor had been on the watch himself for a while. He talked us into joining him; camping out a couple days longer, where we got to know him better. We stayed together, camping, talking and laughing, keeping our eyes on the night sky. Telling stories over the campfire. The old man had some interesting anecdotes to relate. And he couldn't get enough of Patterson's and my dinosaur tales. Turned out he's an astrophysicist, an astronomer, and though retired, still teaches classes at the local college. This morning I called him, and invited him next weekend to the barbeque. He's accepted. You two have a lot in common. You'll like him, I'm sure."

"If you say so, I'm sure I will."

Henry and Justin finished their phone call and hung up. Henry stared out at the thicket at the fringe of his property with a smile of anticipation on his face. He had something to look forward to now. A big Fourth of July celebration when he'd be surrounded with old and new friends. His family. With people. He couldn't wait. After his stint at Area 52 had so abruptly ended, he'd been so lonely at times. He wasn't used to–and never would be–to being alone all the time. He was already planning what to barbeque, and what side dishes he could whip up. Ann had always been the main cook in their family, but he'd learned a few dishes from her he thought he could duplicate, and everyone would like. She'd left him an organized box of recipes. He'd go all out. Steaks. Potato salad. Baked beans. Margaritas. He'd purchase three or four cakes from the town bakery. He wasn't much of a cake baker. He knew his limits.

A plaintive meow arose at his feet. Looking down, he saw Sasha staring up at him.

"Oops, have I forgotten to give you breakfast? So sorry, fat cat. I'll do it now."

The cat meowed a second time.

"All right," Henry stood up, and moved into the house, the cat following. "I'll feed you."

Henry dished out the cat's favorite canned food, leaning down to pet her when he put the bowl on the floor. "Not that you need it. You are already too chubby I think, kitty."

Sasha wasn't listening to him. She was too busy gobbling the food down.

I know I need to stop feeding you so much. Giving you too many treats. Overcompensating, because you are all I have. Still, I need to be careful. I don't want a two-ton kitty cat. The vet wouldn't like that.

Henry's cell phone rang. Leaning against

the kitchen sink, he answered it.

"Hi there, Henry," Chief Park Ranger Collins's husky voice crackled across the line.

"Hi to you, too, Todd. What can I do for you?" Through the kitchen window, Henry eyes were taking in the squirrels cavorting round the squirrel house. It was better than a TV show.

"Are you busy right now?" Collins inquired.

Henrys gaze then slowly scanned the empty kitchen and looked down at the cat. She'd finished her breakfast, and was ambling away. First her chubby body, then her tail, disappeared through the cat door. Lately, since he'd constructed the squirrel house and put it up, she'd been fascinated with yard squirrels, trying to catch them. *She better leave those squirrels outside alone. She didn't have a chance against their quickness and tiny dagger sharp teeth.*

"Nope, not doing much of anything important at the minute. Why?"

"How about you driving into headquarters today to have lunch with me? There's something I want to talk to you about."

Henry felt his mood rise. Lunch in the park with Collins sounded a heck of a lot better than bumbling around the house looking for something else to do to fill his long day. Patterson had left on his new mission days ago, so it would be nice to spend time with another old friend in the tranquility of the park he loved so much.

"I'm on my way." Henry clicked his phone off, snatched up his keys from the hook on the kitchen wall; walked out the door, locking it behind him. He knew Sasha would be okay until he got back. He'd just fed her.

*****

The drive into the park was relaxing, in spite of the light rain. The end of June, it was nice out, not too chilly, so he opened his truck's window. The breeze on his face felt good; made him feel alive. Getting out of the house also helped. He'd been so bored the last day or two. Looking for anything to fill up the hours. It wasn't easy being a widower. There were so many things he no longer wanted to do, so many places he didn't enjoy going to anymore, alone.

Once or twice, he stole a glance at the passenger's seat, or behind him to the rear seat, hoping Ann would materialize. She didn't. She hadn't been visiting him as often since he'd come home from Area 52. He missed her so very much, yet he wouldn't want her ghost to haunt him forever. It was hard to see her; it was hard when she left. It wasn't normal to see and speak to a dead woman. He knew that. So a pleasant distraction, to get his mind off his dead wife, like going out to lunch with Chief Collins was welcomed.

He arrived at park headquarters, strolled into the familiar building, and into Chief Collins office.

"Good, you're here, Henry." Chief Collins got up from behind his desk and came around to stand before him. "How about we get lunch at Annie Creek Restaurant? I've been eating far too often at the Lodge. I need a change. Today is meatloaf day, and I love Annie's meatloaf."

"I remember you do." Henry left the building with the ranger. Jiggling his keys, Henry announced, "I'll drive."

The friends climbed into the truck and Henry drove them to Mazama Village. It'd been a long time since he'd visited Mazama and even longer since he'd eaten at Annie's. He'd almost forgotten how beautiful the Mazama part of the park was. He'd always liked the food at Annie's, especially their cheeseburgers or the pulled pork sandwich. Hmm, pulled pork with lots of barbeque sauce slathered on top, which he hadn't had for a long time, would hit the spot….

They arrived, and parked in front, at Annie Creek Restaurant and went in. The place was packed and they were lucky to get a narrow booth in the back. They seated themselves and when the waitress came over, they asked for coffee first off, and then put in their orders. Henry had never seen their waitress, but it had been years since he'd worked in the park. Once he had known every one of them. That made him a little sad, but he didn't know why.

The coffee came immediately. Great coffee. As they waited for their food, Collins prepared his to taste, adding a spoonful of sugar, no milk, and peered up at Henry. "How are you doing, Henry? Really?"

Henry was ready to fib, brushing the inquiry off as he usually did with everyone, then seeing the knowing look on his old friend's face, decided not to. "I won't lie, Todd, it's hard without Ann. We had so many plans for our retirement. Time together. Projects. Travel. *Poof.* Now all gone. These days, I'm…lonely. At loose ends. I was always so busy. I had Ann to keep me company, and I was never at loose ends like I am these days. It's worse since I returned from that special consulting job with

Justin and Patterson." Collins, as most people, knew nothing about Henry's stint, what he'd done at Area 52. He'd explained to all his acquaintances and friends that he'd gone on a long visit to New York to visit with his grandkids, and to do a little consulting for Justin's company. A half lie. Area 52 would always have to remain a secret from the people who weren't supposed to know about it. "I don't know what to do with myself lately. Heck, I've been watching too much TV, sleeping way too much; I'm building squirrel houses, for Pete's sake."

Collins didn't laugh. "You need something to do, besides hanging around your house, or frequent camping trips here in the park–or making critter houses. That would be enough for most men, but not you. You've led too of an exciting life to be put into mothballs. Not yet, anyway."

"Don't I know it." Henry also couldn't tell Collins that if his *position* at Area 52 had worked out, he'd be anything but lonely, and bored. But it hadn't worked out. So here he was.

"Okay then, Chief Ranger Shore," Chief Collins called him by his old title affectionately, "I have a proposition for you.

The idea came to me when you and Patterson had lunch with the guys and me at the Lodge some weeks ago. Remember I told you I was short of rangers? That I was looking to hire more?"

"I remember."

"I've had no luck. I've tried everything to lure good men to fill the empty slots. I suspect it's because we have those forest fires threatening the borders of the Crater Lake again, and we might, eventually have to close the park sometime down the road. Thus, I'm still incredibly short-handed. Worst in years. So, I thought possibly, because I'm in such a fix, and you seem to be at loose ends yourself, you might be interested in coming back to the park as a ranger part-time? Not as a regular ranger with all the duties, all the day-to-day grunt work, but you could take over some of the visitors' tours, freeing the other rangers to do the patrolling and anything else that might come up. I recall you really liked doing the tours, and the visitors really enjoyed you doing them. You had a real connection with the visitors. What do you say? You want to be a part-time ranger? Three days a week. Wednesday, Thursday, and Fridays, only until dark. I'm not going to lie to you, it would be great to have you here in the park again, and a real morale booster for the other overworked rangers. Everyone has missed you."

Henry was caught off guard. What Collins was asking him was the last thing he would have expected Collins to request of him. A part time ranger? Just doing the tours? He took a little time to weigh the cons and pros. *Cons*: Being a regular ranger, not a chief ranger, with all its responsibilities and headaches; having to go back to work again and be on a time clock, even if it were only three days a week; having to take orders from a ranger that once he'd given orders to. *Pros*: Getting to be a ranger again; wearing the uniform again; getting out of the house; feeling useful again; being around the other rangers, of whom many were old friends; working in the park he loved again; giving the visitors' tours, which he had loved doing, again. Over the years when he was a park ranger, he'd done so many of the tours at every favorite spot in the park, he knew the spiels by heart, he could say them in his sleep, even after years not doing them. Lastly, an extra paycheck, as small as it would be. And it wasn't as if he couldn't use the cash. He loved buying his grandchildren gifts, and visiting New York. Additional pocket money for day trips there would be nice. The city was expensive. Hmmm.

When Henry didn't answer immediately, Collins's expression turned glum. "Do you need some time to think about it?" Clearly, the man was desperate. That, or he missed Henry a heck of a whole lot.

Their food came and was set on the table in front of them. Before Collins could take a forkful of his meatloaf, Henry said, "No, I don't need time to think about it. I'll do it. In fact, it's a timely offer. I have gotten tired of being alone so much, missed working in the park, being a ranger, missed you and the other rangers, too, so sure I'll do it. I always loved doing the visitor tours and making the educational speeches about each spot we stopped at. I got a kick out of them."

Henry then had the thought: *If I'm here in the park more, I might even run into Oscar and his family eventually. That would be great. I miss the little guy.*

Chief Collins leaned over the small table and good-naturedly slapped him on the back, a relieved smile transforming his features. "Thank goodness. I had really hoped you'd accept the position. I *really* need the help."

"I'll take the part-time job, Chief…on one

condition. I have to have Friday the 3rd of July off. I'm having a big weekend Fourth of July barbeque at the house, and I have people coming in and staying for the weekend."

"You got it. Actually, you don't have to start until after the Fourth of July holiday. Is the eighth of July okay to start with you?"

"It is. In fact," Henry added, "I was going to telephone you, and invite you and your wife, Emma, to the Fourth celebration at my house. But then you called me to come here first, so I'm asking you now in person."

"A Fourth of July barbeque?" The Chief Ranger's eyes were smiling.

"That's what I said. There will be good food, family, and friends. It'll start early Saturday morning, and last way into the night. My son, and daughter-in-law, and my grandkids are flying up from New York for it. They'll be staying the whole weekend. I was going to invite a couple other rangers, as well. I'll give you a list before I leave today and, if you would, could you invite them, as well? It'd save me a bunch of telephone calls."

"Sure, I will. Though some of the rangers will have eat and run, or some come later, so I can still have enough men that day to cover the park. But count me and Emma in. Emma loves barbeque. As I do. And I just happen to have that Saturday off. I know it'd be great to all get together again. It's been too long. I haven't seen your family in ages. Should we bring anything?"

"Only if you want to. As I recall, your wife makes delicious baked beans."

"She does. I'll ask her to make a pot of them, and we'll bring it along, then."

"Only if she wants to. I'll have plenty of food there. Justin and I will be doing the grilling. Steaks, hamburgers, and pork steaks."

"I can't wait." Collins leaned back in his chair, patting his full stomach contentedly. Collins had always enjoyed a good meal.

Henry asked various questions about the job, and as Collins answered him, he pondered: *Doing the tours would be like coming around full circle in his life. Starting almost at the beginning.* When he'd been simply a normal ranger, patrolling the park and happily lecturing to the visitors, before he'd become chief ranger living in his and Ann's beautiful cabin in the park, before the dinosaurs, and Ann's death, and…the aliens and their spaceships at Area 52. A full circle. Life was strange all right. But he realized he was happy about the job development. Truly happy.

The restaurant had filled up with the lunch crowd. There was a noisy family, with kids, sitting behind them, chatting, laughing, and eating. There were affectionate young couples conversing over their lunches, and a group of elderly people across the room in hiking clothes who looked as if they'd just come off one of the trails. Ah, it was so good to be back in the Mazama Village; so good to be in the peopled part of the park. He'd never realized how much he missed the visitors, but watching them, and their antics, he knew he had. Over the years of his ranger career there, he'd met so many interesting people. Now he looked forward to meeting more. His life wasn't over yet. He smiled at everyone and most smiled back.

Halfway through the meal, Henry remembered something. "By the way, Chief, has Ranger Finch or anyone else, seen any more of those strange lights zipping around in the skies he was going on about when we were having lunch that day at the Lodge?"

Collins scratched the side of his face where his day-old beard was coming in, and pushed his empty plate away. He'd ordered dessert, and wanted to clear space for it. "He hasn't said anything to me lately. No one else, not even any other rangers or visitors have, far as I know, reported any further sightings, either."

Henry related to Collins how he and Patterson, while out camping, met Professor Hescott in the park, and his claims on what he believed the lights were, when he and Patterson camped out in the park the week before.

Chief Collins let out a short laugh, but Henry caught the hesitancy in it. "People have been saying lights they can't explain in the sky, or unidentified objects, are aliens for decades. I don't believe it. I don't believe aliens exist, much less bother with visiting our little planet. Why would they? If aliens have the technology to light-speed their way here, what could they want from us? We'd be primitives to them. We only went to the moon once, and haven't been back yet. We don't do space travel. My guess is if they do voyage here from some faraway galaxy or universe, they would want something from us. Something we might not want to give them. Our planet, its resources, water, something or everything. Maybe they're cannibals and we look like cattle to them, and they want to eat us." Collins visibly winced. "If aliens do exist, Henry, as far as I'm concerned, they can just stay away. Forever."

Henry had to bite his tongue. *Oh, Collins, aliens do exist. They've been here many, many times before. For thousands of years. I know. I've seen their spaceships. I've seen them.* But Henry couldn't reveal that. That was all top-secret. He'd signed the papers where he'd promised never to speak about what had happened at Area 52. What astounding conversations he could have with people if he could tell them what he'd seen and experienced. It would blow their minds. Darn, how he wished he could talk freely about Area 52 and the aliens. He couldn't.

When they were done eating lunch, and catching up on personal and park stuff, Henry took Collins to headquarters and dropped him off at the front door. "I'll see you this weekend. Any time after eight in the morning. I'll be up getting things ready for the feast."

Chief Collins merrily saluted as Henry drove away.

He hated to return to his house. His empty house. As he walked inside, he felt the same loss he always did. Ann wasn't there. Even after a year and a half, his brain, his heart, couldn't comprehend the reality of it. It hurt every damn time. He wondered if it would ever feel anything but sad.

CHAPTER 4

Justin was sitting on the porch swing with Henry and Isabel. Isabel had flown up with Justin and the family the night before, and Henry had been happy to see all of them. The Fourth of July celebration had been going on all day; the food had been prepared and eaten, the day hadn't been too hot, and there'd been no rain. The grandchildren were playing Frisbee in the yard, running, yelling, and laughing. All his friends, Patterson, Sherman, their kids, Steven James and his wife Doctor Emily, Chief Collins, Ranger Finch, Cutters, and Cromwell, and Professor Hescott were all there around him. Everyone was snacking on leftovers from the lunch, or a variety of desserts, sitting in the kitchen on a table, or out enjoying the beautiful evening.

Patterson, Henry took note, eavesdropping occasionally on the animated conversations, seemed extremely interested in everything Professor Hescott and Ranger Finch had to say about the mysterious lights they'd seen in the park. The scientist and the ranger talked a long time about them. Justin, sitting near them, listening, also appeared fascinated to what the two men had to say. Of course, he would, having been at Area 52.

Earlier, Henry had questioned Professor Hescott, and then Ranger Finch, if either of them had seen the glowing orbs lately. Neither had. Professor Hescott was still camping out in the park, hunting for them, while Ranger Finch said he was more than happy to have not seen any more.

"They gave me the willies," Ranger Finch had confessed. "I don't like things I can't explain. I don't need to see them again. I've seen enough."

When the professor started in on his belief that the lights were alien crafts, Justin remained silent. Of course, he would. All of them who had worked at Area 52 had promised, on threat of imprisonment, not to talk about what had happened there. Not to blab about the alien ships or the beings that must have traveled in them. Henry could see that Justin was having a hard time not commenting.

For Henry, he hoped, since he was going to be in the park regularly with his new job, that over time he might see the strange orbs. He'd love to discover what they truly were.

Henry and Isabel sat and chatted, catching

up. They'd kept in touch. She'd visited him a few times since Area 52 had shut down, and he'd seen her at Justin and Delores's apartment in New York, but it was good to have her there for the weekend. They had time to really visit.

"You like being in the lab with Justin again?" he asked her, smiling at the way Justin and the Professor were hitting it off, since the Professor had stopped conversing with Ranger Finch and Finch had wandered off, probably for more of the chocolate cake. Finch had a real sweet tooth. Justin and Hescott had fallen into an animated conversation about all things scientific and probably would be for for hours. It did Henry's heart good to see the old man happy.

"Oh, I like my new job well enough, I suppose." Isabel leaned her chin into her hands, and whispered aside to him so no one else could hear. "Not near as much as I liked working at Area 52. I not only miss the work, but all the other scientists. I mean, I am happy to be home in my New York apartment once more, so is Mr. Fluffy, but studying those spaceships were a once in a hundred lifetimes' gift and I grieve that I've lost the opportunity. I miss the friends I made, there, too. You and

Justin, and Patterson today, are the only ones I see anymore. The rest have scattered all over the country, taking new positions."

"At least you had a year at Area 52, I only had a few months, and you're still working with Justin," Henry whispered back. "Can you talk about any of it?"

Her sigh was so soft he could barely hear it. "There's not much to tell. Justin and I are just compiling what details and information we can recall from the year we spent at Area 52. Since all our data and proof of what we were doing disappeared along with all the DNA, we're doing the best we can. Luckily, both of us had hand-written journals and notes with our discoveries, theories, and other important information laid out on timelines since the first days we were at the base. I've journaled since my sister was taken. It's always been therapeutic. Those journals *did not* disappear when everything else did, maybe because they were hand-written. So, we have something to work with and study further–those detailed chronicles, and our memories. The government is paying us well. We get to work in our New York labs and go home every night if we want to. At least it's a job. It pays the bills and buys cat food for Mr.

Fluffy."

"I have news, also," Henry told her. "I'm going back to work, part-time anyway."

"Really? Where? Doing what? You're not going back to hunting rogue dinosaurs out in the far reaches of the wildernesses, are you? I think *all* the dinosaurs are at long last gone, thanks to your alien friends."

Henry thought of Oscar and his growing family. No, not all the dinosaurs were gone.

"Oh, I'm done hunting dinosaurs. That last little brouhaha where we were running terrified from those two rampaging blood-thirsty dinosaurs, Heckle and Jeckle, in the bunker, did it for me. If more blood-thirsty dinosaurs reemerge somehow, someone else can go after them. I'm done. I'm going to return to Crater Lake Park as a part-time ranger, mostly giving the visitors their park tours. Three days a week. That's safe. Turns out, Chief Collins is somewhat short on rangers and has asked me to step in and help for a while. Seeing I have nothing else better to do, I accepted."

"That's great, Henry. I recall you did say you loved being a park ranger; especially enjoyed the time you spent escorting the visitors around the park. I'm happy for you. I know you must have been at loose ends since Area 52 shut down."

"I have been." Henry met her gaze and tried not to look too despondent. "You know what it's like when you plan for years for a retirement with your spouse, the things you were going to do, the places you were going to visit, and then one day you find yourself alone. It's been over eighteen months, but most people don't understand that I'm still…lost. I'm not grieving every day any longer, but there are still bad days. Continuing loneliness. People don't want to hear about your continuing sorrow, or how much you still miss your dead sweetheart. How you hate the empty house. I have to keep it to myself. I need to keep busy. It's the only thing that helps. Those months at the base were a Godsend. Wish we were still there."

"Oh, I understand the grief and shock of losing a spouse completely. Henry," she murmured, laying her hand gently on his for a moment before she took it away, "but I'll tell you from someone who's been there, it does get better over time. A lot of time." Her expression was sympathetic. "You just go on with your life. Keep your family and friends close around you. Keep busy. The years will dull your misery. You'll even be happy again one day. You'll see."

Isabel's gaze was taking in the people milling around the yard and porch, plates of food in their hands, as they chatted with each other. "This is good. This barbeque. Having people over helps the loneliness. You returning to the park as a ranger, living the fullest life you can will help, too. That's the best way you can combat losing someone you love and dealing with the resulting lonesomeness, I know. I never would have made it since Bill died if I wouldn't have had my friends, my work, and Mr. Fluffy." Her smile was soft, understanding.

Henry nodded as if he agreed with her. In reality, he knew he'd never be the same without Ann. He was pretending to be all right. He pretended all the time. It was easier…on other people.

Steven James had worked his way to Henry's side, holding hands with his doctor wife, Emily. Henry hadn't seen them for a long time, and earlier, when they'd first arrived, they'd caught each other up on their lives. Steven had finished his schooling, had become a full-fledged nurse, and worked alongside his wife at her clinic. He still sometimes took his guitar into a local coffeehouse, or family bar, and played a couple sets with some musician friends. “Less and less,” he told Henry. “Because my work at the clinic, and my family, takes more and more time. I continue to write songs, and one day I might even record them. One day.”

“You are content with your life, though,” Henry inquired. “Right?”

Steven had hugged his wife, kissing the top of her head. “I’ve never been happier. I love being able to help people when they’re sick. I’ve never felt so useful and fulfilled. I love my music, but I love helping people more. I’m proud of it.”

Henry remembered his daughter, Laura, who’d been a nurse during the dinosaur wars, had also been proud of helping people.

“That’s all that matters.” Henry tried not to be jealous of the man, of the wife and family he had. He tried hard not to be jealous of any of the contented couples he knew. Though, seeing them smiling and giving each other loving looks, and sneaking hugs, he couldn’t help but think: *One day one of you will be gone, and the one who remains will feel this sad loneliness I feel. This ache of the heart, and you’ll never be the same again. You will wander around an empty house that no longer feels like home. Running, but there's no place to run; no place to hide. Alone. Always alone. You'll ask: how did that happen?* And he'd then feel sorry for them. Every one of them. Where there were two, one day there would only be one.

The day was a success. Henry and Justin barbequed the meat, with a little help from Patterson, and the kitchen counter and table were full of the side dishes that had been brought, his guests ate, laughed, and talked among themselves. A good time was had by all. Henry was glad he'd had the barbeque.

Sometimes Henry felt almost out-of-body, peering in at someone else's normal life. But he mingled with his guests, ate the delicious food, talked to everyone, and smiled a lot. There were even moments when he could say he was nearly happy. It felt wonderful to have some of the old gang around him. It felt good to have such a friend as Isabel by his side. It was nice to see how joyful Professor Hescott had been the whole day. Henry had done a good deed.

By nightfall, most of his guests were gone, except for Patterson and his family, Isabel, Justin, Delores and the grandkids. Living so close, Patterson and his family would be the last to leave around nine o'clock. Justin, his family, and Isabel, were staying another day with him. Tomorrow they were going to take the grandchildren to a movie in town, and out to the park afterwards. They'd all get a flight back to New York early Monday morning.

Late that night, when everyone had left, and Isabel, Delores, and the kids were tucked into their rooms sleeping, Henry and Justin sat on the rear porch each with a cup of coffee and a last piece of cake, talking.

"I couldn't help but notice you and Professor Hescott got along quite well," Henry remarked, his eyes studying the starry skies. It was a beautiful clear night. Warm, but with a hint of a cool breeze. The perimeter of woods at the edge of his property was a dark lumpy line, but he could hear the night creatures chirping, clicking, and singing out in the trees. Fireflies blinked on and off in the darkness, and formed a blanket of blinking lights across the yard. Ann would have loved this night.

"Interesting guy." Justin sounded tired. Jet lag most likely, or too much partying.

"Did you two discuss his strange lights in the night sky?" Henry already knew the answer to that question, yet he asked anyway.

He wanted to see what Justin had to say on the subject.

"We did. Apparently, he's been chasing them, or lights like them, for years, all across the country."

Henry exhaled. "He believes they're alien ships."

"They might be." Justin shrugged in the dark. "Wouldn't that be something? Maybe it's the same aliens who took those two spaceships of ours from Area 52? I had to pretend what he was telling me couldn't be true. Aliens really exist? I hated lying to the old man."

Yeah, when we both know aliens really do exist. Henry shivered, as warm as the night was, at the thought of those spirit aliens returning–for any reason. If they did, what would they want? They'd want something. Chances are, it wouldn't be good. He couldn't forget what they'd told him about how humans were thought of by them. Destructive parasitic creatures.

"Of course, I felt bad, knowing what I, what we, know–that extraterrestrials and their spaceships are real, but, like you, I couldn't say anything about that."

"No, you couldn't," Henry said. "Patterson

and I both kept our mouths shut about the existence of the extraterrestrials."

"Anyway, Professor Hescott said he'll continue to hunt for those lights. He's going back into the park again this week. He's determined to track them down."

"I know, Justin. He promised he'd call me if he saw them again. He figured out that was the real reason Patterson was out in the woods with me last week. Patterson knew about the lights and he's searching for them, too. You know what I think?"

"What?"

"Patterson's new government assignment has something to do with those orbs. I believe the government is actively looking for the aliens to return. They're on alert. They want to be ready this time."

"Henry, I do believe you're correct. I've spoken to Patterson recently and I also believe that his new job involves…aliens. It makes sense after Area 52 and his involvement there."

"I think so, too." Henry chuckled. "Do you think the military has found another spaceship somewhere?"

Justin's reply seemed thoughtful. "Wouldn't that be something?"

"It would. Do you think they'd call you in again to help uncover the spaceship's secrets? Another Area 52?"

"Only if dinosaurs were the pilots or connected in some way to the mystery. I'm a paleontologist, remember?"

"I remember."

"Hey, Henry, you mentioned earlier you'll be working as a ranger in the park again. I think that's fantastic. I never thought you were actually ready to retire. And since Ann is gone, and Area 52 is gone, it'll be good for you. Get you out of the house. Could be you might run into those strange lights yourself. If you do, will you let me know about it? Give me a call?"

"I sure will."

"And," Justin slid a conspiratorial glance aside at Henry, "when are we going to take that camping trip into the park's deep woods? Look for Oscar and his family? Ever since you told me the little guy's still alive, and you saw him, I've been wanting to go search for him. See him and his progeny. Get some pictures and DNA samples from him to study. It's almost unbelievable that he lived through the aliens' magic all-things-dinosaur vanishing trick. It's like a miracle."

"It is. Why don't you come down sometime in August," Henry suggested. "The weather is the warmest then. We can take a long hike out into the area I saw Oscar and his pack. Camp out for a time. We might find Oscar, or he'll find us."

"August, huh?"

"Yeah, August. I'll ask Chief Collins for a week off, and we'll go on the great Oscar quest."

"It's a date, Henry. Let's make it August the first to the eighth. Lock in the dates now. If I ask a month ahead of time, I can get it off. At times, it is convenient to have my brother-in-law as my boss. It'd be great to see Oscar again."

"It would. So…August first it is. You got a deal." Henry hoped they would see the little dinosaur. A troubling thought hit him: *the strange lights in the park's skies…if they were alien spaceships…and, as Professor Hescott believed, they were hunting for something or someone…were they looking for Oscar and his family, too? And if they were, why? What would they do if they found him? He didn't like thinking about it.*

Justin yawned, stretching his long legs out on the porch floor, then his arms upwards to the sky. "I'm ready for some shut-eye. It'd been a long day, but a lovely day. Thanks for having us. We all had a grand time."

"Thanks for coming. I loved seeing you, Delores; the grandkids. That picture of me and Ann that Phoebe drew and gave to me as a gift is so lovely, so lifelike. I'm going to frame it and hang it in the living room in a place of honor so I can look at it all the time. She is such a fine artist; such a sweet child. Timothy is a great little guy, too. Their love makes Ann being gone so much easier to bear. I miss all of you so much. You guys live too far away."

"On that topic," Justin rose from the chair he'd been sitting in, "why don't you come out to New York for a visit and spend some quality time with those you say you miss so much? If you're only working Wednesdays to Fridays, that leaves Saturday, Sunday, Monday, and Tuesday free. Four days is more than enough for a nice visit out to the east coast. I'm sure my brother-in-law, as he does for us, would send a plane for you. At no cost to you. A free ride."

"I'll think about it."

Henry was on his feet, too. His bed was calling him. It was late. Sasha had already turned in. She was probably curled up asleep on his bed. The barbeque had been a big success, and Henry was looking forward to another day tomorrow where he wouldn't be lonely, with family.

"Will you consider coming for a while late next month for a visit, Henry, or in September at the latest? Phoebe and Timothy have a long list of places they'd like to show you; things they'd like to do with you."

"I definitely will come. How can I turn my grandkids down?"

They said their goodnights, and Justin headed off to his bed.

For a short time, Henry lingered outside on the swing and breathed in the sweetness of the night. *It had been a good day. Family, friends, tasty food. He hadn't been alone. A really good day. For a while he had been happy.*

Chapter 5

"Sir, please watch your step," Henry Shore, part-time Park Ranger for Crater Lake said, cautioning the woman as she inched closer towards the caldera rim overlooking the shimmering lake. A leather holster holding Henry's gun squeaked as he moved. It felt strange wearing his duty gun again, but it felt good. Normal.

When he realized the visitor hadn't heard him, Henry instinctively reached out and took the man's arm, pulling him away from the edge. With an inward smile, he remembered: *visitors rarely listened.* They traipsed all over the place never looking where they put their feet, lollygagging along; gaping at the sites. Always feeding the animals, though they'd been warned not to because it was against park rules. Some of the wildlife could be dangerous, especially the bears. They weren't like the stuffed teddy bears one could buy in the Rim Village toy shop, cute and cuddly–the real ones could claw and bite. They could kill a human. At least once a year some naive park visitor was mauled or bitten by an animal because they hadn't heeded the rangers' advice. But park visitors and their money,

Henry still recalled, were what kept the park open, and the rangers' paychecks coming.

"It's dangerous to get too close," Henry warned the careless man in the most deterrent tone he could emit. "The rim is composed of shale, loose rocks, and dirt, combined with patches of snow. In some sections it's very slippery." In some parts of the park and along the rim, it was not unusual to have snow on the ground until July. "It's very unstable. Doesn't take much to go sliding over the edge or to start an avalanche.

"And it's a straight plummet of nearly five hundred feet in some places, and in others as far down as two thousand, to the water. Right here it's about fifteen-hundred."

Suddenly Henry experienced a ripple of Déjà vu. He'd been running the tours for a little over three weeks and, as he'd hoped and suspected, the lectures had come back to his brain and lips easily. He'd told the same stories for so many years, when he'd been a ranger, they'd been engrained in his memory. He could recite them in his sleep, and at times it was almost as if he was.

Some of the visitors he'd met knew who he was, ex-chief park ranger and the great dinosaur hunter, were in awe, and wanted to hear his dinosaur stories. He usually obliged them. To them he was famous. It was flattering. When they inquired about Ann and her articles, her illustrations, and her books, he proudly answered those queries as well. It had gotten easier as time had gone by, and his sadness had lessened. He was proud of her. She had her legion of adoring fans as well. He found he liked talking and bragging about her. It didn't make him weep inside any longer.

The man caught his breath, met Henry's eyes, and nodded gratefully. He obediently stepped back. So did some of the others who'd inched too close to the precipice. They were already winded from toiling uphill a quarter of a mile through the close-set trees, slipping on the hunks of lava rock and powdery pumice, weighed down with all the junk park visitors inevitably seemed to drag along: video and regular cameras, cell phones, umbrellas, walking sticks, and enough snacks to last a week.

In the park it was cool, even though it was the end of July. The summer season lasted barely two months until early September. Then the white stuff would begin to fall and continue falling again until early June. There were small patches of snow dotting the landscape around them and thinly crusted up along parts of the rim. Chief Collins had had told him that last winter the park had had over seventy inches of the white stuff. A record.

"You say the lake was once a volcano?" the man who'd come too close to the edge queried, his eyes studying the blue lake gleaming so far below, a huge sapphire embedded in a setting of multicolored rocks and lush evergreens. The view from the rim was breathtaking.

"Yes, sir," Henry replied. "Ages ago Crater Lake was a volcano called Mount Mazama, part of the Cascade Mountain range that stretched from Mount Garibaldie, in what is now British Columbia, to Lassen Peak in northern California. Geologists estimate it erupted about seven thousand years ago. Fiery magma, ash, cinder, and pumice spewed out in avalanches, some of them coming from underground beneath the base of the mountain. The escaping lava streams left a vast cavity that caused the twelve-thousand-foot peak to collapse and form this magnificent caldera.

"Over the centuries the caldera accumulated water from rain and snow and created the lake you see below. Evaporation and seepage, balanced with precipitation, keep the water level fairly constant; there are no inlets or outlets that we know of. The lava cooled over time and now the water's pretty cold, fifty-five degrees at the surface in high summer; much colder at the lower depths. Right now, the surface water is around thirty-eight degrees Fahrenheit."

Henry continued with the rest of the familiar speech, his mind drifting now and then to other things. It had been a busy, satisfying three weeks. Though he was only part-time, the others rangers had automatically fallen into line as if he'd never left, treating him with all the respect and comradery as when he'd been their chief. There were times when one or more of the other rangers would ask his judgment on something, or even look to him for their orders, as if he was still in charge, and he'd have to steer them gently to Chief Ranger Collins. He wasn't chief ranger any more. Henry didn't mind that the rangers deferred to him at times, it was flattering, and neither did Chief Collins. But he didn't want the job even if it was his to have again. Not without Ann. That was his past. He was content working part-time in the park only for as long as he wanted to. He could quit whenever he wanted to. His choice.

He realized he'd paused in the middle of the speech, daydreaming, and his audience was waiting for him to continue. Dragging his mind back to what he was supposed to be doing, he went on, "The pure water supports little life, except for aquatic moss, which, by the way, is found at extreme depths in this particular lake. Originally the caldera contained no fish due to the lack of adequate food and spawning grounds; but over the years the park has stocked it and now there's rainbow and brown trout, and Kokanee salmon in it. No fishing license is required." He tagged on the smile he always did at the end of the paragraph.

Henry didn't notice the man attempting to snag his attention. He was looking in the other direction, still talking. "Later, additional volcanic activity within the caldera produced the cinder cone, a volcano within a volcano, which you see below to your right." He pointed at a diminutive island that rose out of the water and was covered with evergreens. "The island is known as Wizard Island–which, by the way, is as high as Niagara Falls and covers several acres. The island also holds three or four boat houses where some of the tour boats are kept. There are also two smaller cones in the lake, but both are below water level."

Henry watched what appeared to be two water bugs across the lake leaving Cleetwood Dock. They were really sixty-foot boats heading towards Wizard Island. Probably the last tour of the day and running late. Like always. *Nothing much has changed*, Henry mused, *here in the park*. Or at least the park he'd known before Godzilla and the rest of the ravaging dinosaurs, had taken up residence. It made him feel at home, though, and he was happy to be back. The park had always been as much a home to him as the one he'd shared with Ann. It was what he knew.

Below were more people with other tours strolling along the crater's rim. Sometimes their voices could be heard drifting on the wind, snatches of conversations or soft laughter that played in whispers around Henry's head.

He acknowledged, with a closed mouth smile or a tip of his hat, the people in the tour group working their way past them up the two-and-a-half miles from Rim Drive to the fire tower at the summit of Mount Scott. Mount Scott was the highest point in the park at 8,926 feet. It had a wonderful view of the surrounding lands, including the second highest mountain in the park, Cloudcap, and was popular with the visitors.

"There are only six lakes in the world," Henry resumed his lecture in a resonant voice, "deeper than Crater Lake, which, at its greatest depth, has been measured at approximately 1,932 feet. In the western hemisphere, only Great Slave Lake in Canada is deeper, and only by about eighty-three feet."

Henry stared out over the circle of water below, still able to appreciate the beauty of the spot after all the years he'd been there, and been away. He enjoyed his new house in Klamath Falls, though not as much since Ann had died, but of all the places he'd lived in his life, Crater Lake was the most like home to him. It made him happy just to be there.

A young boy with bright red hair peered over the edge, tossing a small rock into the abyss. He was about to toss a shiny piece of quartz, but decided to pocket it instead. Looking up guiltily, the boy pretended to pay more attention to Henry's speech.

No, nothing had changed.

"Crater Lake is approximately 25 miles in diameter and the rim that we're standing on is formed of varicolored lava rocks," Henry educated the group.

"The water is so incredibly blue," one of them, a middle-aged woman with a timid smile commented, unintentionally interrupting him. The visitors always noticed the vivid blue color. It was one of the first things they commented on. That hadn't changed, either.

"I've never seen such a brilliant blue," said another woman, further back in the crowd, supporting the observation. She was holding the hand of a young girl, about ten years old, with braces that glittered in the sun every time she smiled.

Henry explained. "That's because the water is so crystalline and unpolluted it acts as a prism for the sun's rays, reflecting them to the surface. When it's overcast or cloudy the blue isn't quite as intense."

The water below, a mirror, cast back everything around it in hauntingly muted colors. A hawk swooped down over their heads and with a dip of its wings soared into the billowy clouds above.

This has happened before, Henry thought. *I've been here, seen this, before.*

It was getting late. Time to wind up the tour and get the people back down to their RVs, lodge rooms, or tents, safe and snug, before the night fell. The park could get extremely dark after the sun went down.

He sped up the program, shivering with the first arrival of the evening air. “The lake was discovered in June 1853, by a party of prospectors led by John W. Hillman as he was searching for the ‘Lost Cabin’ gold mine. He never found the mine, but while climbing up the slopes of Mount Mazama to get a better view of the area, he and his mule nearly stumbled over the precipice here. Which would have been a really bad step.” Henry pulled out the same old joke. It always did the trick.

A couple of chuckles.

“Though Hillman never found the lost gold mine, discovering the lake was almost as good. I believe this is the most beautiful lake in the world–but, then, I guess I could be biased because I have spent so much of my life in the park. Well,” Henry declared, “it’s time to return to the lodge.”

Out of nowhere, the man who’d stepped too near to the edge blurted out, “Ranger Shore, have you or any of the other rangers, or any of the other people visiting in the park, seen the recent weird glowing lights in the sky? My wife and I,” the man tilted his head towards a slender woman, in khaki slacks and a blue sweatshirt, standing beside him, "have seen them now three nights in a row, and even twice in the daytime. We're camped out in the Mazama Campgrounds. Our friends have seen them, too. Other people in the camp." The visitor was snacking on a bag of potato chips and between words he popped one after another into his mouth.

"What lights?" Henry had plastered a smile on his face, but inside an uneasiness stirred.

He was flooded with a stronger sense of Déjà vu. Last time it had been a monstrous creature that visitors had spotted in the lake and asked him about…now it was lights in the sky. *Here we go again. Yep, things never changed.*

"Yeah, they were really eerie. Sparkly globes of light that flew around high, miles maybe, up in the sky like crazy fireflies, going up, down, hovering above us at times as if they were watching us. But they were silent. They showed up three days, nights, in a row. Has anyone else seen them?"

Henry knew he shouldn't say much about the lights. Though Ranger Finch and Professor Hescott purported to have seen them, so far Henry hadn't. He didn't know what they were.

He didn't know enough to explain what they were. If they were a natural phenomenon or something else. Something benign or dangerous. He didn't want to upset the visitors for any reason. Often unexplained occurrences scared people. That, and he didn't want the park overrun with gawkers and the curious searching for them. He remembered what had happened all those years ago when the news of a monster in the lake had gotten out. Pandemonium.

He hated to withhold information, but he knew it was the best way to go for now. "I wouldn't know anything about them, friend. I haven't seen anything like that myself. Sorry."

The man appeared disappointed, but moved away with his wife when the rest of the group followed Henry down from the rim. It was a trek to the lodge where the visitors had all begun their tour, and it was getting late. The sun was poised on the horizon. The daylight was fading. Henry was tired from walking, the long day, was hungry, and wanted to get home. He not only had to escort the visitors to the lodge, he had a long drive home to Klamath Falls. The passage of time. That was the difference. He wasn't a young man anymore and his body got tired easier than a decade ago. His home, his sanctuary and all its comforts, beckoned him.

But he was bothered about what the visitor had said concerning the lights. He liked his life the way it was now. Simple. Normal. No dinosaurs. No aliens. No weird orbs. Working in the park. Visiting friends. Friends visiting him. It had taken him a long time to get his life balanced again. Somewhat. He still missed Ann every day; thought about her. Things had settled down, though. He realized that he needed, as long as God wanted him to be on this Earth, to be as content as he could be. One day he and Ann would be together again. All he had to do was live what was left of his life, be as happy as life would allow him to be, and wait.

*****

When Henry pulled into the driveway, it was dark. There was a package on the front porch. He picked it up as he went into the house. Inside, he switched on the light, and looked at the address the UPS package had come from. New York. Isabel.

Sasha had been coiled in a ball, sleeping on the sofa. She got up, stretched, and trailed behind Henry, meowing all the way, into the kitchen.

"I know, I know. You're hungry. I'm getting your supper right now. Keep your tail on."

Henry fed the feline. He sat down at the table. Opening the package, a smile settled on his lips. It was a Tupperware full of homemade yeast-risen cinnamon rolls. Isabel had said she'd make some and send them to him, and she had.

He'd flown out to visit Justin and the family in New York the weekend before. The visit was terrific. He'd gone to the zoo with his grandchildren; had gone roller skating with the family. He'd only fallen once. It'd been a really long time since he'd been on skates. He'd taken Isabel out to dinner one night to this exclusive restaurant she'd been wanting to go to, and the cinnamon rolls were her thank you for it. Somehow, they'd gotten on the subject of their baking specialties. Henry's specialty, of course, was grilled meat on the barbeque grill. She'd commented she was known for baking these special yeast cinnamon rolls, and people loved them. Since Henry had always had a fondness for yeast rolls, and said so, she promised to send him some. So, she had. That was sweet of her. She was a good friend.

Over dinner in New York, the two had discussed what they'd been up to since the Fourth of July celebration weekend. "I told you that I accepted that part-time ranger position in the park. I've started, and it's like old times. Like I never left. It feels good getting up early in the morning with something to do; having someplace to go a couple days a week where I can feel useful," Henry said. "What are you doing these days?"

"I'm still working with Justin at the lab in the New York, trying hard to salvage whatever we can salvage from the Area 52 days. Gleaning all we can from our journals that were the only things left behind."

"From what Justin says, the aliens didn't leave much for anyone to compile or study. What will you and Justin do after you finish up with what you have?"

"Funny you should ask that." She had gazed over his head with a wistful look on her face. The restaurant had been piping in music. Haunting old songs from the nineteen seventies. Beatles, James Taylor, the Eagles, and others of the era. The music brought back so many memories to Henry. His youth, his and Ann's youth. Their love and marriage. So many sweet times. "I thought I was going to return to teaching. I miss it. It was my original calling, my career, for many years before I was recruited for the dinosaur studies and began working for the government; ending up in Area 52."

"You're not going back to the teaching, then," he'd queried.

"No, I don't think so. I'd wanted to secure a tenured position at a local college. New York has been my home for such a long time. I grew up here. I lived my whole marriage here with my husband. I love the city. It's so vibrant. Alive. It has everything anyone could ever want."

Henry had agreed. "Yes, New York is a fascinating, exciting city, but I'm a country boy at heart. Give me the woods, the lakes, and the mountains. As you know, I started out as a cop here, for years, in New York. When Ann and I moved to Crater Lake, I knew I'd never leave. I adore Oregon. Crater Lake, and Klamath Falls. It's my home now."

"But you can have the best of both worlds. You can visit New York whenever you want, enjoy what it has to offer. Justin and Delores, your grandkids, love having you here. I like having you here, as well."

"That's true," Henry had responded, "and

you can come visit me in Klamath Falls whenever you want. I'll show you the town. We could even go visit the park again, or go camping if you'd like?" Then he threw in, "As friends, of course."

"Of course. That would be nice. I like playing the tourist. Being out in nature. I enjoy camping," Isabel had replied. "And Crater Lake is a great vacation destination."

"It is. But I'll be here in the city again soon. Justin and Delores want me to fly out for another extended weekend in the fall. They think my grandchildren need to see me more. They miss me."

She had locked eyes with him over the flickering candle on the restaurant's table. Their meal had been delicious and the company had been excellent. "I know they do. Timothy is always asking when you're coming to visit him again. He's a smart kid."

"I know he is. So is Phoebe. I do sometimes wish I didn't live so far away, but Klamath Falls is my home. I can't leave."

"I know," Isabel had retorted. "I understand."

And Henry had been sure she did. She loved New York as much as he did Crater Lake.

"Well," Henry had backtracked, curious, "then I take it you aren't going to teach here in the city?"

"No, not right now." She'd grinned enigmatically at him. "Patterson telephoned me last night and presented me with an offer I couldn't refuse."

"Patterson? He offered you a job? Working with him, I presume?"

"Representing someone else, he did. And yes, with him."

"Really?" Henry had felt a little jealous. Left out again.

"Yes."

"And…let me guess…it's highly classified and you can't blab about it." Henry had studied her face. No hint there.

"You got it. Sorry, Henry," she had answered, shrugging, as she drew her finger silently across her closed lips, "my lips are supposed to be sealed."

"Well, since I already suspected Patterson was on another hush-hush top-secret government project, and, like you, is not allowed tell me what it is, or talk about it, I can only guess what it might be concerning. I have a hunch."

"You do, do you?" There had been a

teasing tone in her voice.

That hadn't deterred Henry. "Yep. I have a *sneaking* suspicion it has something to do with…*aliens*. Again."

Isabel's eyes had sharpened in the candlelight, but hadn't given anything away. "What makes you say that?"

"Because we went camping weeks ago in the park and he seemed *really* interested in these reports of strange lights in the sky, which Ranger Finch earlier and then Professor Hescott had both claimed to have seen. Though he kept denying his interest in them, Patterson seemed unusually determined to see those lights for himself; that's where we met Professor Hescott, on our camping trip. He was searching for the orbs, as well, and had been for weeks. He joined us, and we all camped out together for days, but we never saw any lights in the skies. Professor Hescott swore the orbs were alien ships…hunting for something. He's been chasing them all over the country."

"Interesting." Isabel's face had shadowed. Henry was reminded of what had happened to her as a young woman when the aliens had landed in her family's yard, and abducted her younger sister. Aliens was a sore subject, a land mine, with Isabel.

"You didn't tell the professor that, yes, aliens do exist; that you know they do because you were at Area 52, and you've seen them?" Isabel had hesitantly queried.

"Of course not. As you well know, we're not allowed to speak about what we went through and saw at Area 52. I kept quiet. But Patterson was more than captivated in what the professor had to say and what the old man believed. So therefore, I highly suspect these mysterious lights Ranger Finch and Hescott have seen are somehow connected to whatever secret project Patterson's involved with."

Isabel had remained silent to that.

"Do you think Justin will join you and Patterson with this…new secret project?" Henry couldn't stop from digging just a little more.

"I don't know. I think I've been invited to become part of the team because, besides paleontology, and archeology, I also have an astrophysics degree. Patterson did say that was why they wanted me."

"See," Henry reiterated, "*aliens*."

"Henry–"

"I know, I know, you can't discuss it. Don't worry. I'll stop." He'd reassured her.

But inside, Henry thought he already had guessed what Patterson's–and now Isabel's–secret project was about. And sooner or later, he was sure, somehow, he'd learn if he were right.

"Well anyway, I wish you the best of luck with your new job, Isabel. I really do. Wish I was going with you," he groused good-naturedly. "I feel left out."

"I bet you do." She'd patted his hand. "But keep your eyes open for those mysterious lights in the park. Let me know if you see any of them."

Oddly enough, Patterson had said the same thing to him. "Oh, I will."

Henry had had a pleasant weekend with his family, and Isabel, in New York. He wasn't ready, probably never would be, to love another woman, but it was always good having friends.

He hadn't thought much about the lights in the sky the last few days until he remembered the visitor in the park that very day who'd claimed to have seen them, as well. He and others. Again, Henry had that uneasy feeling. Were they, as Professor Hescott had insisted to him and Patterson, really alien spaceships? And, if they were, what were they searching for?

He had another thought. If they *were* aliens…were they the same dinosaur aliens he'd met in Area 52, or were they different ones?

In the big ship, he'd asked the shadowy aliens: "There are other aliens?"

Many more, the alien had confessed. *The Grays, the Blues, and the Telerines.* And how many more? The universe was vast. Humans knew so little of it. They were too busy messing up their own planet to even care.

The cinnamon rolls, warmed up with butter on them, melted in his mouth. He had them for supper with a glass of milk.

I have to start eating a little better, he chided himself. *More fruits, vegetables, and balanced meals. What Ann had aways gotten onto him about. Maybe tomorrow….*

CHAPTER 6

Scott Patterson was up before dawn, said goodbye to his wife, Sherman, and laid soft kisses on the foreheads of his two children, before he picked up his suitcase, left the house, got in his car and drove to Kingsley ANG Base in Klamath Falls. Kingsley is where General Wallace had said the military transport plane would pick him up.

As the sun was rising, the airplane landed and Patterson was escorted onto it by two soldiers. Once inside the plane, his suitcase was taken and stuffed in a storage compartment on top, and he was led to a seat next to General Wallace. Told to buckle in, the plane coasted down the runway and lifted in flight. They were airborne. *Not wasting any time, are we*, Patterson thought to himself.

"Nice to have you aboard, Patterson," General Wallace greeted him, thrusting out a hand to shake the old FBI agent's.

The man looked older than the last time Patterson had seen him, and that was barely six months ago. Wallace's eyes, behind the thick glasses, were weary. His chocolate hued skin had a gray cast to it. There was an air of exasperation to his manner, as if he had a problem, and had no idea how to solve it. He wasn't the type of man, or soldier, to accept that. So, it made sense that he found what had been going on maddening.

"General," Patterson said to the military man. "Where are we going?" Patterson hadn't been informed where yet, and wanted to know. Not that it mattered. If the General wanted him to take a trip to the moon, he would have. A job, was a job, was a job. He served his country when asked, whatever and wherever that might be.

The General snorted. "You won't believe it. We're returning to Area 52."

Patterson was more than a little surprised. "Area 52? I thought it was shut down, closed up?"

"It was. For a short while, until this new threat arose. The President and his military advisors believed Area 52 was a better location to headquarter our research, offices, and men. Area 51 is too antiquated. The technology too backward, the meeting spaces too cramped."

Yes, Area 51 did exist. A famously not well-hidden secret that so many people, to this day, still debated over if it had ever existed or not; or still existed. The thing was, though not completely shuttered and still in curtailed use, it was the past. The military had constructed Area 52 as Area 51's successor. Area 52 was better in so many ways.

Patterson was delighted to be returning to Area 52. He'd been in Area 51 before, years ago, and as far as he was concerned, it was a depressing hole in the ground that had given him claustrophobia. The narrow halls and gloomy rooms had seemed haunted to him with the old memories of alien conspiracies.

"And Patterson, as you already know, we're calling in experts from various scientific fields, astrophysics, astronomy, xenology, and ufology, and others, to help us decide what to do. The President doesn't want just the top brass and the military to run this project. The threat to our planet is too great to leave it, he feels, just in the hands of men with guns. He believes we need level-headed scientific and diplomatic brains on solving this, as well."

Patterson was aware of that development. He'd been the one to convince Doctor Isabel Hutton to join the team. He'd recommended her. It hadn't taken much convincing. She had the right credentials, was one smart lady, and had a history with aliens. She'd most likely be there when he arrived.

"General, you called and I came. You gave me a vague idea of what this trouble you're having is, alien related in some way you said, but I need to know more. Do you and the government know anything more about the…problem?"

The General seemed to shift uncomfortably in his seat, his expression grim, as his gaze journeyed past Patterson and out the window into the swiftly moving heavens. Outside, the sky was a vivid blue, wispy with pale clouds. "I should wait until the task force is gathered together at the bunker and explain everything all at once, but I imagine it won't hurt to give you a condensed version of what's been occurring."

Yet what General Wallace divulged to Patterson as they flew towards Area 52, still shocked the ex-FBI agent. It more than shocked him, it scared him, and it took a lot to do that.

When the General was finished, Patterson told him about the camping trip he'd taken with Henry Shore; being joined by eccentric Professor Hescott, who had claimed he was searching for mysterious orbs in Crater Lake Park.

"The Professor said he has seen the orbs in different areas of the park. He's part of an Internet website where like-minded alien hunters post their alien sighting experiences. He says the sightings have increased. Some of them have even seen alien spaceships."

The military man sighed, massaging his fingers along the side of his nose. "Those mysterious lights or orbs, whatever you want to call them, Patterson, have been seen all over the world in the last weeks. They're everywhere."

"But," Patterson said, "That's not unusual. Unexplained Aerial Phenomena have been spotted in the skies worldwide for centuries, stretching back as far as the fourteen hundreds, so that's not new. Since its founding in nineteen seventy-four, the National UFO Reporting Center has documented around ninety thousand UAP sightings, with almost 95% of those sightings supposedly easily explained away as military tests, weather balloons, or other terrestrial activity."

"Or so says the government," the General quipped sarcastically. "You are correct, in the past, some, and I say only some, so-called sightings were military tests, weather balloons, or other terrestrial activities, but that was *before*. In the last month, the number of bonified true sightings of extra-terrestrial *spaceships* have increased ten-fold. Something is going on. Something big. Our National Aeronautics and Space Administration (NASA), which is home of the Johnson Space Center, and our top observatories across the country, our scientists, and the President think so, too. That's why the task force has been brought together.

"There's more. A great deal more." The General closed his eyes, taking a deep breath. "We will discuss all of that when we get to Area 52 and the whole team is gathered around."

The airplane landed, Patterson and General Wallace disembarked and were driven to the bunker.

*****

Patterson maneuvered his way down the corridors he knew well on his transport, parked it in front of a double steel door, and entered the conference room. Besides General Wallace, there were six other individuals gathered around the table. Patterson was pleased to see that five of them were the same scientists, now those he considered old friends, from his last stint at Area 52. Doctor Isabel

Hutton, of course, but also doctors Russell Gartner, Lucia Walters, Stanley Louison, and Courtney Waverly. There was only one other person he didn't know. As he strolled into the room, he waved at the familiar faces; some of the scientists waved in return, or nodded. Patterson took a seat beside Doctor Hutton.

"Good to see you, Scott." Isabel smiled a welcome at him.

"Good to see you all, too. It's like old home week here," he replied, staring around at everyone. "We're only missing Justin and Henry." *And wouldn't both of them be tickled to be here with everyone*, he thought. *Especially Henry.*

General Wallace, nodding in Patterson's direction, spread his hands to include the people at the table. "Patterson, you know these five characters," and the General even let a sly smile slip out, "but you have yet to meet the sixth one of the team, this is Doctor Lawrence Emmet. He's head scientist, an alien expert of world renown, at the US Naval Air Systems Command." The renowned scientist was an older man who could have been anywhere in his seventies, with long curly snow-white hair, and the most intense blue eyes Patterson had ever seen with bushy dark eyebrows curved above them. The man's eyes were virtually hypnotic they glittered so brightly. The white hair contrasted with the dark eyebrows.

"Doctor Emmet is also part of the Airborne Object Identification and Management Synchronization Group, or AOIMSG as we call them, which has merged with and succeeded the Navy's Unidentified Aerial Phenomena Task Force, to assess and mitigate any associated threats to safety of flight and national security. The Department of Defense takes reports of incursions–by any airborne object, identified or unidentified–very seriously, and investigates each one. All of their people will be reporting to him, and to us, from this time forward. Both organizations, as well as a couple other government agencies, are also going to coordinate with us as we go forward."

This is big. This is really big. The powers that be must believe we–humanity–are really in danger, if these government organizations are truly working together. A rare occurrence, indeed. Most of the time these organizations don't like to share the glory. They don't work well together. But they are now.

Patterson rose from his chair, and walked over to Doctor Lawrence Emmet and, as the other man came to his feet, they shook hands. The scientist was very tall; so tall he towered over Patterson.

Geez, Patterson thought, *the guy has to be six-six at least. Maybe more.*

"I'm duly impressed, Doctor Emmet. It's an honor to meet you," Patterson told the scientist. "I've been following your career, your published dissertations, and your career for many years."

The tall man seemed taken-aback by the unsolicited praise. "Thank you for the undeserved compliments, Scott Patterson. I simply do my job as so many others do," he answered with a tight smile. "And I also am aware of your considerable accomplishments. General Wallace had told me all about you. FBI agent. Your battle on the front lines against the rampaging dinosaurs. You're a genuine hero."

"Thank you, Doctor Emmet. But, as you, I was, and am, only doing my job. What I'm paid, and paid well, for." A humble smile.

Patterson settled down beside Isabel, who gave him a welcoming grin and a friendly pat on the shoulder, as General Wallace took his place at the head of the table. Patterson could see that Isabel was happy to be there, though there was an anxious look in her eyes.

"Didn't I just see you at Henry's barbeque," she whispered aside to Patterson.

"You did." Patterson winked at her. "I'm surprised that most of the old gang is here. It's nice."

"It is, isn't it?" Isabel replied. "Except I don't think this is going to be as much fun as exploring abandoned alien spaceships. I think we have a real problem."

"What do you mean?"

"You'll see." Isabel gestured at the General. "He'll tell you."

General Wallace, clearing his throat to gain everyone's attention, his gaze meeting Patterson's, launched the meeting with an alarming revelation. "As of the beginning of last month, the reported sightings of UAPs have increased…all across the globe. We don't know why. People are seeing everything from glowing spheres in the sky that zip in and zip out at a high velocity, to actual spaceships, some moving at very slow speeds, and some that are traveling, it is believed, at unbelievably high velocities, and can change direction on a dime. They seem to be watching us. More than usual."

Isabel arched an eyebrow at Patterson.

General Wallace went on speaking. “There have been other, overly aggressive, on the aliens part, *incidents*…as long ago as two thousand and seventeen there were almost daily sightings of UAPs harassing one of our warships near San Diego. But that was rare. Now those kinds of unsettling confrontations have also proliferated exponentially to a frightening level. Lately, military planes have been hassled by similar UAPs. More every week.

“As you probably all know, there were congressional hearings on extraterrestrial activities recently and, in light of what is going on now, the government, though it offered little insight to what the UAFs really are, has recommended the government improve the policies, training and tech needed to further investigate and understand them. They want us to be ready for whatever comes. Thus, here we are. We’re one of the many new task forces being formed to investigate these new possible threats.

“In my opinion, not a minute too soon. Should have been yesterday.”

Patterson waited for what he was afraid General Wallace was leading up to. He had a good idea what it was. He was putting together all the signs, and it didn't look good for humanity.

The General hesitated and then continued, "In the last four weeks a steady stream of UAFs have been captured by night vision cameras by the US Naval Air Systems Command. Even NASA has joined the hunt for the ever-increasing UAPs and has been seeing more and more of them; reporting what they see to the DOD when they do. Different shaped and glowing objects that fly over the sky of the United States and often stop for a heartbeat of time. Some of the objects do not appear to have any propulsion systems, and eventually they flash, and then disappear into the atmosphere. These sightings haven't just been occurring in the United States.

"And, disturbingly, in Ukraine, over Kyiv, unidentified flying objects, according to a new report from the Main Astronomical Observatory of the National Academy of Sciences of Ukraine, having been swarming since the war there began. The researchers have divided the UAP observations into two categories: *cosmics* and *phantoms*. According to the report, *cosmics* are luminous objects brighter than the background sky and have been observed flying solo as well as in squadrons. *Phantoms*, by contrast, are dark objects, usually appearing *completely black*, as if absorbing all light falling onto them. They range from ten to forty feet wide and can travel at speeds they estimate are near to thirty-three thousand miles per hour. In comparison, an intercontinental ballistic missile can only reach speeds of up to fifteen thousand miles per hour."

Patterson thought: *They're observing the war. Not good, with all the atrocities the Russians have been accused of performing. This war shows the worst of human sins. What would aliens think of our race watching this conflict?* He respectfully interrupted the General, "Are we sure these are UAFs?"

"Some believe they are, while others, the U.S. Office of the Director of National Intelligence for one, believe it is possible that at least some of those swarming UAPs above Ukraine are nefarious technologies deployed by China, Russia, or other nations, or non-governmental entities, and may be linked to foreign surveillance or military technologies. That debate continues.

"But the MeerKAT radio telescope, in South Africa, as well as others across the globe, have been witnessing these UAPs as well. They seem to be surveilling any areas of warfare that are occurring anywhere on the planet. The aliens are spying on us.

"To top it all, MeerKAT is also receiving these bizarre flashes, or pulses, from outer space that last about three hundred milliseconds; or longer. The pulses aren't all that uncommon. They've been getting them for years. It's the increased number of continuous pulses that is extremely rare. Someone or something far out in the galaxy seems to be communicating with someone, or something, here on Earth, or around Earth. That, along with other suspicious sequences of events, and the strange UAPs seen all over the world, has put the fear of God into all of us. The government is scared. And when the government gets scared, we are all on high alert, and saying prayers."

"What sequence of events exactly?" Patterson had to press. He didn't need to. He had a really bad feeling. He remembered very well the two spaceships they had had at Area 52 and how technologically advanced they were. What Henry had told him about the invisible aliens, what they had said and warned him about when they'd appeared to him that last night before they took the second spaceship. *Oh, oh.*

General Wallace rubbed his forehead as if it hurt. "All the events I've already mentioned, and some I'm not officially allowed to speak about yet, that point to a possible proliferation or, even worse, an *invasion* of…*aliens*," he mumbled.

"Invasion?" Patterson blurted out.

"The UAPs to be precise. The government believes, of course, they're extraterrestrials. They are taunting us now. Out in plain sight. They're no longer hiding. It's as if there's a conscious effort on the aliens' part to show us, they are here. Come and get us. Stop us if you can. They're antagonistically shadowing and tormenting our military, our warships, and aircraft. They're doing that to all government militaries all over the world."

The General stopped talking, looked at each one of the people at the table one at a time, and then gravely added, "And just as disturbing, reports of human abductions have skyrocketed. Numbers like we've never seen. The government can't keep up. In one Wyoming town alone over twenty individuals have gone missing, and their families have sworn they saw alien ships take their loved ones away…right in front of them. Some tried to stop the aliens, with guns, and nothing they did could halt the kidnappings. The bullets couldn't get through the alien's protection cloaking. Same with the spaceships. The intruders don't seem to be afraid of us; don't seem to care anymore if we see them. They do whatever they want to do to us."

At first, no one uttered a word. Patterson glanced over at Doctor Isabel to see her drained face. He had known, for a long time, about the abduction of her sister thirty years ago. Justin had told him about it. This conversation must be affecting her, and not in a good way. There was a barely concealed panic in the depths of her eyes. Her body, her hands, were trembling.

Doctor Louison's right hand was drumming fingers on the table; his face was solemn. "There are first person accounts of the abductions? How many?"

"Yes, there are first person accounts, Doctor, of thousands of abductions. Worldwide. And they are still increasing."

"What do these first-person witnesses say?" Patterson spoke up.

The General, his hands resting on a stack of official looking folders, sighed softly. "They report unidentified spaceships coming down, hovering over humans, and though the people try in vain to escape, beaming them up. The people aren't seen again. Or, leastways, they haven't been returned so far."

Doctor Courtney Waverly, her expression dazed, asked, "are these adductors all the same variety of aliens; from the same kind of alien spacecrafts? Do they know?"

"Apparently, it's being reported that two very different types of spaceships have been basically involved in the sightings. Some of them are saucer-shaped, and sound suspiciously similar to the two we had here in the hangar at Area 52. According to those who have seen them, the saucers do not participate in the stealing of humans, or so far, not that we know of. They seem to merely be observing. Always around. While the other kind–triangle-shaped and monstrous in dimensions–that sometimes pulsate in rainbow colors, with an eye-blinding radiance, are the ones stealing away humans. The phenomena have become an epidemic in the coastal areas of all the continents."

"As if the spaceships are hiding, lurking, beneath the oceans?" Lucia Walters appeared uneasy now, too.

"Possibly." General Wallace was sifting

through the files on the table before him, rearranging their order. "There's been a lot of speculation over the years to if there are alien bases beneath the seas. The military and the Navy seals are searching now in earnest for possible underwater alien bases, if they exist."

Russell Gartner, reclining in his chair, questioned, "What are we here to do, then, General? We aren't military. I'm only a paleontologist. Same as a couple others of us here."

"You're all around this table because of what you did, saw, and experienced here at Area 52. You investigated the alien spaceships. You were inside of them, studied their technology; the aliens DNA. Some of the only humans to ever have been inside of alien crafts. Aliens we think are similar to some of the aliens that are badgering us now. We need all your expertise." General Wallace inhaled. "We need all the help we can get."

"America, the world, needs your help," Doctor Emmet, gazing around at everyone around him, restated. "All of your help."

For Patterson, that was all that had to be said. If his county needed him, he was there.

The General opened the laptop in front of him. He clicked it on and powered it up. From one of the files, piled on the table before him, he took six USB drives and slid them down, or across, the table to each of the scientists. "Here are live videos of some of the spaceships, and their nefarious actions, and recordings of eye-witnesses' statements. Take and study them. Give me any impressions or insights you might have on anything on them. Anything that you think might be even slightly important.

"I won't kid any of you. The President and his Secretary of Defense, his top generals, after receiving this information…fear possibly a full-scale alien invasion could be imminent. The President is, is of course, tremendously worried."

"So, what's the government, the Department of Defense, NASA–the military–doing about all this?" Patterson demanded.

"What do you think they're doing about it?" The General seemed weary as he fielded the question. "We are, the world is, preparing for war. The President has set us at Defcon 1."

Oh my God, Patterson fretted over what the General had told them. *War. With aliens.* And he had thought the dinosaur wars had been the worst thing that could happen to the world. Apparently not. He had the feeling that any sort of war with extraterrestrials would be far worse. At least the dinosaurs hadn't had intergalactic spaceships, advanced weaponry, and heaven-knew-what-else a higher civilization could or would throw at them. Henry had told him that the aliens he'd encountered in the larger spaceship, before it vanished, had had telepathic abilities. They'd communicated with him without words. *Telepathic malicious aliens with advanced weapons. Yikes.*

After more back and forth nervous inquiries, and discussions, the group broke up. Patterson could tell the scientists were upset, afraid, of what would happen next. He didn't blame them. He wasn't all that happy himself about a possible alien incursion. How many books and movies had he read and seen about aliens attacking the earth? Too many to count. Just like dinosaur wars, thrilling stories when they were fiction, but not so thrilling when they happened in the real world.

"It's late." General Wallace released the scientists. "And after all of you traveling here, I'm sure you want to get settled into your quarters; get some rest. We'll meet again tomorrow morning here at eight hundred hours. If you have any other questions, I'll answer them then."

*****

"I've been given the same room I vacated six months ago," Isabel said to Patterson. "Now I get to redecorate it all over again. If I have time." She shrugged, as she headed for the exit.

If the aliens, Patterson though, give her, us, that time.

The scientists filed out of the room, conversing among themselves as they drifted down the corridor to the rooms they'd been assigned.

"Patterson and Doctor Emmet," General Wallace caught the men before they could leave, "could you please stay behind for a while? I have something I want to speak to both of you about."

When the three were alone, the General pivoted around to face Patterson. "On the phone before you came, you were describing your excursion out into the wilds of Crater Lake with your friend, Henry Shore, where you discovered there has been a rash of UAP sightings. Bouncing, glowing balls of lights behaving strangely? That they had been seen earlier by one of the rangers at Crater Lake and an astrophysicist who was camping out in the park. What else can you tell me about what the ranger and the astrophysicist had to say?"

"Not much more than what I already told you. Henry and I didn't see any orbs or weird lights in the sky ourselves, though we camped out for days looking for them. In two different park locations, in fact. No luck. But Professor Hescott, that astrophysicist and college teacher, claimed fervently that'd he'd been seeing these unearthly orbs of light for months and, whenever he'd hear where they were being spotted, he'd go there if he could. He had been following the lights all over the country. He even camped two nights with Henry and myself hoping to see them again."

"Did you?" The General queried.

"No, General. As I said, I never did see them. Myself anyway. Hescott swears they have been popping up all over, even in other countries–of course, you already knew that. Professor Hescott is part of a worldwide online organization that tracks alien sightings of all kinds, as well as the orbs."

"I would like to have this professor's contact numbers and address, if you have them. I need to speak to him."

"I can give them to you. He and Henry have become good friends. He's visited Henry a time or two and he was at a Fourth of July barbeque Henry hosted a couple weeks ago. Professor Hescott did say that he'd let us know when he saw the orbs, or anything suspicious, again and where."

"Has he seen anything unusual, alien wise, since you three were camping?" The General was keying in notes on his laptop as he asked his questions and Patterson replied. He peered up from his computer at Patterson, waiting for an answer.

"I don't think so. But I haven't seen the professor or talked to him since Henry's get together." Patterson glanced over at Doctor Emmet, who was listening yet had a bored expression on his face; was picking lint off his expensive looking suit. Earlier during the meeting, he had been the only one at the table in a suit, other than the General's uniform. The other scientists, as well as himself, had been dressed casually in slacks and shirts.

Emmet kept glancing at his phone. He seemed to be immensely interested in something on it. The guy hadn't cracked a smile since Patterson had sat down, though he'd seemed distracted enough as if what they were conversing about wasn't all that important. Patterson had the impression the man knew more about the alien threat and what their intentions were then he'd given them earlier. He also seemed to have an entitled air about him. Of privilege. Getting what he wanted, others be damned. It was this unemotional cold look in his eyes. He undeniably was from money. Ivy league for sure. Harvard or Princeton graduate. It was in every dismissive gesture, and subdued mannerism he exhibited as if he were the boss at the table, and not the General. The guy made the hackles on Patterson's back go up. He'd met lots of men like Doctor Emmet before in his line of work. Some of them could be real jackasses.

The General cocked his head in Emmet's direction. "Doctor Emmet, with your position and high government connections, I suspect you know as much as I do, perhaps more, about what might be coming down the pike. Are we under attack from aliens? Or are we going to be?"

Patterson caught Emmet's hesitation, the way his eyes became hooded, which didn't bode well to whatever he would be willing to confess to them. The man wasn't about to share everything he knew, not right now, for whatever reason. Patterson had met men like him before. They thought they knew what had to be done, sometimes had a hidden agenda, and nothing would dissuade them from their preconceived path. To Patterson, they were dangerous men. Since it appeared Emmet would be a crucial piece of their task force, Patterson sure hoped he wasn't right about the guy. One bad apple could ruin the barrel. Oh, how well, he'd learned that over the years.

Then it came to Patterson. Who Doctor Emmet reminded him of…Doctor Albert Harris. The so-called famous paleontologist who'd been head of the fossil excavating team sent originally to Crater Lake by some la-de-da university–that he couldn't now recall the name of–all those years ago during the Godzilla days. Harris had been a prissy, fanatical man, also with an arrogant manner and large ego. He'd wanted to capture Godzilla *alive* to study the monster, for God's sake, for his own gain, no matter how many people died in the attempt. And many had died. Harris's colleagues, team members, and a slew of rangers and innocent bystanders. Patterson had always felt it was a pity Godzilla hadn't devoured Harris, instead of his old ex-FBI partner Dylan Greer, the Deep Rover's pilot, and Henry's good friend Ranger

Redcrow. How come the good ones died young, and the selfish, self-serving narcissists didn't? Well, if Doctor Harris was even still alive. Who knew? Perhaps he'd tried to capture other live dinosaurs in the last decade, and one of them had gotten him. Gobbled him up. The thought almost made Patterson smile, but what he, Wallace, and Emmet were gathered there to confer over, wouldn't allow for that. So, he smothered the smile before it was born.

Patterson wasn't prepared then when the General suddenly proposed, "Patterson, I would like you to work with, work for really, Doctor Emmet here. The President has asked for an inner, elite preliminary team, coordinating with myself and the U.S. military, the US Naval Air Systems Command, and NASA, of course, to actively hunt for and locate, and maybe even bring down, if we can, one of the alien spaceships. Top propriety. We need to know what we're up against…if the aliens decide to attack us.

"And with your time at the FBI, your background during the dinosaur wars of tracking, hunting them down, and exterminating them, and your time here at Area 52, you are a perfect candidate to work close with Doctor Emmet. He'll be the brains; you'll be the brawn."

Patterson couldn't help it, his eyes glanced sideways at Doctor Emmet, who was looking self-importantly smug. *Me, work with, take orders from, this Doctor Harris clone? You've got to be kidding?* Was what Patterson was thinking, but the words never left his lips. He knew better. The General, his country, needed him and he'd do whatever they asked him to do; especially if an alien invasion was looming. He could do nothing less. "Of course, both of you will still work with the whole team, as well. Doctor Emmet will also continue to work with the US Naval Air Systems Command. Anything either of you need, just ask. The government is giving you unlimited resources and cash."

So," Patterson nodded at Doctor Emmet first, and then walked around the table to stand in front of General Wallace, "I'm ready to serve, General. I'll go and do anything that needs done."

"Good, I knew we could count on you Patterson. We always have been able to." The General thumped Patterson on the back. "You go with Doctor Emmet here. There's a plane waiting for the both of you with a destination already plotted. Emmet has all the instructions. You leave…now."

"Now?" Patterson echoed. He'd just gotten to the base, and he had to leave again?

"Now." The General closed up his laptop, put it under his arm, and briskly gave the two a get-going gesture with his free hand. "No time to waste. You will be reporting to a General Woodruff for training; joining a group of experts out in the field like yourself. From the scientific, the regular populace, and the military. The best we have. We need to get ahead of this alien situation. We need to find out what's going on."

Training? Patterson had a terrible mental flash of him running an obstacle course in a downpour, climbing steep walls, hiding behind skinny trees, in heavy body armor, learning how to evade or shoot aliens…that were invisible…with big laser weapons. *Oh, no.*

"Where are we going?" Patterson stood up. Good thing he hadn't unpacked yet. It saved him the trouble.

"Doctor Emmet here will fill you in on that and everything else you'll need to know. I have a meeting with the head of the DOD and, if I want to get there in time, I must leave now." He reached out and shook both

Patterson's and Doctor Emmet's hands. "Good luck, you two. Do us proud. Find us an alien spaceship and take it down. Give us what we're going to need to defeat the aliens, if they do decide they want a war with us. Best preparation is to be prepared."

Yep, Patterson thought, *that would be advisable. Be prepared. But how exactly were they going to do that? He had no idea. How do you find and capture an alien spaceship anyway? And how do you fight invisible aliens?*

The General hurried out of the room, leaving Patterson and Doctor Emmet staring at each other.

Someone had to speak first, so Patterson took the reins. "Where are we going, Doc?"

Emmet gave him a harsh look. "Doctor Emmet to you, Sir."

No skin off his teeth, so Patterson complied. "Doctor Emmet…where are we headed?"

"We're flying down to the Bahamas. Andros Town." Grabbing his laptop and notebooks, Emmet presented him with a smirk. "To the land of sun and fun."

"Ah, you're taking me on a vacation, huh?" A little humor couldn't hurt anything.

Patterson had accepted if he had to work with the man, he'd make the best of it. Chances are the guy wasn't a Harris clone. He didn't really know Emmet yet, and the least he could do was give the man a chance to prove he wasn't another Harris. God, he hoped he wasn't. That stick-in-the-mud Harris had been a self-righteous selfish S.O.B.

"If you call going to investigate suspicious rumors of a group of unexplained aerial phenomena buzzing the island, enduring rigorous training as if we're young men again where we will so learn how to shoot big guns, hunt for, and interrogate aliens," he shivered, but with a sly smile on his face, "then it's a vacation."

Fun, fun, Patterson mused. "No problem. I've spent so many years chasing dinosaurs in the freezing or broiling woods, up and down mountains, up in the skies, in destroyed cities, so chasing alien spaceships and aliens in the Bahamas doesn't sound all that bad to me." *Except for the training*. He wondered if the General had meant physical, psychological, or emotional training? He should have asked. *He was getting too old for that sort of nonsense, especially the physical.* Or, at least, his bones were. They broke a lot easier than when he'd been thirty. He had a vivid recollection of hurting his leg out in Crater Lake's woods on that stormy night, and Frank and Hescott having to help him hobble to Hescott's hut out in the forest. Ouch. His leg still ached at times.

"Training, huh? I'm getting too old for that nonsense, *Doctor Emmet*," Patterson grumbled. "I think I'll skip that part, the rigorous part anyway. And I know how to shoot and hunt for…anything I am sent out to kill. Believe me."

"I believe you, Patterson. I'm with you." To Patterson's surprise, Emmet echoed the sentiment. "I'm way too old to do that training, as well."

Patterson was pleasantly surprised when Emmet laughed, a big hearty laugh. "I think we can both skip that training. Say we did it, and don't. I'll handle the paperwork. My friends will take care of it for us." The laugh changed the way the ex-FBI agent thought of the man. When laughing the way he did, Emmet didn't look or seem so egotistical. "And you never know, while we're waiting for an alien spaceship to flitter by, after hiding out on the beach or in the weeds on the stake-out, we might even be able to grab a good meal and a couple margaritas in a local restaurant or bar, grab a swim–when we aren't actively searching for little green men, that is. No sense in all work and no play. Life's too short.

"You know, we won't be alone in the hunt. And we have no idea how long we will be waiting to capture what we're down there to capture. Could be weeks. Longer."

We have no idea if we'll come out of this little adventure alive, either, Patterson fretted.

Patterson offered the older man a smile for the first time. "Sounds good to me.

"So," Patterson added off-handedly, "you don't seem as worried about this possible alien invasion as General Wallace seems to be?"

"Oh, don't take me wrong, I am. Extremely concerned. It's just that if we live every second of our lives waiting for the doom to fall, that's not much of a life, is it? My life's moto is: Face the threat when and if it comes…and not before. Life is short. Time to be scared, when you need to be. Enjoy our life in between."

"My life's doctrine as well." Perhaps he and the doc could be friends.

"I learned that during the dinosaur wars," Emmet confessed, "I nearly died a couple of times. I had a few close encounters with the prehistoric beasts, you know? They overran a town I was staying at. I barely escaped each time."

Patterson chuckled. "Same here. I'm lucky to be alive when so many of my friends perished during those years."

Doctor Emmet had his hand on the doorknob. "I'm going to go gather my things for flight, and you do the same. I'll meet you at the entrance in, oh, say, about a half-hour. The plane is scheduled to leave at 3:30."

Patterson bobbed his head affirmatively. "I'll meet you at the entrance then in thirty."

Doctor Emmet went out the door first, but Patterson stayed behind and dropped down into a chair again; pulled out his cell phone. Sherman wouldn't be happy to know he could be gone for weeks, or longer. But once she knew he was looking into a catastrophic threat to humanity–though he couldn't tell her any more than that–she'd accept it. Being ex-military herself, she understood these things. She understood duty and sacrifice for one's country. He keyed in her number and waited for her to answer. She took the news pretty well. She always did.

When the call was over, he pushed himself up from the chair. His mind, though, was troubled. Chasing dinosaurs wasn't anything like chasing advanced aliens menacing the world. Not anything like it at all. He remembered the astonishing technology of those spaceships; what Henry had confided in him about the aliens he'd encountered on the big craft. They'd been so advanced. So highly intelligent, intuitive…telepathic. How could humans hope to defeat such advanced adversaries? Humans didn't even have interstellar spaceships, or could read minds.

Please, God, he murmured a silent prayer, *help us humans. This could be the end of us if those aliens are determined to take over our planet. If they are malevolently inclined, stronger than us, and want to war with us.* A war with extraterrestrials would change everything. For the first time in his life, he was afraid. He so wanted to talk everything he had learned over with Sherman, or his friends Henry or Justin, so they could ease his mind, they were always good at that, but he couldn't. He had to carry the frightening news alone, except for Isabel. He could talk to only Isabel about it, and the rest of the team. For now. Or at least, until the world would open their eyes one day and see the alien fleet landing, or worse, blowing up our cities…if it came to that.

He exited the room and reclaimed his luggage, which he'd left sitting outside the conference room. With a tiredness he had rarely felt since the dinosaurs had departed en masse, he trudged down the corridor towards where he was supposed to join up with Doctor Emmet. Still praying.

CHAPTER 7

Professor Hescott had set up base camp at the bottom of Mount Scott, and had been there for about a week. Before that he'd been camped out at Dutton Cliff for a week, and before that he'd spent five days at Duwee Falls. The weather had cooperated and he'd had sunny days, and cool, but not cold, nights. There'd been a massive rain storm further up north in the state, but thank goodness, it hadn't come down this far. He'd stayed dry.

But in all that time, he hadn't seen any otherworldly lights or alien spaceships. He wasn't giving up, though. He had until the weather turned in the park, late September if he were lucky, to remain and keep searching the skies. Once the winter season came in, it would get too cold, and snow would come. He didn't like camping in the snow. He was an old man, after all, and his bones couldn't take the freezing weather anymore.

He'd driven his Gator UV for miles around his campsite in ever larger circles, and even up the paved road all the way to the summit of Mount Scott, two miles upwards, every day. The view was spectacular from up there. He could see for miles and miles all across the park; forever looking for the lights in the sky. He knew that if he was patient, he'd eventually see the mysterious orbs again. His online network of alien spotters across the globe had been reporting more and more sightings. It was an epidemic, a pandemic. How could he not see them again? Suddenly the alien presence seemed to be everywhere. They were reporting them across every continent. Something amazing was going on, and Hescott wanted to be part of it. He had been keeping a journal on his alien encounters, no matter how small a detail, for years, and he wrote in it every evening. The aliens were making their presence known more and more every day. It was so exciting.

Hescott loved camping in the park. He felt at home among the trees, the lakes and creeks, and the wildlife, as well as in the halls and offices of academia. When his wife, Geraldine, had still been alive, they'd gone camping often. She had loved nature even more than he. He missed her. They'd been married a very long time. Whoa, what would she have thought about this alien situation? All these mysterious lights visiting the earth? Because she'd been one of those disbelievers.

"There are no such things as aliens," she'd say. "If there were, and they were hostile, we'd be their slaves or all be annihilated. If they were friendlies, they'd have their own TV show here. They wouldn't be playing hide-and-seek for decades with us. So, therefore, there are no aliens."

Whereas he was a true believer. The way he'd figured it, out in the endless expanse of the universe, in all the galaxies and around all the suns, and on all the planets that rotated around those suns, how could there *not* be other life? It was one of the few things he and his wife had ever disagreed on.

At night, his eyes would closely examine the starry skies as he sat warming himself over his campfire. He'd day dream, or nightdream as it was, about being the first human to make alien contact. Wouldn't that be something? He could imagine himself strolling up to the aliens as they left their spaceship and attempting to communicate with them. He'd let them know he was their friend with slow and gentle hand-signals. No fast moves. No weapons. He'd take pictures of them and with them, if they'd let him. He could write a scholarly paper on that first contact, and publish it worldwide. He'd let everyone know the aliens had arrived.

That is, *if* they were friendly aliens. Hescott tended to believe they would be benevolent. They'd be generous with their highly sophisticated technological knowledge, and their medical advancements. They'd help the human race to heal our ailments; perhaps even contribute to the reconciliation of the animosity between countries and peoples. Hoping for such miracles, was part of his optimistic nature. He sure prayed he was right. He didn't want to think about the flip-side.

Hescott camped, searched the forest during the day, the skies at all times, and waited.

It was on the seventh night the event happened. That night he'd remained awake for as long as he could keep his old eyes open, waiting for the orbs or anything to appear, but somehow had fallen asleep right there at the fire. He hadn't made it to his sleeping bag. As he came awake, he slowly registered a dazzling array of dancing lights behind his closed eyelids. His eyes flew open. He looked up.

And there in the sky, to his right and towering above him, was this extraordinary obsidian silhouette. Its edges seemed to blend into the night sky, but the stars sparkling around it faintly gave it an outline. It was coming closer. Eerily silent. Closer. Closer. His heart began to race, and his hand went to his chest. His heart was thumping so loudly, he was afraid it was going to burst out of his chest.

"Oh, my God," he cried, rising to his feet, his eyes glued to the descending object as it moved nearer. It was expanding in size as it lowered towards him, and he realized it was a giant triangle shape. Not a saucer, sphere or disc shape. Triangular. "This is new. Most of the sightings so far, as I know of, have been of these saucer shaped crafts. Sure, there have been other shapes seen. Some have been tubular, horizontal or vertical. But what is this?"

As it slowly crept across the sky and then passed above him, his mouth fell open, and he dropped to the ground on his knees. His heart was now racing, his body quivering. He'd never seen anything so gigantic in size; larger than a football field. How did it stay up in the air? Wow! It blocked out the whole sky when it finally was directly above him. Approximately a few miles up, he roughly calculated, but so unbelievably near to the earth. Its blackness was deeper than the blackness of the sky around it. The craft had no visible lights anywhere on it. How did it see where it was going? How did it not crash into things? *What the heck was it? Positively alien, for sure. Not the usual variety of craft, though. Then the feeling hit him like a ton of emotion. The craft made him feel...afraid. He was suddenly drenched in sweat, and the night wasn't even warm. It was as if the spaceship was sending out these...vibrations. He wanted to run away. Get away. But found his legs wouldn't work. He couldn't run. Instead, he crouched as low as he could to the ground, attempting to lessen his mass, hide, shaking. But* it *knew he was here.* It *could see him, he knew it.* It *could see him.*

It took a long, long time to pass over him, and during its passage, he was frozen, his eyes couldn't leave it. After what felt like hours, but, of course, had to be minutes, he somehow got the presence of mind, the courage, to pull his iPhone from his jacket pocket and snap pictures of the spaceship. Though there wouldn't be much to see, but an enormous black surface, a triangular darkness, except for lights on three points and a larger one in the center, its whole shape rimmed in stars. But he took the photos anyway.

As he lay there in the dirt, the mammoth airship slowly moved off with no visible means of lift or prolusion, and away, taking its good old time as if it didn't care who saw it, and dwindled in size until it disappeared at the edge of his sight, blending into the night line of trees and woods. For a long time, he could still see its shadow as it moved away into the night. Smaller. Smaller. Gone.

Holy cow! He came to his unsteady feet, wobbling. He still couldn't believe what he'd seen; how terrifying the sensations it had created in him. He needed to call Henry and tell him about it. Once it was completely gone, he even doubted his own eyes. *Had he really seen a black triangle as big as a parking lot? Had he? Or had he imagined it?* Perhaps, he'd fallen asleep at the campfire, and had dreamed it all? He looked down at the phone in his hands, at the pictures on it. No, he had the photos, as blurry as they were, and that was something. Proof. It hadn't been a dream.

He left a message at ranger headquarters, because no one was there, reporting what he'd witnessed. Then he called Henry, even though it was the middle of the night; waking him up. Henry didn't seem to mind. He listened and calmed him down.

After talking to Henry, Hescott ended the phone call. Henry said he could call him anytime if he spied anything else alien. *Huh, or I might just stop by and visit Henry sometime next week once he's home from his camping trip with his son-in-law. We can discuss all this face to face. Yeah, that's what I'll do. He did say I could stop by anytime. So, I will.*

Tomorrow, he'd contact the newspapers and anyone else he could think of to report what he'd seen, though most likely they'd brand him a crackpot, and not really listen to him. People were always claiming to see alien spaceships, and most sightings, as with abduction stories, were viewed with open distain or ignored. Oh well, he would try. He needed to *warn* people.

Once off the phone with Henry, and sending the photos to him, he used his phone to post on his website about his incredible sighting. He wanted as many people to know about it as possible, as quickly as possible. He knew what he'd seen was that important. He couldn't wait to hear what his friends on the website had to say, and make comments on, about his experience. See if anyone else had seen the giant triangles.

For some reason, he couldn't put his finger on why, perhaps the ominous feeling the close encounter had produced in him, he felt something had changed; he was no longer so optimistic about the encounters. He was no longer sure he wanted to meet an alien in person. No longer sure they'd be friendly. The orbs were one thing, but that black monster that left him with feelings of terror, was, to him, a very bad omen. The aliens–more than one variety it seemed–were here. Why? What did they want? Yet part of him didn't really want to know.

CHAPTER 8

On July thirtieth, Justin telephoned Henry, to remind him. "Hey, old man, you ready for our camping expedition in search of Oscar and his kin? August first? We still on?"

"Of course, we are," Henry had responded. "I've been looking forward to it."

"As am I. It'll be good to get out in the woods again; get some real exercise. Delores says I'm getting thick in the middle. I've been stuck in one conference room or lab for too many years. I need to breath fresh air, hear the birds sing, and look up into a real sky, not seen through a window or skylight."

"You will. Eight glorious days out in the wilderness with your father-in-law. Sitting out under the stars, camping, hiking, and thrashing through the forest searching for our friendly dinosaurs. I got the Scamp all stocked and ready for the trip. That way Sasha can come along with us…and it'll be a nice shelter for us if it rains, or if we want to sleep in real beds. So, I'll be driving. Just get here, and park your rented vehicle in my driveway."

"That's fine with me. Taking the Scamp along is a smart idea. I have gotten a little spoiled with my indoor comforts. Though I'm looking forward to sleeping under the stars, if the weather permits. I do hope we run into Oscar and his family. See his physical progression, and what he's capable of now. He was so darn smart years ago, I imagine he's even smarter now, with maturity. And what his DNA could tell us. Especially if it links descendant-wise to any of the Area 52 spaceships' aliens."

"I also hope we see Oscar. I want to be sure he's all right. His family is all right. I'll see you on the first, Justin. At seven a.m. I'll have breakfast ready for us before we head out. We'll have a long journey if we want to go far enough into the park to where I last saw Oscar and his clan. It's a long way from the park's entrance gates. I reckon it should take two days. Not traveling at night, of course."

"Will the Scamp make it through the thicker backwoods' roads?" Justin asked.

"Without inclement weather, snow or mud, most of the way, it should. Besides, I know all the old paths and short cuts that our late friend Ranger Redcrow showed me many years ago. I haven't forgotten them. We'll get pretty darn close to where I last ran into Oscar. The final part of the journey, we'll have to park the camper, and hike on our own two feet further in, because the terrain gets too rough."

"We can do that. I don't mind a difficult hike, on a short stretch anyway. A little extreme exercise might be good for me. See you soon."

"See you soon," Henry had echoed, and finished the call. He was excited over their camping trip. He so wanted to see Oscar again. Be sure the little guy was happy and healthy; see how many more children he had. The night before he'd been looking at old sketches of Oscar that Ann had made from that day Oscar had first come to their cabin and raided their refrigerator. The drawings revived so many memories. Of the friendly dinosaur. Of Ann. Those scary dinosaur days and everything they had gone through. The good times and the horrible ones. They had been his past. His past with Ann. Sometimes it seemed like yesterday, other times it seemed like a lifetime ago. It was.

Ann, he grieved, *I sure miss you. I wish you were coming with us on this trip. You always did get a kick out of Oscar and his antics. He survived the explosion that day when the helicopter sent those drone missiles into One-Eye on the edge of our property; you never knew that he escaped death. It would make you happy he did survive, I know it. You'd love to see the family he has now, all his children; how happy he is. I've lost so much, still having Oscar alive and well gives me something to smile about. Gives me a sense of awe that is so lacking in my life these days. To me, Oscar is a miracle.*

*****

Henry had been busy packing up his duffle bag for his and Justin's camping trip until late the night before their outing. He'd finally gone to bed, and was sleeping fairly soundly when he got a telephone call from Professor Hescott.

"Nice to hear from you, Professor, even if it's in the middle of the night," Henry had answered. "Are you okay?"

"I'm okay, Henry, or I think I am. It happened. I saw an alien spaceship tonight. Not the glowing orbs…but an extraterrestrial *spaceship*. A huge sucker. I'm still shaking."

"You did? Calm down, Professor. Tell me all about it."

Henry's interest was instantly captured, and he was suddenly wide awake. He turned the light on his night stand on. Took out a notebook he had in the drawer so he could write down notes. It would help him to remember. "Where at?"

"At the base of Mount Scott. That's where I've been camping out the last week. The craft flew right over me. It had to be miles above, but, I swear, it was so big it took my breath away. Huge triangular shaped shiny obsidian thing as big as a skyscraper turned on its side, yet silent as the dead. Not the typical orbs, or a saucer of any kind. It was hovering right above me, moving as slow as a snail. It was so dark out; I could only make out its shape by the stars outlining it. Thing was, Henry, it made me feel…so fearful. Like its huge size was squeezing me under it down to the earth. I could barely breathe."

"Did it land?"

"No, it came up from the other side of the mountain, topped it, came low to the earth and passed over me, and then slowly made its way across the park until I could no longer see it. My head is still spinning. I've never felt so afraid in my life, and I have no idea why. It was so *big*! Oh my God, what kind of alien could build such a craft, and pilot it from heaven-knows-where to our earth?"

Henry had no answer to that, because what could he say? He didn't have an answer.

All Henry could do was murmur, "Wow,

that's some story. An ebony flying triangle that made you want to jump out of your skin, huh? Only one?"

"Yes, only one. But it filled the sky, Henry. I've been following UAPs for years, yet never thought I'd see something like this–or react the frightened way I did. I have pictures. But I don't think you'll be able to see much. Some are probably going to be only solid dark photos. There were just faint lights on the three corners of the object. Once and a while a fourth light would appear in the center, strobe once or twice, and then blink out. I did get a few pictures when the triangle was farther away, leaving, where I hope you can, at least, see its shape against the star-studded sky."

"Can you please send those photos to me, Professor?" Henry had yawned on the other end of the phoneline. "I have connections, and I'll also pass them, and word of what you've seen, along to the necessary government agencies. I think Scott would like to see them, too."

"I bet he would. I'll send these photos to you as soon as we get done talking, Henry."

"Thanks. Can you tell me anything else–anything else at all, even the tiniest of details–about the spaceship, Professor?"

"Only that it was so different than the other ones people have been reporting seeing for weeks. These were not orbs or bouncing lights." Hescott's voice had been thoughtful. "And besides being mind-shatteringly enormous, it didn't appear to have any propulsion system, and moved unbelievably slow, for its great size. I couldn't imagine how it could stay up in the air. It was the strangest thing I've ever witnessed. Like I said, it sent chills right up by bones."

"Are you staying in your location for a while?" Henry had asked. He'd written almost every word down, so he could show them to Justin when he arrived in the morning, and send a copy to Patterson.

"Another day or two. I don't think it will reappear, but I want to be sure. I'll stay at this spot until tomorrow, or the next day. In case it might return."

"Will you stay in touch with me, Professor, and let me know if you see it again or anything else out of the ordinary?"

"You know I will, Henry. Bye for now." The old man hung up.

"I'll be damned." Henry scratched the side of his head, staring down at what he'd written. Minutes later his phone dinged and he was studying the photos Hescott had taken. They were sort of blurry, as Hescott had said they would likely be, and mostly a grainy black. Hard to tell they were an alien spaceship, except for the ones at a farther distance. There were three photos where he could barely make out the triangular shape of the craft, and some where, at a distance, he could. The photos were iffy, but better than nothing.

Immediately, he sent them on to Justin's iPhone with an accompanying text explaining what they were, and who had taken them, so Justin could see them, too. He send them to Patterson in the morning.

Justin then called him up and Henry told him everything Hescott had told him.

"My, my," Justin muttered over the phone, "there seems to be a mess of these UAP sightings lately. I wonder what it means?"

"So do I," Henry had agreed.

"Maybe, when we're in the park scouring for Oscar, we might even see something…strange ourselves."

"We might. Seems like a lot of people are seeing these sorts of *unusual things*. But what Hescott saw tonight surprised even me. How many species of aliens are visiting us anyway? Orbs, saucers, and now big dark flying parking lot sized triangles. Are they friends or enemies? That's what I'd like to know."

"I'm afraid, the way things are going, Henry, we're going to find out sooner than we think. As you would say, I have a bad feeling about all this."

"As do I. We'll discuss it more when I see you in…oh, about six hours or so."

"Or so," Justin retorted.

Henry hung up and, having packed the night before for the trip, went back to bed. He could, at least, get a couple more hours of sleep. But he didn't. He was too excited about going out to search for Oscar. Morning couldn't come soon enough.

CHAPTER 9

Justin drove up to Henry's house when it was still dark outside, and joined his father-in-law in the kitchen, dragging his dangerously overstuffed backpack behind him.

"You came early." Henry opened the door, and let the scientist in. "Good thing I'm also ahead of schedule. I couldn't sleep much last night, especially after that middle-of-the-night phone call from Hescott. I'm excited, too, to look for Oscar and his kinfolk, so I gave up trying to sleep, and got up. I made breakfast already. Save us some time getting out of the house. I figured we could always nuke it if it got cold."

"Like you, after learning about Hescott's experience, I couldn't sleep, either, Henry. I thought you'd be up anyway, so Jeff arranged for an earlier plane to get me out here. It's great to have a billionaire, who owns a fleet of jets, for a brother-in-law. I can't wait to get out in the woods. And not just for Oscar. It'll be good to be camping again. I needed this."

"Did you remember to pack everything you're going to need?" Henry placed a cup of freshly brewed coffee into Justin's hands as his son-in-law plunked down in a chair. Justin helped himself to the scrambled eggs, toast and sausage links, Henry had on a plate in the middle of the table.

"I'm sure I've remembered everything," Justin quipped. "I'm more worried about you, old man. Old men's memories are sometimes not so sharp. Did you remember to pack everything?"

"I did." Henry gently shoved the younger man's shoulder, presenting him with a good-hearted smirk. "I'm not that senile. Yet."

"How was your flight here," Henry quizzed Justin as the man began gobbling down the scrambled eggs and sausages like he'd been starving. Nothing new there.

With a full mouth, Justin mumbled, "Calm. But interesting."

"How so?"

Justin swallowed. "I was seated next to an air force active-duty major–O-4 Major Gary Morrison–flying home for a visit with his family. He spun me a very intriguing tale of some UAPs he'd had a sort of run-in with on his last airplane ride."

"A run-in with alien crafts?"

"Yep." Justin got up to refill his coffee cup.

"Were they the triangle or the alien saucer

ships?" Since Professor Hescott had seen a giant triangle and Henry knew saucer spaceships also existed, he had to ask.

"Triangles. Plural. The Major claimed they were followed and taunted–that's how he put it–by a fleet of at least twelve crafts, of UAPs. But, as he described them, they were that triangle shape Hescott said he'd seen; not the normal saucer types the Major alleged a lot of his air force buddies have been seeing in the skies with them before this last month or so. As Hescott witnessed with his sighting, they were ebony triangular crafts that appeared seamless, no windows. Solid darkness, except for lights at the corners and sometimes a faint light blinking in the center. Silent. But they could really *move*.

"The Major told me they swept in from out of nowhere, and played an aggressive tag with the airplane. Coming so near at times, he was afraid they were going to collide with them. -He said he'd never seen so many aircrafts go the speeds these were going, and at their massive size, the extraordinary way they were maneuvering. They moved in ways that seemed to defy the rules of flight, and gravity. One second there, and the next second gone. It freaked him and his crew out. The Major revealed he was even frightened himself. The crafts wouldn't leave them alone, and kept flying off into space, only to return minutes later to continue their game of harassment. The incident lasted for a good twenty minutes. Then suddenly as they'd come, the crafts were gone."

"Oh my," Henry's voice was grave, "that sounds ominous. And he said there have been other similar encounters?"

"An endless number of them in the last month. He couldn't give me a figure, but I could tell he was unsettled by the whole situation. He said so many, a scary number as he put it, of his airman and other airmen in the air force have been subjected to the same sort of chilling encounters when they've been in the air. It's rare to see a serviceman, an officer, as scared as he seemed to be. I think that's part of the reason he was flying home to see his family. He knows something has changed. He wants to see his loved ones while he can.

"He also told me that the military has ordered all of the servicemen not to speak about any of these encounters, especially not to the press, or to anyone, on penalty of imprisonment. He must have been terrified to not care about those orders. I asked him, then, why he was telling me his story, and he said he didn't care what the military, or the government, wanted him to say or not say anymore…he believes with what's coming it won't matter anyway."

"What's coming?"

"He wouldn't elaborate on that, perhaps rethinking what he wasn't supposed to do or say, but I did notice he constantly observed the skies around us as we flew; his entire manner edgy. Looking for alien spaceships, most likely. Thank goodness, we didn't run into any."

"Yeah, thank goodness," Henry echoed. "Along with what Professor Hescott witnessed, and Patterson's secrecy, this makes me wonder exactly what's going on. I figure Patterson knows more than he's telling us, but if your new friend on your airplane ride here was truthful with you…I'm afraid something horrible is happening to our world. Something I don't even like to think about."

"But can't not think about." Justin sent him a direct look, and spoke softly, "An alien come-look-see on a grand scale."

"Yes. Could it be an alien preliminary scouting expedition before an official first contact with humanity? That would be something. Though I don't know why they'd be harassing our military and ordinary aircraft. Taunting us."

"That's what I thought, too. Or, could it be," Justin presented another alarming possibility, "an alien preliminary scouting expedition before an official and massive worldwide…invasion?"

The two men simply stared at each other. Henry had nothing else to say to that, other than, "Well, there's nothing you or I can do about it at the moment. We're not even in the loop. We're clueless–until Patterson, as I believe he knows more about all this than he says he does, tells us what's going on. Or someone else in authority tells us something."

"Yes, we are uninformed." Justin gave him a weak smile. "And I hate it."

"So, do I. I hope we find out what's going on," Henry muttered, "before the invasion begins."

"Me, too."

"Let's put all our unfounded, and unproven, fears away; finish this meal and get going, Justin. I'm anxious to be out in nature with the trees and open sky around me. Where things feel normal. Right now, all I care about is finding our little friend Oscar."

Justin nodded. "I'm with you. Camping is just what we need now to clear our brains."

They finished their breakfast, loaded up the camper with Justin's stuff, the cat, and took off soon after dawn. Henry was happy. He was on an adventure with his friend and there was the hope of finding Oscar. There wasn't much more he could ask for. Except perhaps finding Oscar and his clan alive and well in the park.

*****

Henry and Justin drove all day and when dusk arrived, they parked in a clearing for the night; leaving the Scamp hooked to the truck because they'd be continuing their journey deeper into the park in the morning when sunrise came.

The night was cool, as early August often was in the park, but after supper, bundled in their jackets in front of their campfire, they were warm enough.

"Have you heard anything lately from Patterson…since your wet and fateful camping trip?" Justin was warming his hands over the dying flames. "Me? I haven't seen him since your Fourth of July bash. Not a word, either."

"He's busy with that new top-secret job of his." Henry happened to glance up to the lit camper's window and spied Sasha silhouetted there, staring at them. On the drive Henry had the cat in the rear seat in a cage. The feline was glad to be out of it, and free to roam in the camper, and sleep on one of the beds. Sasha did not like to be caged. He was used to his cat door and his yard.

"Ah, he didn't tell you what he was up to, either?"

"He couldn't. Said it was, you know, *secret*."

Justin snorted. "And how well we know about that. I am dying of curiosity, though. After hearing the air force major's story, I know something big is going on. I wish I was part of it all. I don't like being in the dark, especially if it affects our safety and our world."

"I feel the same way. But," Henry threw another piece of wood on the fire, "just my opinion…I also have a strong feeling Patterson's project has something to do with aliens. And we both know something about that already. I have ever since Patterson's and my camping trip, and that story you told me about your Major friend on the airplane ride."

In the flickering campfire light, the paleontologist's eyes were observing Henry sharply. "What makes you feel so sure?"

"Because from the minute Ranger Finch started talking about seeing those strange lights," Henry repeated what he'd told him before, "and Patterson seemed so attentive, I could tell there was more to his interest than mere curiosity. When Patterson and I ran into Professor Hescott in the park and found out the Professor was also looking for the lights; that many others over the whole world had seen them, as well, I saw the way Patterson reacted. Those lights have something to do with what Patterson is working on. I'd bet anything on it."

"We ought to contact Patterson and hook him up with Major Gary, then. Let him hear the airman's story."

"Yeah, we should," Henry replied. "I don't think we can get good reception this far into the park, but we can call Patterson about it when we return to civilization."

"We should, and we will." Justin rose up to get another cup of coffee from the pot warming on their camp stove, and, cradling the cup in his hands, seated himself again. "What you said about Patterson's special project probably having to do with aliens? You're probably right. Sounds like it to me, too. Again, what I wouldn't do to be part of whatever it is.

"It doesn't make sense we're left out of the loop, after what we both saw and went through in Area 52. We know aliens exist. We know what they're capable of. We should be part of that new team."

"While I agree with you a hundred percent, the truth is, we haven't been invited to join them." Henry shoulders shrugged in a gesture of dejected acceptance.

Justin surprised Henry when he retorted, "*Yet.*"

Henry flashed his son-in-law a funny look. "Is there something you know that I don't?"

"Not really. But we did work at Area 52, same as Patterson and Isabel, and we were well acquainted with the spaceships and everything in them, and you…you communed telepathically with aliens. The way I figure it, if something big is going on concerning extraterrestrials, why wouldn't they seek our counsel or help?"

Henry heard what Justin was saying, but he wasn't sure he was right. "Maybe they could use your expertise, but me? I'm just an old dinosaur hunter. No reason to draft me."

"Except you met the Area 52 aliens. They

spoke to you."

"Well," Henry waved the statement away with a lazy hand gesture, "not many people know that. And *my* aliens might not be the *same* aliens that are pestering the world now."

"True."

"Anyway, I'm content working as a ranger part-time here at Crater Lake. It's like coming home. It grounds me. When I'm rangering here on the rim, or on Mount Scott, or any other of the natural sites, I almost feel normal." And he didn't have to tell Justin why. Justin knew how much he missed Ann.

The paleontologist said nothing to that.

Out in the night woods somewhere owls and other nocturnal creatures were chattering with each other in the uppermost heights of the branches. The air had suddenly become a chilly breeze, the moon was high and its light was a muted ivory as it shone down on the campsite and the Scamp. The fire's flames reflected patches of luminance in the camper's windows. Sasha must have gone to bed, because she was no longer lurking in any of them.

No cat's eyes glowing in the semi-dark.

"Talking about jobs," Henry inquired, though his attention was on the forest around them. He was looking for Oscar or any of his kindred. His ears alert to any odd noises in the underbrush that would signify small creatures coming their way, though he realized they weren't anywhere near where he'd seen Oscar the last time. That was far deeper into the woods. Except for the owls, crickets and frogs, there were no other forest creatures around announcing themselves. "How is yours going?"

"You know, Henry, after the excitement and fulfillment of working at Area 52, piddling around in my New York lab again with the sparce remnants of all the discoveries we were left with, after the aliens took everything, is less than satisfying. I miss Area 52. I think about those spaceships a lot. How awe-inspiring they were. The people I got close to. How important our work seemed. Being back in New York at the old grind just isn't the same. I'd do anything to have all those alien DNA samples we took from the ships and our research back again. Live specimens as we had with Heckle and Jeckle. To be truthful, I'd do anything if I was there again with the alien ships. That was a once in a lifetime placement."

The two sat in silence companionly for a

time, reliving old adventures and trials, friends; listening to the night sounds around them. Somewhere in the distance a wolf was howling and others took up the cry. Henry was relieved the calls sounded very far away. It was strange, even after all this time, that he no longer listened for the cries of dinosaurs. As far as he knew, except for Oscar and his descendants, the dinosaurs were gone. That truth allowed him to fully enjoy being in the park again. No Godzilla, gargoyles, or One-Eyes would jump out at them and attempt to eat them. Just bears, mountain lions, or cougars.

"On a more personal level," Henry eventually moved on to a new conversation, "how are my grandkids doing?"

"They're doing well. Growing faster than Delores and I can believe. I swear, Timothy had all of a sudden had a growth spurt. He's inches taller just since the Fourth of July gathering you hosted. You know, he made all A's in his last semester at school before the summer break. He's so smart, he scares me. He's also showing a genuine interest in science. He's asked me to let him spend a couple days by my side in the lab before he resumes school in the fall. I said he could."

Henry smiled in the campfire. “Could be we have another scientist in the making.”

“Could be.

“Oh, and not to leave your other grandchild out of the update, Phoebe won an art competition for her age group at that summer camp she attended the last two weeks. First place. She painted this beautiful night cityscape as seen from our apartment’s window. It’s stunning. Says she is going to have it framed, and give it to you for your birthday.”

“Really? Another original Phoebe picture for my wall, huh? I love the one she gave me on the Fourth.” Henry was flattered, and proud of his granddaughter. “She’s really taking after her Grandmother Ann, isn’t she?”

“She is, and in more ways than one. She is not only growing into a good artist, she can paint anything, even people, but she loves to write stories. Her English teacher has told me many times that she has a vivid imagination, and she can really spin a tale.”

“That’s our grandchild,” Henry bragged. “And your daughter.”

“Talking about Ann,” Justin met Henry’s gaze in the firelight, his voice gentle, “do you still see her much these days? Do you still…speak to her?" There was that concerned look in his son-in-law's eyes Henry had seen many times before.

Henry rubbed his forehead with his fingers. "Not as much as I once did. Don't get me wrong, I still talk to her all the time, think of her and miss her. I just don't *see* her as often, and she doesn't answer anymore, either. I miss her visits, I won't lie. They made me feel not so alone."

"Sorry, Henry. It is for the best, though. You not seeing her as often. Extreme grief and its repercussions shouldn't last if you ever want to be happy again. As much as you loved her, we all loved her, we all have move on, and continue living."

"Yeah, I know, and the dead should stay dead. But for me she'll never be really gone, Justin. I hear her voice in my head all the time. She's always with me in one way or another."

"I know you miss her. We all do."

"I really do, Justin, every minute of every day, and I will for the rest of my life. But I'll see her again one day. In heaven or in the next life. I can wait."

Justin was rummaging around in his knapsack and brought out a candy bar. "You want one?"

"Sure."

Justin dug out another candy bar and handed it to Henry. "You're going to have to come visit us in New York again real soon. See your grandchildren. Timothy really misses you. He asks all the time when grandpa is coming to see him again."

"I will. Before the kids are back in school. I promise. But, darn it, I guess I won't be seeing Isabel in New York anytime soon when I come. She's off somewhere also doing top-secret work with Patterson and his new coconspirators. Lucky dogs."

Justin chuckled. "Hopefully, she can get time off, for good behavior, and perhaps we can arrange a rendezvous with you two *friends*. They'll have to give her time off. Don't you think?"

"Unless," Henry commented, "what she's involved in is too important for them to let her have time off."

"Well, she stays in close touch with me and Delores, so I'll let you know when she's home for a visit. We can coordinate your visit, if you'd like, to coincide with hers."

"That would be nice, but I won't stay away if she can't get time off. My grandkids need to see me, and I need to see them. But it would nice if Isabel was around as well. She's become a good friend. Either way will be okay with me. You know, Isabel and I also stay in touch just between the two of us. Telephone calls and texts. She even sent me some homemade cinnamon buns a while back through the mail."

"Interesting. Anything I should know about you two?" In the flickering light there was a meaningful glint in the paleontologist's eyes.

Henry laughed. "No. We're only good friends. I keep telling you that. She's a fascinating woman, and we have some interesting conversations."

"Yeah," Justin sarcastically echoed, "just friends."

"We are *only friends*," Henry repeated in a no-nonsense voice. "Stop teasing me, son-in-law. You know that Ann was and will always be the love of my life. My great love. Unlike you, I'm too old to start all over again. I'm not looking for another great love–and wouldn't settle for anything less–not now, not ever. I'm happy with my part-time job, my family, my friends, and my home. My cat. I try to enjoy every day and whatever it brings. I'm finally content."

That seemed to shut Justin up.

The two men lingered over the crackling campfire for another hour, chatting on one subject or another, recalling more of their old adventures in the park, and talking about people they'd loved and lost. They'd been friends a long time; been through a lot together. Had both loved his daughter, Laura. Then they called it a night, and, tired, drug themselves to the sleeping bags they'd laid out under the stars next to the fire, and close to the camper. They'd built the fire up before retiring. Both men wanted to sleep out in the fresh air, under the open sky, because the night was so mild.

Henry lay awake for a time reminiscing over all the years he'd spent in the park; thinking about the past, and Ann. The dinosaur days. The good and the bad times. He'd spent most of his life as a ranger or as chief ranger and the memories were many. He listened to the night animals calling and moving about in the woods around him, and he felt at peace. He always did in Crater Lake.

Before he drifted off to sleep, he whispered, "Are you here, Ann?"

No answer. No Ann appearing as she'd once done. She rarely did these days and he missed those visits, yet he understood why she wasn't coming any more. She wanted him to move on, too. "Ann?"

Nothing. Accepting she wasn't going to show, he closed his eyes, and let sleep take him. It had been a good day, but he was tired. Time for sleep.

*****

The following morning, he and Justin stashed their sleeping bags in the camper. They doused the campfire so it wouldn't spark a forest fire. They prepared breakfast, and had coffee, in the camper; afterwards, they took off deeper into the park's backwoods. If they made good time they'd arrive at their final destination before nightfall to make camp.

By the time twilight drifted in to cover the landscape, Henry brought the vehicle and the camper to a halt at the bottom of a steep hill, and announced, "If I remember correctly, it wasn't far away from here that I ran into Oscar and his family. Over that hill there's another larger hill. In the hollow beyond that second hill is where I set up my campsite for the night, and where Oscar and his gang came out to meet me. The truck and Scamp won't go any further, too many trees too close to each other, so we'll have to hike the rest of the way. That okay with you?"

"Sure, that's okay. About how far is it?"

"Three, four miles; possibly a tad more. We'll spend the night here, and trek into the area tomorrow at dawn." Henry turned the engine off. The day was darker than it should have been at dusk because fat gray clouds were rapidly moving in. The wind had picked up. Rolling down the window, Henry could smell the moisture collecting in the air. He knew the signs. Rain was coming. They'd be sleeping in the camper that night for sure. They'd stay nice and dry. He was glad he'd brought it along even if they had to do the last three, four, miles on foot.

"You ready for some supper?" Henry shot Justin, who'd been lightly napping up until right before Henry had spoken to him.

Justin stretched in the seat, yawning. "I am. I'm starved. What are we having?"

Henry found Justin's hunger amusing. Since the man had snacked continuously the whole day when he hadn't been snoozing.

"Toasted cheese sandwiches. Tomato soup. Apples. I have cupcakes for dessert."

"That'll do." Justin was gazing out the window, a frown settling on his face. "I'm afraid some bad weather is moving in, Henry. I feel it in my bones. Look at those clouds."

"I thought the same thing. I think the bad weather has followed me since that last campout with Patterson." He'd told Justin all about the terrible rain storm he and Patterson had trudged through when they'd first met Professor Hescott. How Patterson had hurt his ankle and Hescott had helped get him to a dry place to recover. "But we'll be warm and dry in the Scamp…and tomorrow morning we'll hike out to where I last saw Oscar."

"I really hope we find him and his clan," Justin declared. "It'd be so great to see the little guy again. I still can't believe he's alive. That little dinosaur must have nine lives, or more."

Henry let out a chuckle. "He's a survivor all right. And quite prolific by what I saw. There must be fifty or more in his family. Or there was when I last saw him."

The men had their supper and later, the rain not having moved in yet, they built a campfire and sat outside around it until it was time to go to bed. They turned in early, both excited about getting up at first light to go in search of Oscar.

Eager, Henry woke up the next morning as the sun was rising and rousted Justin up. They had breakfast, and Henry fed Sasha, who then promptly claimed Henry's empty bed and reclaimed sleep. Henry made sure the cat had enough food and water to last her, and left a window half open so she could sit and look outside. That's all she needed to be happy. Henry didn't plan to be gone for more than a day or two. The men loaded up their backpacks with supplies, and food, and got ready to head out. A light tapping had begun on the Scamp's metal roof.

"Our luck's run out. It's raining, Henry," Justin pointed out after peeking out one of the windows.

"I know, but you and I aren't afraid of a little rain, are we?"

"Nope. As long as I have my trusty rain poncho." Justin had already donned his poncho.

Henry slipped on his boots and then a poncho. "We've trekked through the park in worse weather."

"Many times," Justin said. "In torrential downpours, in snow, and ice storms. We've braved the worst of the elements. No big deal. Let's go."

On the way out of the camper, Justin stopped a moment to pet the cat before he walked out the door. Henry stroked Sasha, as well, and then went out of the camper behind his son-in-law.

The rain was a light veil as they began their steep walk up the hill between the trees. The clouds were heavy and low above them, and the day was a misty gray. The air was warm, but the earth was still chilly under their boots.

"Going to be a foggy one by tonight," Henry predicted, "with the warmth and the cool coming together, and if this rain keeps up. We'll have a wet sleep over, too, if it continues."

"That's why we brought the tarps for our tents. We'll stay dry enough. We owe Oscar far more than putting up with a little rain to see him again. To make sure he and his family are all right."

"I feel the same way."

The men kept forging their way through the woods, enjoying being together out in nature; in the park again, even with the light rain. The overgrowth was thicker, the trees taller, closer together, and the ground difficult to move across. They were very far into Crater Lake's backwoods. Henry has always loved this part of the park. Not many visitors or hikers made it this deep. It was like being in a primitive wilderness.

Every once and a while, Henry would stop and call out to Oscar. He felt silly yelling into the woods like a crazy person, "Oscar, Oscar, we're here to see you! Are you out there?" But how else would Oscar know he was here, if he didn't call out to him? He didn't feel so foolish when Justin started shouting out for Oscar, as well. The two of them thrashing through the forest, calling for Oscar.

"Good thing all the dinosaurs are gone," Justin stated, breathing a little heavier from the hiking. "Or else us screaming out like this might attract something we wouldn't want to attract."

"Yeah, good thing. But there are still wild animals out here that might hear us and want to investigate, so keep your weapon close."

"Always." Justin shoved a low hanging branch aside so he could duck past it.

Hours later, Henry halted in a sizable clearing. "I recognize this place. It was here," he told Justin over his shoulder. "I'm fairly sure this is where I saw Oscar and his family last summer. I remember that rock formation there by that dying tree. Look," he pointed to his right and downwards, "there's still the remnants of my campfire." On the ground there was a ring of rocks and a faded circle of ash smeared into the dirt in the middle.

Justin eyed the space, lifting off his poncho, only long enough to struggle out of his backpack, before he put the poncho back on. The rain was drizzling, just enough that a rain garment was needed. "I'm guessing we put up the tents here then, right?"

"You got it." Henry also slipped out of his poncho, took his backpack off his shoulders, put the poncho on again; dropped his pack to the ground.

"And wait."

"Yes, and wait. We can keep calling out for Oscar and his kiddies, too. But I didn't do that last time, and he still showed up. Somehow, he seemed to know I was here." Henry was already setting his tent up.

Justin followed suit and got his tent out, opened it up, spread it out on the ground, staked it down, raised it, and when it was up, he covered it with a tarp. Soon their camp was set up, and a fire, beneath a third tarp, was crackling.

To Henry it felt like the old days, he and Justin out in the woods camping, except this time they actually *wanted* a dinosaur to show up. How ironic.

Henry was keyed up with anticipation,

eagerly hoping Oscar would find them sooner or later. He really wanted to see the little dinosaur.

Thus, the night began. He and his son-in-law made a simple supper of pre-cooked meat he'd brought from the camper, and opened a can of beans. Later they'd have snacks. Water and coffee.

They hunkered over the fire, scrutinizing the dark trees and the woodlet around them, listening as the rain softly pirouetted on the outside of the tents' tarps. Henry was glad the rain was light. It was the fog creeping in that worried him. It could turn out to be as thick as it was that one night when he and Patterson had been out searching for the red-eyed dinosaurs the year before. That had been a scary night.

The two friends stayed up as late as they could, both hoping Oscar would show up. He didn't. Eventually, when their exhaustion caught up with them from their hike and the fresh air, they turned in for the night in their respective tarp covered tents, and slept.

*****

Henry had been in restless sleep when something made him come awake with a start. He sat up. There was an eerie sound in the night around him. A humming, sometimes soft, sometimes louder, filling the night around him. Then there was a kaleidoscope of dazzling lights rotating around their campsite that were so bright he could see them through his tent's canvas. He scooted to the tent opening, and peeked outside.

Justin was standing beside his tent, gawking up at the sky. "Henry, get out here. You got to look at this. I think those lights up there are alien spaceships!"

Henry scrambled outside to stand by Justin, his eyes on the sky. From what he could tell, off in the distance, high above, miles, in the night sky there was a group of dancing lights coming nearer. Already so brilliant, they hurt Henry's eyes. The orbs stayed close together, but every few seconds they broke apart, and zipped off in different directions, before they regrouped in their original formation. "My God! I bet those are the strange lights that Ranger Finch and Professor Hescott said they witnessed."

"I bet they are," Justin exclaimed, his gaze glued to the distant lights, as well, as they rose, regrouped into intricate configurations, and fell plummeting towards the earth at unbelievable speeds. "Wow, just look at the way they're moving across the skies. Faster than any aircraft we have. That is not the Northern Lights, or reflected lights from cities, or terrestrial activity like experimental advanced military aircraft the government is trying out. Just watching them makes me dizzy."

"They're *hunting* for something," Henry muttered. He was glad their fire had gone out. No need to call attention to themselves. In fact, he felt like running into the woods and hiding. The strange performance in the night skies made him that uneasy.

"And," Justin abruptly cried out, "they're coming this way."

By then, with the orbs now so near, Henry knew it would do little good to run, if those bouncing lights were actually alien aircrafts with aliens in them, but his curiosity overrode his caution. He wanted to see them up closer.

"Let's get a closer look at them, Justin." Hurriedly, he struggled into his boots, and his jacket; retrieved his flashlight, his old duty pistol, and his rifle. He felt better with them in his hands.

"If we catch up with them, I don't think our antiquated weapons will help us any," Justin protested. "Not against what weapons we know the aliens most likely possess. Guns won't stand a chance against alien aggression."

"Get your gun and rifle out anyway. Bring a flashlight." Henry had moved to the edge of their campsite, letting the rain, which was now heavier than when they'd gone to bed, pelt him. He hadn't put his poncho on. Not enough time. His eyes had not left the skies for a moment. He had to see the lights up close if he could. See what they really were.

Justin swiftly tugged his boots on, threw his coat on, collected his rifle, and joined Henry at the edge of the clearing along the forest line. It couldn't hurt to hide beneath the trees' shadows. No sense in being a too visible target.

"They're coming closer," Justin spoke in a nervous whisper. "You don't think they know we are here, do you?"

"I wouldn't think so." But Henry wasn't sure. The aliens he'd communicated with at Area 52, he believed, were so far advanced over humans, he'd put nothing past them. *If* these ships were theirs. He didn't know. These could be totally different aliens. More dangerous aliens. He had the oddest thought: *Maybe one species of aliens visiting them had opened some sort of flood gate...and now others were coming. Like Earth was suddenly the newest, neatest planet for aliens to visit. A new intergalactic resort. Aliens, come one, come all! See the primitive earthlings. Better than a circus or a zoo, full of exotic alien creatures.* Stop it! It wasn't even a surety that the dancing orbs were alien ships at all. They could just be…dancing lights in the sky.

The orbs were growing in size. The sky was an aurora of muted colors swirling around above and around them. All hues of the rainbow as the illuminations beamed off the fog that had, indeed, grown thicker, creeping into the dark forest, and rising high into the sky. It made the lights appear even eerier. Lovely in a way.

Henry felt as if he were standing on an alien world himself. The spooky lights and ghostly noises, the fog churning around them and the nearby trees like a living entity. He shivered in the rain.

"They're hauntingly beautiful, though," Justin mused aloud, "the lights, aren't they? Almost hypnotic."

"Yeah." Henry huffed. "Just beautiful. I only wish they weren't coming in this direction; acting the way they are. I have a bad feeling about all this."

Should we hide? Henry brooded; his breath frozen in his throat. *Would it do any good?* He didn't know.

Henry and Justin watched the oncoming lights as they expanded to eat up the whole sky above them. Now they were strobing crisscrossing spotlights down to the earth.

Looking for something.

"Henry, they're getting awfully near." There was more awe in the scientist's voice than fear, but Henry knew the man, as he knew his son-in-law was more than a little spooked. Justin was trembling beside him.

That's when the lights split apart again. But this time all of them, except one, rocketed in all different directions, and kept going into the troposphere. *Zip, zip, gone!*

"Wow!" Justin shouted. "Did you see them go?"

But Henry hadn't been watching the ones leaving, his eyes were on the one that had remained, and even now was coming closer and closer to them. Becoming bigger and bigger. Right at them.

In seconds it was hovering, its humongous shape spinning like a slow top, directly above them and both men could see it as clear as day, even in the thick fog. It was saucer shaped, silverish, with an aura of glowing light pulsating around it. It was HUGE. As large, if not larger, that the second spaceship that had been kept at Area 52. Yet it was solid, no cupolas of windows. It was also shockingly quiet for its size and proximity.

"Jesus!" Henry mumbled, his voice a croak. "Justin, as much as I suspect that making first contact excites the scientist in you, to be safe, I think we should run for it, take cover somewhere…unless you want to be one of those abductees who get swiped up and, maybe, used for alien experiments. We most likely won't be able to communicate with them, unless they are telepathic like the Area 52 aliens were, but of that I wouldn't hold much of a chance. Even if we tell them who we are, would they even care? I don't relish being their next experiment, in the least. Let's hide."

"Could be you're right," Justin blurted out. "Better safe than sorry. Let's hide."

Without another word, the humans snuck further back into the line of thicker trees, scrunched down, trying to blend into the woods. They hunkered there behind the trees as the branches dropped raindrops on them, and the fog swirled around their bodies.

But the saucer didn't land in their campground clearing–as if it could have fit, it couldn't have–it moved on unhurriedly, strobe lights continuing to search for something; the beams slipping between the tree trunks, sliding over their faces, and moving on. A distinctive hum rose around them. The spaceship was talking, but the humans couldn't understand it.

When it passed by them, the men came to their feet.

"Whew, that was close." A low whistle escaped Henry's mouth.

"Look," Justin cried, pointing to their right, "I think it's landing over that hill there."

Henry didn't know why he did it, but like a moth to a flame, he switched on his flashlight, and headed in the direction where the spaceship had gone. "I'd like to get a better look at it, Justin. From a safe, hidden distance, of course. You coming?" He began jogging through the night woods, dodging trees and bushes, towards where the space craft appeared to have landed.

"I'm coming." Justin shadowed behind Henry deeper into the forest. "I can't let you go by yourself, old man."

The two fought their way through the wet,

dark foliage, climbing steadily up a slowly ascending series of steep hills; holding on to the trees to keep their balance, and pull themselves along.

In time, Henry could see the pulsating lights ahead of them filling the foggy sky. The humming had ceased. The saucer had landed.

They came to the crest of the highest hill above where the spaceship perched below in a scrubby clearing. It had set down on some trees, crushing them beneath its great weight. *Whoa, was it gigantic.*

Crawling into place, getting their knees wet and muddy, under cover behind a row of bushes, Henry and Justin stared down at the craft. It was easy to see everything because the craft glowed as if lit from inside, the illumination spreading over the area around the spaceship.

A door at the bottom of the craft opened. Living entities, of some kind, were coming out of it. Or Henry thought they were living creatures. He couldn't actually see *them*. In reality, they were simply three shifting translucent blobs that dispersed into the woods as the spaceship's lowered door closed again. He remembered that same type of invisibility cloaking the dinosaur aliens he'd communicated with on the Area 52's second spaceship.

"Can you *see* them?" Justin whispered, rubbing his eyes, as he gazed down at the spaceship below. "I can't see anything. Well, wait a minute, I can see *something*. It looks like…weird shapes of rippling air moving through the rain. They must have a cloaking mechanism."

"They do. But all I can see is these moving blurs. I can tell something is there, but the solid part of their bodies is blurry, distorted. If it wasn't raining, I probably couldn't see them at all. It's so strange."

Henry wasn't surprised he couldn't actually see the aliens; he hadn't been able to see the ones on the spaceship at Area 52 until they'd wanted him to. And then only for a fraction of a heartbeat. The aliens were clever at subterfuge. Hiding. They would be. Being advanced aliens. Henry did wonder if the extraterrestrials on the ship below were the same species he'd encountered, or if they were different. What he wouldn't give to know that. Now seeing the craft nearer, even the saucer was different that the ones that had been at Area 52. This one was sleeker, not as round, and the silver color was much darker. They might not be his aliens at all. That was a sobering thought.

He really wanted to snap some pictures of the spaceship, but in his haste to leave the campsite, he'd left his iPhone in his tent.

"You don't happen to have your phone with you, do you, Justin?"

"Darn! No. We left in such a hurry, I left it back at the campsite. Sorry."

Cussing a little beneath his breath, Henry groused, "Me, too. Well, no photos then."

Henry had decided it might be best not to stick around. He had no idea where the aliens were, or where they were going, what they were looking for. They might even be looking for him and Justin. They could have even been heading for their camp. Better to be safe than sorry. He didn't want to be captured. And he and Justin weren't equipped to fight any extraterrestrials. He was pretty sure pistols and rifles wouldn't cut it.

"Let's get out of here, Justin. I don't think it's safe for us to remain here so close to that spacecraft."

"You know, you're right. Let's boogie."

Backtracking the route they'd come; they stealthily, and as quietly as they could, made their way to the camp. Their eyes and ears sensitive for any abnormal sounds or movements in the woods around them. Hard to do because it was dark, they couldn't risk using their flashlights, and the rain was still a steady downfall. Cautiously, they checked to be sure there were no aliens lurking anywhere in it or around their camp before they reentered it.

"I think we're in the clear," Henry spoke in voice just loud enough to be heard over the rain. "No one, aliens included, seems to be here."

"Yet," Justin replied derisively. He attempted to make a telephone call. "No bars. Darn it! I was afraid of that."

"Who were you trying to call?" Henry wanted to know.

"Patterson. He–if he is involved with this problem–should know about the spaceships we saw, and this landing. Then we need to report this immediately to the proper government authorities."

"That we do." Henry tried his cell phone, as well, and wasn't surprised when he couldn't reach Patterson, either. Or reach anyone, for that matter. "We're too far into the backwoods to get a signal."

"I kind of figured that." Justin had

continued to peer around for uninvited alien guests. Apparently, he didn't see–or not see–any.

"So," Henry concluded, "under the circumstances, son-in-law, I think we should pack up, leave at dawn, which is, oh, about an hour from now, and skedaddle out of the vicinity home to Klamath Falls. We can call Patterson on the way, as soon as we can get through. Let Chief Ranger Collins also know what we've seen. We'll have to come looking for Oscar again some other time. Getting information on this *sighting* to the proper authorities right now is more important."

"Not to mention," Justin warned, "we don't know where those invisible aliens are right now. They could have followed us, and might be observing us this very minute. Getting ready to pounce on us." The scientist was looking around as he said it.

"Right. Let's get out of here. Heck with waiting for dawn. Let's start packing up now. Be ready to march out soon as soon as we're ready. It'll be close enough to first light that we won't be hiking in the dark for long. We need to get out of the woods and back to safety in town." Though Henry had the uneasy thought that if the aliens wanted them, no matter where they were, they could probably get to them. Aliens were known for coming right into peoples' homes and bedrooms and whisking them away. Nothing would stop them.

So, tearing down their sparce campsite, and their tents, they rapidly packed everything up, and slid their backpacks on. The minute the first tiny glow of sunrise touched the horizon, they were already on the return trek to the Scamp.

They moved fast; glancing behind themselves often for any signs of aliens on their trail, or of the spaceship they'd seen fly over them, or to see it up in the sky anywhere again. But the skies remained empty except for the clouds and the rain. They made it to the camper quicker than he would have thought they could, and drove rapidly through the park. Henry guessed fear could do that.

After hours of driving, Justin finally got through to Patterson, spoke a few minutes with him and hung up.

"What did he say?" Henry's hands were on the wheel, as he focused on the narrow dirt road ahead of them.

"Oh, he's real interested in what we saw. He said he'd pass the information on to the appropriate authorities, who will probably send a team, as he put it, out immediately to where we were, to check on that spaceship if it's still there; search the area for any other signs of its companions. I bet you the team will be military; it usually is when it comes to alien encounters. He said he'd get back to us as soon as he could. I told him it'll take at least two days for us to get back to your place."

"Hmm. I knew Patterson is involved with this whole alien thing. I just knew it."

"I think you're right," Justin said. "He was *really* interested in what happened to us. He couldn't ask enough questions about the spaceships, the one that landed, and what we witnessed. Where exactly we saw it in the park. He didn't seem surprised. At all."

"I knew it."

All in all, Henry was exceedingly relieved to get home in the evening two days later. No aliens or spaceships had followed them.

When they pulled into the driveway of Henry's home, Patterson was waiting for them.

*****

Once Henry parked the truck, and unhooked the camper from it, the three men went into Henry's house, and Patterson and

Justin sat down at the table.

Justin had brought Sasha's cage in from the truck, and because she'd been so excited to be home, he'd freed her out in the yard. After the men went inside the house, not long after the feline came bursting in through the cat door, and sat patiently by the kitchen sink. Waiting for supper.

Henry fed the cat. After what had happened out in the park, it was good to be home. Safe and sound. The aliens hadn't gotten them.

"I didn't expect you to actually show up here in person, Scott," Henry muttered sideways as he made a pot of coffee. "Though, as always, it's a nice surprise. You're always welcome here, friend. You know that."

"I do. But I wanted to talk to you and the Doc here face to face. Soon as possible. Take your statements while the experiences are fresh in your minds. So, I don't miss anything that might be of importance. Even the smallest detail." Patterson pulled out a recorder. It was state-of-the-art, compact, and brand new looking. It fit easily in Patterson's hand. "You don't mind, do you, if I tape our conversations?"

"Of course not, Scott. Do what you have to

do. Record, take notes. Film videos. Whatever you need to do." Henry settled himself down next to Patterson as the coffee began to perk. The lovely aroma filled the kitchen. It was all such a normal routine, but to Henry nothing seemed normal after what they'd seen at Crater Lake. "But I'm not surprised you're here. I half expected it. I told Justin when we hit the town limits that you'd most likely be here waiting for us. I knew you'd want a firsthand account of what Justin and I saw out there in the woods. You'd want to know about the spaceships and the aliens, and we'll tell you everything."

"I'd appreciate it," Patterson thanked Henry.

"I also have some news about Professor Hescott," Henry added. "He called me the day before Justin and I took off on our camping trip. He saw an alien spaceship, too, in the park days before we did. The Professor took pictures of it, though they are blurry. I have them downloaded on my laptop. I'll give you copies and tell you what he told me. According to Hescott, his alien spaceship wasn't anything like the ones me and Justin saw. Imagine that?"

Henry got up and poured himself a cup of

coffee, sat down again. "Help yourselves to coffee you two."

"So let me get this straight," Patterson got up and poured himself a cup, "you and the Doc here just decided to go out on a camping trip. For fun, huh?"

Henry disliked lying to Patterson, but the only other person who knew that Oscar had survived the explosion two years before was Justin. So, he couldn't tell the ex-FBI agent why they had really gone out into the deep woods. To check up on the little dinosaur. He had to keep that secret between him and Justin only. He had to protect Oscar and his family.

"Yep," Henry answered. "We planned it last month. Justin needed a getaway and time out in nature. We took the Scamp, camped out, did a little hiking, caught-up with our lives over a campfire. You know, like you and I did last month.

"We would have invited you, Scott, but you were off on your new top-secret project. Which, by the way, you still haven't let us know what that's all about." Henry grinned, shrugging.

"You know I can't," Patterson reiterated, looking uncomfortable.

"You want to know what happened to us?"

Justin rose and also helped himself to a cup of java; sat back down at the table.

Patterson took a long sip of his coffee, and looked from Henry to Justin. "That's what I'm here to get. Since I talked to you on the phone, Justin, I've been dying to hear more."

Henry reached down and scooped up the cat and put her in his lap. After what they'd gone through in the park, the fear, and the hasty retreat, it felt good to be drinking coffee in his kitchen. Safe. Or as safe as anyone could be with aliens flying and running around. It was only then he realized how close he and Justin may have come to catastrophe. *If the aliens would have seen them, captured them....*

Patterson clicked on the recorder, and introduced both Henry and Justin and listed their credentials.

Justine began the story by saying, "It was quite an…experience."

"Then tell me," Patterson said for the recorder's benefit.

And Henry and Justin did, and when they were done, and Patterson had asked all the questions he wanted to ask, and the recorder had been switched off, Henry looked right at the ex-FBI agent. "We have already guessed that your top-secret project is about aliens…possibly planning a worldwide invasion or something like it? Those strange lights, those orbs some call them, and actual UAPs have been spotted increasingly all across the globe, more every day, haven't they? That's why you're here. We *know* something is going on. Something terrible. Something involving aliens. So, Scott, how about leveling with us? We're all friends here. Maybe Justin and I can help you investigate what's really going on. I mean we have seen the aliens and their ships. First at Area 52, and now, recently, one up close. A working spaceship.

"And I," Henry gently reminded Patterson, "have communicated with aliens. Don't forget that. Who else do you know who has done that?"

With a sigh, Patterson replied, "I know you did, Henry. You're the only one I know of who has talked to aliens." The ex-FBI agent seemed to deliberate their sincere request for more candidness, looking between Henry and Justin, and then surrendered. "All right. I'm going to confess everything to you two. I have to clear it with General Wallace first, though. Let me call him."

Ah, he's working with General Wallace again, Henry mulled that development over. For some reason, that didn't surprise him either.

Patterson excused himself and walked into the living room. Henry could hear his muted conversation on the phone, not clear enough to understand though, then the man came back into the kitchen. "General Wallace has given you both mid-level clearances. I can partially bring you into the fold. Tell you what we suspect is occurring. Well, some of it."

That's better than nothing, Henry thought. He'd take it.

"What's occurring?" Justin pressed.

"You guessed right," Patterson said in a somber tone, "our government believes aliens are preparing for a first contact…or an all-out invasion. We don't know, as of yet, which one. We don't know who or what the aliens are. Not yet. Friend or foe. We just know they have been showing up lately in greater and greater numbers, and they're not shy."

"I knew it!" Henry snapped his fingers.

"Also," Patterson added, "General Wallace is sending out an exploration team to the park to see if they can witness the spaceships themselves. They'll check in with Chief

Collins before they set up a base there.

"Also, General Wallace would like to see both of you at Area 52 on Saturday. In person. We'll send a plane for you. I'll let you know when the car will pick you up here to take you to the airport. Justin, the General will clear this time off with your boss. They do know each other. Henry, the same with your part-time ranger job. The General will clear it with Chief Ranger Collins. For as long as you both are needed."

Yippee, Henry thought. *Back to the base.*

Saturday was five days away.

"Area 52," Justin remarked. "You're at the old digs again, huh?

"We are."

"Isabel, too?" Henry asked, taking a wild guess.

"She's there," Patterson admitted. "As well as a lot of the old team."

Hot dog.

"Er," Henry couldn't help but ask, "are we part of that team now?"

"I can't say. It's not up to me. The General will decide after he listens to what I have learned here today, and he talks to both of you in person on Saturday."

"I can't wait." Henry leaned into his chair,

a big smile on his face.

Patterson stood up. "Since I have all I need, and I'm done here, I'll leave you two. I had better stop by the house, and see my family before I fly back to Area 52, or Sherman will have my head."

"Yeah," Justin remarked, "you better."

"See you both on Saturday." Patterson got up and went out the door, gesturing goodbye as he went.

When their friend had left, Justin and Henry sat there for a while staring at each other.

"Henry, we could be back in the game."

"We might, son-in-law."

Both of them were ginning.

Justin seemed to be thinking something over. "I have five days until Saturday. If it's okay with you I'll spend the night, and fly back to New York to wrap up some things. See my family. I'll return Friday night. Unless the plans change, and I have to return here sooner to catch our plane. Call me if they do."

"I will. Your room is waiting down the hall," Henry said. "Let's unload the Scamp and put our stuff away. After I'll call Chief Collins and tell him, I need a leave of absence, indefinitely. I prefer to do that myself, even though he'll get another official call. I also need to tell him what we saw in his park. He should close the park for now until it's safer for the visitors. He wouldn't want any of them unduly frightened, hurt, or abducted."

"He's not going to like closing the park."

"But I don't see how there's any other thing to do. Those aliens were walking around. Heaven knows what they're after or what they would do if they came across humans."

"Better safe than sorry," Justin concurred. "Collins will have to put the safety of the visitors first."

"And after I speak to Collins, I'll fix us some supper."

"That's an excellent idea. I could eat."

"Son," Henry laughed, "you can always eat."

CHAPTER 10

The day was bright and warm, nothing wet or cold was falling from above, and the dinosaur was out with his family hunting for food, which they did from sunup to sundown every day. It took a lot of fat creatures to feed his growing family. The young ones, full of energy and playfulness, were far ahead of him and the older ones, frolicking as much as they were hunting.

The dinosaur made sure he kept his brood in sight, kept them safe, and only letting them roam in the areas that most sticks did not intrude into. He protected his kind and had since the first egg had hatched. They were always on the watch out for the larger furry creatures with the big claws and teeth that skulked on the forest. They hid from those. But long past were his lonely days. He was surrounded by others just like him, his family, and he was content, running through the lush woods he considered home.

He had other memories, older ones, of another more dangerous time when he was friends with the creatures he'd thought of as the sticks, far from his now home. He remembered them once in a while, especially the one stick and his mate who had been his friends. When he thought of them, he had a happy feeling inside. He hadn't forgotten them or those days when he had helped them defeat their and his enemies. He recalled where his friend stick had its cave, and had almost gone to see him a time or two. But his family was so time consuming; they always needed him. He would think of seeing the stick and then would forget.

The glowing ball above them was further down towards the trees, when their prey, a tall skinny creature with long legs and pointed ears, was sighted and, with whoops of excitement, anticipation, and hunger, he and his family took chase. The fastest of them moved out ahead and cornered the prey. Brought it down. Then they shared the prey and everyone ate. When they were done, they took off in search of more prey. It took a lot of meat to fill everyone's bellies. It took all the time they were not sleeping.

After another quarry was flushed out, run down, and devoured, the pack, their stomachs full, but their throats parched, headed for the water, and drank until their thirst was quenched. The dinosaurs rolled in the grass by the water, played with each other, happy to be fed and safe, or rested, enjoying their time together. The youngest were jumping, play fighting, or climbing the nearby trees. Looking out over the scene, the dinosaur felt satisfaction. Pride. His offspring were all doing so well, growing strong. Growing clever. Some gaining their new abilities. Some he could already communicate with. There were a few who could do things he had never envisioned. Special talents. His pack was growing stronger all the time.

He was content with his family and his life here in the park. He settled down on his haunches in the shade of a tree by the water, his eyes grew heavy and half closed. Then the world changed. *Alarm! Alarm!* His eyes flew open.

Some of the smallest of his family had begun chattering, squealing loudly, dashing around frightened, as a dark shadow passed above them. The dinosaur looked up. At first, he believed it was the sky growing angry as it often did, when it would shed water, white flakes, or the hard wetness. But it wasn't the sky crying at all. It was a giant dark monster hulking high above them, moving slowly. It filled the sky and its sinister presence alone made the dinosaur shiver. His progeny was afraid, he could feel it in them, especially the littlest ones. They ran to him, crowded around him, making tiny cries, quivering.

And the fear hit him. *They must run, they must...hide!* This creature above them was not their friend. He could *feel* that. It might hurt his family. He could hear the intruder's ugly thoughts in his head, and they were enemies. *Bad, bad enemies*. He screamed out the danger warning for his children to run and hide. *Now!* And all the dinosaurs scampered into the woods, away from the water and the silent monster hulking above them in the sky. They melted into the forest, and crouched into small crevices, behind bushes or rocks, and covered themselves in leaves. They had been taught to hide well.

All the dinosaur knew was that they could all be in danger. He and his children were in great peril.

Stay hidden, he warned them all with silent thoughts, low hisses, and squawks. *Quiet. Do not move. Until I tell you it is safe.*

Trembling among or behind tree trunks, leaves hiding them from the threat in the sky, or under their fallen limbs or leaves, the dinosaurs were motionless, and silent, until the black monster above them left the sky and moved away.

When the dinosaur believed his offspring were safe, he called them all out and led them towards their cave. His gaze continuously on the sky in case the black beast returned.

He and his horde were nearly at their home and safety, crossing the final open space before they would scuttle into the cave, when another floating thing, not as big as the dark one, came down over them. It hovered without making any noise.

Unlike the last time, at the water, the dinosaur knew right off that this huge creature was not their enemy. He could hear things in his head coming from the shiny thing.

We are friends. Do not be afraid.

And the dinosaur wasn't afraid. He could hear many voices in his head coming from the shimmering thing above him. Calm, kind, good voices. He didn't know how they could communicate with him, but he was sure they would not hurt him or his kind. They told him so.

We need to speak to you and your children. We have a warning for you. Do not be afraid when our craft settles down beside you. Come to us. We will not hurt you.

The dinosaur understood what the voice meant. He was made to understand.

The large hovering object lowered itself to the earth, and opened its mouth. The dinosaur, hesitating at first, was coaxed into entering the opening. He went alone, telling his children to go into the cave where they would be safe until he returned. *Do not follow me*, he cautioned them.

Once inside he was surrounded by voices coming from creatures he could not see. He felt them all around him, but they were not there. But he had no fear. He knew somehow, they meant him no harm. They told him of the danger he and his family were in and that they wanted to take them away where they would be safe; where their ancestors had come from millennium ago. And where they belonged.

But the park was his–their–home and the dinosaur didn't want to leave. He wanted to know why they were in danger and once the invisible voices told him, he became upset. He told them about the black monster he'd seen at the water and they cautioned him not to let one of the black monsters find him and his clan. He'd done the right thing, they said, by hiding. The black monsters were dangerous.

After a while, he made them understand

that he and his family did not want to leave his forest home. The invisible ones were not happy about his decision and let him know they would give him time to think about it and decide. They would be back for his answer.

He thought of his stick friends and asked the invisible ones to tell the sticks what they'd told him. And only because they could see how much he vouched for and cared about the sticks, they reluctantly agreed.

A time and place for another meeting were settled on, and after visiting with the invisibles, the dinosaur left the object, and it silently lifted from the ground, and flew away.

The dinosaur made sure his family were safe in their cave, and he left.

He had to warn the sticks. He had to warn his stick friends.

Chapter 11

The sun was barely creeping over the horizon when Henry, abruptly awakened from sleep, heard a series of loud noises–as if someone was pounding on or throwing themselves against the door–on the rear porch. He listened for minute or two, and then closed his eyes, ready to recapture sleep, when the noises repeated themselves. Much louder this time. Someone was banging persistently at the porch's door. He sat up in bed in the dim room, the sunlight a faint glow over everything. He noticed the time on the wall clock. It was five in the morning. Still dark outside. Justin hadn't even woken him up yet, as his son-in-law had spent the night and was leaving by seven to fly home for a couple days, he'd said. The noise came again.

"Darn it," he complained, mostly to himself, dragging himself out of bed, "who could that be this early in the morning? Sasha, is that you? Trying to get in your cat door? I really do need to put you on a diet if you finally can't get your fat butt through it. Why are you making so much noise?"

He stumbled down the hallway towards the

kitchen, half-asleep. He and Justin had stayed up way too late, talking about the ever-increasing sightings of alien spaceships and their terrifying adventure in the park. The possible meanings behind it all. Both men were still unsettled by what they'd seen; what it might mean to the citizens of Earth. Both wondered what they'd learn at Area 52 when they got there Saturday. There was a lot to think and worry about. Then Henry, even when he'd retired to his bed, still couldn't stop thinking about the aliens. He kept forming scenarios of what was or could happen and none of them made him feel any safer. Now he was paying for the late night. Justin, he knew, was supposed to get up early. Not this early, though. He wouldn't even be up yet.

Henry opened the back door, expecting to see Sasha, or at worse a raccoon loose on the porch trying to get in, because that had happened before, but what he did see made him stare in pure astonishment. There sitting on the porch, in the pale morning light, staring at him, was a familiar looking small dinosaur. About four feet tall, its skin looking a little furry. Its head cocked at him, its eyes wide with an intelligent glint. Henry could have sworn the beast was smiling. Nah. Dinosaurs can't smile, can they?

"*Oscar?*"

The dinosaur scuttled up closer and stretched out a claw towards Henry.

Grinning, Henry touched the claw gently with his hand. Their old greeting. He was overcome with the fact that Oscar had come to visit him in his own home again. After two years, he never thought that would happen again. "What are you doing here, little buddy?" But Henry didn't care why Oscar had come, he was just so happy to see him.

"You know Justin and I were just in the woods looking for you. Is that why you're here now? You heard or saw us? And, for some reason, followed us back here…we did leave in an awful hurry….because you, either, missed me so much or…there's something you need to communicate to me? Something important?"

The dinosaur merely blinked at him. Its third eyelid, a nictitating membrane, closing and opening side to side. The creature had grown some, but was still around four feet tall. His skin was a darker color, his tail somewhat longer, his muscles stronger, yet his eyes remained intelligently empathetic, if possible, even more so than the last time he'd seen the creature, Henry thought. The eyes were fixated on Henry. The dinosaur made a series of clicking sounds, gesturing in the air with his shorter front arms, as if he were trying to talk to him.

"Sorry, Buddy, I don't understand. What are you trying to tell me?"

More clicking, more eye contact. Henry still didn't understand what the critter was trying to tell him.

Throwing its shoulders up in what Henry surmised was a gesture of exasperation, Oscar let out a series of low grunts, moved towards Henry, and peered into the house through the glass on the door. He gazed up Henry with a beseeching look; put his claw on the door handle.

"So, you remember your last visit here, huh? And you want to come inside?"

Oscar's face made that funny smile-like expression again.

Henry opened the door wider and let the little dinosaur in. As Henry switched on the light, the creature scurried past him, and into the kitchen. Oscar scampered around the room, touching things, and knocking items off the table, opened the pantry door, peaked in, and left it open; jumped up on the kitchen counter and opened one cabinet door after another, as if he were looking for something.

Jumping down from the counter, and glaring for a long minute at the refrigerator, the dinosaur scampered out of the kitchen, and into the dark living room.

Henry followed him, turning on the lights as he went.

The dinosaur was hopping around the room. He looked behind the sofa, the chairs, and then scuttled down the hallway.

"Oscar! What are you doing? Wait up!"

The little dinosaur was in the first bedroom, once his and Ann's, now only his alone. Henry got to the doorway as the creature was coming out. Oscar hopped past him and headed into the guest bedroom where Justin was sleeping.

Henry had stopped in the middle of the hallway. He'd figured it out. He knew what Oscar was doing. *He was searching for Ann.* "You're looking for Ann, aren't you, Oscar?" Henry asked in a whisper as the dinosaur shuffled past him in the hallway.

Oscar didn't answer, merely kept moving, searching.

When Henry entered the guest bedroom, the dinosaur was poised at the head of the bed, and a surprised Justin was sitting up in it gaping at the dinosaur in his room.

"Henry!" Justin had turned on the nightstand light and was gaping at the intruder. "Henry! There's a *dinosaur* in my room!"

Henry laughed. "Yep, there is."

"It's Oscar, isn't it, Henry?" Justin's eyes went wide. The man rubbed them, waking up the rest of the way.

"It is Oscar. He came to visit us."

Oscar was studying the man in the bed curiously. The creature released a continuous guttural sort of noise from his throat. A dinosaur purr? Could be. Henry had the feeling it meant he accepted Justin as not a threat, as a friend.

"Don't worry, he appears to remember who you are. He won't hurt you."

"That's good. I guess I had better get up." Justin slid out of bed, and grabbing the clothes he'd left on a chair nearby the night before, quickly put his pants and shirt on. His gaze was on the dinosaur the complete time, a big smile on his face. "I can't believe he's right here in the flesh. How did he get here? Why is he here? How did he get in?"

"I believe Oscar heard or saw us when we were out in the woods looking for him and, when we left in such a hurry, he tracked us back here."

"But why is he here? Just because he saw us or missed you?" Justin was dressed, and was standing above Oscar. The dinosaur scooted up to Justin and reached out a claw to him.

Henry could tell by Justin's face, he was delighted at Oscar's gesture.

"Touch his claw, Justin, he's saying hello to you," Henry encouraged the scientist.

Justin did and the dinosaur and the human said hello to each other, touching claw to hand.

"And to why Oscar is here, I'm not sure. He just showed up at the rear door, woke me up in fact banging on it. It's a wonder the ruckus didn't wake you as well."

"If I'm exhausted, as I was last night," Justin excused himself, "I can be a heavy sleeper, as you know."

Oscar had sidled up to Justin, and suddenly he seemed to be *hugging* him. The creature's arms briefly circled around Justin's waist, for a heartbeat, then released him. A dinosaur that hugged. Henry couldn't get over it. How smart was this critter? "Oh, he remembers you all right, Justin. From one of our dinosaur hunts you came along on, I imagine. He knows you are a friend."

Abruptly, Oscar swung around, scurried out of the bedroom, and down the hallway. Henry and Justin trailed behind him.

When the dinosaur pushed open the bathroom door, and went inside, Justin asked, "What is he looking for?"

With a touch of melancholy, Henry answered, "I think he's been looking for Ann. All over the house, since I first let him in. He's been in every room now so far. He was close to her, too."

"Oh, my goodness. It's astonishing that he remembers her that well. It says a lot for his innate intelligence, long-term memory, and sense of empathy. What an incredible creature."

The two humans waited for the dinosaur to exit the bathroom. The beast acted extremely distressed; its head tilted down; its shoulders slumped. Its behavior so human it affected Henry greatly. The little dinosaur was truly sad. He couldn't find his friend, Ann.

It was then Oscar went up to Henry and, stopping before him, laid a look of such sorrow on him, it almost made Henry cry. Then the little dinosaur leaned up again him, patted him with its talons, as if he were trying to comfort him. Henry could almost sense the dinosaur's sympathy.

"I think he knows she isn't here," Henry whispered to Justin, something so primal catching in his throat. "He *knows* Ann is gone. Perhaps he even knows she's dead."

After a brief time, Oscar pulled away from Henry, pivoted around, and took off down the hallway.

Henry and Justin, exchanging bemused looks, were right behind him. Oscar ended up in the kitchen positioned in front of the refrigerator. He peeked over his shoulder at Henry with, Henry could have sworn, a pleading glint in his eyes. His one talon pointed at the refrigerator.

Henry let out a chuckle. "He wants to raid the fridge like he did the last time he was here. I can't believe he remembers that."

Henry walked over and opened wide the fridge door. "Sorry, there's not a lot of food in there this time. There's no Ann to stock it as there once was. But you can have whatever you find, little buddy," he apologized to the dinosaur, as the creature started grabbing items off the shelves, tearing into them, and instantly stuffing whatever he found into its jaws. An expired selling date package of pork chops, a roast Henry was going to make for supper before going to Area 52. Left over odds and ends. Half rotten vegetables, fruit. Oscar devoured them all, smacking his lips after each entrée or scrap of food; often gazing back at Henry or Justin as if to make sure what he was doing was okay with them. Henry would nod, and smile, at the dinosaur, and Oscar would continue eating whatever was in his claws. He even pried open a jar of dill pickles. But, making a face, decided he didn't like them, and dropped the jar to the floor.

Going to have a mess to clean up when he's done, Henry thought. But he didn't care. If that was the price to have Oscar back in his home, he'd gladly pay it.

"He's as hungry as ever, the little glutton." Henry was smiling. The dinosaur's little vandalism had brought back some poignant memories. Last time Oscar had raided the refrigerator Ann had been here. Ann had been alive. Henry pushed that sad truth away. *Don't think about that.* Just be happy Oscar was once more making a mess in his house.

Justin had brought his iPhone from the bedroom and was snapping candid pictures of Oscar. "I still can't believe he's here." Justin had a look of awe on his face. "I know we've seen, fought, ran from, and exterminated all sorts of cunning, malevolent dinosaurs…but there's just something that blows me away about Oscar and his kind. If all the dinosaurs had been like him, perceptively benevolent, we wouldn't have had to destroy all of them. Which to this day I still have guilt over. We committed genocide on a whole species."

"So more humans wouldn't die," Henry somberly reminded him. "We couldn't contain, restrain, or stop their vicious slaughter of us humans. We only did what we had to do. For our species survival."

"Yes, we did. I have no regrets to the decision humanity, in the end, had to make. It was either us humans, or the dinos." Justin had continued to take pictures of Oscar as the prehistoric throwback methodically decimated the food supply in the refrigerator. The dinosaur seemed determined to eat everything eatable there was inside of it. "I guess I'll have to go to the store pretty soon, that is, if I want to eat anything for supper." At least, he had canned goods in the cabinets. In a pinch, he could always eat canned ravioli.

"I wonder if he'd let me take a little bit of cell specimens." Justin had moved to the other side of the munching dinosaur to get a different angle for his photos and videos.

"All you can do is try. My advice is to attempt to ask him first. Maybe he'll let you take a tiny sliver of skin."

"Sure, he will," Justin remarked sarcastically.

"My second suggestion would be not to even try." Henry met Justin's eyes. "If he thinks we're trying to hurt him, he'll stop trusting us."

"I imagine you're right. Perhaps he'll let me swab the inside of his mouth. That wouldn't hurt him."

"You can try. But I wouldn't if I were you. He might bite you. You see the incisors he has?"

As the dinosaur snatched things out of the refrigerator and either consumed them, or tossed them across the room when he found he didn't want to eat them, Henry found himself speaking to the little dinosaur as if the creature could understand his words. Perhaps he could…or get the gist of what he was saying by his developing telepathic abilities. How much stronger had they become in the last two years? He might as well try to gauge them.

"It's been a long time since you were here

that last day," Henry spoke in a soft, comforting tone to the dinosaur. "Do you remember old One-eye and the helicopter crash? We feared you had died in the explosion killing One-Eye. But you didn't. Do you remember any of this?"

Oscar paused in his eating, and twisted around to quizzically regard Henry. At first, the dinosaur appeared puzzled, and Henry asked the last questions again.

Oscar seemed to be ruminating, making a sound like a low chortling in his chest, as if he were talking to himself. He slowly nodded. Then nodded harder.

"Oh, my God. I think he remembers. He knew what I was asking." Henry was taken aback. *Oscar could understand him*. Somehow. As astonishing as it was, the dinosaur's intelligence and telepathic abilities both had increased in the last two years. "I'm going to try something."

In a measured calm, but serious, voice, Henry told Oscar about everything that was happening in the world. The recent sightings of the orbs in the park, and all over the world. The alien spaceships, and what had happened to him and Justin with the solitary spaceship in the park. The practically invisible aliens who had disembarked from it. He told him about Hescott's scary sighting of the large obsidian triangular space craft, and how frightened Hescott had been. He told him everything and Oscar appeared to really listen.

When Henry was finished, he asked, "All right, Oscar. Now let's try another question or more. Why are you here? Are you aware of everything I just spoke about? Are you? *Is that why you're here*? Something about the alien spaceships we're seeing everywhere lately?" Henry attempted to simply pantomime a big flying object, shaping a saucer in the air with his hands, landing in what he hoped would represent the woods Oscar and his clan lived in.

Oscar seemed to ruminate on that for a bit, stared hard into Henry's eyes, then strongly nodded again.

"It *is* about the spaceships," Henry exclaimed.

"This is almost unbelievable." Justin flopped down on a kitchen chair, ran his hand across his face. He glanced first at Oscar and then Henry. "That he took in what you said is astounding, Henry. But I really think he did understand."

"I think he did, too."

"What are we going to do now?"

Oscar had returned to what was left in the refrigerator, but it was basically empty, except for the few remaining condiments. Apparently, the dinosaur didn't like mustard, vinegar, or hot sauce, and after he'd tried them, making faces at the tastes, he tossed the containers cross the kitchen. The ketchup he guzzled down from the bottle, as much as he could get of it. Then he jumped up on the counter, and, after a few tries, managed to open one of the cabinets.

"*Oh no!*" Henry got the little guy's attention, glaring directly at him, and firmly shook his head, "you can't eat all my canned goods, or my dishes. Get down from there." Henry pointed to the floor, and Oscar, giving Henry a doleful look, reluctantly dropped down.

Henry tried to clean up the mess Oscar had left behind on the kitchen floor, sweeping it all up and dumping everything into the trash can. He'd mop later.

Oscar was by the door. When he caught Henry's eye, he pointed at him, and Justin, and afterwards to the door, and only what Henry could understand as meaning *outside*. He did the gesture three times. More adamant each time.

"He wants us to go outside?" Justin deciphered the dinosaur's instructions.

"No," Henry muttered softly, "I'm pretty sure, he wants us to go somewhere with him.

"Is that what you want, Oscar? Us to go somewhere with you?"

Oscar nodded, edged closer to the door, placed one claw on the handle, and pointed outside with the other; his head tilted in that direction.

"Uh, I'm pretty sure, he wants *both* of us," Henry said, "to go somewhere with him."

Henry spoke to Oscar, hoping the dinosaur would again comprehend what he was trying to tell him. "All right. We'll come with you. But give us some time first to prepare." He patted the air with his hands as if to convey *wait, wait*.

Unbelievably, Oscar seemed to comprehend, bobbing his head up and down.

"Where does he want to take us?" Justin was staring at Oscar, who was poised by the door. "I was going to head home today. Patterson is expecting us at Area 52 on Saturday, remember?"

"I remember. But Saturday is still four days away. Maybe, where he wants to lead us isn't a long distance away."

"Or so we hope. What if it's as far away as where we just returned from? I'm ready to postpone, or even cancel, flying home, but if we can't make Saturday at Area 52, we need to call Patterson and let him know what's going on. Make up some excuse or other…to do with the alien spaceships, of course. But not mention Oscar."

"No, we can't mention Oscar. We can't tell Patterson, as good a friend as he is to us, that Oscar is still alive. We can't. He's too establishment. I made a promise with myself not to endanger Oscar by telling anyone else, but you, about his survival."

"Don't worry, Chief, I'll come up with some excuse or other that doesn't involve ratting out the existence of our little comrade here."

"What are you going to say to Patterson?"

Justin winked at Henry. "Trust me. A little fib can't hurt, if it's for the good of all." He keyed in a number on his iPhone.

After a number of rings, Justin must have gotten Patterson on the phone.

"Hello, Scott?" Pause. "It's Justin. I wanted to give you a heads up that Henry and I will really try to make that meeting at Area

52 on Saturday, but we just heard from Professor Hescott about a new alien sighting he's had in the park, and Chief Collins has asked Henry and I to come into ranger headquarters to talk to the Professor about what he experienced, and then to do a little reconnaissance in the park afterwards where Hescott had the encounter. The Professor wants to take us out to the site and show us some things. I figure whatever we find out would be of interest, as well, to you and General Wallace. We're try to make it to the base by Saturday, or as soon after as we can. Is that okay with you?"

Justin was listening to Patterson's response, and he gave Henry the thumbs up. When he got off the phone, he said, "It's all right. Patterson informed me the meeting has now been rescheduled. Something with a higher priority came up for the General. Patterson said he'd been about to call us to let us know. He also said he'd contact us when the meet is back on."

"That was serendipitous. Works for us." Henry gazed at Oscar. "I guess I had better get dressed. Then we'll go wherever Oscar wants us to go."

Henry tried to explain the delay to the

dinosaur, and Oscar appeared to understand. Kind of. He took off through the kitchen, and into the living room. Henry could hear the little guy rummaging through the other rooms. Closets.

Henry rolled his eyes at Justin. “He’s probably hunting for something more to eat. It’s a good thing we never emptied the food from the Scamp. At least we can grab something for breakfast from it before we take off…to wherever we are going. If we can keep Oscar from eating it all, that is. Our backpacks, which we didn’t get around to unpacking last night, are still in there. We’ll grab them, too.”

CHAPTER 12

A short time later, after eating a hasty breakfast and gently fending off Oscar so he wouldn't eat the food right out of their hands, Henry and Justin were getting in the truck. Oscar had tagged along and was outside the vehicle, waiting. The dinosaur knew what he was doing. He was going to lead them to their destination.

Henry was squinting at the line of woods at the end of his property. "We can't follow Oscar out the way he came in. The truck won't fit. We have no idea, either, how far away Oscar wants to take us."

"What are we going to do?" Justin inquired, his eyes on Oscar, bopping around the truck, obviously anxious to get going.

With his fingers, Henry rubbed between his eyes, sighing. "I think…Oscar needs to ride with us and, if he understands, advise us where to go. We'll drive into the park first off, and hopefully Oscar will direct us from there."

"You sure he wants us to go to the park?"

"I'm pretty sure that's where he wants us to go. Where else? It's where he lives. Why don't you get out, Justin, but leave the door open, and stand behind it until I tell you to get in the back seat, and I'll try to coax Oscar into the front with me."

"Oh, that should be fun." Justin chortled, sliding out of the front seat, and standing patiently behind the open passenger side door as he'd been asked.

"I know just how to do it." Henry tugged one of the apples he'd brought from the camper out of his pocket and, leaning closer to the open passenger door, he waved the apple at Oscar. After barely hesitating, Oscar jumped up onto the seat, and took the apple from Henry's hand. He practically swallowed it whole, then looked to Henry. *More?*

Justin quietly shut the truck's door, and got into the rear seat.

It took both men by surprise when Oscar finished gulping down the apple, and then calmly settled on the floor in front of the passenger's seat, peeking up, and gazing out the front windshield. He was barely tall enough to see out.

"I'll be," Justin said, awed, "he

understands what we wanted him to do."

"For now. When I start up the truck, and begin moving, we'll see how he reacts."

Henry switched on the vehicle, hesitantly drove out of the driveway; stopping before he went out on the road. Oscar jumped, grabbing the dash with his front claws, sending an anxious glance at Henry. *Oh oh.* "Buddy, watch those sharp talons of yours. I don't want my dash slashed up. It's okay, Oscar. The truck won't hurt you, as scary and noisy as it is. We're going where you want us to go. Just point the way." Henry pointed first to Oscar and then out the window ahead of them. He strongly thought his intentions at the little dinosaur and, as improbable as it seemed, the dinosaur nodded. *Somehow, he understood.* Oscar pointed a claw to the right, and Henry pulled the truck right onto the highway. He didn't drive too fast at first. He wanted Oscar to learn he was safe. Learn they were following Oscar's directions.

"Wow," Justin muttered from the rear seat, "I can't believe we have a dinosaur in the truck."

"Me, neither." Henry's chuckle was soft. "I didn't think he'd fall for it, but he did. He doesn't even act afraid."

"He's with you, Henry, that's why. He trusts you."

I guess he does, Henry thought, secretly pleased.

The three of them rode down the highway towards the park. Henry knew that was where Oscar wanted them to go. Where else would he lead them? Oscar was all eyes watching the passing scenery; once and a while making strange clicking sounds, or guttural snorts at something or other he glimpsed out the windows. The creature appeared excited, and not upset in the least, to be riding along with them. It made Henry think of a happy dog traveling in a vehicle. He kept expecting the dinosaur to want the window open so he could hang his head out in the breeze.

Yep, my life, Henry reflected, *is a strange one all right*.

When they arrived at the park, Oscar pointed straight ahead, and Henry stayed on the road.

"Where is he taking us, and, as I said before, why?" Justin was observing the route before them, when he wasn't watching the dinosaur in the truck.

"We'll going to find out sooner or later. I'm as curious as you, son-in-law." Henry was comforted they'd brought their weapons. Heaven knew what awaited them at the end of their journey. He hadn't forgotten what had so recently chased him and Justin from the park a couple days before.

As if Justin read his mind, the scientist said, "Do you think those spaceships are still in the park? The one we saw land?"

"I don't know, but to be truthful, I really didn't want to revisit here this soon. Chief Collins said he's thinking of closing the park until this spaceship dilemma has been dealt with. Only Oscar could have dragged me back."

"Whew, at least, we let Patterson know where we're going to be and why. Or partially why. He'll inform General Wallace, so they'll be aware of what we're doing. Could be we might even run into that military team Patterson said the General is sending out to the park."

"Could be we will. It'd be like old times, us and the military hunting for…well, aliens this time, instead of dinosaurs. But, if we run across any soldiers, we'd have to find a way to hide Oscar. The military cannot see him." As Justin talked, he couldn't help but grin at Oscar's antics. The dinosaur was behaving like a wound-up child on his first car ride. The creature gawked out of the passenger's window, making weird noises, or the front windshield, hopping from one leg to another. One time the creature leapt into the rear seat, and either stuck his snout or talons into every crevice and corner, and sniffed at everything, including Justin. The dinosaur stared out the rear window, making snorting noises, or trilling melodiously in his throat, then abruptly jumped back into the front next to Henry. The critter couldn't get enough of riding in the truck. He wasn't afraid at all. He loved it.

Every time they came to a crossroads, Henry would ask Oscar, "Which way now, little buddy?" And the small dinosaur would think for a minute, eyes scanning the landscape around them, and then his claw would come up and point.

Every time, it still amazed Henry.

The whole trip was like an out-of-body experience. How did Oscar understand what Henry was asking of him? How did the dinosaur know almost what Henry was thinking?

Outside the sun was shining, no clouds, or rain in sight. That would make it easier to follow Oscar's instructions navigating through the park and get them to where he wanted them to go. Wherever that was.

Justin muttered, "I hope he knows where he's going."

"Oscar, my boy, are we almost there yet?" Henry queried, an hour past the entrance, and after they'd swerved onto a particularly rutty and weedy lane which would take them deeper into the park. Strange thing was, Henry, as long as he'd worked in the park, didn't recall the lane or where it went to. But Oscar seemed sure of where they were going. He swung his head around and nodded affirmatively to Henry's question.

Then they were close. Oh, well. There was nothing Henry could do but trust the little guy. The dinosaur had never steered him wrong before.

Oscar became agitated. He began

making frightened whimpers and turned to stare at Henry, pointing at a thicket on their left. *Go there. Go there.* Henry thought the dinosaur was speaking to him. In his mind. *Hide!!!!*

"I think Oscar wants us to drive as deep into those trees as the truck will go and…hide," Henry whispered to Justin, as the dinosaur became frantic, rocking his body back and forth on the seat, eyes wide, tail wildly whipping. Henry had to lean against the window to avoid having his face thrashed by it. "Whoa, little buddy! What's wrong?"

Once more Henry had thoughts thrust into his mind. *Hide! Truck. You. Him. Now!*

Hide? The truck, and him, and Justin? "Justin," Henry spoke softly, "I think Oscar wants us turn the truck off and to hide it here among the trees. And we should hide, as well."

"He told you that?"

"In a way, he did," Henry replied, pulling the truck snug up against a group of trees so that it was hidden, as best as it could be, and switched it off.

Oscar instantly calmed down. He

scooted to the window and glared out, and up through the glass, into the sky.

"So, we're just going to sit here?"

"For a while we will," Henry said. "And not move."

"Hmm. He told you that?"

"In a way." Henry tapped the side of his head. "The thoughts just popped into my head."

"Telepathic communication again, as you experienced with those Area 52 invisible aliens?"

"Something like that. I guess, somehow, I'm on Oscar's wavelength; like I was on theirs."

Oscar twisted around to Henry and Justin and put his claw up against his mouth. *He was telling them to be quiet. Really?*

"And also, I think Oscar doesn't want us to make any noise," Henry whispered. Oscar tossed him an irritated look.

A black cloud moved over them, the day morphed to night, and the truck shook. Henry couldn't resist, rolled down his window, and stuck his head out. Looked upwards.

"My god…what the hell is that?" The

words came out before he could stop them. Something gigantic, and dark, was slowly traveling above them about a mile up in the sky. But it was so huge Henry couldn't see where it ended. It was only a solid ebony shape. Pressing down on them. It was silent. It was the scariest thing he'd ever seen, and he'd seen a lot of scary things in his life. Probably because it created a great feeling of dread in him, and he couldn't explain why.

Now Justin was staring up at it through his window, too. "It's a spaceship…but not like anything I've ever seen. I can't even see what shape it is. It must be miles and miles long." Justin's voice was also a whisper. "Flat. Black. Gigantic."

Oscar was throwing them dirty looks. *Be quiet! Quiet!*

The three sat there for what seemed like forever. Eventually the obsidian shape ended and lumbered off into the horizon. When it was far enough away, Henry realized it had been a triangular shape. Flat and a dull black.

"It was triangular," Justin told Henry what he already knew.

"The same type of craft that Professor

Hescott said he saw last week here in the park. In fact, it could be the same one. He swore, though, that there was a whole fleet of them."

"A whole fleet, huh? Scary to think there's that many of them. I've heard about this type of craft," Justin said. "Triangular and as large as a stadium. Obsidian and silent. Slow as a turtle. As if they're not afraid of anything we could do to stop them. Which, unfortunately, is probably true. They've been seen now for years flying over Earth. There was this case of one flying over Illinois in broad daylight, like this one, and people saw it for miles and miles around, reported it. It was a real sensation. No one ever found out what it had been, or where it had come from, or went to. There was nothing anyone could do, but watch it fly over them and dwindle away. Like that one we just saw."

"Now we've seen it, too." The craft was far enough away that Henry was sure they were safe to resume their journey. He got a nod from Oscar. Henry turned on the truck and pulled out from among the trees.

"Oscar, was that big black flying

monster what you brought us here to see?" Henry's eyes were still scanning the sky to see if the monster had any friends. He could just make out the small dark triangle fading away in the far distance.

He could have sworn the dinosaur frowned. Hard to tell with that dinosaur face of his. His head shook. *No.*

Henry inwardly shuddered, remembering the terror he had felt when the giant triangular craft had been suspended above them.

"Which way now, Yoda?" Henry asked the dinosaur in the front seat, and the dinosaur pointed.

They drove for another hour.

Henry brought the vehicle to a stop. "We're not far from Mount Scott."

"We are, huh?" Justin had been watching Oscar as the creature, inquisitive, was continuing to check out everything in the truck. He'd found a way to open the glove compartment and was pulling everything out. Most likely looking for something to eat. He'd already gotten Justin's candy stash the scientist had had in his pockets. Now the little dinosaur was searching under the seats.

Finding nothing of interest, he plopped back down beside Henry, his attention on the scenery around them. He touched Henry's shoulder.

A thought floated through Henry's mind. *Here. Stop here.*

They came into a large clearing, again one Henry had never come across before. Someone or something had scorched it so it was empty of brush and trees. Oscar was sighing. Henry had never heard the dinosaur sigh before. When the truck came to a halt Oscar started pushing at the door, and Henry reached over and opened it for him. The dinosaur skittered out, and scampered to the edge of the clearing. He gestured for Henry and Justin to follow him, and they did.

Oscar picked a spot near a tree with shade, and sat down. He was staring up at the sky.

"I guess," Justin acknowledged, "this is where he wants us to be."

Looking up at Mount Scott, Henry spoke, "I guess it is. At least, it wasn't far from my house."

"True," Justin seconded. "Not as deep into the woods as we were the last week."

The men settled down beside the dinosaur. The whole thing felt so unreal to Henry, but he had a premonition he hadn't seen anything yet.

It wasn't very long after, about another hour or so, when the giant silver saucer came into view and silently lowered itself to the ground in the clearing. It was even larger than the second extraterrestrial craft that had been at Area 52. It was similar, but different. Sleeker. No cupola on top. It must be one of the modern ships.

Justin whistled. Shading his eyes with his hand to better see the space craft silently come to a landing in the burnt clearing, Justin rose to his feet beside Henry. "I would say I wish we'd brought our weapons, but I don't think they would do us any good against whoever or whatever is in that spaceship."

"And you'd be right." Henrys eyes opened wide; his face felt warm. "I always used to get a kick out of all those old alien movies I loved as a kid. You know the ones? Where the spaceship from another planet lands and the military, always the military, starts shooting guns and missiles at it willy-nilly? Tanks surround the vessel and fire at it and anything that comes out of it. As if our puny human weapons could hurt any aliens who have journeyed for perhaps billions of miles at the speed of light, or faster. I'd always laugh. 'You're not going to beat them with those primitive weapons,' I'd shout at the television, or the movie screen." Henry huffed. But he had to admit, regarding the craft before them, he was anxious. Who wouldn't be? He wanted to believe more than anything that these aliens arriving were friends coming to visit them from another galaxy. But he couldn't be sure. No one could. He and Justin could both be either captive or dead in the next couple minutes. He'd be a fool not to be afraid.

"Oscar," Henry snuck a glance at the dinosaur beside him, "are these aliens friend or foe?"

Oscar didn't answer. Not by thought or action.

"I think this is what Oscar brought us to see," Henry said softly. "He wants us to meet these aliens, or them to meet us."

"Didn't we experience this exact scenario before? Except there were a lot of these saucer spaceships, we saw them fly over us, and one landed? We hid, and then ran away?"

"I remember. Now we must ask," Henry exposed what he suspected, "if Oscar made us *hide* from the triangle ships, but brought us here to *meet* these saucer aliens, perhaps the ones in the big triangles could be the bad guys?"

"It makes sense. Possibly we're here to find out what is really going on with all the extraterrestrial spacecraft sightings the world has had lately. We might get some answers."

"We can only hope." Henry glanced down at Oscar. "I only wonder why, and how, these aliens came to make contact, of some sort, with Oscar in the first place. I mean, what connection do these aliens have with Oscar and his kind?"

"Possibly Oscar, as you have pointed out," Justin offered, "being telepathic, apparently, the aliens might have been able to communicate with him? But why would them want to communicate with Oscar?"

"To get to us?" Henry offered.

"But, again, why?"

"That I don't know," Henry rubbed the

side of his face, "but there's more to it, I reckon. And I think we're about to find out what that may be. I have a wild guess: they came to save Oscar and his family. I mean, if Oscar *is* one of their ancient descendants, as I thought when the Area 52 aliens communicated with me, could be the aliens want to save Oscar and his clan; evacuate them from the planet before the war begins. To make sure they're safe. Relocate them to their home planet."

"I thought of that, too, Henry. But that is a wild theory."

"Ha, and why would that be any different than the other crazy or wild things we've lived through the last decade? Intelligent, mostly malevolent, dinosaurs waging all-out battle with us humans, and now aliens coming to harass and abduct us? A world war with extraterrestrials?"

"You have a good point there." Justin's eyes were on the spacecraft.

Henry stood straighter. Something was happening with the saucer.

As they watched, a door came down from the bottom of the spacecraft, and as the last time *something* came out of it.

Something they could barely see. Moving blurs…coming in their direction. As before, the aliens had cloaked themselves.

Justin breathed, "*We have made contact.*"

Henry could see Justin was nervous. The scientist's body trembled slightly next to him. He'd never been visited by any aliens before, as Henry had. But Henry was anxious, too. Who knew, with aliens, what to expect?

"Justin, for what's it worth, when I met those aliens in that spaceship in Area 52 that time, they were benevolent. Or they claimed to be. I felt they were. I believe, since Oscar led us here, that these aliens are the same. The good ones. I'm interested in what they'll have to say."

"I sure hope you're right, Henry, that these are the good ones. Otherwise, we could be today's abductees. What I can't figure out is why they wanted to see *us*. Why we're here."

"I think we're about to find out, son-in-law."

The pulsating semitransparent blobs were levitating nearer. Henry could almost make out a faint outline of tall silhouettes within the blobs. But it was impossible, though, to see what the aliens actually looked like. Oscar was hopping up and down, but not, as far as Henry could tell, from fear, but from excitement. The little dinosaur stopped bouncing from foot to foot, and leaned up against Henry, making his reassuring clicking sounds.

Then, as it had in the Area 52's spaceship, it was as if time stood still. Henry felt the same dreaminess he had in the alien ship when the extraterrestrials had spoken telepathically with him. One of the blobs was now communicating with him…in Henry's mind. He couldn't understand at first, but slowly the words, the thoughts, came into focus and he understood, or understood as well as he could have.

Our descendant here who lives in this place asked us to help your species. We had come to rescue him and his kin from your planet so they will not be harmed, and let what was to happen, happen. But our child here has pleaded for you kind to be warned. Aided if possible.

"Warned? Aided?" Henry echoed, alarmed, speaking out loud so Justin could, at least, hear his side of the conversation, his eyes staring at something in front of him he couldn't see. He felt woozy. He'd felt the same strange way the last time, as well. It was draining. Alien conversing left him feeling off balance. He was fed the images and thoughts, jumbled, but somehow the message rearranged itself, and got through to him.

There is an interplanetary alliance we are part of with others from our galaxy. There are eight of us in the alliance. The alliance searches for planets with species on them they deem unworthy to continue existing; unworthy of the planet they live on. To protect the rest of us. Some in the alliance believe your human race is far too destructive to your planet, too warlike, too vicious, too unchangeable, to be allowed to keep this planet. They say you kill your own, you pollute your land and your air, you are continually at war with each other, and have been since your creation–and you are destroying your lovely Earth. The climate changes your world is experiencing, now escalating almost beyond repair, with your stubborn insistence on continuing to use what you call fossil fuels, and not tending to amending your destruction of your air and atmosphere, will slowly destroy your lands, and seas, until your human kind will not be able to live upon your world. Your climate fluctuations will become too extreme. At that point, your planet will become inhospitable to your human race. To the alliance these are the worst crimes a species can commit. Eventually, your species will become like our alliance...searching for a new home. The alliance cannot allow that. Cannot allow your race to spoil another planet. Habitable planets are far too rare.

Henry, as many people were beginning to witness, knew that the yearly temperature average for the planet was steadily rising. That summer alone, so far, had set record high temperatures all across the globe. The week before in some place in Europe it had hit a hundred and fourteen degrees…a historic all-time record for that region.

"You know the destruction of our planet will become a reality? That our temperatures will soon make it impossible for us to live here on Earth?" Henry posed the question aloud, thinking it at the same time.

Our wise ones have predicted it. At the rate you are polluting your planet, it is inevitable.

"How long?"

Not more than one of your centuries. Less.

"Less than a century?"

That struck gloom into Henry's heart. Justin was staring at him, figuring out what they were talking about.

You are killing your Earth. Planets as beautiful, as vibrant, and livable, as yours are rare in the galaxy. They are so precious. The alliance has been apprised of your Earth's predicament and is judging your species now. Though we have been watching you for a very long time, from your earliest beginnings.

"They–you–are judging us?"

Yes.

"What will happen if all of you judge us guilty of these…crimes?"

They will exterminate you.

There was a sinking feeling in Henry's stomach. Extermination. Planetary genocide. "But you are here warning me.

Us. Why?"

Our child here wanted to let you know what danger your planet is in. He is protective of you and your humankind. He believes you are worthy to be given another chance to change your irresponsible behavior.

"You mean Oscar?" Henry gestured to the little dinosaur who was regarding the invisible aliens with big eyes as he stood between Henry and Justin. Henry wondered if Oscar could see the aliens. If he could understand what they were saying. He had to, if he'd brought the aliens to meet with him and Justin. Oscar must be able to communicate with them.

"What happens if the alliance finds us guilty?"

Once your planet is free of your species, as they do with the other planets, one of our alliance will claim it, and repopulate it with their own species. Many of the others in our alliance live on uninhabitable or dying planets, or have fading suns, and this is how they colonize. As I said, a planet like yours is extremely rare. There are many in our alliance who covet it, and have been waiting long to find and claim one like it for themselves.

Henry's heart was racing, his mouth bone dry. Henry was so shocked at what the alien was *thinking* to him, for a moment he didn't know how to respond. Aliens wanted to exterminate the human race and steal their planet? This was far worse than anything he could have imagined. People had been saying for decades that aliens were visiting Earth; some even said they lived among us, and had for a long time. But they had also been judging us? He almost couldn't believe it, but the proof was in front of him, even if he couldn't see the aliens. Lord, he prayed he was getting the alien's message correct. Part of him wanted to cry out: true, humans were an insidious parasite on the planet, deadly to other humans, but who gave aliens the right to decide their fate? Who gave non-Earthlings the right to condemn humans to extinction for their so-called crimes?

Justin was listening, distress on his face, to the one sided-conversation which was all he could hear. Clearly, he was getting the gist of it from Henry's verbal responses.

"They are coming to exterminate us?" Henry asked the invisible blobs.

It is their plan. If they decide you are undeserving of this planet.

"They, not you?"

They. The others in our alliance.

"Are they the ones in the big black ships?"

The Gemmas. That is what they call themselves. More are coming in their ships. Many more. They are on their way as we communicate. They are eager to possess your planet.

"They're on their way? How soon will they get here?"

In the time you call weeks.

"Weeks?" Henry felt the desperation practically choking him. The dinosaur scourge had been terrifying enough, but somehow this was far worse. Humans could fight dinosaurs, no matter how clever the brutes were, but how could they fight aliens so far advanced they could travel across galaxies? Guns, tanks, and missiles, even nuclear weapons, wouldn't cut it. If these aliens came, the human race could be doomed. Oh damn.

"Can you help us?"

Our descendent, your friend here, believes your race can improve; could get better. He speaks highly of you. You and your species, he asks, should be given one last chance to live to become a better proprietor of your world.

Once more, Henry asked, "Can you help us? Will you intercede with these Gemmas?"

No alien thoughts came into Henry's mind. The alien either couldn't or didn't want to answer. Henry wondered which one it was.

"How will they eradicate us? What sort of weapons do they have? Do we have a chance against them?"

The alien again did not respond. Which truly frightened Henry.

"Can I warn our leaders, our people? Is it too late to change? Can I tell then what is coming?"

Yes. Perhaps your leaders will take this warning seriously and alert your populations. It would help the final decision if the Earth's people would agree to do what the alliance requests of them. Change its self-destructive behaviors; become a better steward of your planet.

Like that would ever happen, Henry brooded.

Without another thought sent to Henry, the two cloaked aliens, or their outlined shapes anyway, began to undulate and drift to their spaceship.

Henry wanted so badly to beg them to come back, tell him what he should do. Give him and Earth some encouragement that his species would not be annihilated. But he couldn't bring himself to beg. He knew it wouldn't help. He knew he should be forever grateful just that they came to him and warned him. He had the feeling that the Gemmas wouldn't have done it.

"Thank you," Henry called out after them. "Thank you for warning us."

When the spaceship's door had sealed, the saucer rose gracefully into the air, and when it was above the trees, it zoomed away faster than a streaking star. In a heartbeat it was gone.

"That was amazing!" Justin exclaimed. "Scary as all get out, but amazing."

"Glad you thought so. Me, not so much." Henry drew in a shuddering breath, his mind overloaded with everything he'd learned from the aliens.

"I heard your side of the conversation." Justin was still looking at the place in the sky where the spaceship had vanished. "Thus, I can roughly figure out what your conversation with the aliens was about. Our world is in danger, right? From aliens. Other aliens. Not those?" There was a look on Justin's face that Henry had never seen before. Restrained terror.

Oscar was observing them. Henry wondered if the dinosaur knew what was going on. He probably did. He was one smart dinosaur. He most likely had understood everything the alien had said. They spoke the same language of the mind, or Henry thought they did.

"We're in danger all right, Justin. Our whole planet and every human on it. We're in end-of-the-world danger." As best he could he explained to Justin what the alien had told him When he was done, Justin had an even more terrified expression on his face.

"We need to inform Patterson and General Wallace about all this. Immediately. This can't wait until Saturday."

"I agree, Justin. We'll try calling as soon as we get to the truck. If we're out of range, we'll call until we are able to reach one of them."

"Oh, Henry, this is bad. This is *so bad*."

"Tell me about it. I feel as if the ground has shifted out from under my feet and huge deep holes are popping up everywhere. Reality has gone out the window. I wish to God this alien threat was only some waking nightmare, but I know it isn't. I'm afraid now, nothing will ever be the same."

"It isn't. It puts everything else we usually worry about, the mundane everyday things, into stark perspective."

Oscar had come up and touched Henry's hand. There was this empathetic glint in the animal's eyes. Henry shivered. It was as if Oscar knew what Henry was upset about. As if he knew what the alien had told him. How much danger his friend, and his friend's home, was in.

"Thank you, Oscar," Henry murmured. "Thank you. It seems you're always helping us silly humans."

Oscar nodded, stood there touching

Henry's hand for another minute or so, tipped his head at them, and swinging his body around, he scurried off into the tree line. For a moment, he twisted around and stared at Henry and Justin, then disappeared into the trees. He was going home. His home. Henry hated to see him go. Not for the first time, Henry acknowledged how unique the miniature dinosaur was. How much of a miracle.

"He's rejoining his family. Going home." Justin was watching the dinosaur merge into the brush.

"I guess we need to do the same." Henry started walking to the truck, and Justin hurried behind him. The sooner they could get cell reception, the sooner they could warn the people who needed to know about what was coming. Above them vultures were circling, screeching out to the sky. Staring up at them, the sun in his eyes, Henry thought they were appropriate harbingers of future things to come. Nothing good.

CHAPTER 13

They weren't far away from where they'd met the aliens when Justin was able to get through to Patterson on his cell phone.

"Don't tell them anything about Oscar coming to take us to meet the aliens," Henry whispered aside to Justin before his son-in-law started talking on the phone with Patterson. "Just that we had an alien encounter and we'll tell him everything when we see him. It'll give me some time to fashion some sort of story where I can tell them what they need to know, without outing Oscar."

"I'll keep it simple. For now. I'll only tell him about the alien meet and greet itself. Since that's probably what they'll be most interested in."

Henry drove as Justin spoke with Patterson. When the paleontologist was finished, he ended the call, and glanced at Henry. "Patterson says General Wallace is sending a plane for us to the airport."

"We're driving to the airport?" Henry inquired.

"No. We're getting special VIP treatment. A military helicopter will pick us up in your backyard in," Justin looked at the truck's dash clock, "three hours–that should give us enough time to get to your place, grab some clothes, and copter to the airport. I know there's enough room for the helicopter to land in your yard. Been done before. Once I told Patterson about the spaceship landing and the aliens we met, your *communication* with one of them, Patterson said General Wallace wants us there *yesterday*. We're flying back to the base. Do you believe it?"

"Area 52? Really?"

"Really. That's what Patterson said."

For some reason, Henry found he was happy about returning to Area 52. Patterson and Isabel were there. "Now I just have to figure out what to tell Patterson and General Wallace about how the aliens found us. Without connecting Oscar to any of it."

"You'll think of something, Henry, I know you will."

"I'm working on it."

Justin hadn't brought many changes of clothes with him for their camping trip, but the scientist was used to traveling light, and they didn't know how long they'd be at the base. Henry would pack a few things, some clean clothes. Better to be prepared. He'd lend some shirts to Justin, if his son-in-law needed them.

For shirts, they were about the same size. Justin had filled out over the years. He was no longer the skinny guy Henry had first met so many years ago.

They arrived at Henry's house and grabbed any items they might need for their trip. Though Henry was agonizing over the world's dire situation, he was also excited to be going back to Area 52. To be, even only temporarily, part of the team again.

"Justin," Henry said as he was stuffing clothes into his suitcase, "I've been thinking. We can just say the alien ship somehow found us. Maybe because I once was visited by aliens at Area 52, and they were able to communicate with me telepathically, they sought me out again. Something like that. Heck, say the space craft landed in my backyard."

"The military will come out here and check that out."

"Let them." Henry sighed. "If they find nothing, they won't know anything. I have to protect Oscar and his family."

"I know, Henry. There will be no mention of Oscar. The aliens, as they are wont to do, came looking for and found you. The spaceship landed out back. I got it. Besides,

General Wallace and the government have other bigger problems to deal with. A possible alien invasion for one."

"Yeah. The aliens. What time did Patterson say the helicopter was arriving?"

Justin, laying a hand over his cell phone for a second, glanced at the clock on the wall. "It should be any minute," he said to Henry. He was talking to his wife, letting her know he would be delayed. That he'd let her know more when he knew more.

Henry put food and water out for the cat, extra food for the feline on the counter, then picked up his cell phone, and called Sherman. "Sherman, I have to leave the house for a while. Go out of town. I don't know how long. Could I ask you to come and get Sasha for me and take care of her until I get back?"

"Sure, Henry," Patterson's wife, Sherman, replied cheerfully. "You know I will. I'll come by this evening to pick her up. Don't worry about her. She likes it here. Loves the kids, and they love her. When are you leaving?"

"Any minute. I'll leave her food out on the counter for you, and the back door unlocked. Just lock it on your way out. You know where the cat carrier is."

"I do. Can you tell me where you're going?

Maybe approximately how long you could be gone?"

"I'm afraid I can't, but," he lowered his voice, "Scott will know how to get in touch with me if Sasha has some problem. Justin, who is here with me now, and I are both going to be with him. If he can I'm sure he will tell you what's going on. And if I can call you to check in on her, I will."

"Ah ha, more secret stuff. What is this, an epidemic?" Sherman was used to jobs that were classified, being married for years to a government agent like Scott, and being ex-military herself. "Don't worry, Sasha will be fine with us. Have a safe trip. Contact me when you can."

"I will. Thank you, Sherman. Give my love to your kids."

Henry hung up as the sound of a helicopter filled the afternoon. "Time to go."

He and Justin grabbed their stuff and went out the door. The helicopter was landing at the end of the yard away from the line of trees. The two men ran out to it, and when the blades stopped whirling, they climbed on board, the copter elevated again, and flew into the sky.

As the helicopter rose higher, Henry met Justin's gaze, a grim expression on his face.

He knew Justin felt as he did. It was going to be hard to tell everyone what the aliens had warned them of. That an alien armada was heading this way, that was most likely not friendly, and humankind was to be judged…and if they failed, they'd have to fight to survive. Henry watched the landscape flow beneath him. His thoughts were troubled. For the first time, he was almost glad Ann was in the afterlife, instead of here with him on Earth. Because something terrible was coming.

*****

The helicopter landed on the airstrip, and, grabbing their luggage, Henry and Justin got off of it and onto the plane waiting for them. As the plane took off, Henry felt a touch of déjà vu. He remembered when Justin had taken him to Area 52 for the first time over a year ago. Except this time there wasn't a yowling cat along with him. Last time he was more excited than frightened. This time he was more frightened than excited.

He'd always loved those Independence movies, but then he'd never, in a million years, imagined he'd be living in one of them.

As the first time, they were met at the base's airport by a window-tinted dark car and driven to Area 52. They were escorted down the same long halls Henry once rode down on his transport and ushered into a large meeting room. Patterson was there. Isabel. Doctors Russell Gartner, Lucia Walters, Stanley Louison, and Courtney Waverly. All who had been on their old team. And one man he didn't recognize. General Wallace sat at the head of the long table. Henry was happy to see all of them, even under the circumstances. It was like coming home.

"Sit down, Doctor Maltin and Mr. Shore." The General gestured to two empty chairs. "You both know most of the scientists sitting around the table."

"Hello Doctors," Henry acknowledged the scientists with a nodding of his head, a smile.

Some of them echoed his hello.

"Hi Isabel." Henry grinned at her.

"Hi Henry," she said. "Nice to see you. Again."

General Wallace waited until Henry was done, and said, "But let me introduce the one at the table you don't know. This is Doctor Lawrence Emmet. Head scientist, and alien expert of world renown, at the US Naval Air Systems Command."

The older man had curly white hair and

piercing blue eyes. Henry estimated he was around seventy or so. The man nodded at Henry and then Justin. Henry and Justin nodded back.

"Good timing, Mr. Shore and Doctor Maltin. Doctor Emmet and Patterson have just returned from a reconnaissance trip from the Bahamas. So we're all here."

Henry wondered what the Bahamas trip had been all about. But he was fairly sure, now that he was part of the team again, that sooner or later Patterson would spill the beans about it to him. Soon as he got the man alone.

General Wallace didn't waste any more time. He was looking at Justin and Henry. "Patterson says you have some vital information for us. Doctor Maltin?"

"I'd better let Henry here give you the story, General. He was the one who the aliens communicated it to."

Doctor Emmet, as well as the others around him, flashed Henry startled glances. Isabel's face was ashen, but her eyes were on him.

"Communicated it to?" Doctor Emmet interrupted. "The aliens spoke to you, Mr. Shore?"

"Tell him, Henry." Justin propped his

elbow on the table, and leaned his chin in his hand; his right eyebrow raising a tiny bit. His eyes secretly reminding Henry to make it convincing, so no one would guess that they'd had help from a little dinosaur who was no longer supposed to exist.

So, Henry told the people at the table about the spaceship landing…in his backyard–leaving out everything to do with Oscar–and the two barely visible rippling blobs coming out to greet them. Told them about the telepathic thoughts he received form one of them. Told them what the alien said before it, and its buddy, disappeared back into their craft, and flew away.

Then, to catch them up on everything that had gone before that so they'd be up to date, he talked about the huge triangular alien craft Professor Hescott had witnessed seeing in the park and how terrified it had made him feel, leaving out the one he, Justin, and Oscar, had run and hid from, because Hescott's encounter had occurred after Patterson had left Henry's house, and before he and Justin had seen the alien ship with Oscar. He had to amend his and Justin's timeline somewhat, and outright lie about where the saucer shaped spaceship had actually landed, leave out Oscar completely, but he thought he did a pretty good job of it, all in all. He hated lying, but he had no choice if he wanted to protect Oscar. He hoped he sounded convincing.

As he imparted his story about the coming aliens, some of the faces around him reflected fear–but, he thought, no surprise. *No surprise.* Isabel, well, he understood her expression as one of remembered terror from when her sister had been abducted. True, everyone around the table, perhaps excluding Doctor Emmet, already knew aliens truly existed, they'd been involved with the extraterrestrial spaceships at Area 52. Some of them were even fully aware that on the last night the second spaceship had vanished, Henry had been communicated with telepathically by the aliens who took it. Ah, Henry realized, what the men and women around the table were afraid of was that their worst fears of an alien invasion could now be coming true. It was no longer a science fiction horror movie. It was all too real. His story only supported that.

When Henry was finished everyone started tossing questions at him.

"How many of these hostile aliens, *Gemmas* you called them, are coming?" General Wallace had a stoic expression on his face. Probably trying not to show his true feelings.

"I don't know," Henry answered truthfully. "The alien didn't *think me* a number, only that there are many more coming. A fleet."

"When will they get here?" Doctor Emmet was tapping his fingers against the edge of the table. Probably a nervous reaction.

"What we call weeks, the alien said." Henry was watching Patterson. The man was clearly troubled. The man was most likely thinking of his wife and children. If Henry still had a wife, and two small children, he'd want to be with them, to protect them, if an alien invasion arrived. Henry could almost see the indecision on his friend's face.

"And you think nothing will save us now? Nothing will save humanity from annihilation?" Isabel presented her questions, her eyes frightened.

"I don't know," Henry spoke in a hesitant voice. "From what I gathered the only thing that will save our species is if we change immediately. Stop polluting the planet with fossil fuels and dirtying our atmosphere, stop warring amongst ourselves, and killing each other. Stop the hate. Stop populating the earth like rabid bunnies. World peace." Henry shrugged. "I may be a pessimist, but I don't think any of that is going to happen."

"I don't think so, either," Patterson muttered, his face suddenly looking twenty years older.

"Maybe," Doctor Emmet contributed his opinion, "if the world population see the alien ships coming, they might be scared into changing."

Doctor Waverly snorted cynically. "I wouldn't bet on it. You men," and she sent a sharp glance at General Wallace, Doctor Emmet, and Patterson, as her fingers lightly fingered through her short gray hair, "and I'm speaking of your gender in general, much prefer when threatened, to just yank out your guns, AK47s, missiles, and bombs, and shoot your adversaries into submission. I don't believe those sorts of weapons will win us a war against these approaching aliens. And, as Mr. Shore says, getting the countries of the world to become friends, eradicate war, and killing each other off, and do the right thing environmentally, is a pipe dream. That'll never happen, or not quick enough anyway. If these aliens have the power to destroy us, unless we change our evil ways, then we don't have a prayer."

Doctor Gartner had hung his head in his hands, but now gazed up. “Then are we simply going to give up?” He was asking everyone around him at the table. “Accept our fate? Let the aliens *kill* us off like we’re bad ants?”

General Wallace was shaking his head. “No, Doctor Gartner, if we have to, we’ll fight to the very last man, or woman, on Earth, you know that. Humankind will not surrender, judged by a sinister alien race from billions of light years away. They have no right. This is *our planet*. They can’t have it. We’ll fight!”

Henry thought of something. He turned to General Wallace. “I told you what Justin and I know, what happened to us, how about now telling us what all you esteemed scientists and military individuals here already know. Why was this group formed? What are you all here for? What do you know?”

The General stretched against the back of his chair, closing his eyes for a moment, before he answered. “The military has been aware for months that alien spaceships, mainly two different types, saucers, and massive black triangles like your Professor Hescott saw, have been visiting our Earth in greater and greater numbers. Sightings and human abductions have increased to a frightening level. Then four weeks ago our government spied what they believe is a …an armada of unidentified UAPs far out in space, but coming in our direction. This group here," the General nodded at the scientists, "is just one of many all over the world. Trying to decide what to do about these coming ships. Trying to figure out why they're coming here and what they want.

"Now," he looked at Henry and Justin, "we also know these are not friendlies coming our way. You two gave us another piece of the puzzle."

"You've known aliens were coming for a while?" Henry's stomach lurched.

"We have," General Wallace replied.

"Does the military, the government, anyone, know what they're going to do about it?"

"The President is working on that now, along with the top military men and minds in the country."

Working on it? Henry was suddenly tired. Words of future courage wouldn't win the coming war. He felt as if he were in a nightmare and he couldn't wake up.

"What are we going to do *now*?" Doctor Louison, someone who had remained silent until then, pressed.

"Not much," Patterson interceded with an answer. "Get ready. Prepare our defenses."

It was Isabel who had to ask, "Let the public know?"

General Wallace's head bowed; his voice, when he spoke next, was gruff. "The President is not letting us release that information to the general public…yet. He believes it will cause a major panic."

Yep, there will be a major panic all right when the giant flying triangles come down to hover above the towns, cities, and countries of the world. A real honest-to-God world-wide knock-over-and-down-your-neighbor-to-get-somewhere-you-think-is-safe panic. People will go insane. Is this how our world ends? Aliens exterminate us? And how will they do that? Bombs? Giant lasers? Infect us with some biological agent that will slaughter us all? Henry shuddered just thinking about it.

A solider came into the room and going up to the General, leaned over and said something into the man's ear. The soldier left.

General Wallace came to his feet. "Sorry, I've been called to a very important meeting. I have to attend. The President has asked to be brought up to speed on these latest developments from Mr. Shore and Doctor

Maltin. What information you both brought us." He swung his gaze to take in everyone else at the table. "I will see you all later. If I am being called away from the base, I'll let you know before I go."

Looking at both Henry and Justin, he added, "I'd like you two to remain here on the base as consultants. Doctor Maltin, because you were head of the last scientific team here on the base when the alien spaceships were here. Henry, since you seem to have a telepathic connection to one of the alien races, you might be of some use, help, with what's to come. I'd like you both to be here if we need you."

Henry's smile was slight. "I'll be here." He was excited to be back at Area 52, but not for the reason he was back. "So…I'm on the team again, huh, General?"

"Yes, Henry," the General cleared that up, "it seems you are. You and Doctor Maltin. Since you both have connections to aliens, in one way or another. Welcome back. You have already been assigned rooms. Doctor Emmet will give you your keys."

The General said his goodbyes to everyone, followed the soldier, and exited the room.

The other scientists left behind began to talk among themselves.

Henry twisted around to Isabel, his eyebrows lifting in a mischievous way. “We’re back on the team! The old gang is together again.”

“We are,” yet Isabel had a serious look on her face, “but I wish it was under better circumstances. Give me rogue dinosaurs loose in the facility, and empty abandoned alien spacecrafts any day. But live extraterrestrials, possibly with hostile intentions, a fleet of them, coming to Earth, is something totally different. This is a really scary situation.”

“Tell me about it!” Scott Patterson had left his chair and had come up behind them. He laid a hand on Henry’s shoulder, and one on Justin’s. “I’m really glad you two are here, though. It wasn’t the same without you.”

Henry peered up at Patterson. “I knew your new top-secret project had something to do with aliens! *I knew it!*”

“Sorry I couldn’t tell you the truth, Henry. Orders, you know. I had the idea that somehow, though, you’d already deduced what I was up to when we were on our camping trip and ran into Professor Hescott. All those nights looking into the night skies trying to catch a glimpse of the mysterious orbs. But you're here now, you know everything, or everything I know anyway, and your special ability might come in handy when we need it. If we need it."

"Yep, Justin and I are here now." Then, remembering what General Wallace had mentioned earlier, Henry asked Patterson, "So you and Doctor Emmet just returned from the Bahamas? What was up?"

"There were reports of alien sightings down there. Lots of them. Alien airships coming up from under the water. We went down to interview some of the people who'd seen the phenomena. See if we might witness some ourselves."

Justin looked up at Patterson. "Did you?"

"No. But we talked to many people who have seen them. They were spooked about it. The incidents have greatly increased the last month or so. We hung around for a couple days and came back."

Patterson then took an empty chair on the other side of Henry, and leaned in. "I can't believe you two had an actual physical contact with aliens. Later tonight, we're going to have to have a drink together, the three of us, and you can tell me every little detail about it.

Second time for you, Henry. They must like you."

Justin chuckled. "They must. Or anyway the good aliens do."

"As opposed to the bad aliens in the big triangles?" Henry threw in. "If they are the bad ones." Yet Oscar had acted as if the extraterrestrials in the ebony triangular spaceships were to be avoided at any cost. The little dinosaur had been so openly scared of that ship. Supposedly that was why the three of them had hid like frightened children until the craft passed by them. Of course, he couldn't tell anyone about any of that. He was relieved he could use Professor Hescott's unsettling experience to illustrate the sensations of danger, the threat, the black triangles created in humans.

Isabel had been eavesdropping on their conversation and felt the need to contribute to it. "We already knew there were two separate alien races checking us out the last month or so. Now we know one of them is more dangerous than the other. We didn't know which alien species is in the fleet the military has detected coming our way. Now we do, thanks to you. And evidently, they're not friendly."

"I don't know," Justin interjected, "if there's a *fleet* of aliens coming to Earth, it can't be good, I would think."

"An honest-to-God alien invasion." Patterson exhaled, worry darkening his features. "I think I've seen this plot in a bunch of movies…and it rarely ends well."

"It never ends well," Henry said.

"What are you, the General, the government, going to do about these advancing ships?" Justin quizzed Patterson.

Doctor Emmet drew up a chair across the table from them, and was the one to answer Justin. "What any government would do. What, I pray, all the governments over the globe are doing right now as well as us. Our President, his Secretary of Defense, his Cabinet, and our military elite are in meetings right now, and our military will be put on high alert as soon as the alien ships get closer. As your alien said, they're weeks out. The President doesn't want to panic the people, so he wants to keep this quiet for as long as he can."

"Humph," Henry responded, "until the alien ships show themselves hovering above D.C, and other major cities of the world, huh? Maybe when they start shooting at us?"

Doctor Emmet sent Henry a dirty look. "Mr. Shore, even you realize that this invasion news would cause worldwide mass chaos."

Henry gave up. He knew Doctor Emmet was correct. If aliens began to attack earth, the world population would go insane. That's what human beings did. "In that, I hate to admit, you are right, Doctor Emmet. The people would lose their minds if they knew about the advancing alien fleet."

"Therefore, we're preparing as best we can," Doctor Emmet went on. "The military is gathering their forces; making plans for battle, or for whatever we will have to do. The President, after being alerted to what you have told us about your alien encounter and what the aliens communicated to you, is in virtual meetings with the other leaders of the world, as we speak, attempting to get allies in the coming fight."

"The President believed my story?"

"I'm sure after General Wallace vouched for you, and told the President about your earlier experience with the base's second alien spaceship before it disappeared–and those aliens who communicated with you then. What happened to you. He'll believe. That where General Wallace just went. To talk to the President about what you. But truth is, the President has also known about the alien presence here for as long as he's been in office. All presidents do. I imagine he wasn't surprised to hear they're finally on their way.

"Problem is, I bet most of the other countries probably will not believe an alien force is coming to destroy us. They'll think we're lying to them."

"What's new?" Justin grumbled. "Human beings are stubborn creatures. They believe nothing unless they can see it for themselves. And sometimes not even then."

Henry caught Doctor Emmet's attention. "If we even get the opportunity to fight. From what I intuited from my alien mind meld; we might not even be given a chance to explain or save ourselves. I have no idea of how these aliens will judge us, if they haven't already, and what they'll do. They might nuke us from space–whatever weapons they will have–or send a biological agent down to exterminate us. Or they might have some other ways of killing us we haven't a clue to. Aliens, you know."

Doctor Emmet's intense scrutiny of Henry was uncomfortable. The man didn't appear to be concerned about aliens coming their way.

His attitude better at hiding it behind a tough exterior. He reminded Henry of their old friend, Agent Dylan Greer. Hard on the outside, perhaps not so hard on the inside.

Some of the other scientists had wandered over to say hello to Henry and Justin; welcome them back. Ask questions about Henry's alien encounter. They were curious to what he had to say. They were happy to see their old boss and the dinosaur hunter. Henry was glad to see them.

"Henry, Justin," Isabel asked after the scientists had had their queries satisfied, and had vacated the room, scurrying off to who knew where, "let's settle you both into your rooms, drop your stuff off, and go get some supper. What do you say?"

"I say that's an excellent proposal." Justin scooped up the keys with room number tags attached, that Doctor Emmet had tossed on the table, and got up. He looked at them.

"I believe, Henry, this is your old room number, if I recall correctly." Justin handed the key to Henry. "And my room, it conveniently turns out, is right next to yours."

Isabel also came to her feet, and snuck a peek at Justin's key tag. "And both of your rooms are just across from mine."

Henry glanced at his son-in-law. "You don't get your fancy suite back?"

"Apparently not. I'm not the boss here anymore. No fancy room for me. I get a normal- sized one just like yours and Isabel's," Justin answered Henry.

"Who is the boss?" Henry questioned Isabel. She'd know. She'd been there longer.

"Doctor Lawrence Emmet," a deep voice interrupted, "head scientist at the US Naval Air Systems Command, and famous alien expert. The man standing behind you."

Doctor Emmet was indeed standing behind them, next to Patterson. Emmet put his hand out to Justin. "I'm sorry I've taken your rooms, Doctor Maltin, but it's an honor to finally meet you. I've heard so many great things about you, and how efficiently you ran Area 52 last year." After he shook Justin's hand, he reached out to shake Henry's. "And I've heard a lot of good things about you, as well, Chief Ranger Henry Shore. Patterson here has raved about both of you."

"Has he? But I don't mind if you have my old rooms," Justin admitted. "I was hardly there. I basically lived in the labs, or around the alien spaceships, or in meetings. I'll be fine in a regular room next to my friends. As long as it has a bed and a shower, I'm happy."

"Good to hear." Doctor Emmet smiled at them for the first time.

Patterson spoke to Doctor Emmet. "The four of us," he gestured at Isabel, Justin, and Henry, "are going to supper. Would you like to join us, Lawrence?"

"I'd like that."

Surprised, Henry thought Patterson seemed quite friendly with the new boss. That meant something to Henry. If Patterson got along with the guy, Emmet must be a good man.

"So would I," Justin added. "I have a lot of questions about everything. Now that Henry and I are part of the team again, perhaps you can answer some of them."

"I'll try," Emmet replied. "As much as the General, the military, and the government have revealed to me and as much as they've allowed me to disclose. This whole *event* began barely weeks ago. I've been here myself only a little under a month. The rest of the team about two weeks. There's so much we don't know yet."

The five of them made their way into the hallway, and seated on their electric transports, they drove to the dining room.

Coasting down the hallways he

remembered so well, Henry wished he was in Area 52 for a different reason than for the one he was. Aliens coming to murder all of them for humanity's past sins. He'd been in a lot of tight spots in his life, but none as tight as this one. Because in his mind and heart, he couldn't see how the human race could evade this coming punishment. So many humans wouldn't believe aliens were coming, so many wouldn't accept how creatures from another galaxy would want to destroy them. Humans fought against and were notoriously skeptical about any truth they didn't want to face. Henry had no trouble accepting the truth that aliens wanted to terminate the human race…if the prize was a new home planet for them.

But, regardless of the possible coming apocalypse, it was nice to be back at the base with his friends. For now, he held on tightly to that small gift.

CHAPTER 14

Gathered around the supper table, friends, and colleagues, they chatted among themselves as they ate their meals. Henry hadn't realized how much he'd missed the excellent food, until he began eating. So much better than his own cooking.

Doctor Emmet swung around in his chair to talk to Henry and Justin more easily. "I'm so intrigued with your alien experience I'd like to know more. I'm intrigued. Can you tell me everything–everything–you can recall from the time you saw the saucer approaching, landing, and your encounter with the aliens? Don't leave out even the tiniest detail."

Henry sent a questioning glance at Justin. *I guess since he's the boss I have to answer him.*

With Justin inserting his lesser recollections here and there, Henry tried to give Doctor Emmet what he'd asked for. A complete minute to minute account, as much as Henry could dig up, of his alien encounter. It was tricky, not contradicting any of his other facts he'd already given the group earlier at the meeting. That and keeping Oscar's part out of it. But he thought he did a pretty good job of it all in all.

When Henry was finished, Justin started asking his own questions of Doctor Emmet. "How did we first detect these oncoming spaceships? How much does the government know about these alien ships approaching the Earth? Do you know how many there are? Have they tried to contact us yet? What are we planning to do about it? If you are allowed to tell us, I mean." The old boss in him taking over.

"There's not much to tell, Doctor Maltin. You probably know that NASA's James Webb Space Telescope, JWST as we call it, the powerful next-generation space telescope, designed to scan into the farthest reaches of the Universe, and perhaps look back in time to see how the stars and galaxies might have formed after the Big Bang, is now up and running, and aimed out into the cosmos. Scientists first noticed the coming alien spaceships with the JWST.

"Needless to say, it was quite a shock to them, and our government, when the spaceships kept coming in our direction. But until you and Henry arrived, and divulged what you experienced and know, we weren't sure if the ships were friendly or unfriendly. Or even if they were coming here, or headed somewhere else. With your information, we now fear Earth *is* their destination."

"As if a whole armada of exterritorial spacecrafts speeding to our Earth could be friendly, right?" Henry huffed. "If they were friendly, why send so many ships? I'd imagine, if a friendly hello was what they intended, two or three spaceships would do the job."

"That was one of our initial concerns, as well." Doctor Emmet had gotten a light supper. A bowl of chili, and a glass of milk. He was a very neat eater, wiping his mouth after every few bites.

Justin, on the other hand, had a full plate before him on the table. Meatloaf with double sides. A piece of cake for dessert. A cup of coffee he'd already refilled once. How his son-in-law could keep from gaining a lot of weight, Henry hadn't a clue. The man was always eating.

"Have the approaching aliens tried to contact us *in any way* yet?" Justin asked Doctor Emmet. "Contact anyone on Earth?"

Isabel and Patterson were listening to the conversations with interest. Patterson was just finishing up his meal; drinking coffee. Isabel had a plate before her, but had barely touched her food.

"Not as far as I know. If they have, General Wallace hasn't let me in on any of it. Yet. I do know NASA, the observatory on the hill in Hawaii, and the W. M. Keck Observatory, are all scanning the skies right now for when the alien fleet will get close enough for them to see. All the observatories in the country, and perhaps most of the world, are searching for that alien fleet, as well."

"The world's populace is going to go berserk when they learn…yes, aliens truly exist and they're coming here. Soon." Isabel had that worried look in her gaze again.

"Though why anyone would be surprised that there are aliens out there. I can't imagine," Doctor Emmet stated. "There are a billion, not a billion planets, but a billion solar-like systems out in the Universe. Any person with a brain would be naïve to think we were all alone in the universe. We're not."

Justin swept his hand at the scientists sitting around the table. Some of them still lingered over their meals. Most were subdued, doubtless because of what was facing them and their world. "You don't have to tell anyone here that aliens really do exist. We all know that. The people here anyway. We were custodians of two remarkable spaceships from another world. We're believers for sure."

Emmet said to Henry, "Especially you, Chief Ranger Shore. Once known as a famous dinosaur hunter…now you're an *alien whisperer*. The only human, I know of anyway, who has spoken to an honest-to-God alien. Aliens." Doctor Emmet had finished his supper and came to his feet. "I hate to leave good company, but I have my duties. As well you know, Doctor Maltin. Paperwork, and a list of calls to make. General Wallace is supposed to let me know later tonight how the meeting with the President went. What they plan on doing next. I'll keep you all apprised of any new information I receive or any orders."

When Doctor Emmet had left the dining room, Henry remarked, "He seems like he'd be a good boss. A fair guy."

"So far, he is. And you can speak to him, about almost anything, and he'll listen. I didn't care much for him when I first met him. Thought he was arrogant. A stuffed shirt. But on our assignment to the Bahamas, he showed me he was anything but. He's so much like my old FBI partner, Greer, that in the end, it was easy to like him. Gruff exterior, but more sensitive inside. Once you get to know him some. We're becoming friends." Patterson was leisurely drinking a cup of coffee. His slow movements showed his exhaustion. Everything he'd been through the last couple of weeks, and that impromptu trip down to the Bahamas, had probably sapped his energy.

"Lawrence knows what he's talking about," Patterson continued. "He has a great deal of pull and a lot of high connections in the government. He's well respected as an alien expert. He's been studying the possibility of aliens for years; written books about UAPs and abductions. He was a true believer long before he was privy to the alien spaceships we had here."

Henry took in the remaining scientists around him he'd come to know so well. He looked directly at Patterson and Isabel. "What exactly are you all doing here? I mean Justin and I were asked to come because we saw a spaceship land, and I telepathically communicated with an alien. What are your jobs here? Why are you all here?"

Isabel was the one to enlighten him. "Mainly because we dealt with the two alien spaceships. We have knowledge of them and, perhaps in some ways, the creatures that inhabited and flew them. General Wallace thought perhaps we could be on the front line if…if we have to fight them."

"It makes sense." Henry frowned. "But I don't think the aliens that are coming are the same ones that created those two spaceships we had here. They're a different species."

"The ones who fly those miles long black triangles that have been seen?" Isabel's fingers skimmed around her empty coffee cup's rim in a lazy circle. She'd had a salad with chicken in it for supper. No dessert. Which tipped off Henry how flustered the alien menace had made her.

"Yes."

"How do you know this?" Isabel flashed him a sharp glance.

Henry realized he'd made a mistake and tried to cover it up. "Or that's what our friend Professor Hescott believes. As I said, he's seen them. Saw one up real close. The horrified way they made him feel gave him the idea they were not good aliens."

"Soon enough," Patterson contributed to the debate, "when the alien fleet gets nearer to Earth, we'll know which one is it. Saucers or triangles. They're still too far out in space to tell."

"Sooner or later." Justin stretched in the chair. The day, and all it had held, had worn him out, too. He wanted to go to sleep and not think any more about spaceships and invading aliens.

"Though what difference will it make?" Isabel mumbled, her expression dead pan. "One fleet of aliens rocketing towards our defenseless little Earth is as bad as another. We're doomed."

Which Henry feared was true. Though, because of Oscar, he and Justin knew which aliens were coming. The black triangles. But he couldn't tell anyone that. He had to use Professor Hescott's experience, keep to himself what Oscar had communicated, and pretend ignorance to what he really knew.

Sometime later, the supper crowd broke up and Henry, Justin, Patterson, and Isabel, were getting ready to go to their rooms for the night. Henry and Justin needed to unpack and settle in. Justin wanted to call his family.

"Would any of you fine gentlemen like to have a cup of premium coffee in my room? My special blend?" Isabel invited them as they were getting off their scooters in the hallway. "I'd like to catch up."

"Sure," Henry said. "I can visit for a bit. I

can never turn down your special blend java."

The others voiced the same sentiment.

Henry and Justin dropped their backpacks off in their designated rooms, and they and Patterson joined Isabel in hers. Henry didn't know how she'd done it in two weeks, but her room looked almost as good as before she'd left the base the year before.

"You've decorated your lodgings nicely, Isabel. Again. You don't waste any time, do you?"

"Thank you. I haven't had much else to do since I got here, not so far anyway, so I thought I might as well pretty up my room. It was easy. I'd had my furnishings warehoused in a storage unit in a nearby town until I could get them sent back home. I was so busy, I kept putting it off. Good thing I waited. They were supposed to be shipped just two days before I was called back here. Perfect timing. It was simple to have everything hauled back here when I arrived."

Over coffee, the friends discussed their situation.

"It seems to me, "Justin professed, "there are a great deal better alien specialists out there–no offense, guys–than us."

"We have the best, or one of the best, in the

world." Patterson was stretching his arms and shoulders, yawning a little. "Doctor Lawrence Emmet. He wanted the rest of our old team reassembled here because of our history with the spaceships and this facility. You especially, Henry, even before this last episode you had with the telepathic invisible saucer aliens in your backyard, because the aliens seem to like you. Enough to communicate with you.

"And you, Justin, because you ran the whole show last time and are familiar with the base. I think he said something about maybe making you second in command here."

"Really?" Justin seemed pleased.

"Really. It's not for sure, but he did mention the possibility. Would you be interested?"

"I'd have to think about it. Clear it with Delores. She was happy to have me back in New York, close to home. With what might be coming–." Justin stopped in the middle of the sentence, then tagged on, "I'll have to think about it."

Patterson let the subject drop.

"I did notice that Emmet seemed fascinated with the telepathic part of my encounter story when I powwowed with the aliens." Henry let out a muted snort. “I know that General Wallace said that our government is getting ready for whatever comes. What, if I may ask, will they do if the alien armada does show up and parks itself above our cities?”

Patterson’s laugh was caustic. “You ever saw *Independence Day* the movie?”

“Hasn’t everyone?”

“That’s what the government’s doing right now. Recreating the *Independence Day* scenario–except minus the captured alien behind bars, in the film, they were poking and prodding. They’re collaborating with other world leaders, gathering our top scientists, assembling the military, polishing the weapons of war, the planes, drones, missiles, bombs, and the soldiers to fight. Trying, for now, to keep everything secret from the public so we don’t cause a global full-out crazy-town panic.

“Problem is, our predicament is not a fictional SF movie. It’s real. I’m afraid when we meet our big bad aliens, the outcome is not going to be as positive as the one in the movie was.”

“Yeah, we don’t have Will Smith,” Henry quipped.

Patterson was staring at the wall, his face

contemplative. He released a heavy sigh. "Henry, I've been dreaming a lot lately about...dead people. Every night since I got here and found out what we're facing."

"Dead people?" Henry was alarmed at the resigned weariness in his old friend's voice.

"Yeah." Patterson looked directly at Henry. "Last night I dreamed of Dylan. Remember him?"

"Of course, I do," Henry replied. "Dylan Greer, your old FBI partner. He was an interesting character. An honorable man. A real warrior. He helped us catch and kill Godzilla. I remember well our watery cave hunt and that dinosaur. The stories Dylan told."

"More than anything, he was my friend. The night before I dreamed of that old guy, Zeke, Ann's boss at the newspaper...and Lassen. Remember he was one of the pilots who drove that submersible, The Deep Rover, into Crater Lake? Every night, I've been dreaming of someone who's in the great beyond now. Deceased agents I worked with in the FBI. Old friends from my childhood who have died. George Redcrow, your ranger? I dreamed about him, too."

Patterson glanced sheepishly at Henry.

"Even Ann has visited me. And others I've known along the way in my life, who are all dead now. I swear they're haunting me, and I don't know why."

Henry was staring at Patterson. A shiver crept up his body. Patterson wasn't the sort of man to dwell upon the past, or the dead. He lived in the present. Did what he had to do, no regrets. Henry didn't know what to say. Henry dreamed of Ann sometimes, now that he wasn't seeing her as often as he once had; but she'd been his wife, and he missed her.

"What do you think it means?" Patterson probed. "Dreaming of all these dead people?"

"I don't know, friend." Henry was shaking his head.

"It's these damn aliens coming, that's what it is," Isabel declared with a frustrated shrug. "It's got us thinking and dreaming of death. Others and our own. I've had trouble sleeping since I found out what's going on. I won't lie, I'm frightened almost out of my skin. I'm wishing I didn't know what I know. But I'm not dreaming of dead people. Yet."

Justin said nothing. He was drinking the coffee he'd poured from the coffeepot on the counter, listening; his mind seemed far away. Henry was pretty sure his son-in-law's thoughts were still on their adventures that morning with both alien ships. The incidents had affected him in a strange way. He was unusually quiet. It was one thing to live a year with two lifeless alien spaceships down in the bowels of Area 52, to walk through them, examine, and study them and all the other-worldly technology inside, when you knew there were no aliens in them; another to see two working alien spaceships flying around in the park's air space, and that, yes, aliens were piloting them. Real, live aliens.

Now for Henry, after what happened to him the year before in the largest spaceship, proof of living aliens wasn't as much of a surprise, but to everyone else at the base, and all the humans of the world, it would be.

The friends sat around discussing the coming aliens and what threat the world might be facing; what they could do to protect themselves and their families, for just a short time longer. Then everyone's exhaustion caught up with them. The party broke up and Henry went across the hall and let himself into his room. He switched on the light. The space was bare, except for the basic original furnishings. A television on the wall, a table and chairs, a bed, and a chair by the bed.

When he'd left the last time he'd taken his little decorating touches with him. Under the circumstances, he didn't think he'd be redecorating. What would it matter…*if.*

He took a shower and went straight to bed. He missed his cat, but even that was a muted emotion. He laid awake for a brief time fretting about what the future was going to bring. What was he actually doing here? What could *he* do to stop the alien war? One ex-chief park ranger, old dinosaur hunter, man with a broken heart, with a pistol and a rifle? On the other hand, what could the entire human race do to stop a pack of attacking aliens?

"Hey, Ann," he whispered into the dim room, "where are you? I really need to talk to you. Do you know what's going on in our world? Do you know what is happening? Do you know about the aliens?"

The room was silent. He was alone.

Ann didn't come to see him as much as she once had. He still spoke to her often, though it was more like talking to himself. He missed her and he missed her ghost. It was as if he'd finally and totally lost her.

"Ann, Ann." He sighed, closing his eyes. "I need you. I'm afraid. Afraid of what tomorrow and the days after will bring. The end of the world wasn't something I wanted to ever have to live through…or die through. Alone." Facing something like this alone was so much harder.

Ann didn't appear and soon, disappointed, yet accepting, Henry fell asleep.

*****

The following two weeks were a strange time for Henry. A strange time for everyone on the team. They knew what was coming, but, so far, the world's main population didn't. They were sworn to secrecy with everyone, except their team mates, even with telling their families. They weren't allowed to speak openly about the coming spaceships in front of the soldiers.

Henry was interviewed numerous times by the higher ups in the military and by other alien experts. Men in uniforms or men in white lab coats. They asked him about his telepathic communication with the aliens in the park; asked him how he knew he had understood their messages correctly. Why they chose him to speak to? What could he tell them? "I don't know why they picked me. I don't even know how I do it." Of course, he had a theory why, from the beginning, he'd been singled out to be the alien whisperer…his connection and friendship with Oscar. He'd thought the little dinosaur was distantly related, and in sympatico, with the Area 52 aliens. Because Oscar trusted him, the aliens did, too. But he couldn't tell any of the uniforms or the lab coats that. He didn't want any of them to know about Oscar.

Henry did a FaceTime meeting, arranged by Doctor Emmet and General Wallace, with the President of the United States. Now that was quite a memory for the future. Just a shame it had to do with the possible end of the world. He'd voted for the man, so it was a privilege to be considered important enough to have a meeting, to speak, with him. Ann would have been so proud of him. No president had ever interviewed her. As General Wallace put it, the President wanted to converse with the man who could mind-talk to aliens. It was a personable, though short, virtual meeting, considering the state of affairs. The President was polite and posed quite a few questions; about Henry and his dinosaur hunting days, and then about his experience with the aliens, both at Area 52 and in the park. His special ability to commune with them. Someone, most likely the General, had told the President all about him and his adventures. Henry had been flattered by the President's interest. Imagine, all he had had to do to get a private conversation with the President of the United States, was to be a mind-reader of aliens. Who knew?

"If we find we might need your unique talent, Mr. Shore, can I count on you to help us out? If the aliens want to speak to us, will you be one of our ambassadors?"

"Of course, Mr. President. I'm at your disposal. Whenever or wherever you need me, I'll be there." Oh, boy, if that happened, he might be able to see inside another alien spaceship. Then he remembered the way Oscar had reacted to the triangle craft. The little dinosaur had been so scared. Well, maybe it wouldn't be so great to go inside one of those ships. But he'd do it for his country, if it was asked of him.

"Mr. Shore, my people will be in touch if that occasion arises, and we will have you flown out here at the government's expense, or wherever we need you to go." On the screen the President smiled at Henry over the computer miles. The man's face showing nothing but amiable, and polite interest. The perfect politician. "Thank you." And the

President of the United States signed off.

If the aliens ever reveal themselves, Henry brooded. *If they even want to meet with us. Because Henry knew the aliens who were coming, according to what he'd understood from Oscar, didn't want to talk. They wanted to exterminate them.* But he humored the leader of the free world and said the words the man wanted to hear. He felt bad about it, but what else could he do?

The days went by and the tension increased among the people in the base. Everyone realized that the alien fleet was coming ever nearer each day, but no one knew how or what would happen when they got to Earth.

Every day Henry wondered what the heck he was doing there. The other scientists were diligently working with the military, collaborating with them over what they'd learned from the base's extraterrestrial spaceships the year before, telling them about their technology, and the alien DNA; trying to formulate some sort of plan if, and when, the aliens arrived in America's airspace. Trying to figure out how they might be beaten or killed. But since they didn't know who the aliens were, or what would hurt or kill them, they were whistling in the dark. To Henry, all their plans and preparations were heart wrenchingly frustrating. There were other scientists and military working across the country; the world, General Wallace told them, to be ready for whatever would come. Preparing for war, but praying somehow for a peaceful resolution.

There was as yet no response, no messages in any form at all, from the approaching alien force. It was as if they were in stealth mode. The government was trying desperately to make contact and negotiate with them to save humanity. The world's governments were also trying to reach the coming extraterrestrials. The aliens remained silent, and kept drawing closer, and closer.

*****

One night most of the team were at supper in the dining room. There wasn't much small talk going on as the food was consumed. Everyone was deep in their own thoughts. The mood was solemn. Henry had been at the base for over two weeks and everyone knew how close the aliens were to Earth now. Very close. Everyone was frightened.

Some of the scientists would drive or fly home on the weekends to be with their families. Doctor Emmet was very lenient with the absences. After all, it might be the end of the world, so being with loved ones was important. During the week, there was a lot of FaceTime with spouses, parents, and children. Henry FaceTimed with his grandchildren, and flew home with Justin to see them once, but he had no real reason to fly to his own home. There was no one there. His cat was at Sherman and Patterson's house, and according to Sherman, Sasha was content with the kids and their cat. If the world was ending, might as well let the cat be happy. At least someone was.

About the time Henry and the gang finished their meal, Doctor Emmet strode into the dining room, unsmiling, and announced, "General Wallace has returned to the base and he wants to speak to us. Please be in the main meeting room in fifteen minutes or sooner." Then Doctor Emmet pivoted around on his heels, and hurried out the door.

"Oh, my," Justin stood up. "I wonder what's up?"

"It can't be good." Isabel pushed her tray away, and also came to her feet. "Doctor Emmet seemed really worried."

"He did, didn't he?" Henry was out of his chair, too.

Everyone was moving towards the door. Everyone was silent. There was nothing to say.

As they sat around the same table in the same room they'd first all met at over two weeks before, General Wallace, his face lined, and his eyes weary, didn't waste any words or time. "I've just been alerted. The alien fleet has come into our atmosphere. There are twelve ebony triangular shaped aircrafts intruding into the Earth's airspace. Within a short time, if they keep coming, the world will soon be able to see them."

"Where are they heading?" Justin asked. "Does the government know?"

"They think straight to D.C. If the trajectory holds." The General had a file before him that he was riffling through.

"Have they made contact with the aliens yet?" Henry felt numb. He guessed most of the people at the table felt the same. This is a nightmare…not real. Or a real bad joke. Alien invasions only happened in fiction books, on television, or in the movies. Except, *this was real*.

"No. We've tried and tried to contact them, but they aren't responding in any way. The President is frantic to do something. He's already put the military, all the government agencies, on high alert. When the spaceships come into view of the American people, he'll have to act. If by then the aliens are still mute…we will most likely be going to war."

Oh boy, Henry thought. *Here we go. The apocalyptic thrill ride has begun. Everyone just start praying and hang on.*

After the General fended off the questions he couldn't or wasn't allowed to answer, he excused himself, and left. He had a lot to do. War and all.

The rest of them sat around for a while, not knowing what to say.

Eventually they slipped off to their rooms to call or FaceTime with their loved ones, or to worry in solitude.

Henry wondered how many would flee the base in the morning.

CHAPTER 15

Oscar was sleeping peacefully, curled up among the little ones crowded in around him, when he first sensed something was wrong. He opened his eyes, lifted his head, and sniffed the air. The cave they called home was dark in the rear where the family lived, but his eyes were used to that darkness. The pack was snoozing after a long day of hunting. But it must be near the rising of the new sun, he thought, though there were no first tinges of light seeping into the mouth of the cave. He was sure he had slept through the entire dark time, though. The light must be coming soon.

He'd been on edge, anxious for no reason he could understand, for many light and dark times. The forest had changed. It seemed to be strangely silent. Afraid of something bigger than itself. The tiny creatures that drifted above them were no longer noisy. The animals that fed, wandered, and lived around them were skittish. Most were hiding, rarely coming out, and only to hunt and feed. Things in his world were not right.

Ever since those strange beings from another place had come to visit him in their huge objects that could move above the ground, above the trees, the forest had been different. Ever since the beings, he could not see, but knew were there, who had somehow made him hear what they had wanted him to hear, and understand, his thinking had been confused. He'd brought his friend the stick to meet with them as they had requested. The strange beings from another place had come out from their huge object and had communicated with the stick. Oscar had understood everything they had told his stick friend. He heard it in his head. The strange beings were warning the stick of something bad coming to his home. The bad being more strange beings in great flying objects…but not good beings like them, but bad. Very bad. Oscar had done his part. Done what the strange beings wanted him to do. Or so he had believed.

The strange beings had wanted him and his family to go with them. He had no idea where. They had been adamant. They said they would return for them and they should prepare. But Oscar had made his decision, he and his kind would never go with them, and he had let them know that. He would never leave the forest. His home. Never leave their cave. Oscar didn't want to. He loved his woods, his snug cave, the waters in holes around them. But something was wrong in his forest…something was wrong in the world. Oscar was worried.

Crawling and climbing over the others still sleeping, Oscar made his way to the mouth of the cave, and peeked out. He could see the tip of the fiery ball that brought light to the world rising on the other side of the forest, yet it was pale and clouds hid its usual brightness. The time of light was arriving, but it was dim out, almost as dim as his cave.

The outside was not calm as the inside of the cave was. There was a heavy fall of water dropping from up above. The world was a murky greenish-gray, and the wind was howling so loudly he could barely hear anything beyond the cave's entrance. Except, there was something…something deep in his head pulling him out into the falling water and darkness. He, and the stronger, older ones of the clan, would still have to go out into the forest, hunt, and bring food back for the tiny ones that couldn't go out and hunt yet for themselves. The larger predators would kill them too easily. Oscar must feed and protect the little ones at all cost.

He squatted on his haunches for a long

time, staring out into the outside, and listened. *There it was again.* Something was calling him. Something wanted him to leave the safety, and dryness of the cave, and venture forth into the woods. *Come to us. Come to us. We will guide you.*

One of his offspring, a very small one, had come from the sleeping group behind him to sit beside him. Oscar looked down at the baby and was filled with pride. This was one of his children. One of his family. He remembered with a wave of sadness how he'd lost his first family a long time before. He had grieved for them, but luckily, he'd hidden the other eggs where his nemeses, the bad dinosaurs, couldn't get to them. This brood of new young was from those precious eggs, and the ones that were born from them. He was very protective of all of them. He did not want to be alone again.

The little one snuggled up against him. Oscar laid his claw on the dinosaur's small head lovingly. Oscar cocked his head as the beckoning from the outside came to him again, louder, more insistent. Making a series of chirps, snorts and chattering, Oscar in dinosaur language, told the baby dinosaur to go rejoin its mama. Do not follow him. Tell the others to stay in the cave until he returned. No dinosaur must leave the cave.

When the little one rejoined the others, Oscar moved slowly out of the cave, and into the wet world beyond. The call in his head was getting stronger. He must listen, and he go to them. For he now realized who was summoning him. It was the strange beings in that giant shiny object he had met with before with his friends the sticks beside him; the strange beings he had brought his friend the stick to see. They were back.

What could they want of him now?

He trudged his way through the gloomy trees and clingy undergrowth following the voices in his head. The wetness coming down from the skies didn't bother him. His thick hide protected him from all sorts of wet and cold. He was used to the climate of the forest. He traveled for a long time as the voices grew stronger n his head, leading him, until he broke out of the brush into an open space. There before him was the same huge shiny object he'd visited before.

Something came out of the big shiny object and stood in front of Oscar. A few somethings. He couldn't see anything, but he knew they were there. One of them was speaking to him silently.

The strange being from another place spoke to Oscar for a long time. It told him something it said was very important. First it reiterated that Oscar and his clan should come with them to its home world far away before the big war came to them all. Oscar again said he and his family would not go. They were staying in their home.

You and your kind are not safe here once the war begins, the strange being spoke in Oscar's head. *The Gemmas are almost here and they will destroy you as well as the humans who live here. The humans will all be killed.*

Oscar didn't know who the Gemmas were and he didn't care. He only heard that the humans, which he knew as the sticks, were in terrible trouble. Extermination. He had to help them. The sticks weren't all bad. Some of them were his friends.

All the sticks will be destroyed? Oscar was confused. Why?

And the strange invisible being told him, as best he could explain it to the little dinosaur, why.

Oscar was still confused at first. He didn't really understand. Only that his friends the sticks would be no more–unless he could find a way to help them? The world he called his home would be changed forever?

That's when he asked to speak to more of the strange beings and they took him into their home, and for a long time Oscar was inside the big shiny object communicating with other strange beings. They showed him around their home, it was so much bigger than his home or his friend the stick's dwelling, and Oscar was scared, but he kept communicating with them. He tried so hard to make them understand that the sticks did not deserve to all be killed off. Perhaps, in the end, they did understand. He hoped so.

When he was released to return to his cave, the wetness from the sky was even worse. It pummeled his hide and made him shiver. He could barely see where he was going. But his instincts guided him to his cave again as he knew they would. It was home. Where he felt safe. It was where his family was. Where he belonged.

But he must go warn his friend the stick. As soon as he could. No matter how wet the world was. Now. From what the strange beings had told him, there was no time to waste. Once he was sure his family was all right in their home, he started the long journey to his friend the stick's cave. He had to hurry; he didn't have much time. The sticks didn't have much time.

Chapter 16

The following days were full of tension, and yes, contained fear. Everyone at Area 52 was waiting for the alien armada to arrive and come into view of the people of the world. It would be any day now, they were told. Any day. The military predicted either tomorrow or the day after.

The night before the President had finally gone on the air and told the country about the *visiting aliens*, as he called them; trying not to cause a panic. *They* would soon be visible high up in the sky. Not to worry, people. We have this all under control. Thing was, they didn't. They didn't have any of it under control. The aliens had entered our atmosphere, all twelve triangular dark ships, silent as the grave, and had not made contact with anyone–not our government or any other government across the globe, not any of the worldwide observatories on high alert. The President, as General Wallace had explained it to Henry, Justin, and Patterson, was giving the invaders the benefit of a doubt that they were coming in peace. A friendly first contact. Until it was proven different.

"I bet the military doesn't believe it's a *friendly visit* for a microsecond," Justin had complained to Henry and Patterson after the General had exited the room. The three men were the last left at the table. Everyone else, or those still at Area 52, had gone to their rooms. Some to pack. The base had pretty well emptied in the last day or so. There was nothing any of them could do now. Their reports had been turned in to the government, though they hadn't had much advice or any real answers to what could be used to defend the world from the aliens, if they decided to attack. How could they plan any fighting defense when no one knew who the aliens were, what their strengths were, or even what they looked like. What they *really* wanted. Whatever would happen would happen. It was in the hands of the leaders and the militaries of the world. Every scientist at Area 52 felt as if they'd failed. They'd tried their hardest, their best. But without more definitive information on the threat, they hadn't come up with any viable solutions.

"No, they don't," Patterson commented sarcastically. "In confidence, the General told me that we're ready to shoot, if they start shooting first. All the International governments feel the same. This could be it."

"It?" Henry asked.

"The end of our world, if what you reported, Henry, is correct. If the aliens are here to destroy us. I just pray that our defenses react quickly enough if those extraterrestrials fire on us first. Then I just pray their weapons aren't so far advanced that we can't even begin to fight them."

Henry and Justin didn't say anything to that. *As if any of that would save them if the aliens were serious about obliterating them. No one knew what weapons the aliens possessed. No one knew how powerful they were.*

"It's a good thing the rest of the world doesn't know what Henry knows," Justin mumbled. "The real intention of those aliens. We'd have a war right here on Earth, right now. Panicked humans go insane sometimes so quickly. Fear can make us destructive demons. We'd blow ourselves up before one alien showed its…face. If any of them have a face, that is."

But the rest of the world didn't know what Henry knew. The President had decided to keep that little secret partially under wraps; only telling his top generals and advisors. Henry had suspected, though, that the President hadn't actually believed one hundred percent about his mind-communicating aliens. Most sane people wouldn't believe such an outrageous thing. Besides that little problem, the President, General Wallace had conveyed, was afraid the country would go even more nuts than it already was if he'd told them everything. So he hadn't.

The eyes of people all over the world were rising to the sky. Waiting. The aliens were coming. Everyone had a different take on what it all meant.

"I hear there are *welcome aliens'* parties going on all over the planet." Patterson had a disgusted look on his face. "Orgies, too. Some people are so delighted with the visitation nothing else matters. It's just an excuse to party. Idiots."

"I heard," Justin confided gravely, "some people think it's the end days and soon Jesus will come down from the clouds to start his reign here on Earth. He's coming with the aliens. People are quitting their jobs. Selling everything they own. Some are fighting in the streets. People are getting hurt. Dying. It's absolutely crazy. And the aliens haven't even shown up yet."

"Are you two heading home tomorrow?" Patterson asked Justin and Henry. "I am. I want to be with my family if this situation hits the fan. I'm not active military, I'm a free-lance consultant, so I'm free to leave whenever I want."

"Probably." Justin sighed, rubbing the bridge of his nose after taking his gold rimmed glasses off. "I'm taking Henry with me."

Henry shrugged. "I have nothing at my home to go to. I want to be with what's left of my family now. Justin, Delores, my grandchildren. Sasha? I know she's happy with Sherman and the children. She'll be all right there."

"Isabel?" Justin said. "She's coming with us. She's in her room packing now. She'll meet up with us later."

"That's good." Patterson was looking around the room as if trying to capture every detail in his memory for some future time. "No one should be alone now. We should be with our families."

"Scott," Justin reminded him, "you know you and the family are welcome at my place, too. If you want to come. My brother-in-law will send a jet for all of you. Heaven knows what commercial flights are going to be like."

"I'm grateful for the kind and generous offer, Justin, but I want to be home with my family. In my home. If anything happens."

"I understand." Justin smiled at the ex-FBI agent. "But the offer is always open. Anytime, friend."

A soldier came hurrying into the room and marched up to the three men. She was slim, her blond hair done up neatly in a bun; her army uniform, though clean, was slightly wrinkled. Her eyes under arched eyebrows were a dull green, her face pale. All the military on the base now knew what they and the world were facing. An open alien arrival of perhaps unfriendly extraterrestrials. The soldiers were trying to look brave, but Henry could see how worried they were by the expressions in their eyes. Their tense behaviors. Though they put on a good show.

"Henry Shore?" she inquired glancing at first Patterson and then, when Patterson cocked a thumb at Henry, addressing Henry. "You have an urgent telephone call from a Sherman Patterson. I can have it transferred here if you'd like?"

"Yes, I would. Thank you," Henry told her.

The servicewoman nodded and left the room.

Henry gave Patterson a tentative smile. "I wonder why your lovely wife is calling me?"

"Something to do with Sasha, maybe?"

Henry was suddenly a little worried. He couldn't bear to think of something having happened to his cat.

Justin had walked over to the end of the table and moved the phone closer to Henry so he could answer it.

Leaning over so he could reach the phone, Henry put it to his ear. "Sherman? You sure you're calling the right person? Your husband is sitting right beside me."

"Say hi to my sweetie then, would you? I'll speak to him after I finish with you. But no, this call, I'm afraid, is for you, Henry. I went over to your place this morning to get some more of your cat food for Sasha. Guess what? Someone broke into your house. I thought I should let you know."

"What, someone broke into my house!" Henry, with everything else going on, was disheartened. He didn't need this now. Had the madness already begun…were gangs of thugs already breaking into houses, looting, and vandalizing? Were people committing suicide, diving off buildings, or drinking poison? Inwardly he shuddered. "How bad was it?"

"Sorry, friend. They left quite a mess. They must have broken into the rear porch window.

Glass and blood are everywhere. Strange thing is, they ransacked the refrigerator, throwing things, half-eaten, all over the kitchen."

Oscar!

Henry gasped, and his eyes locked with Justin's. "They emptied the refrigerator? Threw food everywhere?"

Justin straightaway got what Henry was trying to tell him. His head barely nodded, yet Henry knew he got the message.

"Yep. I' afraid your food supply is irreversibly depleted. Not that you had much in there to begin with."

"The rest of the house?" Henry's mind was busy piecing together the puzzle.

"The rest of the house seems to be fine. Though there was one other odd thing." Sherman took a second to talk aside to someone, probably one of her children, and came back to finish. "There are scratches all over your porch door. Inside. Looks like animal scratches to me. If I didn't know better, I'd say it was dinosaur talons made those scratches. But, as we all know, the dinosaurs are gone."

Yes, as we all know the dinosaurs are gone. Not really. There is still Oscar and his brood. Sherman, like Patterson, knows nothing about that, though.

Justin interrupted in a soft voice, "Henry, we can take a flight to your house to check on it before we fly to New York. My brother-in-law won't mind us using his jet for that."

Patterson was observing both of them closely. Henry hated keeping the Oscar secret from him, and mulled over just telling him. If the end of the world was coming, what difference would it make? But something kept him from confessing. *Not yet.*

Henry resumed his conversation with Sherman. "I'm coming home now, Sherman. To gauge the damage. Justin is giving me a lift on his brother-in-law's private jet." Henry spoke aside to Patterson. "You want a fast ride home, Scott? You can hitch one with us. We're heading to my house."

"Sure." Patterson seemed relieved. Probably knowing how hard it would be now to get a regular plane ticket to anywhere. "I'd appreciate the ride. It'll get me there with a lot less hassle and quicker, too. Thanks. I don't want Sherman and the kids to be alone when the aliens arrive. We need to be together."

Henry waited for what he was afraid Patterson was going to ask. *Why do you care if your house has been broken into with the dire circumstances we find ourselves under? What does any of that matter anymore? If we're probably all gonna die.* But Patterson didn't ask. Taking a long look at him, Henry could see the man had other weightier things on his mind. His family for one. What was going to happen when the alien ships arrived? Would they all still be alive this time next year? Or next week? No one knew.

"Oh, by the way," Sherman mentioned, "your cat is fine. Except I don't think you're ever going to get her back. The kids have bonded. They think they're going to keep her."

Any other time Henry would have laughed. Not today. Not now. "Tell the kids, sorry, they can't have her. She's mine.

"Here's your husband."

Covering the phone for a moment with his fingers before he handed the receiver to Patterson, Henry whispered, "You haven't *told* her yet? Doesn't she get on Twitter or Facebook, watch television? The President spoke to the nation last night about the approaching aliens. And real soon here the alien spaceships will be all over the news media and televisions across the world in full living color, when they are hovering over Washington, D.C."

"Oh, Sherman knows about that," Patterson replied. "She just doesn't know the entirety of it. Everything we're aware of because of your little tête-à-tête with those invisible aliens. She, like most of the planet, doesn't know the aliens have come here to kill all of us. Like a lot of the human race, she doesn't know why they've come. I didn't tell her about that little nightmare. I didn't want to scare her more than she was already," his mouth whispered, a frown on his lips. "I kept praying our government would find a peaceful solution. Or someone would. Doesn't look like it, though, if the aliens won't even make contact with us. Won't talk to us. I'm telling her *everything* as soon as I get home. When I am by her side to help her accept it. Once I tell her I won't leave. Simple as that. I belong with my family right now–until we know what is going to happen. They're my first priority." He took the phone from Henry.

Henry was on his feet when he gestured for Justin to accompany him outside the room. "We'll let you two have a little privacy," he said to Patterson. "We'll be in the hallway waiting for you."

Once outside Justin pivoted around to Henry. "You think it was Oscar who broke into your house, don't you?"

"I'm sure of it. Every time that little thief visits me, he raids the fridge. Either devours or tears up everything in it. It's his unique calling card. And I'm sure he's the one who clawed up my rear door. It's a clear message. *Come home. Now.* He needs to see me and tell me something. Badly."

"How will we find him, Henry? If he's returned to the park? The alien fleet is supposed to come within sight over us in a day or two. We think things are insane out there now…just wait until that happens. *Whew.* Complete and utter pandemonium. Worldwide."

"I don't know, but we need to get to my house as soon as we can. That's the first step." Henry had noticed that Patterson had ended his phone call, and was coming out to join them. Time to go. "We'll decide what to do once we get to my house."

"All right," Justin murmured.

The three men headed to their rooms to clear out any of their personal items they wanted to keep. For Henry, it wasn't much. He'd never really moved in, suspecting his stay would be short. Then Isabel would join them, and they'd leave Area 52 for the second time. Going home. Never to return. Or, at least, Henry didn't think he'd ever come back. There'd be no reason for it, especially if the world ended.

"We're going to make a side trip first, Isabel," Justin told her when she came out of her room, pulling her wheeled suitcase behind her. "Henry's house was broken into, and he wants to check it out. Also, we're giving Scott here a ride, as well, since we'll going in that direction. Then we'll fly on to New York."

"That's sweet of you. Flying Henry to check out his house first. I can't believe someone broke into it." Isabel hadn't minded. The aliens weren't supposed to come for two days or so. They had time to make a side trip and then get to New York for the *arrival*.

Henry looked around his little room before he left. The memories of his time there flooded over him. Some good, some not so good. At least when he was here the first time, he wasn't scared the world might be coming to an end. Now the future was dark. Darker than ever before. For everyone. Soon would be the day. Soon would be the day the human race found out whether it would be allowed to continue, or would be ended. Henry acknowledged he was more afraid of the outcome than he'd ever been during the dinosaur wars.

Oh, how he wished Ann was waiting at home for him. Still alive. He really needed her with what was coming. But she wouldn't be there. She'd never be there again. Perhaps he'd be joining her sooner than he thought.

*****

Jeff Smith's luxury jet got them where they wanted to go in short order. They rented a car, and dropped Patterson off at his house; lingering only a short while to say hello to Sherman and the kids, and for Henry to briefly cuddle Sasha. The cat had been so happy to see him, she'd jumped up into his arms, purring, and snuggled against his chest. The cat had missed him.

Leaving Isabel to visit Sherman and the kids longer–they'd pick her up after they returned from Henry's place–Henry and Justin drove to Henry's house. Since Isabel didn't know about Oscar's miraculous rebirth, they'd sort of coaxed her to stay with the Patterson's until they were done checking on the damage at Henry's. She wasn't hard to convince. Isabel and Sherman were becoming friends since the July Fourth weekend get together at Henry's barbeque; though they'd known about each other for years because Isabel had also been part of the Area 52 family. When he and Justin drove off, the two women were yakking over coffee and upside-down pineapple cake Sherman had baked in honor of Scott coming home, and the visit from his friends.

"We'll have coffee and some of that delicious looking cake," Justin had promised Sherman, "when we return from Henry's. He's anxious to see how bad the mess is and make sure his home is otherwise okay."

Henry and Justin drove over to Henry's house.

The first thing Henry saw when they stepped up onto the rear porch was the broken window and the scratches on the door. Blood all over the wooden porch floor.

"It *was* Oscar," Henry exclaimed. "I'd bet a hundred bucks on it." He slapped his hand against his thigh, excited.

Justin bent down into a crouch to get to the blood splatters below the smashed window. "I hate that Oscar got cut breaking in, I hope he's okay, but now I have my blood samples. If I ever get a chance, I'll examine them." The paleontologist produced a small plastic envelope from his shirt pocket, carefully scraped some of the dinosaur blood into it, and folded it carefully, replacing it in his pocket.

Henry unlocked the door and he and Justin moved into the kitchen. Sherman had been correct. The kitchen was a mess. Most of the food in the fridge was gone. There hadn't been much in there, but whatever there had been, the dinosaur had scarfed up. What he hadn't eaten was scattered haphazardly over the floor. He wasn't worried about the mess. At the moment, he had more serious things on his mind. Where was Oscar? What had he wanted?

"How in the world did he ever get into the refrigerator?" Justin marveled out loud. "He would have had to open it somehow."

"The critter had already worked out how to pull at the handle, and open it." Henry chuckled. "He's one smart dinosaur."

"He sure is."

"I just wish I knew why he came here; what he wanted to tell me." Henry was peering around the kitchen, as if Oscar might have left him some secret message or something. Of course, there was nothing but bits of food across the floor. He quickly cleaned up the mess, not that there was much left to clean up. Oscar had pretty much emptied the fridge.

To be sure the dinosaur wasn't hiding

somewhere in the house, they searched every room. No Oscar.

They looked outside, stalking around the property, calling out Oscar's name. Yelling; banging some pots and pans they'd brought from the kitchen. They moved along the edge of Henry's large yard, where it met the forest, kept moving and kept shouting.

No Oscar.

Standing there at the line of trees, Henry didn't know what else to do. *Oscar, Oscar, where are you?* A soft rain had begun to fall; the day was turning murkier. A mist was floating low to the ground. Henry and Justin were getting wet. Henry didn't care. He only wanted his dinosaur friend to show up. The end of the world might be coming, and all of a sudden, Henry really wanted to see his little buddy one last time. It was almost an ache, a deep yearning in his heart. He couldn't have Ann, so he wanted Oscar. How could a person love a dinosaur? But he did.

"I guess he's gone home." Henry couldn't hide his disappointment. "I just have the feeling he wanted to tell me something truly important. Now I'll never know what it was."

"What are you going to do about your broken window, Henry?"

"Sherman said she called Walt at the hardware store in town. He's going to come out in the day, or so, and fix it. Bill me later. It's nice to live in a small town; to know all the businesses and their owners."

"I imagine, in that respect, it would be. Though I love living in a big, bustling city myself. There's so much to see and do in New York. Or there was, anyway." A note of despair had crept into Justin's voice.

With bowed heads, dodging the largest raindrops, they made their way to the house as the rain became a deluge coming down around them. They were both soaked to the skin and wanted to get out of the rain. But when Henry, who had kept glancing backwards to scour the woods, twisted around and finally looked at the house...*there was Oscar sitting there on the porch waiting for them as if he'd never left*. Then Henry could have sworn, the little dinosaur waved at him. Waved? Nah, it had just been an involuntary gesture. Dinosaurs don't wave.

"*Oscar!*" Henry yelled, a big grin spreading across his countenance. He began to walk faster, almost a dead run, Justin straggling behind him.

As Henry stepped onto the porch, Oscar

hopped up to him. The creature put out a claw and Henry, still smiling, touched it with his hand. "I am so happy to see you, Oscar!" Henry would have hugged the little guy if he thought he could have gotten away with it, but he didn't try. Oscar had to make the moves towards him, not the other way around.

Henry plunked down on the top porch step, beneath the porch roof, to get out of the rain. Justin gingerly trod around him and the dinosaur, and went to perch on the porch swing above them, his eyes never leaving Oscar. Justin, as always, seemed enchanted with the small creature.

Oscar settled down beside Henry. \

"What did you want to tell me, Oscar? Why are you here? I have the feeling it is of utmost importance. Am I right? Does it have to do with the bad aliens? The ones coming? Can you let me know what you want me to know…somehow?"

The dinosaur, peered out at the rim of trees, their shapes now muted by the rain and the light fog, cocked his head at Justin on the swing, and then gazed back to Henry. The creature made a series of strange sounds. Chirps and squeaks, a vibrated humming that came from his chest. As if he were trying to communicate with his human friend. The dinosaur tilted his head one side to the other as if it was frustrating him, trying to communicate. His manner seemed to convey worry, or to Henry it did. His eyes gazing directly into Henry's eyes, the dinosaur laid a claw on Henry's head. Henry nearly jumped, it surprised him so much, but he forced himself to remain motionless.

Justin was gaping at them now. The scientist blurted out, "What is he doing?"

"I don't know–."

And suddenly Henry's mind was filled with thoughts and snatches of *images*. Not his. They were coming so swiftly, it almost made him dizzy. Disjointed, and so faint the images were difficult to decipher or understand, but, concentrating hard, he could just make some of them out.

My God, Henry thought, *Oscar is trying to talk to me through our minds. Wow!*

As the pictures slowly formed in Henry's mind, they told the story the dinosaur wanted to tell him, and Henry's mouth fell open. He held his breath as the images continued. Assaulting his consciousness as soft as snow. The messages were simple and eventually he *understood. Oh my God.*

The mind meld lasted only a handful of minutes, but felt much longer, then Oscar took his claw off Henry's head, flashed him one last knowing look, gave him one last affectionate touch, and then bounced down the steps, scurried off across the yard in the heavy rain and churning mists, and disappeared into the woods.

Justin couldn't wait to hear what Henry had learned. "What was that all about?"

Henry was on his feet now, and there was awed shock in his eyes. "Oscar just *told* me what we should do…if we don't want the bad aliens–I believe he meant the ones in the ebony triangle ships–to exterminate us. Oscar might have just saved us humans and our world."

"He did?" Justin reaction was one of incredulity, but also one of relief. Hope. The scientist honestly smiled for the first time in weeks.

"He did. Come into the house and I'll tell you what he made me understand we must do. If I got the message correctly."

Inside, Henry sat down at the table. He told Justin what was going to happen and what had to be done.

"If I understood Oscar correctly," Henry

spoke slowly, "our little friend has somehow *interceded* for us with his alien friends, who I believe, are Oscar's far distant future ancestors, and part of that intergalactic multi-alien alliance that the triangle aliens, the Gemmes, are also part of, among others. Oscar has begged his aliens to plead with the Gemmes, and the rest of the alliance, to give the human race a reprieve, a second chance at survival…if we *do not show any forceful aggression towards the alien fleet whatsoever when they arrive; no firing on them, no attacks–not one gun raised or missile sent against them–at all in any way*. If we do not move against them, they will leave after a certain amount of time without annihilating us and claiming our planet, taking our open restraint as a sign, a promise, that we, the human race, understand what we, as a species, have been found guilty of, and have *agreed* to change our ways. Immediately.

"If the alien alliance agrees, we will have a second chance to fix the crimes the human race is accused of in the Intergalactic Organization's mind. They will give us time–Oscar didn't know how long. I don't think Oscar understands increments of time. What I took from everything Oscar attempted to tell me was this: if we, the human race, haven't changed our evil, greedy, murderous, earth decimating ways, the aliens will return and destroy us. Every last one of us, and take our Earth. I believe Oscar vouched for us humans because he believes we can change, be better, and the aliens listened. This time."

"Oscar told you all that?"

"In his way. I don't know how he did it. Telepathy of some kind. He's gotten so much better at it. I got his thoughts. I hope I got them right."

"How long, did Oscar say," Justin pointed up at the rainy sky, "will the triangle aliens stay up there waiting for our reaction?"

"I don't know. Oscar didn't say. Like I said, he doesn't understand our concept of time. I got the impression, though, it will be a test of sorts. If we make any aggressive moves towards the alien ships, any of us I assume, worldwide, it's an instant fail. No second chances. Then we die."

Justin lowered his head, shaking it. "Now I guess you have to convince the world to stand down when the aliens show up. Don't react with any hostility, don't attack them. Good luck."

"I have to try. But I have no idea how to do

that, Justin. Who's going to listen to a retired Chief Park Ranger? I'm a nobody."

"You're not a nobody, Henry…you're the man the aliens have mind-spoken to. You're the alien whisperer. You've communicated with aliens now…twice. That's got to count for something."

Henry threw his son-in-law a dirty look. "Yeah, if anyone believes me."

"The President of the United States believed you."

"But did he really? Or was he simply pacifying me because General Wallace and Doctor Emmet insisted he hear me out? General Wallace told both of us that the government was in a panic trying to figure out what to do about this coming alien armada. This situation has never happened before. They've been grasping at straws. We have no idea what orders our military have been given on how to handle the alien threat; what is going to happen when those enormous triangles appear over Washington, or wherever they're going to park–and just hover in the skies above us. When through the media, television, and the internet, Instagram, everyone on Earth will see them? I imagine this is one of the government's worst nightmare scenarios."

"I imagine it is." Justin gave his father-in-law a serious look. "As soon as we get to Scott's, we need to ask him to connect you to General Wallace. The General can listen to you, and get you, at least, another virtual meeting with the President. You can tell your story, and pray the powers that be will listen and won't fire on those aliens."

"From where I am right now, it seems a very long shot. And what if I'm wrong…and I *didn't* fully understand what Oscar was trying to tell me? What if the aliens do attack us immediately?"

"You have to trust yourself, and Oscar. You know you have this eerie rapport with the aliens, so why not with Oscar as well, if he's their descendant? You do what you can do. And then we pray."

"Yeah," Henry said, "but, again, how am I going to tell that story without blowing Oscar's cover? I can't say my little dinosaur friend–who's supposed to be dead, but isn't–mind-melded with me, after telepathically communicating with the saucer aliens, and told me what had to be done so the bad aliens in the big obsidian triangular spaceships don't blast us into space, or however they're going to exterminate us."

Justin thought about that. "We could…tell everyone a saucer landed in your backyard. These days it wouldn't seem so unbelievable. The government knows aliens exist, and soon, even the disbelievers, since the President spoke, will, too. The General knows about your weird experiences with the alien ships at Area 52. He was there. Right now, all that matters is you get that message–Oscar's message–to the General and he, somehow, gets it to the President. Then it's up to them."

Henry dropped his head into his hands. "They're not going to believe me, Son. When those colossal triangles appear who knows what the government, the military, will do? Humans have a long history of shooting first instead of talking or negotiating for peace. You saw how mammoth that triangle spaceship was. The fear it evoked in us. It was almost supernatural, that fear. I've never been so afraid as when you, Oscar, and I were hiding from that one we saw. Blood-thirsty dinosaurs are nothing compared to those cursed black crafts. Just wait until a herd of those monsters show up here on Earth. The world is going to go nuts."

Justin exhaled, his whole manner reflecting

weariness. "We do what we can. Come on, let's get back to Scott's house. Start the ball rolling. I could use a hot cup of coffee right about now. Better yet, a large shot of whiskey, or two. It's been a day."

"It has. And I could use some coffee myself. No whiskey for me. I'm already in the Twilight Zone and I don't need anything else messing with my reality." Henry stared at the mess in the kitchen. "I'll clean this up some other day. If I ever come back here, anyway. Wait a minute, Justin."

Henry dashed into his bedroom, grabbing the pictures of him and Ann that sat on his dresser. He wasn't going anywhere without them. He pulled an extra suitcase he had from the closet, and tossed more clothes into it; toiletries from the bathroom. He hadn't taken much to Area 52 two weeks ago, and who knew if he'd need more now going to Justin's apartment. Best to be prepared, was his motto. He'd bring along Sasha's cat carrier as well. It was on the porch. Sasha was going with him to New York. He couldn't leave her behind this time. She was all he had left of Ann.

Then he and Justin left his house. Perhaps for the last time. He didn't look back once. He didn't want to cry.

CHAPTER 17

"Okay, let me get this straight. This just happened?" Patterson couldn't hide his amazement. "While you were at Henry's house an alien spaceship–out of the blue, so to speak–a saucer you say, landed in your back yard? Just now? And, Henry…the aliens *spok*e to you again like they did last week in the park? Into your thoughts? You're not kidding me?"

"No, I am not kidding." Henry tilted his head at Justin. "Justin was there, as well. He saw it all. Except the aliens, neither one of us actually saw them, like before. They were cloaked somehow. Basically, invisible to our eyes. I heard their thoughts when they came out of their spacecraft. Which we could see easily enough. Big shiny saucer. Similar to the large one we had at Area 52…but even bigger. Must be the new futurist model."

Henry and Justin were sitting at Scott's kitchen table with Scott, his wife, and Isabel, having coffee and cake. The children were playing in the next room. Scott didn't want to frighten them with talk of aliens and invasions. They, as most children, already suspected something was different, yet hadn't been told anything yet, so no need to scare them even more.

Isabel and Sherman were listening to the conversation with unconcealed interest. Sherman, ex-military that she was, had no fear in her eyes. She was ready to pick up arms for her country and family anytime she was needed. Isabel, though, was another story. Henry imagined she wanted nothing but peace, any way she could get it. Her eyes were troubled. Neither one said anything, but remained quiet as they listened to what Henry had to say.

"And what did they tell you this time, Henry?" Scott was sitting close to Sherman. They were holding hands.

Henry, every once and a while regarding Justin furtively, wove the story they had concocted on the way over from Henry's house. When he was done, Scott was grinning. "If this is true, the world will be saved. *If*, as you say, we can persuade the powers that be to not fire on them or act aggressively in any way. It's a nearly impossible order, but what have we got to lose? We have to try. I can't believe these saucer aliens have interceded for us with the other ones. Why would they do that? What do they have to gain? If, as you say, they're one of the members of that alliance?"

Henry hadn't been sure at first how to answer that. A half-truth seemed like the way to go. "Do you remember Oscar, our little dinosaur friend who helped us a couple of times during the dinosaur wars? He led us to that crashed helicopter? Led us to One-Eye and then where One-Eye had stashed his eggs? He grew kind of fond of me and Ann."

"I remember Oscar," Scott replied, with a warm expression on his face. "I was sad when he died in that missile explosion that killed old One-Eye. That funny little dinosaur saved our butts more than once. He was the only dinosaur I didn't fear or hate. Shame he had to die."

"Yes, he did save our butts more than once. And I learned last year, when I had that out-of-body bizarre mind meeting with those Area 52 aliens on that second spacecraft, that they were Oscar's far distant-in-the-future ancestors. They seemed to know I was his friend, and he was mine. That Oscar had trusted me; was fond of me and Ann. I guessed they read my mind and discovered that connection. Oscar's friend was their friend. I think the same thing happened today. Because I cared, we humans, cared for Oscar and his kind, we were friends with them, we are being given one last chance to change. To be better humans. To treat each other better. To treat the planet better. The saucer aliens interceded with the others in the alliance and, mainly, the Gemmes, the ones in the massive ebony triangular spaceships, the ones who mostly want to eliminate us and claim our planet for themselves; the Gemmes were the ones who convinced the rest of their Intergalactic Alliance of Planets that we are a vicious, virulent species and deserve to perish. But after the saucer aliens vouched for us, forced the issue–and I believe they are the strongest in the alliance besides the Gemmes–we have been given one final chance. This will be our last warning, though.

"The Gemmes are soon to appear in our skies over D.C. Tomorrow perhaps. According to the message I just received, if we do nothing, they will eventually leave. If our military fires on them, anyone fires on them anywhere across the globe, we will have war. And I don't think we have a chance of winning. They're too advanced, too strong. We must *not* attack."

Scott had a grave expression on his face, tinged with a tiny bit of optimism. "I'll telephone General Wallace immediately and let him know you've been visited again by the saucer aliens; tell him what they *told* you. What we have to do to save the human race."

Justin and Henry exchanged a hopeful look of their own as Scott placed a kiss on his wife's cheek, and with a smile, went into the room off their kitchen, which served as his home office, to make the call.

Scott was gone for what felt like a long time. Almost an hour. As the four left in the kitchen waited, they spoke among themselves about everything else besides the alien problem. Sherman talked about her and Scott's children. Isabel talked about how hard it was to leave Area 52 again. Justin caught everyone up on what his children, Henry's grandchildren, were up to. Henry was the only one to remain silent. He was thinking about Oscar and their last meeting. It made him smile. He liked that Oscar had resumed visiting him at his home. No one mentioned aliens. Not once.

When Scott walked into the kitchen, he met Henry and Justin's gaze. "Justin, can we use your brother-in-law's jet to fly to Washington, D.C?"

"Now?" Justin asked, a little surprised.

"Now. I spoke to General Wallace and he conferred with the President–"

"Of the United States?" Henry exclaimed.

"Yes, the same President you spoke to not too long ago on FaceTime. And he would like you and Justin to come visit him at the White House. As soon as you can get there."

"Visit him at the White House," Henry echoed, not sure he'd heard right.

"As the General put it, our President wants to see the man who communicates with aliens face-to-face this time. He wants to talk to you, Henry. Now. I think he wants to see what measure of a man you are. In person. I'm told he's an excellent judge of character. He'll be waiting for you in the Oval Office. You'll have no problem getting admitted. They're expecting you. You, too, Justin, since you saw the spaceship as well. Isabel's been invited as well, because the president knows she was at Area 52 with both of you and was also privy to the whole alien spaceships investigation; knows about her abducted sister. This thing the President has to do–not show any aggression when the aliens arrive–to just wait patiently until they decide to leave…and convince all the other world leaders to do the same…he needs to actually speak to you and

Justin. Look you in the eye, Henry. Decide if you're sincere or a crazy man. I vouched for you, though, and so did the General."

Henry would have laughed, but things were too serious for that. The fate of the whole world depended on if he could make the President of the United States believe him." That shouldn't be too hard, should it?

Justin inhaled deeply. "I'll call my brother-in-law and ask him if we can use the jet for a little while longer. But, under the circumstances, I have no doubt he'll give me the green light. Then I'll give Delores a heads up to what we're doing, and that I'll be a little late getting home. I don't think she'll mind. Besides, D.C. is so close to New York, it'd be just a short flight from the White House to our apartment if I need to zip home for anything."

Everyone stared at each other. Isabel was the one who nudged Henry. "We better get going then. There's no time to waste."

"No there isn't," Sherman said. She and Scott were still holding hands.

"I'm taking Sasha along to the White House," Henry announced. "I hope the President doesn't mind. I can't leave her here again, as much as she likes it. She belongs with me. Especially now."

"She does," Sherman grudgingly conceded. "I know you've missed her. She obviously missed you."

"Let us know what happens with the President," Patterson said to Henry. "Keep us updated if you can."

"We will," Henry responded. He was nervous, but eager to meet the President in person and to press his case. So much counted on the President believing him.

Henry, Justin, and Isabel came to their feet. Henry corralled the cat into the cat carrier, and grabbed a bag of cat food and treats for her that Sherman had had ready. They all said their goodbyes. Wished Henry, Justin, and Isabel good luck and saw them to the door; waved as they walked out into the driveway.

In minutes they were in the car again, Henry driving, and on their way to the airport. Justin called his brother-in-law first to let him know what was going on and to get his blessing for their quest. Then he called his wife and explained it all again to her. She wished them all well and said she'd pray for them to accomplish what they were trying to do.

Within an hour the three, four counting the cat yowling in the carrier, were in the air flying to Washington and their destiny.

Henry was afraid to look too long out of the windows, afraid he'd seen the alien fleet. He didn't.

Chapter 18

As Henry, Justin, Isabel, and the cat in the carrier, arrived at the White House, they were expected, and were quickly escorted by a group of men in uniforms through the front door, down the hallways, and past historic rooms, to meet with the President, who waited for them in the Oval Office.

There had been so many troops stationed inside and outside the White House, on the grounds, so many more than Henry had anticipated. The soldiers appeared tense, though their stern faces and postures concealed it well. Most of the soldiers were vigilant almost to the point of paranoia. No doubt, they were on high alert with what was coming. Waiting for something to happen. And Henry knew what they were waiting for.

Henry, nor any of the others with him, had ever been in the White House before and they were awed by the years and years of American history they were walking past and through.

"This place is so impressive," Isabel spoke softly as they moved through the corridors. She was staring at everything as they walked past, her eyes wide. "The famous and infamous people, the major history-changing occasions, the world-changing decisions, this house has seen are mind-blowing. I feel immensely honored and humbled to even be here. And getting to meet the President seems, wow, unreal."

"It sure does," Henry concurred.

"You're right, Isabel, this does feel as if we're in a dream," Justin remarked, as the soldiers led them towards the Oval Office. "Someone pinch me…am I dreaming?"

"If you are then all three of us are. Dreaming, I mean," Isabel responded in a whisper. It was as if she were afraid to speak too loudly in such a revered building.

"About as an unreal feeling as the reason we're here," Henry grumbled. He'd been practicing how he would tell the President what he had to tell him. No matter how he phrased it, it still sounded insane. What was he doing here? An ex-Chief Park Ranger and old dinosaur hunter? He prayed the President would believe him. Otherwise, the human race would be doomed.

Sasha was whimpering in her cage. Henry stuck his fingers through the front grill to pet and soothe her. "It'll be all right, girl," he comforted her. "I know you don't like being locked up, but there is nothing to be afraid of.

We're just wandering through the White House like regular tourists. Hush, hush, girl. You're about to meet the President of the United States. Be a good kitty. They say he likes cats. He even has one as a pet. Maybe you might get to meet him."

When they were finally ushered into the Oval Office, there was the President of the United States sitting at the Resolute Desk, grimly smiling up at them. He was alone and that detail surprised Henry. The man looked older now than he had when Henry had FaceTimed with him not that many days ago. There seemed to be extra wrinkles lining his face, and more gray in his hair. His eyes, a vibrant blue, were filled with a tiredness that could only be described as something that was etching worry in his soul. The weight of the country, Henry imagined, was on the man's shoulders as the aliens were approaching. Henry thought to himself: *I wouldn't want to be in his shoes right now. Too much responsibility. What must it feel like to carry over three hundred million people, their hopes, and fears, on one's back? To have to make the life-or-death decisions a president has to make?* Henry didn't think he could do it. He wouldn't want to do it. When he had been Chief Park Ranger at Crater Lake during the dinosaur wars, he had had to make life-and-death decisions for his men and women rangers, and that had been difficult enough. He still carried guilt over some of his more deadly decisions. These days, since Ann had died, it was hard enough to manage his own life, must less anyone else's.

The President stood up, as they entered, to greet them. "Mr. Shore, Doctor Maltin, and Doctor Hutton–my alien experts–thank you for coming. I've been assured by reliable sources that you three people know more about the alien threat, about aliens in general, than most anyone else on the planet."

"I wouldn't say that. Mr. President," Justin protested humbly. "There are others. I'm sure, even more qualified than us."

The President objected. "In my mind, with what I've learned about the three of you, you three are some of the best."

Along with Doctor Lawrence Emmet, Henry thought. *But Doctor Emmet wasn't with them today.* Heaven knew where he was. Probably at AOIMSG Headquarters watching the aliens approach.

The President stood up, came from around the desk, and first grasped Isabel's hand warmly, smiling at her as if she were an old friend, instead of someone he had just met. "Doctor Isabel Hutton, it is so good to meet you, even under these frightening circumstances. I have been briefed on all your hard work the last few years at Area 52. Your history with the spaceships and aliens. Spoken with many of your colleagues, who raved about you. I know about the abduction years ago of your sister. I'm so sorry for your loss. But I am grateful you're here to help me and the American people deal with this emergency. We need all the help we can get."

Isabel's face went white when the President mentioned her sister, but she put on a smile and thanked the President for his kind words.

Then the President pivoted around to Justin and shook his hand. "And Doctor Maltin…I've heard great things about how you led Area 52 last year; and the decade before that with all your work during the dinosaur war days. Your scientific discoveries that helped us to end their reign of terror over the world. I've been following your career for a long time. I'm proud to finally meet you. You are well respected in your field. Thank you for coming today."

The President saved Henry for last. The man took Henry's hand and shook it vigorously, while staring into Henry's eyes as if he were trying to see into Henry's soul. See if he was a man he could trust, believe in. *See if the alien whisperer was for real or a fraud.*
"And Chief Park Ranger Henry Shore, now retired, besides being a famed dinosaur hunter from the dinosaur war days, who reportedly saved endless people's lives, and who also consulted for Area 52. I have also been following your career for a long time, through reports and your talented wife's–Ann, right? – articles and book, as well, Mr. Shore."

"And," the President squinted at the animal in the carrier, "welcome to your little furry friend."

"The cat's name is Sasha, Mr. President," Henry said.

"Hello there Sasha," the President nodded at the cat in the box. Sasha just stared out at him. Then let out one mournful meow.

The President laughed.

"She doesn't like being in the carrier," Henry explained.

"I guess I wouldn't like it, either."

The President turned back to Henry. "Mr. Shore, I've been told, you actually spoke *telepathically* with the aliens in that second ship before it vanished as the first one had? Is that true?"

"It's true," Henry replied, meeting unswervingly the President gaze.

"And I've also been informed, by individuals I trust, that you have also recently telepathically communed, again, with one of the alien interplanetary alliance members, one who is allegedly on our side attempting to help us. They gave you an extremely urgent message they want the world to hear?"

"They did," Henry replied respectfully, gulping. *Here goes nothing.*

"Getting this message out to the world is, according to my advisors, perhaps the only hope our species has to avoid an alien war."

General Wallace and Patterson, Henry thought, had more than fully briefed the President about their mission. Henry was impressed. He was also uneasy. The fate of the world, in some ways, was riding on his back. *Oh boy. How could anyone carry that weight? What if I got Oscar's message wrong? If the aliens came and we do nothing, and they strike first? Obliterate humankind? No, he couldn't think that now.*

The President graciously gestured them to

the couches across from him. “Please, all of you, sit down. We have some talking to do.”

Henry set Sasha’s cat carrier on the plush rug beside him. He was sure the others, as he was, were overcome with simply being in the Oval Office. It seemed such a hallowed room from the moment they’d entered it. Not only was the office gorgeously decorated and furnished, a beautiful room by any measure, but knowing that it had been the home of so many presidents over so many decades, and visited by so many famous people, and distinguished foreign visitors, through the years, who had all left their mark on it, made it almost magical. History. It was pure history. It made Henry proud to be an American.

The President had sat down in a chair across from them. He was a fit looking, but thin man, not very tall, but still his bearing and the way he carried himself, projected confidence. He had that charisma that so many high politicians possessed. He would never enter a room without being noticed.

He returned his attention to Henry. “Mr. Shore, I will say, it is nice to see you in person this time instead of on a computer screen.” The man tented his fingers on the edge of his legs. His body leaning slightly towards his guests before him. His manner earnest.

"As you probably know," the President caught them up on the situation, "the alien ships coming have not communicated in any way with us, though we have signaled them many, many times as they grew closer to our planet. So far, we have no idea what their intentions are, good or evil. As you can guess, it has created a great deal of anxiety and fear among us and among the American people; the entire world, really, because no country has been able to get a response from the aliens. No one knows what they want.

"I, as well as the other world leaders, have put our militaries on the highest alert, readied our defenses, and are prepared to fight if we have to. But, realizing the high level of technology and most likely the deadliness of the aliens' weapons, I would prefer to negotiate with them. Find out what they're here for and why. Thanks to you we knew they were coming, but now they're almost here, and we need more information. Do we fight them or do we wait until they make the first move? General Wallace said they told you something of ultimate importance; can you tell me about it?"

Linking his eyes with Justin's, for support,

in between his words, Henry revealed to the President of the United States what he'd learned from Oscar. But following his and Justin's partially fabricated story to protect Oscar's existence, he fibbed slightly and said the aliens that had landed in his backyard had given him the thoughts. The President listened, watching Henry closely, every once and a while swinging around to Justin and asking him a question. After all, the scientist claimed to have been at the alien landing, as well, though he hadn't received any telepathic thoughts from them.

When Henry was done relating his tale, the President summed up the latest message. "So, this, er, apparent invasion is a…grand test of a sort? They want to know if we have received their warning, the message they gave you, that we, the human race, must change if we are to be allowed to continue to exist? If we do as they ask–do not react to their arrival in any hostile way–then they know we *got their message* and we have agreed to what they want us to do? Tin this particular instance, the test is one of non-aggression? Unwarranted and belligerent aggression being just one of the evil habits we humans, in their opinion, have? Others being the way we brutalize and kill our fellow humans, continuous and never-ending wars, and how we detrimentally mistreat the planet's ecosystems? If we attack them without provocation, we will have failed their first and, therefore, only test? It would show we're not willing, or even able, to begin changing our bad behavior, and they will, without hesitation, destroy us, and take our Earth for themselves? Do I have it right?"

Isabel was sitting, perched on the edge of the sofa. She smiled encouragingly at Henry. *You're doing good*, her look said. She reached out and laid a hand on his for a moment.

Henry sighed aloud. "Yes, Mr. President, that's about the sum of what I understood was what the aliens from the saucer spaceship were trying to tell me, and wanted me to impart to you, and to the world. These aliens, the ones in the silver saucers, want to help us for some reason I don't fully understand, and they interceded for us with their alliance members to give us one chance. Thank goodness, most of the members of their alliance don't take this species genocide lightly. They only kill off the worst species they come across."

The President sat there deliberating, his expression grim, as everyone else in the room held their breath, waiting. Henry could see the man was undecided about what he should do. It was a first for any American president, or for any president or world leader for that matter…having to deal with a squadron of aliens coming to earth; having to persuade other world leaders to stand down when threatened by aliens in their airspace. “I, as well as many other people, of all the humans on the planet, wonder why it is you the aliens have decided to communicate with. Do you know why?”

Again, Henry tried to explain about Oscar and the special friendship they had had with him and Ann, the times Oscar had helped the rangers and him, and how the aliens at Area 52 had appeared to him the year before, also communicating telepathically with him because they had a distant connection with the little dinosaur, and possibly trusted Henry because of that odd friendship.

The explanation seemed to somewhat satisfy the President. But even as Henry had been telling his Oscar story, he thought it sounded unbelievable. Weak. But it was the best he could do. He was so nervous, sitting in the Oval Office with the President, he was surprised he could even string two sentences together, much less make his story sound credible.

"My generals of all the armed forces, my advisors," the President stated, "want me to strike first. Take no chances. They fear because the alien fleet won't communicate with us, that they're coming to attack us."

"Strike first? As we humans have always done? That won't work for us this time, Mr. President. These aliens I believe are way too advanced for that. If you do," Henry spoke softly, "that will be the end of us. Perhaps we could defeat them, if it were only the Gemmes, but they are not alone. Apparently, there are many alien species in their interplanetary alliance. I don't know how long it would take for the others to get to Earth, but if they all come against us, with their advanced technology and weaponry, we wouldn't have a chance. Gaining our planet as the final prize is more than enough incentive."

"How long, did the saucer aliens say we had to stand down and not fire on their ships?'

"They didn't say. I'm sorry. Until they leave, I would say." Henry wished he had a better answer for the President, but he didn't.

The President nodded. "All right. I have to speak to my cabinet, my generals. Congress. I can't make a decision this important on my own. I am not a dictator. I must get agreement. I'll also conference virtually with the other world leaders, let them know what's going on. And pray they believe us, believe me."

The President's benevolent gaze took in all three of his visitors one at a time. "You're all welcome to stay here at the White House for as long as this situation lasts, if you'd like. Until we see what happens. We have extra rooms." The President gave them a faint smile.

Of course, they did, it was the White House. Henry shook his head. "Thank you, Mr. President, for the kind offer." He glanced at Justin and Isabel. Both were also shaking their heads. "But I think the three of us want to stay with my son-in-law at his New York apartment until we see what happens. Justin's wife and children, my grandchildren, are there. I believe I speak for all of us. We want to be, we need to be, with our families right now. Justin's apartment is very close, so if at any time you need to talk to us, you can call, or need any of us to return, it's just a short, quick flight back here. We have access to a jet and can charter it anytime at short notice."

"My apartment is about a forty-minute flight from here, Mr. President," Justin chimed in.

The President dipped his head. "I understand completely. My family has gathered here in the residence as well. I want us all to be together, no matter what happens.

"Again," the President came to his feet, walked up to the three of them, and warmly shook their hands, "I want to thank you for coming. Thank you Henry for giving me that message from the aliens. I am going to try to persuade my people of the legitimacy of what you told me. We, the people of Earth, owe you a great debt of gratitude. We are blessed to have you and your telepathic connection to the aliens. I trust you. I just pray the world will listen."

Behind them Henry could hear Sasha meowing nervously in her carrier where he had left her by the sofa. She knew something big was up. Animals always knew. She'd be happy to be in the apartment, be with her friend, Miss Kitty Cat, again.

A woman in a dark blue skirt and jacket, a file in her hands, a scared look in her eyes, hurried in and whispered something to the President. The change was immediate. The President locked eyes with Henry and Justin. "The aliens are here. They came early. I've been told they are above us in the sky right now."

The President spun around and moved briskly to one of the Oval Office doors, the east one Henry thought, opened it, and walked outside. It was twilight and the sun was fading on the horizon. The grounds around the White House, the stately lawns, the trees, the garden around them, were tinted that subtle golden hue that sometimes a setting sun produced. It was a beautiful sight.

Stunned, Henry, Justin, grabbing Sasha's cat carrier, and Isabel followed the President out into the Rose Garden. They gawked upwards into the sky. Henry heard Isabel gasp, and suddenly her hand was taking his free hand. He could feel her trembling. Justin was staring upwards as well, his face as white as the house behind him.

There, filling the sky, were three huge obsidian triangular alien spaceships, each one as big as a football field, and another seven or eight further up above them, looking smaller because they were further away.

"*Oh my God,*" Justin whispered, but loud enough to be heard, "*they're here.*"

"Yes," the President declared, "it seems they are."

Now they were surrounded by Marines in

their uniforms, standing tall, guns at the ready. "Mr. President," one of them said in a no-nonsense voice, "we need to get you somewhere safe."

The President nodded at the soldier, and turning, addressed Henry, "I need to go face my generals in the War Room. Talk to the Congress. They're probably all going crazy. I have to make sure they do not fire on these…visitors.

"You'll be escorted out of the White House and driven safely to the airport so you can catch your plane home," the President told Henry. "And if I need you, Henry Shore, I will have someone come and get you. All right?"

"Whenever you need me, Mr. President, I'll come."

"Excellent. Thank you, Henry." The President took one last look up at the sky full of black triangles. They blocked the dimming light. Then he spun on his heels and marched back into the Oval Office, his Marines going with him.

Henry, Justin, and Isabel continued staring at the gigantic ebony triangles hovering low over D.C. and the White House. The spaceships were truly chilling. They hovered, silent as death.

Oh, Ann, Henry brooded, I wish you were here. *I shouldn't say this, but I am scared. I miss you.*

Isabel's grasp on his hand tightened, and he looked over at her. Her face was shadowed with terror.

"It'll be all right, Isabel," he told her, putting Sasha's carrier down on the ground, he wrapped his arms around her. At least he had his friends. Justin and Isabel, and Sasha, by his side. He wasn't alone.

"Henry," she replied in a haunted voice, "I don't think anything will ever be all right again. I have a very bad feeling about this."

Henry glanced up again at the invaders. God, he prayed she was wrong.

"We need to get to the jet and fly out of here," Justin stated firmly. "We need to get home while we can…if we can. Everyone will be trying to get out of Washington. Not only will the roads be bedlam, but the skies, as well. The government will most likely close all air space pretty quick."

Henry accepted Justin was correct and they had to move. They followed the soldiers through the Oval Office and backtracked their earlier route out of the White House. They were shuffled into a dark sleek SUV and driven to the airport. The streets and highways were crowded with lots of yelling, angry, insane people, most in cars, but some just walking, and Henry was relieved once they left the city behind.

They could still see the hulking triangular spaceships from the airstrip. Their pilot took off and they prayed they'd make it safely to New York. They barely did. As they landed, they learned that right after they'd taken off all planes had been grounded until further notice.

"We made it here just in time." Justin exited the plane and led them to a vehicle sent by his brother-in-law to take them to the apartment.

Once inside, Henry thought they'd left the ugly monster spaceships behind in the skies of Washington, but no such luck. The alien ships, hovering menacingly over the capitol city were all over social media, and on television. Delores and the kids were watching them when Justin, Henry, and Isabel got to the apartment. The kids were fascinated, couldn't take their eyes off the screens.

Sasha, though, was more than content to be with her old friend Miss Kitty Cat. At least, someone was happy.

The following hours were torture. Henry,

as the rest of them in the apartment, held their breath, watched the news constantly, devoured what little information the government was releasing, and prayed that war would not break out.

Henry spent quality time with Phoebe and Timothy, giving them attention and love. Trying to calm their fears. "Everything will be all right," he kept telling them. "The aliens aren't going to hurt us. They're only visiting, checking us out. They'll be gone soon."

Timothy believed him, Phoebe did not.

In the mornings, as if anyone could sleep, the gang gathered at dawn at the kitchen table for an early meal and to talk. Talked to soothe their fears, talked to make a connection to another human being. To keep from going off the deep end.

On the second morning, everyone in the house woke up to a new horrifying development. All but one of the triangular spaceships had left their original location over Washington D.C. They'd flown to major cities all across the globe and now floated over them. Still silent, still voiceless. It was all over the news media and on every television screen. The world was going bonkers.

The days drug by. The sinister shadows of

the silent aliens and, to all the world except a few, the mystery of what they wanted were hanging heavy over everyone. Over the world. The spaceships sat up in the sky, barely moving. Watching. But Henry knew why they were there, what they were doing. They were waiting to see if their warning had been heeded. If the human race could keep from taking their usual aggressive behavior–just this once–in our long combative history. Henry prayed every day that the countries of the world would hold back, not to throw the first punch out of fear, ignorance, and false pride. He prayed hard.

Whenever Henry was forced out of necessity to venture out onto the streets of New York, to get supplies, he would walk past zombie people gaping up at the ebony monster hulking above them, their eyes disbelieving, and panicky. Or they'd be scurrying here or there like fearful mice, their heads down, not daring to look up, to get their tasks done, and slink back to their shelters. But their fear was palpable. They were waiting for the aliens to begin firing, begin killing, and conquering. Or for the government to do something. Anything.

Henry, even when his eyes weren't on the

black spaceship, could feel it hulking above him. Wherever he walked, he knew the interstellar craft was up there following him anywhere he went. In the stores, in Justin and Delores' apartment, he could still *feel* it. And he had thought the dinosaur days had been harrowing. Now, instead of waiting for a blood-thirsty dinosaur to leap out at him and take a bite of him, he had to contend with an even far worse predator drooling above him.

Among humans worldwide there were vicious verbal disputes, unprovoked hostilities, mobs looting and rampaging in lawless gangs. The media played the horrific scenes twenty-four seven over and over and over. It was as if sanity and the rule of law had dissolved. People had regressed into wild animals. The suicide rate across the globe sky-rocketed, especially among the elderly, and ill. Henry feared for the world, and not merely from the aliens. It often haunted him: what if the aliens had lied? What happened if the aliens had never meant to keep their peaceful promise to leave without destroying us if we did not retaliate? What if they were really here to commit planetary genocide? If so, what were they waiting for? The weapon of mass destruction to come to readiness up in their ships…for reinforcements? *The what ifs and unnerving doubts drove him nearly crazy.*

But the spaceships remained frozen up in the skies. Chillingly quiet. Hovering over major cities. Waiting.

While every human held their breath.

*****

On the third morning of the aliens' surveillance from above, while the children were still in bed sleeping, Henry confessed to Justin, Delores, and Isabel, "The President called me last night. It was short and sweet. The man has a lot on his shoulders right now. He wanted us to know he had succeeded, so far anyway, in keeping everyone–all the leaders of the major countries–from firing on the alien spaceships. It wasn't easy. Telling them what the aliens wanted. That this is a test and we can't afford to fail it. And that what the aliens definitively want is for humans to change our destructive ways; stop warring, killing each other for no reason, and to begin taking better care of our precious planet, before it's too late. The fact that the alien spaceships are hanging over us, not blowing us to smithereens right off, is enough, the President concluded, to make most of the foreign leaders' tentative believers. For now, anyway. Unless the aliens fire the first shot. Then, heaven help us, all bets are off. *Boom! Boom! Boom! Interplanetary war.*

"Yet the world's leaders are waiting as our President has begged them to do. But it's easy for them not to do anything at the moment, they're all scared out of their wits.

"Russia has determined the aliens' cloaking technology wouldn't let any of our missiles or bombs through anyway.

"China wants to just send nuclear warheads at them…but have agreed to wait a while as asked because they're not sure the warheads will even affect the spaceships.

"Great Britain is fairly sure the spaceships' exterior cannot be breached by any weapon we Earthlings possess anyway. I don't know how they know that, but there it is. So, all we can do is wait. Pray the aliens leave eventually as we've been told they will. Then will come the truly difficult trials…being better humans, and caring for our planet with more reverence."

"Good luck on that," Justin cracked, from where he was standing next to the stove, a spatula in his hand. Delores and Justin had been making everyone pancakes. The delicious aroma wafted through the kitchen.

For a moment, as Henry drank his first cup of coffee, he felt as if everything was normal. Just a normal day like any other day before. Except he could feel that ugly alien spaceship up in the sky above them.

"All we can do is hope." Isabel was in her robe, her eyes rimmed in circles, as she sat on a chair at the table. She'd told Henry she had had trouble sleeping, too. Frightened some of the aliens would beam down and snatch her up like they had her sister, or they'd get tired of being nice and start lasering them off the planet. Since the alien ships had arrived, Isabel had been a wreck.

The night before Henry and Isabel had stayed up later than the others, talking; unable to capture sleep. Airing their fears and hopes for the future, if there would be a future. The apartment had been quiet and most of it dark, and they'd conversed in lowered voices so they wouldn't wake anyone. They'd sat in the kitchen on stools at the counter, the lights dimmed, and had snacked on cookies and coffee.

Henry was glad he had a friend like her. He could tell her anything, she understood. About Ann and how much he missed her. How lonely he still felt. She gave him the woman's point of view. There was a moment, only a fleeting moment, when Isabel had laughed softly at something silly he'd said, where he looked at her and realized she was becoming more to him than a friend. It took him by surprise. He wouldn't call it love yet, because Ann was still in his heart and always would be. But there was *something*. Something fragile and precious growing in his heart for her. When he was with her, he didn't feel that aching loneliness he'd felt so often the last year. And then the truth of what was going on in the world would hit him again, and he'd think: *what difference would it make? Attempting to love someone again...now? When, in truth, these could be the last days of humanity. So why bother?* There were so many ways the alien stand-off could end in catastrophe. *If* he had misunderstood Oscar's mind message, or Oscar had misunderstood what he'd been told. Or, *if* the aliens were more devious than he and Oscar knew, eviler, and would kill them all off, just because they could, and take possession of their planet anyway. No, this was not the time to fall in love again with anyone. But it was nice to have a friend like Isabel.

*****

On the fourth morning of the alien's surveillance from above, the gang again woke up around first light and padded out in their pajamas, nightgowns, and robes, and took comfort in the companionship of family, good friends, hot coffee, and homemade cinnamon rolls Isabel made for them. It was the only real time they could talk freely about everything, when the children were still sleeping. Neither Phoebe nor Timothy got up before nine.

There was a small television set on the kitchen counter and it was, as usual when anyone was in the kitchen, turned on to the world news. The screen was full of the alien spacecrafts, and the bedlam erupting all over the world. It was getting worse every day. Humans did terrible things when they were scared.

"*They're still here*," Isabel groused, her eyes on the television as she took another roll off the cookie sheet sitting on the stove.

"Yeah, they're still here." Delores was wearing her blue robe that the kids had gotten her for her birthday the month before. It was fluffy. It looked warm and comfortable to Henry.

The sun was stealing into the windows and its light crept through the room. Henry welcomed the sunlight. It meant they'd made it through another night. No alien attacks. The situation lately reminded him of the fortified siege at the old ranger headquarters years ago during the height of the dinosaur wars when they'd been waiting for the creatures to attack. Praying they wouldn't. Different cast, but same show.

At one point, when the four of them were lounging at the counter, eating their rolls, and trying to act normal, even laughing at one or another's humorous anecdotes about some incident or other that happened to them outside on the street the day before, Henry glanced over to the empty stool at the end of the counter and he could have sworn, for a heartbeat, Ann was sitting there, smiling at him. She was as young, as lovely, as when he'd first met her so many years ago when he'd been a rookie cop in New York. He'd met her when she was twenty and he was twenty-four. He'd been shopping at the local market, picking out a cantaloupe in the fruit department, and he'd looked up to see her standing in the aisle with an amused smile on her pretty face.

"I wouldn't take that one, if I were you."

"Why not?" he'd bantered back.

"Because it looks bad."

He'd been confused. "In what way does it look bad? How can you tell?" He'd rolled the melon, examining it. "It looks fine to me."

"Take my word for it," she'd teased. "It's not. Just a hunch."

"A hunch?" Then he'd laughed. He'd thought at the time she'd only wanted to meet him.

They introduced themselves and kept chatting amiably as he finished his weekly shopping. He got her telephone number. It had been instant love at first sight…for him anyway. She took more convincing. A year later they were married, and their beautiful life together had begun.

It was so good to see her, even if she faded away all too soon. She must have been worried about him; wanted him to know she was thinking about him, cared about, and still loved him. Always and forever.

After the children got up, they joined the adults and they all spent time together. Then Justin left the apartment to go into the lab, at the President's earlier request, still working with other Area 52 scientists, and scientists across the world, to study the alien conundrum. Not that it would do any good.

Nothing was known about the black triangle aliens, but the scientists wouldn't stop searching for answers because of that. Justin said it was better than sitting around all day, twiddling his thumbs, waiting for the sky to fall. But he was never gone for long. There were laptops, emails, telephones, and FaceTime. He wanted to be with his family if something would happen.

*****

On the fifth morning of the alien's eerie surveillance from above, the gang was going to gather once more at the kitchen counter to share breakfast, and conversation, and help keep each other's mood up.

"They're still here," was the first thing Isabel, in robe and slippers, griped as she shuffled into the kitchen, and sat down, a cup of coffee cradled in her hands. Her shoulders were slumped.

"I noticed," Henry remarked, rubbing the sleep out of his eyes. Today he wasn't in his pajamas and robe. He was fully dressed. He told Isabel why. "The President telephoned me again a little bit ago. He's requested Justin, Doctor Lawrence Emmet, and myself to come to the White House this morning around nine for a special meeting. He said he was having trouble with Russia, China, North Korea, and a few other leaders, agreeing not to fire, or make a first strike, on the invaders. They want to *see me, talk to me*. Virtually anyway. Hear what I told the President from my own mouth. They're having trouble believing what we, as humans, have to do. They need persuading. The President thinks sticking me on a screen and spilling my guts in person, will help. Needless to say, I'm a little nervous. Who am I to talk to world leaders?" He shook his head, still not believing where his strange life had taken him.

"Then after that meeting," here Henry stumbled some in his explanation, "the President is going to speak to the nation, again, on television, and he wants *me* by his side to tell the country what I learned from the saucer aliens. He thinks it will also help calm everyone if they hear it from me in person. He said I convinced him, so he's sure, with my reputation from the dinosaur days and my honest demeanor, as he put it, I can convince the world's leaders and the American people. I sure hope he's right…and I don't freeze up on screen, or pass out. Either time." He inhaled, his nervousness hard to suppress.

"The President," he then finished, "is

sending a government helicopter for me and Justin. It'll be here in about an hour."

"Does Justin know yet?" Isabel grabbed a donut from under the glass cake cover to have with her coffee. She looked sleepy; her hair uncombed. No makeup. They were all comfortable enough with each other to just be themselves.

"I just told him. He is getting dressed. He's excited all right. Should be out any time now."

As if on cue, Justin rushed into the kitchen, and poured himself a cup of coffee. Delores was right behind him. She was in her nightgown and robe. Her hair tousled; her face fresh from sleep. Justin, though, was dressed in his best casual clothes. Like Henry, no suits for him.

"Oh boy," Isabel expelled a deep breath, "this time tomorrow you're going to be famous, Henry! You, too, Justin."

"I don't care about any of that," Henry asserted. "I just pray I can sway those other trigger-happy world leaders to not blow-up humanity's last chance of survival. Make them understand they *cannot fire*–or attempt to fire on, as I don't think it would do any good–on the triangles."

"All you can do is your best, Henry,"

Delores said. She was getting a box of Raisin Bran from the cabinet, milk from the fridge, and the sugar bowl. A peach to slice on top of the cereal. "Everyone's on their own this morning for breakfast. I'm having cereal and fruit."

Isabel spoke up, "Cereal sounds good to me." The woman rose from her stool and, after Delores finished pouring her bowl full, took the box from her, and an extra peach, took out another bowl from the cabinet, and made herself the same breakfast.

"Aren't you going to eat anything, Henry?" Isabel plopped down beside him.

"I'm too nervous." Henry observed Isabel as she ate her cereal. His stomach was doing flipflops. Nerves. Why was he forever getting into these predicaments? He simply wanted the world to leave him in peace, but instead, it wouldn't leave him alone. In this instance, he had no choice, though. It was his planet in peril. His world. His life, as well as all those he loved.

Those darn aliens...why did they have to entangle him into the middle of all this mess? Yet, if he could help, he had to help. What other choice did he have?

"Don't worry," Delores, was crunching on

her Raisin Bran, "I hear the White House always has a table full of food put out for early morning visitors. There'll be plenty for you to eat…after your big television debut. A fancy breakfast spread. You won't starve." She grinned at Henry, spooning in another bite.

"I'll have to get the kids out of bed in time to see you both on television," Isabel said. "At the White House. Phoebe and Timothy will get a kick out of it. Their dad and grandpa in the White House with the President of the United States, saving the world." Her chuckle was a bit tainted by the fear they all were living under. Delores was a realist. She knew how ominous the world's predicament was.

Sasha and Miss Kitty Cat were both sharking around the humans' feet, meowing for their breakfast, too.

"Okay, you two bottomless fur-pits, I'll get you your breakfast." Henry fed the cats and spent a little time playing with them. It gave him something to do. When the felines had fat bellies, and were tired of their human playmate, they scampered off to romp in the other room. Meows and friendly hisses could be heard. Sasha seemed to like being with Miss Kitty Cat. They were old friends.

The helicopter came exactly on time, it

landed on the apartment's open top floor helicopter pad that was made for helicopter touchdowns when needed, and Henry and Justin boarded it.

It was eerie soaring up into the sky with the titan-sized obsidian triangular spaceship miles above them blocking out the sun. It was scary, too. Henry was relieved when they'd passed from under it, and moved into clear skies.

In the helicopter, as they regarded the city and its buildings slide below them, Justin and Henry tried to have a conversation. But the twirling blades of the machine were so loud they eventually gave up. Exchanging looks of restrained excitement at what was ahead of them, they sat back, and enjoyed the scenery for the short ride.

They landed on the White House's lawn and were immediately flanked and accompanied by soldiers into the building. He didn't want to stare up at the dark spaceship hanging over the White House, but he couldn't resist doing it. Damn, the thing was *huge*. He realized he was sick to death of the black monsters hovering over them. In New York, here, everywhere. The news had reported more of them that had arrived since the first ones had come. They were all over the globe.

Waiting. Watching. In the worst desperate way, he wanted them to just leave. *Leave!*

Henry and Justin entered the White House and he was filled with the wonder of it all over again. *Wow,* he pondered, *he'd been to the White House twice in one week. If Ann could see him now. How proud she'd be of him. Perhaps, she did see him from heaven.*

The President met them in the media room, shaking their hands and appearing relieved they'd made it. Henry thought the President looked ten years older than when he'd last seen him. His face etched with deeper lines, and his eyes bloodshot with exhaustion. His face had a nervous tick Henry hadn't seen before. Poor man. Responsibility for a species survival was a heavy burden.

Within minutes, after introductions all around, Henry and Justin were seated at a table and speaking virtually with a panel of heads of state and foreign leaders. Doctor Emmet was there, as well, but outside of the camera's eye, sitting with other high-level officials, watching. He waved at them. They waved back. Then the fun began. Translators helped the participants to understand each other. It was a grueling couple of hours trying desperately to make pig-headed dictators believe what Henry, and then Justin, had to say. The leaders were itching to start sending missiles and bombs up at the aliens. *Fight! Fight! Kill! Kill! Crazy! Crazy!*

Russia wanted to send nuclear weapons up at the alien ships. China did, too. North Korea, and others, wanted to attack them with their jets and missiles. Such short-sighted hot heads. The leaders kept making excuses as to why they shouldn't attack first, and Henry, as well as Justin, had to keep explaining why they shouldn't. Henry also told the foreign leaders what the aliens had warned that humanity had to change…they had to start treating each other, and their planet better; stop killing each other. Cease the warring. *Immediately*. Or lose their planet forever, and face total species eradication. As he spoke, going into further details of the aliens' demands, Henry, though he couldn't understand the different languages, he could understand well-enough the skepticism, then the anger and frustration that had played across the leaders faces. World leaders did not like to be scolded; not even by all-powerful aliens. He didn't keep anything back. At the end of the conferences; Henry wasn't sure if they'd succeeded in compelling the foreign leaders to not blow the aliens to the sun–or trying to. Yet he and Justin had done their best, and that was all they could do.

Then, after the foreign leaders signed off, the American television broadcast began. The President, behind the presidential podium, talked to the nation first; then introduced Henry and Justin and, in their own words, let them tell their stories. The President, before he requested the two men to come up to the podium and speak, confessed to the nation about the two ancient alien spaceships that had been lodged, and examined, at Area 52, for years; then he went on to talk about Henry's first telepathic encounter with the saucer aliens there the year before. It was a good lead in to Henry and Justin's stories.

Then when Henry's turn came to speak to the country, he attempted to be as honest, and as straight-forward as he could; leaving out nothing but Oscar's role in the meetings. He hated telling the fib to keep Oscar out of the narrative, but he was sure it didn't matter one way or another. Except to Oscar and his family. He thought he did a fairly decent job, though he never was much for public speaking in front of millions of people, and especially with so much at stake.

Afterwards, Henry felt as exhausted as

when he'd been fighting the worst of the dinosaurs doing the most dangerous dinosaur days. He was drained. Also pessimistic about what would happen now. Since the alien crafts had appeared, the country had fallen into an even deeper morass of mayhem; the world, too, it seemed. The waiting to see what the suspended alien spaceships would do was driving even more humans to the brink of madness. The President thought appearing on television would also help that particular situation. Henry wasn't so sure. Everyone was too freaked out by the aliens to listen to reason. But he and Justin had done what they could to help.

Please, he pleaded silently to a God he prayed was listening, *don't let our world be destroyed. Save us, please.*

Isabel had been on the money. There had been food at the White House. A bountiful and scrumptious brunch, laid out on a long linen covered table, which the President generously invited them to share in. Good thing, Henry, once the foreign leader conference and the TV broadcast was done, found he was starving. He and Justin made pigs of themselves. Henry couldn't stop himself. It was strange lately how good food suddenly meant so much. *As if every meal might be their last.*

Doctor Emmet was perusing the breakfast buffet with them. He didn't eat as much as they did, but Henry would have bet the doctor had sampled the food earlier while he had been busy talking to the pig-heads. Or when he and Justin had been speaking to the nation.

The President thanked them again before they left the White House, and ordered the helicopter to take them to their home in New York.

"I pray your speeches today will help humanity," the President said. "I pray the aliens will leave us in peace. That we don't have to fight them. But we will if we have to."

"I also pray we don't have to fight them, Mr. President," Henry replied sincerely. But he didn't know what would happen now. No one did.

Henry had almost forgotten the alien behemoth was waiting out there above them. Its shadow turned the day cold for him. He was so aware that at any second an attack could explode on them. What he wouldn't have done to know what those aliens were thinking now. It was so stressful not to know.

It was a relief to return to the normalcy of Justin and Delores' apartment. Where the overhead hulking alien spaceship could not be seen, unless one peeked out a window. Henry found himself avoiding windows. Everyone told him how good he and Justin had looked on television. How genuine they had sounded. Henry was glad of that. When he'd been telling his story on television, to him, he had sounded like a demented person. *Telepathic communication with invisible aliens? Yeah, sure.*

"You're a world hero, Grandpa." Phoebe gave him a big hug when he came in the door. "You too, dad." She gave Justin a hug as well. At sixteen, Phoebe was turning into a beauty. She looked so much like her late mother, Laura, that sight of her always caught at Henry's heart. She had told him that she didn't have a new boyfriend, because she was too busy with her part time job at a local ice cream shop, which she wasn't working at since the alien ships appeared, her studies, and her artwork. She wanted to earn a scholarship to college, be a scientist like her father, specialty not chosen yet, and nothing was going to stand in her way. She was a determined young woman, didn't waste her time with anyone who wasn't as serious as she was, and knew what she wanted. Or she had known what she'd wanted before the aliens had come. Now every dream she had, like the rest of the world, was on hold. Her chestnut-colored hair was nearly down to her waist; much longer than her mother had ever worn hers. She was tall for her age, her eyes a deep brown. Her face was classically pretty. When she smiled, she was beautiful. Henry was so proud of her. It broke his heart to think she might not have a future.

"Wow, Grandpa," Timothy said, crawling into Henry's lap, and leaning his blond head against Henry's chest, "you were in the White House with the President! I saw you on television. My grandpa was on TV. Wait until I tell my friends." The boy was beaming with pride; his blue eyes twinkling. He was tall for only being seven years old. As his sister, he was taller than most other boys, but very skinny. He had developed a small stutter in the last year, but unless the boy was really nervous, he covered it up pretty well. He loved animals. Maintained he wanted to be a park ranger one day, like his grandpa had been, so he could live out around the wild things. He had a pet white rat he called Stinky, and a ferret he had named Mr. Ferret.

Henry and Justin's TV adventure was the

main topic of the day. Everyone sat around the counter, and Henry and Justin answered questions for a long time. All smiles. But Henry never forgot, for even one second, that the alien ship was levitating above them, silent and watching. He could only pray that the world had listened to the President, to him and Justin, and would settle down some. That the other countries' leaders and their militaries wouldn't try to blast one of the spaceships out of the sky. That night Henry took up the cooking apron and fried hamburgers and potato slices for everyone. After dinner, to calm everyone's fears, the adults and children sat at the kitchen table late into the night, played board games, and then cards. They all tried to forget what was hovering outside above them. Tried to forget the countdown they all were under. Prayed that no rogue country attacked any of the alien ships.

*****

On the sixth morning of the alien's surveillance from above, Henry rose from his bed and started checking the Internet news feed on his iPad. He was the first one up. It was barely dawn. But he hadn't been able to sleep any longer. The day before, with all its excitement, had wired him. He hadn't left his room yet. As he scrolled through the morning news he was relieved, and delighted, to see that the President's broadcast, and his and Justin's honest recounting of their alien encounter where Henry was made to understand what the aliens wanted, and he had desperately tried to make the people of the world understand as well, had seemed to calm some of the fears of the peoples of Earth. All the world's leaders had broadcast his and Justin's account on their airwaves, with translation ribbons running below, of course. According to the news, it had helped. The craziness, the looting, random killings, and even the suicide rate, globally had subsided a great deal overnight.

"Well. I guess Justin and I did the right thing telling the world what we knew, as hard as it was," he murmured to himself as he put the iPad down in front of him. Delores had left a plastic-covered plate of Danish and fruit slices, apples, and pears, on the counter for the morning snack and he took a Cheese Danish to have with his coffee. He turned on the television set by the sink, low so it wouldn't wake anyone, and his eyes were glued to the images of calm coming over the planet. Things were changing…things had changed. It made his heart glad.

How strange that so many people had believed him and Justin. But then again, the world only had to look upwards and how could they not believe *now* that aliens existed? It was just another step to believing what he and Justin had revealed.

The rest of the house got up eventually, even the children, and they had something to eat. The cupboard, though, was pretty much bare. The refrigerator, too. It took a lot of food to feed four adults, two children, and two cats.

To break the monotony and help time go by when Justin asked him if he'd like to go to the store with him to get groceries, Henry agreed. They couldn't let the family starve, no matter what tomorrow might bring. Henry also saw the advantage of stocking up before all the food was gone. Since the alien ships had arrived, the stores emptied fast. Going out for groceries and supplies lately meant going to a whole string of stores to get what was left on the shelves; that was if they could find much of anything. That was why the buffet spread at the White House had been such a treat. The last five days there were a lot of things that weren't available in the stores any longer.

At least that morning there was less of a

chance of being screamed at, robbed, or beat up by someone who'd gone off the deep end. Not since the President's broadcast. Things had to be better out there, or so Henry and Justin hoped.

But out in the city, the streets were empty. "Where is everyone," Justin asked.

"Either hiding or still sleeping." Henry's gaze looked up at the black spaceship. "Or hiding in their homes thinking about how to be better people."

"That would be nice, wouldn't it?" Justin casually retorted.

After visiting at least six stores, they got what supplies they could, and returned to the apartment.

The remainder of the day and the following day they stayed inside with their family and counted the hours. Watching TV, checking the Internet, to what the world was doing. The changes had begun to rapidly snowball and it was kind of…miraculous. Henry could hardly believe it, but oh how he wanted to.

"I can't believe it!" Justin's expression was awed. "Our appearance on television, our pleas, were heard. It worked!"

"It appears that way." Henry's eyes were glued to the television screen.

Worldwide, things were changing. People seemed to be kinder, more compassionate, to each other everywhere, the murder rate, the television news reported by late that evening had fallen drastically. Then the real miracles began to transpire throughout the world. Russia was pulling out of Ukraine completely; peace had been declared. North Korea had stopped testing its missiles, and sprouting off about sending them anywhere, opened the border to South Korea; and were now talking about discontinuing their nuclear program.

China declared peace, no more missiles or bombs to be made. They acknowledged Taiwan's total sovereignty, and promised friendship from now on with every other country in the world, no matter how poor. They vowed to lay down their arms.

America, too, was discontinuing its nuclear programs and its war preparations; and offered to increase help to any third world country with food and medical supplies. Countries all across the planet were opening their borders to those in need, with no limits.

The gangs in Africa swore peace with their fellow Africans. Their members laid down their arms. No more kidnappings, torture, or warfare. Countries were promising to stop polluting the land. There was more, but Henry was so overwhelmed with what was happening in the world he was almost afraid to hope that what the aliens had demanded was coming true. Humanity was changing. Mending its evil ways…or as much as humans could.

Yet for the first time ever, Henry had hope for the human race and their war-ravaged and suffering planet. Perhaps, humanity could change. But he couldn't help but worry: *These benevolent changes, how long would they last?* Knowing human nature, he was cynical. At least, humankind was trying to be a better steward of its people and its ailing Earth. Now the quadrillion dollar question was: *was it enough change quickly enough for the aliens to give them another chance?* They would see.

*****

On the eighth morning of the alien's frightening surveillance from above, Henry got up and scuffed into the kitchen in his slippers for his morning coffee. He hadn't had time to turn on the TV yet. Coffee first. He was drinking it when Justin came dashing into the kitchen, still in his sleeping clothes, a delirious smile on his face. "Henry, Henry! Look outside! *The alien spaceship is gone! It's gone!* Turn on the television!"

Henry got up from his stool and switched on the kitchen TV. The images filled the screen.

It was true. It was all over the news. *The spaceships had disappeared. Poof! They were all gone. Every last one of them across the globe.* The aliens had kept their word. Humanity showed they were willing to try to be better, so the aliens were giving them one last chance.

Thank you, Oscar! Henry rejoiced silently. *If your alien friends wouldn't have interceded for us humans at your request, we'd be a dead species by now. You're the one responsible for this miraculous outcome. Oscar…you saved the world!*

"Maybe the aliens watched our broadcast, too," Justin muttered.

"Maybe they did." Henry grinned in return. "And maybe they understood it. Translated it, perhaps? Intelligent as they seem to be."

"Perhaps they did. And if they saw that, they must have seen the changes the world has begun to go through. They must have. But they are *gone*, Henry! That is all that matters."

Yes, that was all that mattered.

The rest of the family came out of their

rooms as Justin's booming voice called everyone to wake up, and they all started hugging and kissing each other, their eyes on the TV, so happy the aliens had left. The human race would not be terminated. This time.

Minutes later, the White House telephoned Henry and connected him with the President. "You did it, Mr. Shore. You and Doctor Maltin did it. I wanted to thank you again…but I also wanted to tell you that right before the aliens left our atmosphere, they sent us a short ultimatum. In their language. Our linguistic experts are studying it, and hope to have it decoded as soon as they can."

"That's wonderful, Mr. President. Are you sure they're really gone?"

"Yes, Mr. Shore, they're gone. Long gone. NASA, the U.S. Space Command Joint Operations Center in Colorado Springs, the MeerTRAP Telescope, the James Webb Telescope, and all the other important observatories across the globe can't see a glimpse of them anywhere in our galaxy. They've left it entirely. Their ships space-travel incredibly fast."

Henry had to ask, "When you get that ultimatum decrypted, Mr. President, would you tell me what the aliens said?"

The President hesitated briefly, then answered, "We owe you and Doctor Maltin at least that. Yes, I will."

Henry got off the phone and found himself embracing Isabel, who was crying tears of joy. For the first time in eight days, longer than that, really, they could breathe again. The family, all smiles and laughter, sat down to have a celebratory breakfast. They chatted happily about the future, because now they had one.

Henry, with Justin and the others listening in on the speaker mode, called Patterson and Sherman to share in the good news.

"When I get back home," Henry told everyone he spoke to, "we're going to have a big *Goodbye Aliens* party at my house. Everyone is invited."

Outside they could hear the cheering, and happy yelling, out in the city. They went down to the first floor and out onto the street to join the ecstatic crowds. It was like New Years, Christmas, and V-Day all rolled into one. Everyone was overjoyed.

Oh, Ann, Henry thought as he cheered with the others around him in the sunshine, *I wish you were here to see this. I wish you could be here celebrating and cheering with all of us.*

All in all, it was a very, very good day.

CHAPTER 19

Epilogue

It was a week later and Henry had been home for four days. He'd lingered at Justin and Delores apartment for three extra days after the alien ships had vacated Earth's airspace. He had appreciated the company of Justin and Delores, and being with Isabel, and his grandchildren. He'd enjoyed wandering around New York with his family with everyone's new better, kinder, outlook. People stopped to smile and talk to everyone else; offered to help anyone who needed help. It was astounding how nice all the humans were being to each other. The thieves had stopped thieving, the bullies, and gangs, had stopped beating other people up, and the murderers had stopped killing people. Rapes had fallen to virtually zero. Antisemitic incidents had all but disappeared. Humans banding together against the aliens threat because they were all humans. Again, Henry wondered how long that would last. But while it did, he was taking advantage of it. Being out among the New York crowds was like being in another alternative reality…one where the evil, selfish, greedy people had all vanished; or, at least, gone into hiding for the time being.

Nope, this was not going to last. And knowing that made Henry soul sick–and inherently frightened for the future of mankind. He had no doubt that one days those aliens, or some other aliens, might visit Earth again and might pass a final judgement on if the human race should survive or not. It could happen.

In time, though, as much as he'd liked being with his family, he'd wanted to go home. Justin's billionaire brother-in-law sent him home in style on his jet as a thank you for all he had done to save the world. Henry didn't turn down the gift. He had to admit, Jeff's jet was a lot more luxurious than any public flight.

It was evening when Henry staggered in through his front door, lowered the cat carrier to the floor, releasing Sasha, made his way into the bedroom, and dropped his suitcase beside the bed. He'd unpack tomorrow. His exhaustion was more than physical, it was emotional, and psychological. The last couple weeks, months actually, had drained him of every ounce of his energy. He needed normalcy, peace, and quiet, alone time, now for a while. It was still sad to walk into his home, and not find Ann there, but he had come to realize that home was still home. He loved it. Cherished it. It was his sanctuary…the home he and Ann had lovingly planned, built, and lived in together. He was glad to be home.

Hours later, he had finished taking a shower, was dressed in his comfy clothes, and was relaxing in front of the television. His eyes were on the screen, full of rejoicing humans all over the planet talking about the new world order, but his mind was miles, days, away. He kept reliving his encounter with the alien ship, the invisible aliens, Oscar's surprise appearance, and what he'd mind-messaged to him; his visit to the White House, meeting the President, and speaking on the air to the world. He remembered the sheer horror of the giant alien spaceships hovering above the cities. Whoa, had all that really happened to him? He smiled. If Ann were alive, she'd tell him to put it all in a book. Well, perhaps he might. He'd have to get a ghost writer, though. He wasn't the journalist his wife had been.

Henry was half-asleep in the living room chair, the cat snuggled in his lap, the light dim, the TV droning on the other side of the room, when a series of knocks came at the door. He was instantly awake, out of the chair, the cat jumping to the rug, and moving towards the rear door in the kitchen. He opened the door. It was Scott Patterson.

"Patterson! Nice to see you. Didn't we just chat earlier today?"

"We did."

"But come on in anyway."

"I heard you were home from Justin when he called me back again later in the day to just talk, so I thought I'd come by and see the national hero of the century." Patterson chuckled good-naturedly as he came into the kitchen. He had a covered dish in his hands which he handed to Henry. "Sherman sent you some supper…and a big piece of her homemade peach pie, knowing how you love it so. She thought it was the least she could do for a national hero."

Henry took the offered plate gratefully and set it on the counter. "Well, thank Sherman for the supper, and dessert. As you know, I do love her peach pie. I never got around to eating a meal tonight yet. I was just going to scrape up something later out of the fridge if I got hungry enough. But since there's not much left in the fridge, this meal is quite timely."

"That's what Sherman thought, too.

You've been gone a while, so she figured a hot meal would be appreciated."

"It is. Can I get you some coffee? I might not have a refrigerator full of food, but I do have coffee and powered Coffeemate."

"Sure."

"So, what can I do for you, Scott? Kind of late for a social visit," Henry remarked, turning the coffee pot on, and taking out two cups from the cabinet above the sink. But Henry didn't really mind, it was good to see his friend.

Patterson seated himself at the table. "For one thing, I wanted to hear firsthand about your adventures in Washington D.C at the White House, and in New York. You know, Klamath Falls was too small, I suppose, to have an alien spaceship stationed above us. I only saw them on TV. I want to hear about that. I would bet you have lots of photos, don't you?"

"I have some."

"Oh, by the way, you looked really good on TV when you were addressing the world. You sounded quite compelling. It worked. I was proud of you."

"Stop it, I'm blushing. But thanks."

"*And,*" Patterson continued, 'I have an

important message for you from the President of the United States. He gave it to General Wallace, who happens to be a close friend of his, to give to me to give to you."

Henry's interest was captured. "A message from the President?" He put the cup under the coffee maker, hit the start button, and watched the coffee come pouring into the cup. It smelled heavenly. Then he made another cup and brought them both, and two spoons, over to the table. The sugar and the Coffeemate were already there.

"I am sure, you will find the message very interesting. The General said the ultimatum was one the President got from the retreating aliens. It was translated."

"And?" Henry had prepared his coffee, but wasn't drinking it. Frozen, he was waiting for what Patterson had to say. "What did the alien's ultimatum say?"

"Just four words: *We will be back.*"

Henry put his hand against his forehead, and lowered his head. The words from his lips were hard to push out. "That's all? No time frame? No, *when* they will be back?"

"No." Patterson lifted his cup to his lips to drink. "General Wallace said that was all there was."

"Hmm." Henry swung his legs over in his chair, patted his lap, and Sasha jumped into it. He stroked her soft fur. Her purring was comforting to him. "They want to keep us guessing, I'd say."

"That's what I'd say."

The two men locked eyes. They knew each other so well; they could just about read each other's minds. The cat meowed. And jumped down to the floor. She ran out the cat door. He wasn't surprised at the message. He'd expected something like it.

"Can't guarantee how long humanity will behave itself," Patterson commented in a mournful tenor. "It's not in our nature to remain good. We are a violent species."

"We are. And Humans have a bad habit of forgetting. But time will tell. There isn't anything you or I can do about that. But pray."

Henry nodded. *And pray we aren't here to see the final human downfall. I hope I'm long gone.*

"Now," Patterson said. "Tell me about the President, the White House, and what it was like to have that black monster spaceship hanging over you in the city? I'm all ears. Show me the pictures."

Henry chuckled, got up, uncovered his

supper, popped it in the microwave, and warmed it up. Bringing it and a fork to the table, he told Patterson everything he wanted to know, and, pulling out his iPhone, showed him pictures.

An hour later, Patterson said goodnight, and Henry saw him to the door.

"Drop by tomorrow, Henry, about five in the afternoon," Patterson said as he was leaving. "For supper. Sherman is dying to ask you questions, too."

Henry bet she was. "I will. Goodnight, Scott."

"Goodnight, Henry."

Henry listened as Patterson's car drove away and the sound dwindled into the night.

He was cleaning up his supper remnants when his cell phone rang. Who would call this late?

"Henry, it's Nehemiah Hescott. Professor Hescott?" the old man's deep gravelly voice came on the phone. "I just thought I'd ring you up and tell you I saw you on the tellie. Wow, you were at the White House with the President…you met the aliens! I'm jealous."

Henry laughed. "You can have them, Professor. Meeting the aliens was an experience I didn't want to have and really don't want to have ever again. I've never felt so helpless."

"But you have to admit it was awesome…your experience. Was it the black triangle aliens?"

"No, Professor, it was the aliens–who I think of as the good aliens–from the saucer spaceships. As you probably know yourself, the aliens in the monster ebony triangle ships aren't any aliens we want to deal with. As I said in the broadcast, they wanted to eradicate us; take our planet for themselves. They're very dangerous."

The professor paused for a minute, then tagged on, "I'm going to be out your way tomorrow late afternoon sometime. I was wondering if you'd mind if I stopped by for a visit? I'm so curious to hear all about the aliens and your meeting with them." The excitement in the old man's voice was easy to hear.

"Sure." Henry yawned, covering his mouth so the professor wouldn't hear. "Stop on by. We'll have ourselves a nice visit. You can come with me to Patterson and Sherman's house and have some supper with us. About five. I'll only have to tell my stories one time instead of two."

"Good, good," the astrophysicist replied eagerly, seemingly pleased that he'd been invited to supper. "See you tomorrow. Around five or so."

"See you tomorrow, Professor."

"Tomorrow." Henry ended the call, and yawned again.

His body weary, his steps dragging, Henry shut off the lights, and went to bed. He was so tired. It would feel good to be in his own bed.

*****

The next morning Henry, happy to be home, the alien crisis behind him, and the world safe, woke up as the sun was just rising above the horizon. The golden light filled the bedroom, and throwing the quilt back, he got out of bed, and padded to the bathroom. Oh, it felt so good to be home! Sasha, who'd been sleeping with him, launched off the bed and followed him, meowing plaintively.

"I know, I know, kitty, you want your breakfast. Give me a minute or two, and we'll both get something to eat. He thought there was a loaf of bread in the freezer somewhere, one place Oscar had not ransacked, too cold, and he could have toast, with the unopened strawberry preserves he'd hidden way up in the top cabinet so the hungry dinosaur hadn't gotten to it, and coffee. Just thinking about it made his mouth water. He'd have to get into town soon and do some shopping to restock his pantry. He didn't like not having any real food in the house.

A short time later, Henry was showered, dressed in his comfortable lounging clothes, cat fed and out romping around in the yard, as Henry sat on the back porch swing in the early morning sunlight, cradling a cup of hot coffee in one hand, and a piece of strawberry covered toast in the other. A plate sat next to him on the swing with a large stack of toast. They tasted delicious with the coffee.

He gently pushed the swing with his foot as he gazed out into his back yard. He could hear the woods' animals chattering and chittering out in the trees. See the birds flitting around the yard and eating at the birdfeeders he and Ann had put out years ago. A family of squirrels were playing along the line of forest at the end of his property. A couple others were at the squirrel house. Glaring at him. He'd have to take out some nuts for them. He thought, for a moment, he spotted a red fox running around the bushes.

He was content. It was a beautiful September morning. Not too hot, not too chilly. Just perfect. He sighed and picked up another piece of toast. He was thinking of topping his coffee and heating it up a little in the microwave, he liked his coffee hot, when he spotted something larger making its way through the distant line of foliage.

Henry began to smile, a large, happy smile, as a mid-sized animal broke out of the tree line and began to scamper towards him.

Oscar! It was Oscar come to visit him! How did the creature know he was home? Henry laughed out loud. He didn't care, it was just so darn good to see his little buddy. He had about begun to believe the little dinosaur had a touch of magic in him. Maybe he did. Nothing, after everything that had happened in the last decade to Henry, would surprise him anymore.

"Hi there, Oscar!" Henry cried out, truly thrilled to see him.

The little dinosaur was only feet away now. "Ah ha, so you've come back to the scene of the crime, huh? Sorry, the icebox is still empty from your last raid. I haven't had time to replenish it yet. But I will soon, I promise." The small prehistoric critter had loped across the grass, jumped up on the porch, and–surprise, surprise–scrambled right up on the swing beside Henry. Henry used his feet to hold the swing still. The creature leaned against Henry's side for a moment as if the was giving Henry a hug, dinosaur style. Then Oscar's expressive large eyes looked hungrily at Henry's plate of strawberry covered toast. It licked its jaws with its long tongue. The dinosaur met Henry's eyes. Pleading. Henry laughed again. "Food always does it, hey buddy? You always come here and find the food. Could that be what draws you here?"

The look on the dinosaur's face and the way he cocked his head, was almost as if he were giving Henry an answer. *I come for you, my Stick friend, not only the food.* The telepathic message, and Henry hoped he'd gotten it correct, warmed Henry's heart.

Henry pushed the plate closer to the animal. "Go ahead, help yourself, friend. You deserve it and more. When you're done with that, I'll make you more. After all, Oscar, as far as I'm concerned…you saved the world. You saved our world. So, eat up."

Henry, a sense of contentment settling on him, watched the dinosaur scarf down the toast. There were red strawberry stains smeared all over the dinosaur's face. Ann might be dead, but Henry knew now he wasn't alone. He never would be.

Henry's gaze moved past the munching dinosaur, and suddenly there was Ann sitting on the other side of the creature on the swing, smiling back at him. Henry returned the smile.

"Hi, Ann. It's so good to see you. It's been a while."

I know, she answered silently. *You did good, you and Oscar, saving the world from the aliens. I knew there was a reason that God took me instead of you. I'm so proud of both of you. I just thought I'd come and visit. I've missed both of you so much.*

"Same here, wife," Henry told her. "Same here."

And there they all three were…sitting on the back porch swing in the shaded sunshine, the sweet aroma of flowers and green trees around them, watching their little dinosaur buddy eat strawberry toast, and enjoying the morning. Together.

Henry could not have been any happier. There were still miracles in the world. The aliens were gone, the planet saved for now, and Oscar and Ann had come to visit. What more could he ask for?

THE END

Please, if you would be so kind, leave a review of this book on Amazon and Goodreads…I'd sure appreciate it.

This was the seventh of my Dinosaur Lake series.

If you missed any of the first six, here they are:

***Dinosaur Lake**, which was a 2014 EPIC EBOOK AWARDS *FINALIST* in their Suspense/Thriller Category.*

Dinosaur Lake II: Dinosaurs Arising
Dinosaur Lake III: Infestation
Dinosaur Lake IV: Dinosaur Wars
Dinosaur Lake V: Survivors
Dinosaur Lake VI: The Alien Connection

** And if you liked this book, you might try any one of my other 34 published novels and 13 short stories because I also write and publish horror, romantic horror, time-travel, dinosaur books, and murder mysteries; now all also available also as paperbacks, and audio books at Audible Audio.*

Rocket, and my beloved late husband, Russell…see you on the other side, Husband.

About Kathryn Meyer Griffith…

Since childhood I've been an artist and worked as a graphic designer in the corporate world and for newspapers for twenty-three years before I quit to write full time. But I'd already begun writing novels at 21, over fifty-one years ago now, and have had thirty-five (romantic horror, horror, romantic SF horror, romantic suspense, romantic time travel, historical romance, thrillers, one non-fiction short story collection, and nine murder mysteries) previous novels and thirteen short stories published from various traditional publishers since 1984. But I've gone into self-publishing in a big way since 2012; and upon getting all my previous books' full rights back for the first time, have self-published all of them. My seven Dinosaur Lake novels, and Spookie Town Murder Mysteries (Scraps of Paper, All Things Slip Away, Ghosts Beneath Us, Witches Among Us, What Lies Beneath the Graves, When the Fireflies Returned, and Echoes of Other Times) are my best-sellers.

I was married to my beloved Russell for over forty-three years and he, sadly, passed away in August 2021. I have a son, two grandchildren, and a great-granddaughter, and I live in a small quaint town in Illinois. I have a quirky cat, Sasha, and we live in an old house in the heart of town. Though I've been an artist, and a folk/classic rock singer in my youth with my late brother Jim, writing has always been my greatest passion, my butterfly stage, and I'll probably write stories until the day I die…or until my memory goes.

2012 EPIC EBOOK AWARDS *Finalist* for my horror novel **The Last Vampire** ~ 2014 EPIC EBOOK AWARDS * Finalist * for my thriller novel **Dinosaur Lake**.

***All Kathryn Meyer Griffith's books can be found here:** http://tinyurl.com/ld4jlow

***All her Audible.com audio books here:**

http://tinyurl.com/oz7c4or

Novels and short stories from Kathryn Meyer Griffith: *Evil Stalks the Night, The Heart of the Rose, Blood Forged, Vampire Blood, The Last Vampire (*2012 EPIC EBOOK AWARDS*Finalist* in their Horror category), *Witches, Witches II: Apocalypse, Witches plus Witches II: Apocalypse, The Nameless One erotic horror short story, The Calling, Scraps of Paper (The First Spookie Town Murder Mystery), All Things Slip Away (The Second Spookie Town Murder Mystery), Ghosts Beneath Us (The Third Spookie Town Murder Mystery), Witches Among Us (The Fourth Spookie Town Murder Mystery), What Lies Beneath the Graves (The Fifth Spookie Town Murder Mystery: sixth, All Those Who Came Before, When the Fireflies Returned (Seventh Spookie Town Murder Mystery), Echoes of Other Times (Eighth Spookie Town Murder Mystery), Egyptian Heart, Winter's Journey, The Ice Bridge, Don't Look Back, Agnes, A Time of Demons and Angels, The Woman in Crimson, Human No Longer, Six Spooky Short Stories Collection, Haunted Tales, Forever and Always Romantic Novella, Night Carnival Short Story, Dinosaur Lake (2014 EPIC EBOOK AWARDS*Finalist* in their Thriller/Adventure category), Dinosaur Lake II: Dinosaurs Arising, Dinosaur Lake III: Infestation and Dinosaur Lake IV: Dinosaur Wars, Dinosaur Lake V: Survivors, Dinosaur Lake VI: The Alien Connection, Dinosaur Lake VII: The Aliens Return, Memories of My Childhood, and Christmas Magic 1959.*

Twitter: https://twitter.com/KathrynG64
My Blog:
https://kathrynmeyergriffith.wordpress.com/
My Facebook author page:
https://www.facebook.com/KathrynMeyerGriffith67/
Facebook Author Page:
https://www.facebook.com/kathryn.meyergriffith.7
http://www.amazon.com/-/e/B001KHIXNS
*You Tube REVIEW of Dinosaur Lake:
https://www.youtube.com/watch?v=EDtsOHnIiXQ&pbjreload=101

***E-mail me at rdgriff@htc.net I love to hear from my readers.* ***

Made in United States
North Haven, CT
05 June 2023